D. K. Broster

Ships in the Bay!

e-artnow 2021

D. K. Broster

Ships in the Bay!

Historical Romance Novel

e-artnow, 2021
Contact: info@e-artnow.org

ISBN 978-80-273-4131-3

Contents

I THE DUTCH PRIZE	12
II ODYSSEY OF MR. MARTIN TYRRELL	40
III SANCTUARY	75
IV THE KINGDOM BY THE SEA	106
V "CAME THE BLIND FURY——"	139
VI THE END OF THE MASQUERADE	158
VII "DANGER'S TROUBLED NIGHT"	179
VIII UP ANCHOR!	212
IX THE CLEAR HORIZON	240

"That mortal breathes not, and never will be born, who shall come with war to the land of the Phæacians, for they are very dear to the gods. Far apart we live in the wash of the waves, the outermost of men."

Odyssey VI. 201-205

"You gwyne to have considable trouble en yo' life, en considable joy. Sometimes yo' gwyne to git hurt, en sometimes yo' gwyne to git sick, but every time yo' gwyne to git well again. Dey's two gals flyin' about in yo' life. One uv 'em's light en t'other is dark. . . . You want to keep away fum de water as much as you kin en don't run no risks, 'kase it's down in de bills dat you's gwyne to git hung."
 Huckleberry Finn, Chap. iv

TO

C. S. EVANS

whose unvarying kindness demands a better tribute, but whose name seems to make appropriate the dedication of this tale of the Principality.

I
THE DUTCH PRIZE

"We sail the ocean blue,
And our saucy ship's a beauty
We're sober men and true,
And attentive to our duty."

Pinafore Act I

"But who is this, whose godlike grace
Proclaims he comes of noble race?
And who is this whose manly face

　Bears sorrow's interesting trace?"

Patience Act I

I
THE DUTCH PRIZE

(1)

The summer day had dawned very clear, and the wind, blowing light but steady from the north, promised not only fine, but brilliantly fine weather, most congenial, since hay harvest was upon them, to all the farmers of Western Pembrokeshire in this year of grace and war 1796. It swept over the wide, airy, almost treeless expanses of Dewisland, studded with innumerable white-washed farms, ruffling the young barley and wheat; the tall pink valerian on the ruins of the Bishop's Palace, down in the Vale of Roses, swayed to its passing; the little blue scabious in their thousands on the cliff saluted it, and the now fading thrift which the scabious had replaced: while the sea itself, on either side of the out-thrust fist of St. David's, from Skomer Island off the one coast to Strumble Head on the other, was the livelier and the more azure for its passing.

Nor was the breeze displeasing to Miss Nest Meredith, driving her father, the Precentor, and an antiquarian visitor in a low pony-chaise towards the western shore, in order that the latter might inspect the ruins of the old chapel erected there to St. Justinian, the teacher of St. David himself. For the breeze not only tempered the heat in the high-banked and flower-bedecked channel which was the road thither, but to some extent kept away the flies from Patch, the fat, slowly-trotting old pony, who need hardly have been taken from his stable for so short an excursion but that Mr. Thistleton, lame from birth was dependent upon some means of transport.

The dust rose behind and drifted slowly on to the banks on either side-on to the troops of ferns, the hundreds of foxgloves, the recurrent patches of pink campion which harmonised so well with them and the yellow snapdragon which made so vivid a contrast, and on to the spires of the majestic, woolly-leaved mulleins planted at regular intervals, apparently by some celestial under-gardener, which were just beginning to twinkle into bloom. The distance from the Precentory to Porthstinian was less than two miles, yet Nest, as she drove, had time to feel sleepy with the heat and the dust-muffled clop-clop of Patch's advance. Papa, she could hear, was talking to Mr. Thistleton about the restoration of the Cathedral's west front, now in progress, but she did not listen. Soon, as she knew from past experience with visitors, they would be discussing with equal zest the curious chimney, alleged to be "Flemish," of the farmhouse at Rhosson, which they would shortly reach and wish to stop at; indeed but a couple of minutes had elapsed before she caught the word "Flemings" already passing between the two gentlemen.

They were out of the lane now, and on their left Trefeiddan Pool, small and shallow, glittered in the stretch of moorland between them and the craggy eminence of Clegyr Boia, where the chieftain who made himself so objectionable to St. David was reputed to have had his fastness. Now a farmhouse sat beneath its slopes, just as Rhosson beneath another sudden hillock. Pool, moor and crag were all upon a small scale. A little further and they were at Rhosson; Nest pulled up Patch almost mechanically, Dr. Meredith and his guest alighted; the former pointed, they viewed; finally they entered the farmhouse.

Nest Meredith untied the ribbon of her big shady hat and fanned herself awhile with it, the sun glinting on her golden-brown ringlets. Patch stood with drooping head, only his long tail busy. The scent of hay was in the air, for one or two fields near Rhosson were already cut, though none was yet carried. In front, the rough road, rising slightly, cut off the view, but away to her right a strip of intensely blue water showed up the brown, seared promontory of St. David's Head itself, shaped at that distance like an outstretched crocodile-not that Nest had ever seen a crocodile. She had only to turn round to see the great tower of the Cathedral emerging, with no sign of the building to which it was attached, from the hollow which held the shrine of Dewi Sant.

It had never occurred to Nest Meredith, the daughter of the Cathedral's chief dignitary-for here at St. David's, where there had never been a Dean, the Precentor or Chanter held that position-to criticise the unprecedented site which the Cathedral itself occupied, down in the valley of the river Alan, while the little town was grouped along the ridge above. She was too much accustomed to its unique position; indeed, rather proud of it. But her married sister Jane, when she came from her present home in Lincolnshire to visit them, would often speak in disparaging terms of old Peter de Leia, the builder of this, the third church to rise over St. David's bones. But of course she did this out of her father's hearing; yet when Nest reminded her that Bishop Peter did not choose the site, Jane would reply impatiently: "My dear Nest, if we all went on slavishly copying our forefathers, what would become of progress?" Jane would never have talked thus about "progress" before her marriage, and Nest feared that the development must have some connection with the alarming fact that her husband, if not she herself, read Tom Paine and Rousseau, even though it were mere intellectual curiosity and not real sympathy which led Mr. Stalybridge to investigate the subversive ideas of these writers, which all true-hearted Englishmen must so abhor.

It was certain on the other hand that no such literature was ever perused by Nest's naval brother William, he who in these days of possible French invasion was contributing towards keeping the shores of Britain inviolate. Yet even William had once declared, à propos of the Cathedral, that he did think those old fellows might have chosen the quarterdeck instead of the hold while they were about it; and that it was, from a sailor's point of view, almost a crime to have wasted such a good daymark as the great tower would probably have made, by erecting it in a rabbit run. In such unsuitable terms had he referred to the charming green valley of the Alan, yellow a month ago with flags, and now all white and fragrant with the meadow-sweet.

Ah, here were Papa and Mr. Thistleton coming out of the farmhouse, Mrs. Lloyd curtseying behind them. Into the pony-chaise they got again, the vehicle swaying to the Precentor's weight, for he was a large man and of slightly full habit-not more so, however, than was consonant with and indeed conducive to dignity. Nest flicked her whip, and Patch slowly put himself once more into motion.

The pony-chaise topped the slight rise, and as they began to descend again Ramsey Sound came into view, a wide blue floor streaked with silver currents, cutting off the high ground ahead which, to the visitor's surprise, revealed itself as an island of some extent. Further out to the right swam Careg Rhosson and other islets. Mr. Thistleton gave exclamations of surprise and appreciation.

"Yes," said Dr. Meredith, "that is Ynys Dewi, or Ynis-yr-hyrddod, as it is sometimes called. As with Bardsey Island, twenty thousand saints are said by tradition to have been buried there, which, as Ramsey is only a couple of miles long, must have necessitated somewhat crowded sepulture. It was there that St. Justinian, who appears to have been a severe disciplinarian, is said to have been slain by his servants; but his body, according to legend, walked over the Sound, carrying its head under its arm, and was originally buried in the spot we are approaching. His chapel, which you can now see, in consequence, I suppose, of this holy feat, used to be resorted to by those crossing to and from Ramsey Island, either to pray for a safe passage or to give thanks for one. We must get out here, I am afraid; this is too steep for Patch." And leaving that steed, never known to stir unbidden, the three of them went down the rough track towards the little roofless shrine.

But Nest did not go in with the two gentlemen; she wished to see, rather, what was occupying the attention of the small group of men on the grassy point just beyond, overlooking the minute landing-place which gave the spot its name of Porth. One of the men had a telescope to his eye. Perhaps he was looking at a seal or two come over from their breeding place in the caves on the other side of the island, and Nest dearly loved to watch seals. Now she could see the whole expanse of the Sound and Pont-y-Geist, the terrible line of jagged teeth running right out from Ramsey into the narrowest part of the channel, past which the tide raced and foamed

13

always; but it was something under the lee of the mainland which caught her attention. Round to the left, close inshore, but at some distance from Porthstinian, a ship was anchored.

Miss Meredith's heart gave an unpleasant jump. When one lives on a seacoast in time of war, still more, as in her case, between two seacoasts, even a strange sail in the offing may raise alarm. And here was an unknown and rather curious-looking vessel moored in the Sound, while a boat which had evidently come from her was already well on its way to the little landing-place.

The group of men, all known to Nest, had turned at her approach and saluted her.

"I hope that is not a French ship, Mr. Watkins!" said the girl, trying to keep the apprehension out of her voice.

"No, no, Miss Nest *bach* ," said the man with the telescope reassuringly. "Though indeed you might well be thinking that she should be a foreigner, for foreigner she was once, for sure. But now she will be a prize; look you, she do fly the British flag!" He held out his telescope. "If you was to look through this, miss, you 'ould see the way her mainmast has been shot about; and indeed to goodness the boat on the davits there have a great hole in it!"

Nest took the telescope and, since it was not the first time she had used such an instrument, she was able quickly to eschew the succession of bobbing circles, blank save for the blue heaving which filled them, in favour of a small section of the captured vessel. Lighting, however, upon the figure of a man in the ship who, having evidently just washed his only shirt, was hanging it over the side to dry, she hastily lowered the telescope with a blush; but, unwilling so soon to relinquish it, sought instead for the oncoming boat and, after several false casts, was successful in hitting it off. There first appeared in her field of vision the back of a grizzled and rather bald head, swaying to the oar at which its owner was tugging; then, as she slightly shifted the telescope, she came upon the stem of the advancing boat itself, with the water shearing up like crystal on either side of it; after which there swung into view the shoulder of the rower in the bow and the back of his head. He was evidently a young man, for, though he wore a blue, tasselled woollen cap, she could see how thick was his dark brown hair. His neck was tanned, but not wrinkled like the other man's. She gave back the telescope with a word of thanks.

"Good morning, Watkins; good morning, John Llewelyn!" said her father's voice behind her. "I see, miss, that you prefer science to art, the new to the old!"

"Yes; for, Papa, see!" explained Nest in excitement, "there's a ship in the Sound — a prize-and a boat is coming ashore from her. 'Twill soon be in!"

And soon, indeed, the boat with its crew of four was gliding into the recess in the cliffs (for it was not much more) which formed the landing-place. The party from the Precentory watched from above while Watkins shouted down to ascertain what it had come for. One of the rowers scrambled ashore, an individual in a blue frieze waistcoat and wide canvas trousers, and shouted up in a hoarse voice:

"Prize crew from the *Fair Penitent* , letter of marque of Liverpool, taking back a Dutch prize, and bein' short of water and the wind contrary we've put in for a cask or so. Will 'ee show us where to get it?"

"I incline to wonder," murmured Mr. Thistleton above, in Dr. Meredith's ear, "that they don't ask for something stronger than water!"

Mr. Watkins went down, and was seen to be informing the privateersman of the nearest source of supply, while Nest from her eminence inspected the crew of the boat. They did indeed look somewhat ruffianly: all bearded and middle-aged, save the young bow oar with the blue cap who, though unshaven, was not hirsute to anything like the same extent. From where she was, Nest could not distinguish his features, but she noticed that though at first he had sat with his head bent over his oar, he was now gazing about him with every appearance of interest.

Presently he with the two others shipped their oars, got out of the boat, each with a couple of water-kegs, mounted the steps cut in the cliff and passed within a few yards of the spectators, subsequently disappearing up the sloping road.

"Brave and worthy fellows, no doubt, in spite of their somewhat unprepossessing appearance," commented Dr. Meredith. "We must remember the risks they run, the hard life they lead. Did their leader say that it was a Liverpool privateer which captured the vessel there in the Sound?"

"Yes," replied his guest. "A privateer with a very odd name-the *Fair Penitent*, if I heard aright."

"Very odd," agreed the Precentor. "It is, I think, the title of an old play."

"Perhaps her owner has literary leanings," suggested Mr. Thistleton, as they started back towards the pony-chaise. "Or, more probably, an admiration for Mrs. Siddons. I believe, now I come to think of it, that the *Fair Penitent* was one of the tragedies in which she used to enact the heroine when she was playing in Liverpool and Manchester twenty years ago, before she came to London. Liverpool possesses many privateers, does it not?"

"Scores, my dear sir, scores. As many, or more than Bristol. We see them sometimes passing the Bishop and Clerks out there. And slave ships also; the port has a great trade to the Guinea coast. But I cannot remember either a privateer or a prize ever putting in here before."

Patch being roused from his meditations, they now drove slowly home again. Of the privateersmen there was no further sign, and conversation, abandoning present day affairs, flowed once more round the relics of the past.

(2)

Nest Meredith's home, the Precentory, was one of the many buildings which had adorned the precincts of the Cathedral of St. David's in the days of the former greatness of the see, when its Bishop had been little less than a prince, and the shrine of the Saint a very great and famous place of pilgrimage. In those ages an embattled wall, with four gateways, had encircled the whole close, a veritable ecclesiastical city-state. *Fuit Ilium*; now in places that wall had crumbled, and but one gate remained; part of the Cathedral itself had long been roofless, the beautiful Bishop's Palace was in ruins, and St. Mary's College, John of Gaunt's foundation, also; while of the various prebendal dwellings and archdeaconries some were mere skeletons, of some no traces were left. But among those which had survived was the Precentory, and this had moreover been added to and improved, and presented an appearance at once pleasant and dignified. It stood, not like the Cathedral on the floor of the green hollow, but some way up the lip, looking at the great church as it were sideways, and more directly across the Vale of Roses, the "Merry Vale," meadow-like, shallow and open, where the little river Alan, once perhaps a large stream, wound unobtrusively along to the tiny harbour of Porthclais, its meeting place with the sea. Below the house was a terraced garden, the supporting wall of which abutted on a little road which crossed the Alan on an ancient bridge and separated the Precentory from the "Chanter's Orchard," a field stretching to the river.

It was to this sloping garden, and to the shade of a mulberry tree, that Nest brought out some sewing this afternoon. Under the same tree sat already her Aunt Pennefather, the Precentor's widowed sister, who kept his house for him, mild, almost visionary, learned and poetical. The dignified cap which crowned her brow was a trifle askew, yet the stitches which she was putting into a much smaller cap were as microscopic as those of the least intellectual of sempstresses.

But Nest, though she sewed for a while, was really longing to go for a walk, being unusually active in that respect for a young lady of her generation. It was all very well to be drawn along at a snail's pace behind Patch! ... And suddenly some deity-Hygeia perhaps-provided an excuse for satisfying this desire, by bringing to her ears a scrap of a conversation between her father and Mr. Thistleton, who had just come out into the garden, and were standing not far away.

"It was most careless of me, Precentor! The leaf upon which I made the notes of the proportions of that chimney must have been loose, and I greatly fear that I let it slip out while in St. Justinian's chapel!"

"But to the best of my belief," replied Dr. Meredith, "you never took out your notebook there. No, depend upon it, you dropped the page in Rhosson farmhouse itself, and the Lloyds, who are good, careful people, will have picked it up and kept it. I will send someone over there to make inquiries. No, my dear Thistleton, you cannot go yourself, even in the pony-chaise, for I am to take you in half an hour's time to drink tea with Mr. Salt the antiquary up at Bowen's Folly. If you will excuse me I will give orders about sending to Rhosson at once."

Throwing down her work Nest sprang up and ran after her father into the house. "Papa, you will be wanting Richards to drive you up to Mr. Salt's, and John Parry is so stupid that he will not be able to explain anything to Mrs. Lloyd. I will go to Rhosson and ask them if they have found the leaf of notes. It is only a mile and a half, and Bran needs a run."

The Precentor hesitated, then yielded. "Very well, my dear, since I know that walking gives you pleasure, and that John Parry is not very intelligent. I could however send him with a letter-yet, now that I come to think of it, I am not sure that Mrs. Lloyd can read. Go then, child, if you do not fear the heat. I shall not tell Mr. Thistleton, however, until after you have started."

It was not really very hot now, but Nest took her new parasol with her. She was proud of this adjunct, of which there was not yet another in St. David's. And beneath its shade she walked slowly along the route already traversed behind Patch this morning, accompanied by Bran, her mongrel brown dog, who had the formation of a lurcher but the pelt (possibly) of a retriever. Nest, however, deprecated criticism of his appearance, but exalted his intelligence and warm heart.

The lane was really like two long garden beds! Never, even in Devonshire, which she had once visited, had Nest Meredith met honeysuckle growing so thickly as here at home; never elsewhere, surely, were foxgloves so determined to go on blooming up to the very last infant buds of their spires. Further inland, it was true, the lanes had fewer flowers, but myriads of ferns. And yet the lanes were not overshaded like some of those in Devon, for they had no hedges on top of their banks; and the air of Dewisland was not soft and damp, but tingling with the wine of its twin seas, and magical always with the scent of flowers-even when no flowers were to be seen. Yes, Dewisland was Dewisland, and like no other place in the world!

Miss Meredith's quest was crowned with success. Bidden into the closely shut, never used parlour in all its stiff array, where there hung a picture much admired by her in childhood, of the wreck of a full-rigged barque, entirely carried out in coloured wools and enclosed in a black frame with a large natural whelk shell adhering to each corner, Nest received (in Welsh) the lost sheet of notes, dropped, by good fortune, inside the house itself. Looking affectionately at the woolly disaster on the wall, she asked if the Dutch prize were still in the Sound, and was told, No, that she had sailed some three quarters of an hour ago, of which Mrs. Lloyd was glad, for she did not like the look of the men whatever, and once when they came past they were swearing most horribly, she was sure, though she could not understand what they said. After which, with mingled triumph and respect, she asked leave to show Miss Meredith her daughter's new baby.

(3)

Calling off Bran, who was barking, from a safe distance, at the enormous sow in the yard, Nest started back. The sight of Mrs. Lloyd's infant grandchild had set her thinking of her own nephew, aged six months, whose presence, with that of his mother, was shortly to enliven the Precentory. It was strange to know oneself an Aunt. Undoubtedly it made one feel very old. On any count, indeed, twenty was a considerable age. One should, said Aunt Pennefather, begin to have serious thoughts at twenty. Yet Nest feared that her thoughts were no more serious than at eighteen, save that with riper years had inevitably come reflections-nay, more, conclusions-on the transitory nature of human affections, both male and female. For certainly last winter she had believed herself deeply in love with a gentleman, a stranger to the neighbourhood, whom she had met at a ball in Haverfordwest, and had even begun to picture herself going into a decline upon his account. There had not, however, been time for this process to take effect, since this infatuation, nourished on air, had lasted but a month, its demise, too, being materially assisted by the fact that young Mr. Perrot of Camrose had then begun to pay her somewhat marked attentions, continually finding, for instance, that business required him to ride eleven miles or so into St. David's instead of four into Haverfordwest. These attentions Nest enjoyed without in the least making up her mind about their author; then, suddenly, they ceased. So she had good reason, she told herself, to feel that she knew something of life and its impermanence. In her less cheerful moods she sometimes felt also that one so disillusioned should prepare for old age and spinsterhood by learning Latin, or following some intellectual pursuit equally sustaining to the mind. The cultured Aunt Pennefather, although she had married, knew Greek as well.

Reflecting on the advent of Jane and her infant, Nest, before she had gone very far, paused to look over the gate of a hayfield and, tempted by the thought of a short rest upon her homeward way, opened it and went in. The swathes of dried grass and daisies had been roughly piled into haycocks, but these were too high to sit upon without partial demolition, while the grass stubble, as she knew from experience, was apt to prove a prickly seat. However, as she penetrated further, her gaze lit upon a haycock on the further side of the field which seemed to have overbalanced in some way, and towards this pile she bent her steps. "I can leave the field by that further gate," she told herself, "so that I am not going much out of my way. How sweet the hay smells!"

She reached the haycock in question about the same time as Bran, who had loitered behind for some purpose of his own, and now rushed up panting.

"Lie down, good dog!" adjured his mistress. "It makes me hot to look at you!"

But the good dog did not lie down; far from it. Pricking his ears, he took a good sniff at Nest's chosen seat and began to bark at it.

Nest involuntarily took a step backwards and clutched her muslin skirts to her. Undoubtedly there was a mouse in the pile of hay. But she was brave; she did not flee, since it could only be a fieldmouse after all, which she did not dread nearly as much as the domestic variety; moreover, there was no other haycock so convenient. But how tiresome of the creature to have chosen this haycock, of all others! "Oh, Bran, pray stop!" she cried, for the animal's barking was now of an unmitigated frenzy and he was in addition beginning to dance about and to scratch at the pile. "See, I'll drive the mouse out for you!" And, with great daring, but with due precaution also, still holding her skirts very tightly and keeping as far away as possible, she stretched out her arm and poked the point of her new parasol into the yielding hay.

Yet even as one eating cherry jam from which the stones are thought to have been removed and are not, Miss Meredith received a jarring surprise. The interior of the hay possessed quite different qualities from its exterior; it was by no means yielding; yet whatever lay within had not the stark solidity of stone or wood. She had poked something living . . . something, too, from the feeling of it, much larger than a rabbit or hare-creatures which would moreover have leapt out at a touch, if not before. . . . This, whatever it was, gave no sign, uttered no sound. But the whole neighbourhood resounded with Bran's passionate barking. And at his mistress's

18

exclamation and backward movement he, doubtless from an instinct of protection, was stirred to something bolder than mere vociferation, and, making a spring at one end of the pile, he seized a bunch of hay in his mouth and shook it as if it were alive. Then, dropping it, he made a second fierce dash at the same spot as though he had found something better worth attack.

And, in a sense, he had, for, to Nest's equal amazement and terror, a human hand and wrist darted forth from the hay and, catching Bran by the collar, succeeded in holding him off, while at the same instant a violent earthquake movement convulsed the whole heap. Next moment the hay was falling back on all sides from about the figure of a disreputable young man who, wrestling with the infuriated dog, was endeavouring to get from his semi-supine position to his feet.

"Bran! Bran!" cried his distracted mistress. "Bran, come a way! Oh dear, oh dear, what shall I do?" For whether the individual emerging from the hay after the manner of Venus Anadyomene from another element were a haymaker of retiring tastes, or a bad character of some kind, she did not desire the growling and writhing Bran to rouse him to complete wrath by taking a piece out of his person.

"*Bran!*" Desperate, Nest advanced, and with difficulty seizing the dog by his collar, tugged hard. Thus, her effort coinciding by luck with a vigorous thrust on the man's part, she did succeed in pulling Bran away; and, more from fright than from any other motive, began to belabour him with the treasured sunshade, while the man, leaping to his feet the moment he was free of his assailant, disappeared like a flash round the nearest haycock.

"You naughty dog!" exclaimed Nest, trembling all over. She beat him again, her tepid blows awakening no protest. "How dare you-when I was calling you off!" Bran, panting, rolled over on to his back and gave an exhibition of the most abject and foolish contrition. With shaking fingers Nest fastened to his collar the leash which she had fortunately brought with her, stood a moment to recover some of her composure, and then started to walk quickly over the stubble towards the gate which she had already observed and which she knew must give on to a little lane leading back to the road. All thoughts of sitting awhile in the hayfield had now left her; her one desire was to get out of an enclosure where every haycock might, for aught she knew, be instinct with-what? Of what sort was the apparition with hay in his hair who had struggled with Bran and vanished so quickly? She could not imagine; all that she had had time to receive was an impression of youth, dark-haired, dark-chinned, of odd, shabby clothes with hay adhering to them, and of hurry. But the man could not merely have gone to sleep there and the haycock then have collapsed on top of him; he had been too thoroughly concealed for that. And people did not conceal themselves, especially in such an unusual way, unless there was a reason for it . . . and the reason was always a disgraceful one. Besides, he had been alarmed at discovery . . . or perhaps alarmed at Bran . . . or both. Thank Heaven, indeed, that he had run off as he had! But what an adventure! What would Papa say? And Aunt Pennefather, who alternated very inconsistently between disapproving of her niece's freedom of movement and denouncing in her mild, poetical way, the shackles imposed through immemorial ages upon the female sex?

Nest came through the little gate, from the scent of the hayfield to that of the lady's bedstraw and honeysuckle of the narrow lane, and she had closed the gate behind her before she became aware of a masculine figure. It was he, the man from the haycock, standing a little to her left on the opposite side of the lane, against the high bank of flowers, looking at her!

The young lady's heart thumped sickeningly; she backed by instinct against the gate behind her. Bran growled and tugged at the leash; but its loop was round his mistress's wrist. Afterwards Nest wondered exceedingly why she had neither screamed nor run down the lane, which, since this alarming figure was on the further side of her, she could at least have tried to do.

The man, however, seemed to realise that she was frightened, for he remained motionless, save that he pulled his forelock as a gesture of respect, while Nest stared with alarmed eyes at him and his attire-at his coarse check shirt, open at the throat, his white flannel waistcoat bound with black tape-he appeared to have no coat-his wide, short trousers of faded blue fustian, with six inches or so of bare ankle between them and his shabby brass-buckled shoes; and most of all she noticed the menacing-looking sheath knife which hung from his worn leather belt.

"I . . . I won't touch you miss!" he said rather hoarsely. "I only wanted to thank you for calling your dog off me."

"I thought . . ." began Nest, but her breath fluttered so much that she did not complete the sentence; nor indeed was she quite sure what she had meant the end of it to be. If anything, it was the expression of a hope that he had gone completely. Certainly she would have infinitely preferred that to his lingering to thank her!

"I wasn't doing any harm, miss," went on the young man humbly. "I be come to these parts hoping to find work-on a farm, maybe."

"But surely," began Nest, a little reassured by his still remaining at a distance, and also by a certain gentleness in his voice, which, though it held some kind of a country accent that she did not recognise, yet did not sound entirely uneducated, "surely you are not likely to find work ——" ("by hiding under a haycock" was on her lips, but she dared not quite bring out the words. After all, if she angered him he might still attack her.)

Something like a smile came round the mouth which was left revealed by the four days' or so of dark growth on the upper lip and chin. "I can guess what you was goin' to say, miss! I do-does-want work none the less. 'Tis hay harvest, and there be farms about here, and the hay scarce cut as yet."

"Some of the farmers here might indeed be glad of an extra labourer," said Miss Meredith, considering the prospective applicant. He was undoubtedly young, and probably strong, though there was a gaunt look about his ill-shaven face.

"Thank you, miss. I will go and try my luck, then . . . I suppose you couldn't oblige me with the names of one or two likely farms?"

"But . . . I don't know anything about you," answered Nest doubtfully. It took some courage to say it. However, she always had Bran.

But the shabby young man did not seem to resent the statement of this undeniable truth. "No, miss, you don't," he agreed and, bending his head a little, started to finger a flaunting yellow toadflax in the bank beside him. "But some farmer, belike, would take me on for a time without a recommendation."

"But where do you come from-you are not of these parts, surely?" asked Nest in a puzzled and still more dubious tone.

He did not answer, but began to rip off the laughing mouths of the toadflax, and it was something about his attitude, with head bent . . . Why, the boat this morning at Porthstinian . . . the bow oar . . . yes, even that white flannel waistcoat! It came back to her; and as if to confirm her recognition she now saw, tucked into his belt, a blue cap with a tassel.

"Why, I know where you come from!" she exclaimed, before she could weigh the advisability of her words, " —from the Dutch prize! You are one of the men who came ashore for water this morning!"

At that the privateersman raised his head and looked sharply at her and then up and down the little lane. Nest's heart jumped again with a recrudescence of alarm. "But I can always make Bran bark at him," she thought. Indeed it was obvious that Bran was ready at any moment to renew this exercise, not having ceased for a moment to strain at the leash and to keep a lowering eye upon the stranger.

The latter however made no movement in the least threatening. "You'll not tell anyone that, will you, miss?" he asked, and his tone was imploring, not a doubt of it. " 'Tis true; you did see me in the boat this morning-but I can trust you, can't I, you being a lady? And, miss, can you tell me, has she sailed, the *Vrijheid* ?"

"Is that the Dutch prize? Yes, she left some time ago, so they told me at Rhosson farmhouse."

"Thank God for that!" said the young man under his breath.

"Then you have run away from her?" asked Nest with more of disapproval than of interest in her voice.

"Yes, miss. That is to say, from the privateer as took her."

"But why?"

"I . . ." He looked down and hesitated. "I could not stand the life on board; 'twas too hard."

"Then why did you join a privateer?" inquired Miss Meredith a little scornfully. Never having experienced hardships herself, she yet considered that the other sex should look upon them, at least in time of war, as a privilege. Moreover, the Liverpool privateers shed a kind of vicarious glory upon the Welsh coast.

"I did not join one, miss," replied the runaway to this, "I was pressed-kidnapped, you might say."

"Perhaps then you are not really a sailor at all?"

"No more I am, miss."

"But, even if you are not a sailor by profession," remonstrated the (for once) warlike young lady, "you must surely feel how glorious it is to fight our enemies the French . . . and now the Dutch too . . . and to keep the seas clear for British commerce? Or perhaps you did not have to fight, but only to . . . to work the pumps or sails or something of the sort," she concluded rather vaguely.

This time the ex-privateersman's teeth, white and even, showed in a grin, and advancing for the first time (while Bran growled) he pulled up the loose check sleeve from his left arm, and drew Nest's attention to a puckered red mark, nearly a foot long, on the outside of the forearm-the scar of a recently healed wound. "I had that from a French cutlass when we fought the French brig, of heavier guns than ours, off Ushant in May," he said, and went off into a description of this action of which Nest could understand but few details, partly because she was so much surprised to see how the narrator's eyes were sparkling, how the humility had evaporated from his manner, and-though she did not realise this till afterwards-almost every trace of country accent from his voice. This deserter must positively have enjoyed the admittedly bloody fight in which he had been wounded! Why then had he run away from the-what was it called-the *Fair Penitent*?

"But will not the captain of the privateer be very angry when he finds that you never returned to the prize?" she asked.

"He won't know till he gets back to Liverpool. But I had to risk . . . what would happen to me if the rest of the boat's crew found me . . . and what will still happen if anyone . . . splits on me," he added in no cheerful tone.

"And what will that be?"

He did not reply.

"That was why you hid in the hay, then! . . . Did they look for you, the others?"

"Yes. I think they came into the field. If they had had a dog with them, as you had . . ." He shrugged his shoulders. "That was soon after I had given them the slip. Thank God that they have sailed . . . unless *you* mean to give me up to a magistrate, miss? If you don't no one else will. Only those men who were at the landing-place this morning could know me again, and I shall keep away from there." He looked at her with unconcealed anxiety in his grey eyes. Underneath everything he was, as Nest had by now recognised, not really rough of aspect, and even good-looking; the eyes in question, for instance, had lashes as long as her own.

But the phrase "a good-looking scamp" had come prickling into her mind. He was doubtless hoping to work upon her because of his looks and because she was a woman! Nest felt very experienced and disillusioned as she came to this conclusion. She gave a jerk at Bran's leash, that warrior now showing after all a tendency to relax his vigilance and go to sleep.

"I see no real reason why I should not inform the authorities," she said, with all the decision of a matron; but before she had had time to add, as she meant to do, "I do not say that I shall," the deserter, with a short, sardonic laugh, had broken in.

"Will you undertake to come to Liverpool, then, and see me flogged or keelhauled, or both?" His tone was suddenly and curiously that of one speaking to a man, and to an equal, not to a superior. "I don't suppose you have ever seen either process. I have; and I assure you that you would not enjoy witnessing them!"

Brutal, brutal words! Nest turned pale and shrank back once more against her gate.

"I am sorry," said the young man curtly. "But you see, madam, that you do not like the notion. I suggest, then, that you do not take upon yourself the responsibility of procuring me five hundred lashes or so. However, if you really intend going to a justice of the peace about me, at least I need not wait for the consequences. I must look for work in some other district; and I will therefore bid you good day before you can lay your information."

Bewildered as well as outraged-because he had so completely changed since the beginning of the interview-Nest would have let him pass without further parley, glad indeed to be relieved from the strain of this extraordinary encounter. But not so Bran, the intelligent and warm-hearted. For some time he had been sitting quite quietly (until, just now, his mistress had jerked the leash), though with his eyes fixed upon the stranger; but his opinion of him was not really changed. Individuals unlawfully concealed in haycocks, who caused his mistress (and himself) alarm, and were the occasion of his being chastised for doing his plain duty, were not going to slink away like that, as long as there was a tooth in a faithful dog's jaws, and the chance that that mistress, who had just reminded him of his duty, now had the end of his tether in her hand and not round her wrist. . . . Yes, better late than never! As the objectionable man passed, Bran launched himself like a knight in the lists, his leash flying loose behind him, got in a soul-satisfying bite through the fustian trousers somewhere in the region of the knee; was flung off; came on again, filled with the wine of battle; was caught by the throat by hands a great deal stronger than Miss Meredith's; was choked . . . choked more . . . was down on his back in the dust, struggling, suffocating. . . .

"Don't kill him, O, don't kill him!" cried the terrified Nest, the tears running down her face, for every moment she expected to see the sheath knife come out. "I'll do anything . . . help you in every way . . . give money . . . only don't kill him! I did not set him on, indeed I did not!"

Kneeling on one knee, pinning down his now feebly writhing assailant, the assailed lifted an angry face with set teeth and dark brows drawn together. He was going to strangle Bran! . . . Next moment, with a half-contemptuous exclamation, he had loosed him and got to his feet.

Bran too got up, very shakily, and going, with his tail tucked in, to the bank on his mistress's side of the lane, was sick; after which he shivered violently and lay down, all the knight-errantry squeezed out of him. The distracted Nest bent over him, half scolding, half petting, till, bethinking herself of Bran's victim, she turned round and saw that he was engaged in tying a not over-clean red cotton handkerchief round his right trouser leg, just below the knee.

She drew a long breath. "Has he bitten you badly?"

"It feels like it," responded the young man grimly. "I will take a look at it presently and wash the place. I hope I haven't hurt the dog overmuch; I don't blame him, on the whole."

This magnanimity nearly reduced Miss Meredith to tears again. "Oh, I cannot tell you how sorry I am! And you must have the bite attended to at once! It might be dangerous . . . though of course my dog is not in the least mad. Will you . . . will you come to the Precentory —I am Miss Meredith, the Precentor's daughter-and ———"

"To the Precentory —I?" he interrupted with a laugh half scornful and half amused. "A runaway sailor at a Precentory! No, I'll go to some farm ———"

"There's Rhosson, just back there; and Mrs. Lloyd is very kind."

He shook his head. "No, too near the landing-place. But I will find another farm, never fear, miss; and get taken on for the hay harvest, too, with luck."

Nest began to fumble in the little reticule at her waist. "You must allow me, please . . ." For "Miss" had come back into the conversation, and the country accent; and the young man must be poor, she thought, since he had been pressed for a common sailor. It was merely imagination which seemed, just now, to have given her a glimpse of something different.

But if it was embarrassing to intend bestowing money upon him, it was much more so to find that the intention must go unfulfilled, for she had not a penny with her. Very flushed, she desisted from the search, and said awkwardly instead: "Will you not tell me your name . . ." and stopped because he looked amused; then added quickly, "You may be quite easy; I am not going to a magistrate, after-this."

The runaway at that smiled fully; and when he smiled he *was* good-looking, scamp or no. "Mark Thompson, that's my name." Then he glanced at Bran, still lying dejectedly close to the bank. "I'll let you be going on first this time, miss, I reckon-not that I bear your dog any grudge; he's a good-plucked one for sure."

Nest murmured appreciation of this generous attitude. "And you will go to a farm, and have the wound washed as soon as possible," she adjured. "Perhaps indeed it ought to be cauterised."

"Thank you, miss. Perhaps it ought."

She pulled Bran to his feet. "And I hope that you will succeed in finding work."

"Thank you kindly, miss." Once more the forelock was touched; and next moment the Leghorn hat and the high-waisted pink muslin dress were going away down the narrow lane and disappearing into the wider one which met it. Their owner did not look back. The ex-privateersman waited another moment, then, compressing his lips, he leant up against the flowery bank, untied the red handkerchief, rolled up the leg of his loose trousers, and looked at the blood running down his calf from the blue and lacerated wound which was the memento of his meeting with Miss Nest Meredith, the Precentor's daughter.

(4)

Nest Meredith walked home rather fast, followed by a very different Bran from the bounding dog who had set out with her. Both their thoughts were occupied with the same person, yet they could not share them with each other. The immediate question for Nest was, how much she should tell her Papa, and she had not made up her mind upon this point even when she entered his study to see if he were back.

He was, and Mr. Thistleton, too, of course.

"My dear young lady," said the latter when, a little shyly, she presented him with his sheet of notes, "had I known that *you* were going in search of what I lost, I should never have mentioned my carelessness!"

"I think that is what Papa felt," answered Nest, a dimple showing for a moment. "But you see, sir, the distance is not great, and the gratification of recovering your notes would have repaid me for a much longer walk."

"For a lady, my daughter is really a prodigious walker," explained the Precentor. "I have known her compass as much as five miles in a morning! And this walk, I am sure, gave her nothing but pleasure-is that not so, Nest?"

His daughter's hesitation was so fleeting that it would have needed a very acute perception to notice it. "Oh, yes, indeed, Papa; as you know, I love walking!"

"Yet I expected to find you back before us," went on Dr. Meredith, "instead of the other way about."

"I did not hasten back," said Nest, dropping her gaze. "I . . . went into a hayfield on the way home, which delayed me." That was true; though the delay had not occurred in the hayfield.

Outside in the hall, with its panelled ceiling and old music gallery over the door, she stood rather guiltily reflecting, under the eyes of two prebendaries and a bishop. It was true that she had not yet had the chance of telling her father privately about her encounter, and, owing to Mr. Thistleton's presence, might not get that chance for a little while, but she was not sure that when it came she intended to take it. Would it not be a little like going to a magistrate with information about the runaway, a thing which she had told this Mark Thompson that she would not do? Besides, Papa might be rather horrified at the episode; might even feel inclined to curtail the freedom which had always been hers, since she grew up, the right of roaming unaccompanied about this countryside where she was so well known and loved. The question of telling Aunt Pennefather she never even debated.

Old Dixon, the English butler, was arranging something in a corner of the hall. Perceiving her standing there, he made an inquiry.

"Have Bran been fighting, miss, this afternoon when he was out with you? Richards say just now that he won't eat his supper, and have gone into his kennel, all skeery-like. But he didn't see no marks on him."

"Oh, *poor* Bran!" exclaimed his mistress involuntarily. Then she pulled herself up. "No, he has not been fighting, Dixon," she replied, and passed on up the stairs to her bedroom. She had not told a lie, since "fighting," in the case of a dog, had surely a strictly technical meaning, which did not cover conflict with a human being.

Thoughtfully she laid upon the bed the parasol which had so unavailingly chastised the culprit, and went and looked out of the window. But the Cathedral seemed to be gazing across at her with sternness —a vast reproof; in purple stone; so she came away again.

At the evening meal the talk veered round at one moment from the archæological questions which had been engaging Dr. Meredith and his guest to the Dutch prize brought into the Sound (of which Mrs. Pennefather now heard for the first time) and surmise was expressed as to whether the vessel were still there; had Nest heard when she went back to Rhosson this afternoon? A little nervous of approaching the subject at all Nest was thereupon constrained to tell them that the prize had sailed; and in the course of further talk was incautious enough to mention its name.

24

"The *Vrijheid*—indeed! Is that what she was called?" observed Dr. Meredith. "I presume that signifies 'freedom' or something of the sort. But how did you learn the name, Nesta? From Mrs. Lloyd, I suppose?"

Nesta's napkin slid suddenly from her lap and she stooped after it instead of replying.

"Miss Meredith has doubtless better eyesight than ours," Mr. Thistleton meanwhile gallantly observed.

"Not so very much, I think," interposed the Precentor, who prided himself upon his. "I looked very carefully as I stood at Porthstinian this morning, and could not see a sign of a name upon the vessel."

"You forget, Papa," said his daughter with a nervous little laugh, "that I had the use of Watkins's telescope." And if her colour was rather high as she made this misleading statement it could be assigned to her hasty dive under the table. But she knew that she ought to have bitten her tongue hard to keep back that implicit lie! It was not Watkins's telescope which had disclosed the name to her . . .

"The telescope," here remarked Mrs. Pennefather in her remote voice, and with a dreamier look than usual in her dreamy eyes, "the telescope is a contrivance which I have never been able to employ with profit."

"I did not know, my dear Gwenllian, that you had ever tried," returned her brother.

"Yes, yes. In younger and happier days I used sometimes to direct my dear husband's instrument towards the glories of the nocturnal sky-but in vain!"

"But surely, Aunt Gwenllian," objected Nest, glad to escape from the purely marine capabilities of the telescope, "you must have seen something! The moon-it is so large through a glass-or *some* stars!"

"Alas, they were never revealed to me," replied Mrs. Pennefather mournfully. "The night was ever starless to my vision." Here she shut her eyes for a moment and her lips moved; possibly she had realised that this last sentence might be considered to scan and was committing it to memory for future use. And yet there was nothing of the *poseuse* about Aunt Pennefather; she was a perfectly sincere and warmhearted woman, who contrived to run Dr. Meredith's house with success in spite of her poetry and her classics. Nest sometimes found her absurd, but she was very fond of her. She thought now, "It is plain that Aunt Gwenllian always shut the eye which she put to the telescope!" But she did not find much amusement in this reflection, for she was pursued by the feeling that this was the point at which to confess, without giving it the air of a confession-rather, indeed, to narrate in a sprightly manner-her meeting with a member of the crew of that Dutch prize, first under a haycock and then in the lane, and its conclusion, with Bran's attacking and biting him.

But it was just that bite of Bran's which seemed to make this avowal impossible.

Moreover the convenient opportunity had slid by. Her father and Mr. Thistleton were talking of their recent visit to Mr. Jerome Salt, the antiquarian and historian, which Mr. Thistleton appeared greatly to have appreciated. The Precentor remarked that he was glad that he had been able to read the letter inviting them there, for Salt's calligraphy was really becoming illegible, as he acknowledged himself. "He says," added Dr. Meredith, "that with this translation of Giraldus Cambrensis on hand, as well as his historical composition, he will have to think of employing an amanuensis." Nest asked what an amanuensis might be.

It was later in the evening, when Mrs. Pennefather, still with the air of a not very effective sibyl, had poured out tea for them, that the idea of taking an evening stroll-or hobble, as Mr. Thistleton put it-occurred to the two gentlemen. The soft lucent twilight, which lingers so long in the extreme West, made it seem earlier than the testimony of the clock would allow. And when Nest pleaded to be allowed to accompany them, her father, though he said that young ladies ought by this time to be in bed, and that she would probably catch cold, gave his assent, urged thereto by his guest, who said that Miss Meredith wished no doubt to see the ruins of the Bishop's Palace by moonlight, which was a most proper and romantic desire.

It was true that the moon was up; she hung just above the Precentory, but her rays had no power against the remaining daylight, did not even strike a gleam from the Alan when the little party crossed it on the tiny bridge, nor did they light up the beautiful arcading along the top of what Nest in a sudden burst of enthusiasm affirmed to be the finest ruin in the whole world. And certainly, even without the aid of moonlight, the Bishop's Palace looked beautiful enough, even if a trifle spectral, as they went through the ruined entrance gateway and found themselves in the grass-grown quadrangle. Mr. Thistleton, who had been here by daylight, expressed a wish to enter again the Bishop's Hall on the left, and Dr. Meredith preceded him in thither with the lantern, brought in view of such a desire-for, though roofless, the interior of the Palace was much darker than outside. Nest, however, did not follow their example, but stayed without, looking at the noble entrance doorway to the King's Hall in front of her, where over the double ogee of the archway still looked down the statues of the third Edward and his queen. In her heart she was perhaps hoping that the moon would by some miracle kindle suddenly to a real romantic brightness; but as this did not happen she finally and slowly ascended the entrance steps. She advanced, however, no further than the inner doorway, because she knew that in the great hall the floor had collapsed in one or two places, and as the whole range of buildings was supported upon vaulting she had no desire to slip in the gloom into one of the cavities.

Behind her she heard her father's footsteps, and his voice calling out warningly: "Nesta, Nesta, do not go in there without a light!"

She turned to reassure him. It was at that moment that she received the impression of a sudden movement somewhere behind her, and the sound of a thud, as if someone had dropped or sprung down into the vault below. She gave a half-stifled scream.

"Papa!" she called out in sudden alarm, "there is someone in here —I am sure of it!"

"Nonsense, my dear," said the Precentor, joining her on the steps, to which she had retreated. "You heard a rat, I expect-though to be sure that would alarm you more than a human being. Go and ask Mr. Thistleton for the lantern, then; he is just coming out of the Bishop's Hall."

Nest caught her father's arm. "And leave you alone here with . . . No!"

"Nonsense, child, there's no one here! Ah, there's Thistleton; ask him to be so good as to come this way with the light."

Nest darted down the steps on to the dew-wet grass. "Mr. Thistleton, Papa says——" And there she stopped, assailed all at once by a most unwelcome suspicion. What if the person she felt sure was in the ruins were he, the fugitive from the privateer-though why he should be lurking there she could not imagine? But if it were, she had betrayed him, for all her protestations of this afternoon!

"Thistleton, pray bring the lantern here a moment," called Dr. Meredith, peering meanwhile through the inner gateway. "My daughter thinks there is someone hiding in here. I am not of her opinion, but we might as well make sure."

Mr. Thistleton limped briskly up, the lantern shedding a circle of light on the weed-invaded steps. Nest did not follow him. Of course it could not be that young man, even if there were anyone there at all.

Suddenly her heart beat harder. Out of the silence and the shadows above her had come her father's voice, sharp and peremptory:

"What are you doing down there, sirrah? Come out at once and account for yourself!"

And on that there was a sudden scuffling of feet, as suddenly terminated, which suggested that the discovered intruder had not only scrambled up from the lower level of the vault, but was trying to make a bolt altogether. But the operation of clambering up had evidently put him at the mercy of the two gentlemen, and they had seized him before he could get past them. At least that was what Nest, outside, supposed.

"Stand still, stand still now, my man; we will do you no harm! But I demand to know what you are doing in these ruins-in the precincts of the Cathedral!"

"Oh dear, oh dear," thought the uneasy Nest. "If it is that privateersman, he may be desperate, and 'tis much more likely that *he* will do Papa an injury!" Bitterly repenting her cry of alarm she tiptoed up the steps and peeped in.

Yes, it was the young seaman, standing defiantly, under the further archway, between her father and Mr. Thistleton, both of whom had hold of him, the Precentor, no weakling, clutching a shoulder with one hand, an arm with the other, while Mr. Thistleton, holding aloft the lantern, gripped the intruder's other arm with his remaining hand. And even had Nest recognised neither face nor clothes, the fact that the captive had his right trouser leg rolled up above the knee, and the red handkerchief tied round his bare calf, would infallibly have identified him for her. She remained in the outer doorway suffering from a sort of paralysis.

"What are you doing here?" reiterated Dr. Meredith.

"Only taking shelter for the night, sir. I'm sorry if I ha' done wrong." The tone was less defiant than the pose. "I thought-seeing that this place was a ruin, like . . ."

"Too much of a ruin to be an honest man's sleeping-place! Why did you not seek shelter in some more fitting spot, some outhouse or barn?"

"And what is amiss with your leg?" queried Mr. Thistleton, glancing down at it.

The fugitive Mark Thompson answered neither question; he said, even more meekly than before, "I didn't intend no harm here, I assure you, sir."

"You are likely to do harm to yourself, then, making a bedchamber of that damp hole," retorted the Precentor.

"But I was meaning to sleep up on this level, sir, in a corner; then when I heard the young lady coming in, fearing I should frighten her, I slips down into yonder hole, so as she shouldn't see me."

"You are a very plausible fellow, whatever else you are," remarked Dr. Meredith. "But you have not yet told me what you, a stranger, are doing in this neighbourhood?"

"I was hoping to find work at a farm, sir," replied the young man, even as he had earlier replied to Dr. Meredith's daughter.

"Then why have you not gone to one?"

"I have, sir, and . . . they set the dog on me." He gave a glance down at his leg, and Nest drew a long, almost audible breath. "So I thought, sir, that maybe an Englishman like me had not a good chance here, and that I would do better to be pushing on in the morning towards Haverfordwest or Pembroke."

"Set a dog on you!" exclaimed Dr. Meredith. "I do not believe there is any farmer here who would do such a thing-unless indeed he caught you trying to steal! I expect that is the explanation, if you would only admit it. At what farm did it occur?"

The ex-privateersman looked slightly confused; perhaps he was regretting his accusation. "I can't get hold of these Welsh names, sir, saving your presence," he explained. "And I dare say they didn't like the look of me, though indeed I had no thought of stealing and only wanted to find work."

"Hold the lantern a little higher, will you, Thistleton," suddenly said the Precentor. "I cannot help thinking that I have seen this man somewhere before."

"Just my own impression," observed Mr. Thistleton, complying. "He reminds me somewhat of those seamen whom we saw landing this morning from the Dutch prize."

In the outer doorway Nest clasped her hands tightly together. Oh, he was lost, poor man, and through her unwitting fault! She had sent him to a prison, to a flogging, perhaps to keelhauling, which sounded a terrible punishment enough, though she was not sure of its nature . . . and her dog had already bitten him severely!

But on the face now so mercilessly illuminated by the lantern beams there dawned a look of bewilderment. "What Dutch prize, sir? Was you thinking as I came off a ship?"

"Nesta," said Dr. Meredith suddenly over his shoulder, "Nesta, are you there? Come here then, and tell us whether you do not think that this is one of the men who landed at Porthstinian this morning? You were watching them longer than we were."

Oh, if only she had not stayed within call-if only she could slip away now! But her father had seen her standing there on the threshold. She came forward feeling as though her limbs might have belonged to the stone Queen Philippa above the doorway. Whatever her desire prompted her to do, she *could* not lie outright to her father!

"What did you say, Papa?" Her voice seemed to stick in her throat.

Dr. Meredith repeated his question, while Nest, half looking, half not looking at the captive, felt the latter's gaze scorching her like a burning glass.

"The man whom we saw in the boat——" she began, very slowly, dropping her eyes to the ground.

"Well, look at him, my dear!" exhorted her father a trifle impatiently. "There *was* one younger than the rest, I remember, and I have a strong impression——"

For one fleeting second the eyes of witness and accused met. In Nest's at any rate there was anguish. Next moment the Precentor was the recipient of a strong impression of another sort, which reached him through the agency of a human fist, in the middle zone of his waistcoat; and though this partook far more of the character of a vigorous shove than of an actual blow, it loosened his hold of its author like magic and sent him staggering back several paces. Simultaneously, or almost so, the lantern was wrenched from Mr. Thistleton's hold and sent clattering down into the vault; and in the resulting darkness a form rushed past Nest and leapt down the steps. The captured intruder was gone.

The Precentor was too much winded, Mr. Thistleton too lame, both of them too much taken by surprise, to set out in pursuit; indeed the former, more damaged, however, in his dignity than in his bodily frame, was leaning gasping against the doorway with his hands to his diaphragm.

"Papa, Papa!" cried Nest, running to him, "are you hurt? Did he really *hit* you?"

But the Precentor, though breathless and outraged, was still a truthful Christian gentleman. "He . . . he pushed me . . . exceedingly hard. Young scoundrel . . . certainly up to no good . . . must make sure that all our . . . doors and windows . . . securely fastened!" Having recovered a little, he finished by saying: "Come along, Thistleton; 'tis of no use to pursue him now; we had best get back to the house as soon as possible."

In the press of this intention the question of the assailant's identity was, fortunately for the unwilling witness, crowded out. Abandoning all considerations of æsthetics or archæology-though not, indeed, quite unconcerned with ethics-the three hurried back to the Precentory, to find it wrapped in perfect security and calm, and Aunt Pennefather already retired to her bedroom for the night. Nest, conscience-stricken and unhappy, did the same; but she had hardly reached her room before her father came to her door to reassure her.

"You must try not to let that unpleasant little episode keep you awake, my dear child," he said. "Mr. Thistleton suggests that the vagabond was probably a gipsy, and I recall now that the young sailor from the prize, whom I thought at first that he resembled, was not nearly so dark complexioned. I do not imagine that there is the slightest likelihood now of his trying to break in and steal, so do not dream of robbers, my dear."

Nest did not dream of robbers, nor of gipsies. But she lay a long time sleepless in her little dimity-draped bed wondering if after all Papa were not right, and whether the young man from the *Fair Penitent* had not been lurking in the precincts with some ill intent. Why else should he have concealed himself there instead of going to seek work on a farm? For since she had the best of reasons for knowing it to be untrue that a farmer had set a dog at him, it was probably equally untrue that he had been to a farmhouse at all. . . . Yet suppose he had said: "Your daughter's dog attacked me"? He had not; he had preferred to tell a lie. And he had made his dash for freedom just in time to save her from either betraying his identity or herself telling a deliberate falsehood on his behalf. The look in his eyes, which she still remembered with vividness . . . had it meant that he wished to spare her that difficult alternative? At the moment she had half fancied so.

But for the first time it came to Nest, what if *behind* his taking the violent step of deserting from the privateer there were something more than just distaste for the hard life there? For he had not looked effeminate-far from it; and he had described the fight with the French brig with undoubted gusto.

In any case speculation was wasted on a man whom she would never see again, for it was very unlikely that Mark Thompson would ask now for employment at any farm in the neighbourhood. And since she did not feel that, after her deceitful silence, she could tell her father anything about him, she only hoped that with time the burden of that deceit would grow lighter, and that she would not, as just now, feel ashamed to receive his good-night kiss. Meanwhile she tried to turn her thoughts on to the impending arrival of sister Jane and her baby, who would be here the day after to-morrow; and picturing this joyful event at last fell asleep.

(5)

William David Frederick Stalybridge's name seemed almost longer than himself, though not as long as his embroidered robes, in which he had something the semblance of a tadpole with a white and inordinately flowing tail. No such irreverent simile, to be sure, occurred to Nest when she visited him in the room set apart as his nursery, or, feeling very important, walked slowly to and fro upon the terrace bearing him in her arms. It was delightful having this little creature here, it was a joy to see Jane once more, the young mother so proud of her offspring (to whom, in spite of her strictures on the position of the Cathedral, she had given the Saint's for a second name). As for the Precentor, he was in great spirits, and Mrs. Pennefather had quite abandoned Cicero and Euripides for Dr. Brownlow's *Nursery Guide*, though she was understood to be perpending some Lines to a Great-Nephew.

Although the whole household, with the exception of the Precentor himself, appeared to revolve round the tadpole, yet he could on occasion be left, since he had a nurse to tend him and still passed much of his existence in sleep. His mother and aunt were therefore able to take a walk together without feeling that they were neglecting either a duty or a privilege. On the fourth evening after Mrs. Stalybridge's arrival, making their way up to the cliffs, they strolled thence eastwards, looking down, as they skirted the top of Caerfai Bay, upon a long smooth green swell breaking on the sand between cliffs of pinkish purple. The grassy bank upon their left was thickly embroidered with flowers; rough gorse-sprinkled land stretched upon the other side of it, but after a while, when they had passed a little green promontory where the wraiths of a myriad sea-pinks still shivered in the breeze, they were aware of the scent of hay. They had come to a field wherein, not far from the bank, two men were piling hay into a wain, while further back other figures were busy raking it into swathes ready for the fork.

"Griffiths of Tan-y-bach has quite a good crop this year," said Jane, stopping and looking over the bank with an appraising eye. "Considering, that is, that this land along the cliff cannot be very productive."

"Last time I walked this way," observed her sister, "there was a quantity of that pretty tall blue flower-viper's bugloss, is it not?—growing just there among the grass. I wish I had plucked some of it before it was all mown down. The only other place where I have seen any growing this summer——"

She broke off abruptly. From idly looking for traces of the withered bugloss in the heaps of hay her eyes had wandered to the laden cart and to the two men in attendance on it; and now, with the unfinished sentence withered also, she was staring at the haymaker who was tossing up the heap with a pitchfork to the man on top of the pile. It was her acquaintance the deserter.

He was cleanly shaved now, and had not quite so piratical, so gipsy an air, though he still wore the same clothes, save that he had discarded the flannel waistcoat. And indeed, though it was not a hot day, the sweat, even at that distance, could be seen glistening on his forehead, and his mouth was tightly set as though the pitching up of the hay were a considerable effort. He did not once look at the two ladies on the further side of the bank, though their heads and shoulders at least must have been fully visible; it seemed as though his task were absorbing all his energies, for when the lad at the horse's head led the animal to the next heap, he did not immediately follow the cart, and, when he did, used his fork after the manner of a staff.

"How lame that man of Griffiths' is!" observed Jane.

Nest made no reply, but she was unconsciously twisting the ends of her muslin handkerchief about her fingers. The man on the cart shouted something impatient in Welsh, and he with the hayfork quickened his hobbling pace.

"It can't be because of *that*!" said Nest below her breath. But in her heart she knew that it must be.

"What were you saying a moment ago about viper's bugloss?" asked Jane. Receiving no answer she said, "And what are you dreaming about now, Nest? You'll find no flowers here now; the grass is all cut." She went on a pace or two, then stopped again. "Why, 'tis Griffiths himself on the cart. Good evening, Mr. Griffiths; I hope you are pleased with your hay!"

The small, black-haired man perched upon the cart looked round. "Why, I declare to goodness 'tis Miss Jane!" he exclaimed in his high-pitched Welsh voice. "Indeed you are welcome, ma'am! Will you please to wait until I do get down?"

So Jane waited while the farmer slipped down from his eminence. Nest had made a movement to go on, but saw that she would be obliged to wait also, though she would have given anything not to do so. She felt that she could not endure to meet the eyes of the man whom Bran had injured, and to whom her own timid foolishness had nearly proved disastrous the other evening; and she was sure that this interview with his employer must end by attracting his attention. Yet she could not turn her back and affect to be gazing out to sea, because that would naturally offend Mr. Griffiths.

In great discomfort she heard her sister asking after the farmer's family and receiving news of them; in greater still she heard her then remark-no doubt merely from lack of a better topic-upon the lameness of one of the haymakers. Had he met with an accident?

"Yes, Miss Jane, by what he says," replied Griffiths. "Leastways 'tis a dog-bite, and a nasty one, too. It don't get no better, and it do make him very lame, and I think I shall have to get rid of him whatever now that the hay is carried. He is a stranger and I took him without any to speak for him; a poor hand with a scythe he is, and indeed to goodness a cripple is very little use on a farm."

It was just at this moment that the subject of these disparaging remarks came limping towards the hedge to pick up his waistcoat, which was lying near it, the cart, now sufficiently loaded, having started to jolt back to the farm. This time his eyes quite naturally lit upon the two ladies in converse with his employer, and he paused for just the half of a second, the colour in his tanned cheeks deepening. Then without further sign he picked up the waistcoat, stooping rather awkwardly for it, and hobbled after the cart.

At the conjuncture of Bran's victim seeing her and of his master's words Nest would willingly have sunk out of sight behind the bank. Her impulse was to exclaim, "Oh, Mr. Griffiths, must you turn him off? It was my dog which bit him." Had she been alone she might have obeyed it; but in Jane's presence prudence restrained her.

. . . Or cowardice, she thought ashamedly a moment or two later, as, after a few more words with the farmer, they took their leave, and turning homewards retraced their steps along the cliffs, facing the first rosepink of the sunset. But for Nest the beauty had gone out of the evening.

(6)

By next morning, however, Nest (though not inwardly free from tremors) had so far got the better of her cowardice that she was standing, about half-past ten, in the porch of Tan-y-bach farmhouse resolved to do what she should have done yesterday evening. Two black-and-white collies, one old and the other young, half friendly and half suspicious, were vociferating just outside the porch, and at least three other guardians of various sizes had appeared in the yard behind. This canine garrison would have reminded her, had she needed reminding, that it was Bran's week-old misdeed which had driven her to this step. All yesterday evening she had been haunted by the limping figure in the hayfield, and by her own share, unwilling though it was, in Mark Thompson's present plight. And if her belief in his truthfulness had been shaken by his unexplained presence in the Bishop's Palace that night, it was nevertheless quite clear that he had genuinely sought work on a farm, since he had obtained it-only to lose it again-because of Bran.

Wrought upon by these thoughts, and finding her sister deeply occupied this morning with her offspring, Nest had seized the opportunity of slipping away, and in about twenty minutes had found herself at Mr. Griffiths' farm on the cliffs. There was no sign of the ex-privateers-man, nor indeed of any farm hands, so she began to fear that she might not find the owner at home either.

The noise of the dogs soon brought Mrs. Griffiths herself to the door—a stout, handsome woman, pulling down her sleeves over her arms as she came. Great surprise and pleasure were hers on perceiving her visitor, whom she besought to come in and drink a cup of buttermilk.

"No buttermilk, thank you, Mrs. Griffiths," said Nest; "but I will come in if I may. No, pray let me sit in your kitchen! I suppose Mr. Griffiths is out on the farm?"

"Well, no, miss. He's gone to Haverfordwest this morning. Was you wishing to see him?"

Nest, disappointed, acknowledged that she was. "But since he is from home, I can talk to you instead, Mrs. Griffiths. 'Tis . . . 'tis about that man I saw working in your hayfield yesterday evening-the man who is so lame."

"Yes, miss?"

"I was sorry to hear Mr. Griffiths say that he felt he would have to discharge him on account of his lameness. Did the man tell how he . . . I mean, do you know what made him lame?"

"Well, Miss Nest," said Mrs. Griffiths dubiously, "he did tell us it was a dog-bite, and Griffiths he saw the place—a nasty place whatever, he said-but Thompson 'ouldn't tell us properly how he came by it."

"I can tell you that," said Nest, who had flushed up to the roots of her hair. "It was my dog, Bran, who flew at him, I am sorry to say, and that is why I wanted to see your husband about the man."

"It was *your* dog, Miss Nest!" exclaimed Mrs. Griffiths. "Dear, dear! Was Thompson rude to you-did he frighten you, *anwyl* ?"

"No, no, not at all," said Nest stoutly. "No. I met him . . . in a lane, and he asked me quite civilly if I could put him in the way of some work. But Bran took a dislike to him and, just as he was going off, flew at him and bit him. And the man behaved so well over it that I was wondering whether I could not persuade Mr. Griffiths to keep him on, seeing that his lameness is really my fault?"

"Well, Miss Nesta *bach* ," replied the farmer's wife, looking appreciatively at the pretty, appealing face within the shady bonnet, "sure I am that Griffiths would do anything in reason to oblige you, yes, indeed, but besides that the young man was really a danger to himself and everybody else while the hay was cutting—I should think he never did so much as handle a scythe before—'tis too late at all now, for Griffiths did give him his wages and discharge him last night."

Nest's face fell. "Oh, I am sorry for that, Mrs. Griffiths! Not of course that I blame your husband. Do you think that the young man will be able to find work elsewhere? Do you know where he has gone?"

"To Llanunwas, I think, miss, on the way to Solva. And if he could not get work there whatever, he thought maybe he could find some in Solva harbour; he did say he was used to boats, and a lame man can row better than he can fork hay. And do not be thinking, Miss Nesta, that we did turn him off last night without shelter or supper, although he is a stranger and an Englishman and we do know nothing about him-no, indeed to goodness, Griffiths 'ould never do that! Thompson had his supper and a bed and some breakfast too this morning before he went off."

"Oh, you must not think that I am blaming Mr. Griffiths!" protested the visitor. "Of course he could not keep a man who was too lame to work . . . and, yes, I suppose Thompson might find something to do at Solva," she added reflectively. "I wonder indeed that having been a sailor he did not go to Solva in the first instance."

"Oh, he had been a sailor, had he, miss?" inquired Mrs. Griffiths with interest. Nest bit her lip to think that part of the secret which she was keeping even from Papa should have escaped her. However, it was not a very vital part-not, at any rate, in the hands of Mrs. Griffiths now that Thompson had left Tan-y-bach.

"Yes, or so he said," she answered negligently. "But I really know nothing about him; only, seeing that it was my dog who bit him . . ."

"Yes, yes, indeed, Miss Nest! And I am sorry that Griffiths should have been obliged to dismiss the man. . . . Must you be going now, Miss Nesta? I hope his Reverence do keep his health, and Miss Jane, and the lovely babe, as I do hear it is?"

"I suppose," said Nest just as she was turning away, "that the man will have gone to Llanunwas by the road, because he might have got a lift that way?"

"No, no, he did go by the cliffs, because he thought he might ask for work at the mill down yonder in Caerbwdy; but I am sure he 'ould not get it, and he will be nearly to Llanunwas by this time."

But will he? thought Nest when the door was shut. Mrs. Griffiths seems to reckon without his lameness, and as she probably has not stirred off the farm for years, save in her husband's gig, has forgotten how steep is the path just here down to Caerbwdy and up the other side, and how much steeper and longer is that down to Porth-y-Rhaw. Shall I . . . shall I?

But if she went after him, what could she do? Nothing, absolutely nothing, except to say how sorry she was, and give him what money she had with her.

Besides, what an extraordinary, and, had he been of her own station, an unbefitting thing to do-pursue a young man who must very little desire to see her, along three miles or so of cliff! What would Jane, what would Papa say?

Nest stood hesitating there in the sunshine, while the dogs fawned upon her. Then she deliberately turned her back on the direction of St. David's, and crossed the remainder of the field towards the descent into the first little valley running down to the sea which had to be traversed. As she went down the winding path between the bracken every foxglove among it nodded at her, but whether in approval or warning it was impossible to say. A bramble caught her thin yellow frock, flounced and flowered, which took a great deal of careful disentangling; it was evident that the blackberry bush at least did not favour the pursuit. And Nest herself thought, What shall I feel like when I come upon him, if I do; and what shall I say? . . . I shall pretend, of course, that I was just taking a walk along the cliffs, and be very much surprised to see him, and ask him what he is doing there . . .

So she planned as she went down into the combe where the small stream tinkled along almost hidden in wild mint, and was so shy that when it reached the shore it burrowed under the pebbles, and met the sea only as half a score of dispersed trickles. Down here stood the little water-mill; should she inquire whether a man from the farm above had asked for work there, or had even been seen passing? But a glance showed that the wheel was idle; the mill for some reason or other was not working to-day. So she continued along the stream until she could most conveniently cross it on the bank of pebbles at its mouth. Mounting again the other side, she was on a long stretch of turfy grass, and could see, away to the right, the sea breaking white round the bases of the humpy, close-pressed islets at the end of Ramsey Island; fifteen miles away, the shape of Grassholm dim in the haze; and in front and on her left hand the whole sickle-sweep of St. Bride's Bay. Last time she had been here, in June, the grassy bank which accompanied her had been one long nodding line of pink thrift; but now it was clothed in some places with the gold of lady's bedstraw, in others with the heaven-blue of the smaller scabious; and the ground at its foot was carpeted with the purple of the wild thyme. No wonder that the air was scented!

Nest walked on; the fields receded further from the edge. Still there was no sign of Mark Thompson; yet she had hardly come far enough for that. Soon she began to approach a lesser dip, Ogof-y-Ffôs, where the ancient stone dyke, of purpose unknown, which started miles away on the other coast, came to an end. Here there was no shore, for the stream, a very small affair indeed, did not visibly meet the tide, but fell, or rather trickled, when it reached the edge of the green trough, a good thirty or forty feet into the sea below. And it was here, near this outgoing, with his back to her, that a man was half sitting, half lying on the sloping turf, staring, apparently, at the Cradle, that strange jumble of rocks projecting into the sea about a mile away, between him and the invisible entrance to Solva harbour. He wore a very shabby hat; beside him lay a staff and a bundle tied up in a handkerchief. Nest recognised the clothes; the dirty white waistcoat and the faded blue trousers. It was undoubtedly Mark Thompson.

She stopped. He had not seen her, and owing to his position and the fact that the track which crossed the depression did not follow the verge but cut across the middle of the dip, he might not recognise her even when she got down. She was thus faced with a position of some delicacy, for if she were obliged deliberately to attract his attention she could not very easily feign surprise at seeing him. Fortunately, perhaps, a couple of stones slipped from the path, and the rattle carried to the ex-privateersman's ears. He turned his head in an uninterested manner; turned still further round, and then scrambled slowly to his feet, removing his hat.

Nest was by this time on much the same level, but a good ten yards lay between them. This distance the young man made no effort to lessen. He simply remained where he was, whether remembering that formerly his close proximity had alarmed Miss Meredith, or conscious that there was no reason for attributing to her any desire for further speech with him. So that Nest, after a moment's hesitation, was obliged to advance towards her quarry; and somehow all her design of affecting surprise at seeing him went by the board.

"I have just come from Tan-y-bach, Mr. Thompson," she began, and the trouble in her voice was evident. "I was extremely sorry to learn there that Mr. Griffiths had discharged you on account of . . . on account of your being lame."

He looked at her with a certain astonishment showing in his long-lashed grey eyes, cast them down, and fumbling with the ragged brim of his hat replied, " 'Tis very good of you to give the matter a thought, miss-very good indeed!"

"But of course I have given it a thought," returned Nest with vivacity, "seeing that it is, I fear, my dog's fault that you are lame. I am . . . I am much concerned about it."

The ex-haymaker shook his head. "Your dog only did his duty, miss. I don't wonder at his distrusting . . . a man in these clothes."

There was a kind of dull yet amused bitterness in his voice. Now that she was nearer to him Nest thought that he looked rather ill. Thin in the face he had been before-she had noticed that in the lane-but not, surely, pale with that curious effect of pallor beneath tan, as now.

"Mr. Thompson," she said after a moment, "have you had any treatment for that bite?"

"I have washed the place, miss."

"But that, evidently, is not sufficient. If you are so lame it must be that it is worse-and painful, too, I am afraid?"

"I've no doubt, miss, that it will heal in time," said he.

"Yes, but meanwhile . . . and you have lost your employment on account of it. Mr. Thompson, you must go to a medical man. Dr. Walters——"

"That's impossible," he cut in shortly.

Nest coloured. "But, naturally, Dr. Meredith would pay for treatment, since it was my dog which bit you." Then she remembered that Dr. Meredith was unaware of this fact, and could not be told of it.

The sardonic look which she had seen before appeared for a moment. "If Dr. Meredith was to pay for anything, miss, I reckon 'twould be for to have me clapped by the heels in gaol. But I wouldn't have you think neither," went on the runaway in a softer tone, "that I would have used violence on the reverend gentleman that evening, seeing he was your father, if I could 'a helped it!"

"But it was my fault," asserted Nest impulsively. "It was my fault for so foolishly screaming. If I had not — —"

But she broke off in astonishment, for Mark Thompson had suddenly hurled away the disreputable hat, and muttering, "I cannot keep this up any longer!" advanced several steps nearer. "Madam," he said in quite a different tone, "you do nothing but blame yourself when you have, on the contrary, shown the most extraordinary kindness and courage, both in keeping my secret from the beginning, and in striving so generously to avoid recognising me on that unfortunate occasion. Believe me, it was partly in order to save you from an unpleasant dilemma that I was driven to resort to force. I deeply regretted it; I hope you believe that?"

Speechless, Nest took a step backwards, as there burst upon her the full shock of the discovery which she knew now that she had been more than once on the point of making already. Not so talked any privateersman, runaway or no. That hybrid, intermittent accent and diction were as much thrown aside as the speaker's lamentable hat; the mask was off with a vengeance. She grew crimson.

"You are not a sailor or a labourer at all!" she exclaimed indignantly.

"But I admitted, madam, at our first meeting, that I was not."

"Yet you pretended to be . . . you spoke as if . . . and all the time you are a gentleman!"

"Your tone, madam, if I may say so, seems to imply some doubt of it!" returned the masquerader pleasantly.

"If I had known, I should . . . I should not have . . ." Nest turned aside, tears of annoyance in her eyes, and began to poke at the close-growing wild thyme with the point of her shoe.

"You mean," interpreted the runaway, "that had you known I was . . . an educated man, let us say . . . you would have gone to a magistrate and had me taken back to Liverpool to pay the penalty of my desertion?"

"No, sir, indeed I should not, but — —"

"At any rate, it seems that it was because you believed me of inferior station that you were willing to save me from that fate, and very nearly to tell a lie on my behalf to your father — a deed," he added in a softer tone, "which I shall remember all my life with wonder and gratitude."

"I did tell a lie," returned the heroine, almost crying. "At least, it amounted to a lie."

"For Mark Thompson, who never existed! 'Tis all the more miraculous and kind, then! Will you allow Mar — — the real individual to kiss your hand in sincerest gratitude, and then to go upon his way?" As she did not answer, the ex-haymaker very gently took her hand, lifted it to his lips, and let it drop again passive; Nest had once more turned her head away.

"I fully understand," went on the agreeable voice, "that while Miss Meredith can without fear of scandal be seen talking to a ragged unfortunate in whom she is good enough to interest herself, she would not wish it to be known that she had spent the same amount of time and charity over a man of her own class, even though the same rags covered him-and his plight was in fact much worse than that of a mere runaway sailor who could not find work!"

This exact penetration of her feelings at once astonished and exasperated Miss Meredith. If he realised that, then he had no business to deceive her as he had done about his social position-and with such ease too! She ought to have recognised sooner-at moments she *had* almost recognised-that there was something odd about this deserter. Then curiosity and alarm began to battle with outraged feelings. What did the concluding phrase of that short speech signify?

There was not much time left in which to find out, for its maker was obviously preparing to move on, since he was limping back to the spot where he had left his staff and bundle and was stooping to pick them up. What *was* his real plight then? An awful thought suddenly smote Nest-suppose he had committed forgery and that the gallows loomed in front of him? Forgery was the kind of crime which (she imagined) only an educated man would be able to commit. But surely not a man so young! Dr. Dodd, of whose fate not quite twenty years previously she had heard, had been, she believed, middle-aged . . . No, it could not be that; he must have been involved in some unfortunate "affair of honour" in which he had killed his man. That at least was a more respectable, even romantic, misdeed, though of course one must disapprove of the custom of duelling.

The duellist (or forger) now had his stick and bundle and was going after his discarded hat. Nest followed him.

"Sir," she said, not without timidity, "I wish that you would tell me what your plight really is. I assure you that I would not divulge it."

The runaway faced her, his meagre belongings in his hand. "No, madam, I have troubled you too much already. I do not, believe me, wish to burden you still further." But his tone was not repressive, and he gave her the attractive smile which she had seen once in the lane. No, he couldn't be a forger!

"But even though you are not . . . what I took you for, perhaps I could help you in some way," she persisted.

He shook his head, still with the smile. "You *have* helped me, madam."

But the more he resisted the more Nest found herself anxious to know the facts.

"It is true that I am only a girl without influence; but my father, if I explained matters to him . . ."

"But-forgive me for saying so, madam, you do not know what there is to explain! If you did, you would realise that neither the Precentor, nor, I imagine, the Bishop himself could procure for me the only thing which would help me now!"

"Oh, sir, you *must* tell me! What is it that would help you? Do you mean money?"

The shabby young man shook his head. "A sack of money could not buy what I need." He came a little closer and lowered his voice. "If your prayers have influence with heaven, Miss Meredith, what I need is a Crown pardon."

But Nest retreated a step. "A Crown pardon!" she gasped. "But that means . . . you mean you . . . Oh, what have you done then, Mr. Thompson?"

"My real name," said "Mr. Thompson," looking at her hard, "is Tyrrell, Martin Tyrrell. I think I had better not tell you what I am accused of," he added, with a slight accent on the "accused," "for I fancy that you are very patriotic here."

"Patriotic? Yes, we are patriotic; but what has that to do with it, sir?" she asked. "Why should you be afraid of patriotic people?" (Surely, surely, he had not run away from the *Fair Penitent* out of disloyalty-the idea was too repellent!)

Mr. Martin Tyrrell, late Thompson, continued to look at her rather defiantly, and a tinge of defiance was audible in his voice also as he said: "After all, I think you at least, madam, have a right to know the truth about my situation. It is this: there has been a warrant for treason out against me since last May-and probably a warrant for murder also!"

This stunning information, so much exceeding anything that Nest had imagined, had the effect of sweeping her legs from under her; at all events she found herself, a moment or two later, sinking into a sitting posture on the slope. Her eyes, wide with horror, were still fixed upon the maker of this shocking avowal; finding voice at last she got out: "Treason . . . *treason* ! . . . Then you are a Jacobin, a revolutionary of some kind!"

"Not in the least," answered Mr. Tyrrell, quite cheerfully this time, presumably because his dread secret was now disclosed; and he too lowered himself on to the turf at a little distance. "No more than the oldest canon of your Cathedral; no more than your dog, Miss Meredith, who so strongly objects to anyone resembling a sans-culotte. I am merely unlucky; more unlucky than I could have imagined any man with honest intentions becoming in so short a space of time. But I realise," he added quickly, "that you have only my word for this. I do not know whether you can place any more reliance upon it because, like yours, my father is in orders, though he is not a Cathedral dignitary, but merely a poor country parson!"

"How terrible!" murmured Nest, referring of course not to the less exalted position of the Reverend Mr. Tyrrell, but to the whole situation, intensified to her by a half-vision of her own father receiving, for instance, the news of his son William's pursuit by the law on two capital charges. And somehow it did not occur to her, any more (apparently) than to the fugitive, that this statement about his father's profession, though he tendered it as a proof of good faith, had exactly the same claim to belief as his previous statement about his ill-luck, no more and no less. "Is your father aware of your misfortunes, sir?"

"I am not certain how much the dear old man knows," replied Martin Tyrrell with a sigh. "Enough to wreck his peace of mind, at any rate, for I expect the parsonage was searched for me, and though I hope he would not credit the charge of treason, yet appearances could be made to look so black against me on that count, and are so black upon the other . . ." He paused, now wearing a very gloomy look.

"If your father does not know the truth," said Nest impulsively, "you must, sir, communicate with him in some way! Does he even know where you are?" And as the ex-privateersman shook his head, she went on: "But perhaps you are meaning now to make your way back to him? Forgive me for the question, but-have you money enough for the journey?"

"Again it is not a question of money, madam. I cannot go home in any case. It is there above all that I should be looked for-just as I dared not return in the *Vrijheid* to Liverpool, where . . . I know they must be waiting for me. I deserted from her rather than risk that. No, until I came ashore here the other day I have had no chance at all of writing to my father, and now I am afraid to do it, lest it should lead to my capture, which would be the worst blow of all to him. His correspondence," he explained, "is probably watched with that object, and any letter in my handwriting, of which the authorities doubtless have specimens, would be opened."

"But that is terrible for your father," said the girl once more. "Something should be done to relieve his anxiety. What if I asked my own father to write to him? No," she caught herself up, "I am afraid ——"

"No, indeed," agreed the runaway. "I certainly could not expect Dr. Meredith to intervene after the other evening's doings in the ruin, which alone must have given him a pretty unfavourable impression of my character-again my persistent ill-luck!"

For a moment Nest plucked at the wild thyme in silence. "There would be nothing to prevent *my* writing to your father," she said at last in a small voice. "You could instruct me, sir, in what to say."

Martin Tyrrell's face lit up, and he leant forward. "You cannot mean that," he said eagerly; "it is too kind, too . . ." In a sudden gust of emotion he also had recourse to the unfortunate thyme, and tugged out an entire tuft, roots and all. Studying it rather attentively he went on, in a voice which was not quite steady: "The thought of what my poor father must have been suffering all these weeks on my account has been, I think, the bitterest element in my cup. If indeed you could . . . somehow . . . but I ought not to ask it . . ."

"It seems to me, sir, that it is only right that I should do what I can in so distressing a case," replied Nest firmly. "But I must know what I am to put in my letter, must I not-the tale of your . . . of your misfortunes?"

Mr. Tyrrell wrinkled his forehead. "But if I tell you I shall make you an accessory after the fact. Heavens!" a look of horror suddenly overspread his sunburnt features, "you are that in some measure already!" He made as though to spring up, but subsided again. "I ought not to have told you my name; I have perhaps even by that rendered you liable to punishment as an accomplice!"

"Pray do not be so horrified, sir," returned the young lady with outward composure and a not unpleasant thrill of excitement. "The law, I am sure, does not regard females-and females under age especially-as accountable for such things in the same degree as men. And to be of service to your father (she did not say "to you") I ought surely to be in possession of the facts, or as much of them as you are disposed to tell me." She looked at the ill-starred Mr. Martin Tyrrell, sitting upon the same carpet of thyme-but at a proper distance-the blue waters of St. Bride's Bay shimmering behind him, with a sympathetic and expectant air.

And after gazing all round the little valley, which was perfectly deserted but for a raven or two, Mr. Tyrrell let himself slide some feet further down the slope, perhaps hoping thus to render himself invisible to any passer-by, while Miss Meredith would appear to be enjoying a solitary prospect of the ocean. Then he began his story, while the stream dripped to the rocks below, and now and again the shadow of a wheeling gull swept over the sunlit turf of Ogof-y-Ffôs.

II
ODYSSEY OF MR. MARTIN TYRRELL

" 'Sir, I am bold to ask thee first of this. Who art thou of the sons of men, and whence? Who gave thee this raiment? Didst thou not say indeed that thou camest wandering over the deep?'

"Then Odysseus of many counsels answered her, and said: ' 'Tis hard, O queen, to tell my griefs, for that the gods of heaven have given me griefs in plenty.' "
    Odyssey VII.

II
ODYSSEY OF MR. MARTIN TYRRELL

(1)

To whatever lies Martin Tyrrell had found himself committed in the two months since disaster fell upon him, including those mendacities uttered to Miss Nest Meredith at his first meeting with her, and to her father at his second, it was the unadulterated truth which he was telling that young lady at Ogof-y-Ffôs this morning. He cherished no revolutionary aims; he *was* the son of a parson; and he *had* been very unlucky.

But unlucky only since last May, since his untoward visit to Ireland-unless indeed one were to trace the springs of his misfortune a good way further back, to the ultimate cause of that visit, to the stay, that is, of his pretty sister Lucy at the house of a friend in London a couple of years earlier, at a time coinciding with that of the sojourn in the capital of Mr. Gerald Roche of Ballydare in the county of Cork. The Irishman, meeting her, fell head over ears in love with Miss Tyrrell's delicate and appealing beauty; he had money, land and position, and there was nothing against him, in the eyes of the Reverend Henry Tyrrell, save his nationality; and so Lucy's father, with the fear of a runaway marriage before his eyes, gave an unwilling consent to the match. From many points of view he might be considered to have done well for his almost portionless daughter, but County Cork seemed very far away from Northamptonshire, and no one in 1794 would have singled out the Irish as eminently peaceable subjects of the British Crown, nor their country as one of its happiest and most prosperous appanages. As for Martin, though he liked his brother-in-law well enough, he regretted that the Irish Sea had such power to cut him off from his sister. He was much attached to Lucy-there were but the two of them-yet he had only once visited her at Ballydare, and she had only twice crossed to England since her marriage.

The Reverend Henry Tyrrell, vicar of Selham St. Peter, near Thrapston, came of good stock-of well-to-do stock, too, though he, a younger son whose father had dissipated the family property, had never known what it was to have other than a lean purse. He had pinched and saved to send Martin to the University, and the young man, aware of this, was not ungrateful. He had done well at Oxford, though chafing sometimes at the restrictions imposed on him by his narrow resources. But, with a clear knowledge of what the payment of any debts of his would mean to his father, he had contrived to keep clear of financial scrapes; though he did at one period commit himself to an extravagance which, had he had any inkling of it, would have caused the Reverend Mr. Tyrrell much greater distress of mind, if not of pocket.

At the time when Martin was up at Brasenose, that is to say between the years 1790 and 1793, the principles of the French Revolution were proving a draught of heady wine even to sober Englishmen. A good many-and not all of them young men, either-were convinced, with Fox, that the fall of the Bastille was much the greatest and best event which had ever happened; it seemed to them to herald the new era of progress and enlightenment for which many generous minds were longing. And so, despite his quite genuine repudiation to Miss Meredith of any present Jacobin leanings, it must be recorded that for about a term, and although (perhaps because) the atmosphere of the University of Oxford was exceedingly unfavourable to such opinions, Mr. Martin Tyrrell of Brasenose College did proclaim himself an admirer of the National Assembly, did declare his conviction that sovereigns might be deposed, did belong to a minute and ephemeral society calling itself the Friends of Freedom, and did write both prose and verse eulogising Liberty and the freedom-breathing soil of France as contrasted with the enslaved earth of his native country.

But when reform in France was so quickly succeeded by bloodshed and anarchy, and when the Liberty which he had hymned, thinking that she bore in her hand an olive branch, grew more and more to the semblance of Bellona brandishing a torch, then Martin reacted violently against the distemper which had seized him, and Burke himself was not more hostile to the Revolution than he. By the time he had completed his residence at Oxford he was determined to embrace the career of arms, and looked forward to defending his country (whose soil no longer struck him as so desperately enslaved) against the hordes of Revolutionary France. The Reverend Mr. Tyrrell, having soldiers and sailors enough in his family tree, raised no objection to this course; the difficulty lay in raising sufficient money for the purchase of a commission, after the outlay caused by Martin's University education. The obvious plan was to turn that education to account; and but for that upheaval in France which he had once praised, Martin, when he came down from Oxford with a degree in the summer of 1793, might have found a pleasant and well-paid post as bear-leader to some young nobleman making the grand tour. But the Continent was now closed to such travels, seeing that Austria and Prussia had been at war with the newly-formed French Republic since the previous year, and in February the latter had declared war upon England and Holland. Mr. Tyrrell's wealthy cousin, Sir Sumner Tyrrell of Hartley Castle, with his swollen rent roll, could easily have found the money for Martin's commission and never missed it, but nothing would induce the gentle old parson to apply to him. Martin had never really known what was the cause of the coolness between the cousins, but, if it was something that even his father could not forget or stomach, then he was not going hat in hand to his rich kinsman. So he turned to tutoring in England, an occupation which, though abhorrent to him, he stuck to with determination. And gradually the day of release grew nearer, with its prospect of seeing real war and adventure, instead of voyaging with stupid youths over the uneventful seas of Livy or contending with their remarkable renderings of Horace.

But before the necessary sum was quite saved adventure was to come to the aspirant with only too much completeness.

(2)

"This is a letter from Lucy, sir," said Martin, looking up from his breakfast on a wet morning of early May, when all the thrushes in the Vicarage garden were questing about the lawn for worms. "She invites me to go over to Ballydare to pay them a visit as soon as I can."

The Vicar put down his cup, wrinkling the forehead which was only too ready to show signs of worry or perplexity. "Lucy-she is well, I hope? —wants you to go to Ballydare? Nothing wrong, I trust?"

Martin laughed. "How apt you are, my dear father, to anticipate misfortune! Lucy has her husband, if anything were amiss; you know how devoted a couple they are. She would hardly turn to me for assistance!"

The Reverend Henry Tyrrell's troubled look relaxed a little. Gentle, delicate, ineffectual, married late in life, he had never really recovered from the loss of his wife some ten years earlier.

"I do not like the accounts of the events in Ireland which we see in the newspapers, the disloyalty which appears to be rampant there, the spread of this 'defenderism,' as they call it, amongst the Papists. I have for a long time been anxious lest there should be an outbreak against the Protestants in the neighbourhood of Bantry. Needless to say, I would not have had our dear little Lucy marry a Roman Catholic, but I sometimes think that, if she had, I should be less uneasy about her safety in County Cork."

"No, you would not, sir," replied his son affectionately. "You would then be teasing yourself about the dangers of her situation with regard to the Protestants, picturing Ballydare raided by Whiteboys, or whatever they call themselves nowadays —'Orangemen,' is it not?"

Mr. Tyrrell shook his silver head and poured himself out a fresh cup of tea in the hesitating manner in which he now did everything. The smile was off Martin's face as he looked at him; a little frown appeared for a moment between his own incisive eyebrows, and his glance strayed down again to the letter by the side of his plate, and to the sentences in it which said so pleadingly: "I am very uneasy about Gerald; I cannot tell you more in a letter, and pray, pray do not mention even this much to Papa, but *come over as soon as you can*! There is no one here in whom I can confide."

The letter threw no light on the nature of his sister's uneasiness. Was it possible that Gerald, but a couple of years ago so madly in love with Lucy Tyrrell, was already betraying Lucy Roche? No; Martin rejected the idea almost at once. The appeal must mean that his brother-in-law had for some reason fallen into ill odour with his Catholic neighbours in County Cork-just exactly what Mr. Tyrrell had been saying that he feared. Martin slid the letter unobtrusively out of sight into his pocket.

"Lucy sends you her fondest love, sir, and wishes, I am sure, that you, too, could take the journey to Ireland."

His father directed a rather wistful glance at the spot where Lucy's letter had lain. "Does she say anything else of interest?"

"Nothing at all," replied Martin firmly. " 'Twas merely a short letter suggesting that I should pay her a visit if I could arrange it."

"I see," said the old man resignedly. "But can you do so, Martin? What about young Heseltine?"

For Martin was acting temporarily as tutor to a young gentleman in the neighbourhood of whose presence the University of Oxford had decided for a time to deprive itself.

"I only engaged to lick that ill-conditioned young cub into shape for three months," quoth his son, "and my term of servitude finishes to-morrow, a fact of which, my dear father, I had already informed you. But you were thinking of your next sermon, or of Betty What's her name's rheumatism . . . There is no difficulty on that score. You will not object to my leaving you for a couple of weeks or so, to pay Lucy a short visit?"

"No, no," said Mr. Tyrrell, "go by all means. I shall miss you, my dear boy-you are very good to your tiresome old father. But I shall make shift, I shall make shift. It will serve to inure me against the day when you leave me for service abroad with your regiment."

(3)

It was a soft, misty evening when Martin finally arrived at his brother-in-law's house of Ballydare; the mountains were blue and shadowed, and there was no colour this time in the distant glimpses of Bantry Bay. The whole countryside struck him, as on his only previous visit, soon after Lucy's marriage, as beautiful almost to aching point-for Martin was sensitive to such things-but strangely, poignantly sad. Now to this impression was added, this green spring evening, a feeling of some unknown menace. What could it be that Lucy feared?

It was a relief as he sprang out of the chaise to see Lucy herself, smiling and waving her hand to him, on the steps of the old white house.

"By gad, she's lovelier than ever!" he thought; and then he kissed her affectionately, and felt the nervous pressure of her arms round his neck, and her whisper in his ear: "O, Martin, I am so thankful you have come!"

His arm about her waist, he went with her into the great, damp old-fashioned drawing-room, with its windows giving on to none-too-well-kept lawns and ragged cedars. There, by the generous turf fire whose heat and fragrance were welcome after his journey, he took her hands and said: "Dearest Lucy, what is wrong? I have spent so many hours wondering, but I think that I have guessed at last. Your husband is being made to suffer for his loyalty!"

She shook her head, her mouth trembling. "Oh no, no! Alas, it is not that—I could wish it were!"

"*You could wish it were!*" repeated Martin in astonishment. His first, rejected suspicion returned to him. "You do not, surely, mean that you suspect him of . . . unfaithfulness? Is he at home, by the way?"

"No; he is in Dublin, but he comes back to-morrow. Oh no, a thousand times no! He loves me as dearly as I love him . . . and, Martin, in the autumn I am going to have a child!"

"Dear sister!" exclaimed the young man, taking her into his arms again, and thinking, "That no doubt is partly why she is so agitated. Come, sit down here with me by the fire. This is indeed good news! How pleased our father will be! And you-are you not glad?"

Lucy sat down and put her handkerchief to her eyes. "Martin, it has been my dearest dream. But now my baby, when he comes, may be the child of . . . an outlaw."

"Lucy!" exclaimed her brother in high dismay, "what on earth do you mean?" But all the answer he received was a sob. "Lucy, for God's sake, explain yourself! What has Gerald done?"

" 'Tis not so much . . . what he has done, as what he has become . . . and what he may be going to do! Martin, he has . . . gone over to the rebels; he has joined this society which they have reorganised, the United Irishmen. He is hand and glove with men like Mr. Arthur O'Connor of Connorville, and . . . and others whose names would mean nothing to you. I don't know what will become of him!"

Martin loosed his hold of her. "Good God! Gerald Roche, a Protestant and a loyalist, if ever there was one-or so we thought!"

"He is a Protestant still; he has not changed his religion, Martin. He says that religion has nothing to do with it; and for that matter I believe that most of the United Irishmen are Protestants, for the movement started in Belfast. Mr. O'Connor is certainly not a Catholic . . . He has been here twice to see Gerald, and Gerald is always going off to meetings, and that is why he has gone to Dublin now, I am sure, though he gave me another reason. And Martin —" she clutched him again, her pretty face quite haggard in the firelight —"Martin, I cannot help knowing (not from anything that Gerald told me, but from something which I overheard Mr. O'Connor say, the last time he was here) that the United Irishmen are planning to despatch an emissary to ask the French Republicans to help them, to send a force to invade Ireland in their interests, so that the country may rise . . . But invasion will fail . . . and the rising will be put down . . . with severity . . . and then what will become of Gerald?"

"What is it that you want me to do?" asked Martin after a moment of horrified silence.

"I hoped that you might be able to persuade Gerald to think better of it."

"*I* persuade him, if *you* cannot, Lucy!"

Lucy turned her head away. "The trouble is that when we talk of these things, he almost persuades me!" And as her brother gave an exclamation, she went on feverishly, "Martin, there *is* something in what these men say! It is not right, it is not legal of the English Government to seize without trial those poor peasants in Connaught suspected of being Defenders, and send them to serve in the Navy in order to get rid of them! And then there are those dreadful persecutions of the Catholics in Armagh by the Protestants, who are wrecking their homes and driving them out of the county-while the magistrates do little or nothing!"

"I do not suppose," said her brother judicially, "that they find there is much to choose between the two parties. And is it not a fact that the Orange Society was formed last year by the Protestants in order to protect themselves against the aggression of the Catholics? Was there not just at that time a pitched battle somewhere in Armagh where the Catholics were the assailants?"

"Yes," admitted Lucy, "the battle of the Diamond."

"And you really believe, Lucy, that these difficult internal questions can be settled by invoking the aid of our inveterate enemy, France, now doubly, trebly our foe on account of the subversive ideas with which she is poisoning Europe?"

"But I thought that when you were at Oxford, Martin, you were all for the Revolution and the glorious ideals of liberty which it had brought into the world?"

Her brother reddened. "I was a raw youth then. Long ago I saw that I had been led astray by an ignorant and boyish enthusiasm."

" 'Tis not so very long ago, Martin . . . And these Irishmen are not boys, but grown men, men of intellect and education, many of them of good social standing."

"A pretty use, then, to which to put all these advantages-the corrupting of loyal citizens!" commented the young man with all the indignation of the oldest and most crusted Tory. "I should most certainly like to talk to your husband! But it is a shock to me to find that my own sister is tarred with the same brush!"

"No, no, I'm not!" she cried. " 'Tis only that it is so difficult for me to argue with Gerald when he tells me of the horrors and injustices which take place every day in Ireland, when some take place almost under my own eyes! And I cannot ask any of the loyalist gentlemen of our acquaintance in the neighbourhood to try to dissuade him from the path he is set upon, because I dare not let them know that he *is* set upon it-it might not be safe. So there is no one but you, Martin, for I know that I can count upon my brother not to use his knowledge to hurt my husband. I beg of you to have the matter out privately with Gerald when he returns. I am so sorry that he was not back in time to greet you-Oh, dear Martin, do not look so stern; do not say that you are displeased at my plan, that you will not do your utmost to save him from this folly!"

"You call it folly, Lucy, and yet you seek to justify it! I suppose that is because you are what is called a good wife?"

"I call it folly," said his sister, with more firmness than she had yet shown, "because I am sure the plans of these men are not likely to succeed."

"As a loyal Englishman," observed Martin, "I can thank God for that! With regard to this scheme of yours, I presume that your husband is not aware of it, but does he even know that I am in his house at all?"

"Oh, yes," said Lucy with a little smile, "he knows that; he was pleased that I should ask you to come, and he joined his invitation to mine-did I not say so in my letter? I was so troubled when I wrote, so afraid lest I should say too much. You did not let Papa guess that it was upon Gerald's account that I wished to see you, did you, Martin? Yes, yes, Peter, serve supper in a quarter of an hour-can you be ready, Martin?" And as the door closed behind the old servant she said, half laughing, but with tears in her eyes, "You must be starving, dear traveller-forgive my selfishness!"

"I do not call it selfishness, dearest Lucy," said Martin gently, "and when Gerald returns I will do my best."

(4)

But Gerald Roche did not return next day after all. Lucy augured all sorts of ill omens from the delay, was sure that "those men" had entrapped him still deeper into their scheme; but Martin, with masculine commonsense, asserted that the cause had probably something to do with his Dublin tailor.

Next morning, when he had just finished shaving, Lucy came knocking at his door, and when he admitted her, half-dressed, she held out a letter with a face of tragedy.

"I knew that I was right! Oh, Martin, it means ruin!"

Her brother read:

> *My dearest Lucy,*
>
> *I am grieved to the heart at not returning to Ballydare on Wednesday as I had intended, but I am unavoidably detained in Dublin by affairs. It may even be that I shall find myself obliged to* (here, though the words "go to" had been run through with the pen, they were still visible, but the actual destination was too thickly crossed out to be read) *take a short journey, so do not, my dear love, be alarmed if you hear nothing from me for a little while. I hope that your brother will be able to keep you company until my return and, indeed, for as long afterwards as he pleases, by which he can show me that he forgives, as I hope he does, my absence at this moment, which I greatly regret and for which I sincerely apologise.*
>
> *Your devoted husband,*
>
> *Gerald Roche.*
>
> *P.S. —Tell Doyle not to forget the warm mash for Countess.*

Lucy watched her brother read this not very informatory missive; then she sat down upon the tumbled bed and dissolved into tears.

Martin for his part stood staring hard at the sheet of paper as though he thought it could tell him more if it would, held it up against the light to see if it were possible to make out the obliterated word, and found it was not. Then he sat down and put his arm round his weeping sister.

"Lucy, dear, do not cry so! Are you not making a mountain out of a molehill? I am sure you do not wish to be one of those wives who tie their husbands to their apron-strings. If Gerald does stay longer in Dublin, even if he should take this short journey of which he speaks——"

" 'Tis not really a short journey that he means," broke in Lucy, swallowing down a sob. "He wrote that to account for his absence even from Dublin. He means that he is being sent by those men upon a long one! I am sure of it, I am sure of it! And you see that I was right, Martin, and not you, about the reason of his not arriving yesterday; 'tis no business with his tailor that is keeping him!"

"But what journey, long or short, can he be setting out upon?" asked Martin, frowning. "It must be unexpected, by the look of it."

"Listen," said Lucy, seizing him by the arm. "When I overheard Mr. O'Connor talking to him that day about the possibility of French assistance, he said that since no emissary of theirs could hope to get to Paris without English spies knowing of it, they would have to get into touch with the Directory in another way, and that was, through the French diplomatic agent in one of the neutral countries, and preferably at a port. And it is my belief that they are sending Gerald on this mission, because he speaks French so well-perhaps you did not know that, but he does; he travelled a good deal in France, before the war."

"By gad!" exclaimed Martin, rather impressed by her conviction. "In that case, the scratched out word in Gerald's letter may well be the name of the place to which O'Connor and the rest are sending him?"

Lucy nodded. "I tried and tried again to read the word before I brought the letter to you. Oh, how could Gerald be so unkind as to keep from me where he is going!"

Her brother jumped up from the bed and, going to the window, made another effort to read the blotted word, but in vain. Lucy too had risen, and stood by the bed with her loosened hair flowing round her, looking unutterably forlorn and frail, and Martin remembered that she was going to have a child. Anger against Roche seized him; what was he thinking of, so cruelly to agitate his wife at this time!

He went back to his sister and took her in his arms. "Lucy, dearest, what if I were to post off at once to Dublin, see your husband-if he have not already set out-tell him that he is making you ill, and that he must give up for the present, at least, this notion of . . . well, we'll call it taking a short journey? His letter does not sound as though he were necessarily leaving Dublin immediately, and I might well be in time to find him."

Lucy snatched at the offer. "Oh, Martin, my dear Martin, would you indeed do that for me? Truly you are a good brother-more than a good brother!" Her pathetic gratitude went far to repay Martin for thus incontinently taking the road again; and he said, with no visible trace of reluctance, that as no time should be lost, he would start for Cork and Dublin immediately after breakfast.

That repast over, he was strapping up his valise when Lucy came in with something in her hand.

"I know that you have not a great deal of money to spare, dear Martin," she began shyly, "so you must take this for your journey, since you are making that journey entirely upon my account. 'Tis my own money-Gerald is very generous. No, I shall not consent to your going at all unless you take it!" And, as he waved away the roll of notes, she added coaxingly, "Now do not be foolish, kindest of brothers! Surely you can accept money from me when it is for my own service!"

"It is true, I suppose, that you are the only lady from whom I can accept such a thing," said Martin, relenting. "But this is far too much, Lucy; the half would suffice."

"No, no, keep it!" she insisted. "You never know to what expenses you may not be put, particularly if you go post, as you must do if you are to catch Gerald. You can return me what is over, if you insist, when you come back."

Martin disliked taking the money, but it is one of the curses of limited means that one cannot make the generous gestures one would wish, and he would really have been somewhat put to it to face the possible expenses of this undertaking, since he certainly must not economise if he wished to arrive in time to stop his brother-in-law from setting out for that foreign town or country whose name lay concealed beneath those obliterating scratches.

That letter Martin took with him on his journey, but all his diligent study of it advanced him not a jot, save that the last two letters but one sometimes looked to him faintly like "*on ,*" though of this he was far from sure. There was also something that might have been a "*t* " in front of them. The initial letter might equally well have been "*H ,*" "*A* " or "*N* ." But it was more from curiosity than from anything else that he gave so much study to the aggravating word, for he had a good hope of catching Roche, and reasoning with him, at the hotel to which Lucy had directed him, the "Green Stag," in a small street on the right bank of the Liffey.

(5)

"Mr. Roche left this afternoon, you say?"

Martin stood in the dark little entrance hall of the "Green Stag" and repeated in an irritated tone the information which Mr. Ignatius Murphy, the landlord, had just imparted to him. He had, naturally, realised the possibility of being too late, but he had made such haste! The annoyance which he felt against his brother-in-law had not lessened during his journey; now it mounted several degrees higher, and was joined by something like dismay. It might not be easy to find Gerald now.

He stared at the large visage of Mr. Ignatius Murphy, wreathed in a propitiatory smile. "Do you know where Mr. Roche was going?" he asked.

"I declare, your honour, that I have not the smallest notion," replied Mr. Murphy, altering the quality of his smile but not diminishing it.

"Was he going out of the country-to England, for example?"

"Sure if your honour was to place the crown of all the Pope's Indies upon me head I couldn't tell ye!"

"I *must* find out where he has gone to," said Martin crossly. "I have a message for him from his young wife in County Cork-my sister."

"Dear now, if that's not the misfortunate thing!" observed Mr. Murphy, lifting his hands, the smile turned down now to a mere sympathetic glow. "Why wouldn't I be askin' himself when he left where he was goin', the way I'd be able to tell your honour!"

But help was at hand. Behind Mr. Murphy a pretty, rather slatternly head was poked round a half-open door. "If the gintleman wants to know where Mr. Roche will be off to," said the head, "there's one in Dublin can surely tell him, and that's ——"

"Whist now!" exclaimed Mr. Murphy swinging round "Will you be holding your tongue, Bridget!"

"——And that's Mr. Oliver O'Driscoll-Lawyer O'Driscoll," proceeded Mrs. Murphy. "Sure if Mr. Roche's lady, the pretty young thing-himself was after bringing her here once-wants news of her husband, bless her heart, 'tis Mr. O'Driscoll will be giving it!"

The smile which had hitherto seemed glued there had surprisingly left Mr. Murphy's visage by now; he looked distinctly put out. "Let your honour not be listening to the woman!" he said quickly. "Sure she knows nothing whatever about the matter, and 'twill be wasting your honour's time entirely to go to Mr. O'Driscoll."

"Nevertheless it is worth making the attempt," said Martin. ("And all the more that you seem so anxious to prevent me," he added to himself.) "Where does Mr. O'Driscoll live? He's a lawyer, you say-but it is too late to go to his office to-night."

It was Mrs. Murphy who answered from behind her door, her husband having turned aside, muttering something uncomplimentary about thim that was always after interfering. Martin thanked her, intimated that he wished to engage a room for the night at the "Green Stag," and, after removing the stains of travel, partook of a badly cooked meal served on a damp table-cloth, and then set out to find Mr. O'Driscoll, congratulating himself on the piece of good fortune (as he considered it then) which had sent Mr. Murphy's more communicative spouse to give him the lawyer's name and address. He had never heard of him before, and wondered if he were Roche's usual legal adviser.

Mr. O'Driscoll, however, was not at home that evening, so Martin found upon arrival at his door in Conroy Street. He was said to be supping with a Mr. James Malone, in the square yonder, and thither Martin, after a moment's cogitation, betook himself.

Mr. Malone's dwelling was more impressive than Mr. O'Driscoll's had seemed to be; evidently he was a person of means. The manservant who opened the door said, in response to a query, that himself was not entertaining any other gentleman; there was only Mr. O'Driscoll in it, and their honours just after taking their second bottle in the library. Stimulated by half a crown he admitted the inquirer, and Martin shortly found himself being ushered into a large room with tall curtained windows, several bookcases, a monumental table, and a bust or two; and was announced in an abnormally loud voice, not by his name, though he had furnished it, but as "A gintleman to see Mr. O'Driscoll, your honour!"

Each of the two occupants of the room was comfortably disposed by the fire with a bottle at his elbow. One of them rose on Martin's entrance; a thin, precise stick of a man, the typical lawyer. The other, who clapped his hand behind his ear in the manner of the deaf, slewed his considerable bulk round in his chair, and Martin saw that he was elderly, with a noticeable paunch and hair growing in thick grey curls over a massive brow.

"I must tender my sincere apologies," began Martin, addressing both these individuals, "but I need not intrude upon you for long, gentlemen. I understand that Mr. O'Driscoll can inform me of the present whereabouts of my brother-in-law, Mr. Gerald Roche of Ballydare——"

"I can't rightly hear what he says, Malone," here interrupted the stout man, looking up at the other. "What's this about Roche's mother-in-law?"

"*Brother-in-law* ," enunciated Mr. Malone as he stooped to the blunted ear of him who, surprisingly, was Mr. O'Driscoll after all. "This gentleman has come, I understand, to ask you for Mr. Roche of Ballydare's direction."

"And why, in the name of all the saints, should he come to me for it?" demanded the stout attorney. His voice, to Martin (who had now made the necessary readjustment of identities), sounded a shade disconcerted, but his heavy features betrayed nothing.

The owner of the mansion advanced a little towards the newcomer. "Mr. O'Driscoll has the misfortune to be hard of hearing, sir," he explained. "Would you have the goodness to speak somewhat loudly and slowly?"

Feeling as if he were addressing a public meeting, Martin began in what he hoped was a carrying voice: "I am Mr. Roche's brother-in-law, sir, and have come to you because his wife, my sister, who is in delicate health, is anxious about his whereabouts and his safety."

"Safety?" queried Mr. O'Driscoll, raising his thick eyebrows. "What do ye mean by that term-why wouldn't Mr. Roche be in safety? And anyhow I'm not after keeping him in me pocket, Mr. . . . I haven't the pleasure of your name yet?"

"It is Tyrrell," proclaimed Martin. "I should have sent in my card, sir," he said apologetically to the master of the house, "but in my haste I came away without one."

The legal-looking Malone inclined his head, as though to signify that the omission was condoned. "You are of the Irish Tyrrells, perhaps, sir?" he inquired. Martin replied that he was English, and the real lawyer, apparently overhearing this, broke in, "If it's telling Malone ye are that ye're descended from him that shot an English King, sure I'll be apt to forgive ye for breaking in upon me second bottle. Pray sit down, Mr. Tyrrell, and himself will be ringing for another, will ye not, James?"

"Pretty cool, upon my soul!" thought Martin, and said to Mr. Malone, "I beg that you will do no such thing, sir. I am in haste, and only desire to know where I can find my brother-in-law. I understand that Mr. O'Driscoll, if he will be so obliging, can furnish me with that information."

"May I ask you, sir, why you should imagine that he can?"

Seeing no reason for observing silence on this point, Martin told him that he had been advised at the "Green Stag" to apply to Mr. O'Driscoll.

"Murphy of the 'Green Stag' told you to come here?" There was surprise, a rather displeased surprise, in Mr. Malone's voice.

"No," said Martin, "not Murphy-his wife." Was it fancy that he detected on his hearer's visage something of what had been on Mr. Murphy's very dissimilar countenance as he muttered unflattering sentiments about meddlers? Mr. Malone, however, soon recovered himself, and after saying in a reflective way: "Ah, so you are staying at the "Green Stag," Mr. Tyrrell?" he looked at Mr. O'Driscoll, and Martin observed that that gentleman was pulling a speaking trumpet from his pocket.

"I think," said Mr. Malone suddenly, "that he wishes you to speak to him through that instrument. Pray do not shout, but articulate clearly."

The cornucopia-like object now held out receptively towards Martin rather daunted him. However he sat down by its owner and inclined towards its mouth. "If you would be so kind, sir — —"

"*Deaf*, Mr. Tyrrell, *deaf*, not blind!"

"I said '*kind*,' sir. —If-you-would-be-so-kind-as-to — furnish-me-with-Mr. —Gerald-Roche's —present-address — I —should-be-greatly-obliged!"

The cornucopia having collected these words lowered itself. "I can't oblige ye, sir, for I don't know it," replied Mr. O'Driscoll, closing his mouth firmly.

"Have you no notion at all," persisted Martin, " —not even of the direction he has taken?"

"What's that about the ocean? If Gerry Roche has gone to America 'tis the first I've heard of it. Ye know more than I do, Mr. Tyrrell!"

Martin began to be aware of the first cold heats of desperation. "I asked," he said very loudly, "whether you had any notion at all of where he is?"

"Faith, that I have! I'm thinking," responded Mr. Oliver O'Driscoll, with equanimity, "that ye'll likely be finding him at his house at Ballydare."

Martin gave vent to a sound of impatience, and this time seized the horn, and shouted down it: "But I have just come from Ballydare!"

"Ye've missed him on the road, then," returned Mr. O'Driscoll, snatching away the cornucopia with a wince, and transferring it to his further hand. "I am sorry, Mr. Tyrrell, but whoever 'twas that sent ye to me was wasting your time."

It seemed like it, particularly as the oracle had now withdrawn the only means of intelligent communication with himself. Martin got up.

"Could *you* not help me, sir?" he asked, addressing Mr. Malone, a stage nearer desperation now, and convinced somehow that Mr. O'Driscoll was lying.

"I deeply regret it, sir," replied Mr. O'Driscoll's host with courtesy, "but as I have not the pleasure of Mr. Gerald Roche's personal acquaintance, I am not in the least conversant with his movements."

In the ordinary course of events, when two persons assure you of their entire ignorance of the whereabouts of a third, you can do little but acquiesce and, supposing that you have come purposely to elicit this information, withdraw disappointed. But to go away unsatisfied was not yet in Martin's mind, for he did not believe in this ignorance. There was something. . . . Besides, why had Murphy not wished him to come here? He resolved to precipitate matters, and, looking hard at Mr. Malone with, it must be admitted, something of University superiority in his air, remarked:

"I am not disposed to admit the cogency of that argument, Mr. Malone. For even if you do not know my brother-in-law personally, as you say, I believe that you know something about him which accounts in a large measure for his having left Dublin-and that is, that he speaks the French language very well!"

It was an arrow drawn, not exactly at a venture, but at a very uncertain mark; yet it went home somewhere, for Mr. Malone unmistakably stiffened, and his fingers began to beat out a little tattoo on the table by which he stood. Mr. O'Driscoll in his chair must have been watching him narrowly, for he cried out sharply, "What's that he says, James?"

Dispensing with the cornucopia Mr. Malone bent towards him. "Mr. Tyrrell observes that Mr. Roche speaks French very well."

There was a second's pause. The heavy grey eyebrows twitched. "Ah, sure that's extremely interesting," returned the lawyer. "But I don't know that it concerns you and me very much, eh, James?"

"You must pardon me," announced Martin in a loud, clear voice, modelled upon that which Mr. Malone had just employed towards the deaf man, "but I think it does, Mr. O'Driscoll. A knowledge of the French tongue is an useful-an indispensable accomplishment for a man who goes to interview . . . the French resident or minister at a town —a port-in a neutral country!"

It was out now. Malone gripped his arm suddenly from behind, and the corpulent O'Driscoll, who had obviously heard him well enough this time, heaved himself with unexpected alacrity out of his chair. "May I ask what you mean by that, Mr. Tyrrell?" he demanded.

"Oh, you know well enough!" returned Martin, throwing caution to the winds with a feeling of exhilaration. "French aid for insurrection-to arrange for that needs the sending of an emissary who can speak French fluently. Now tell me where Gerald Roche has gone, so that, if it is still possible, I can stop him in this folly, which will kill my poor sister!"

Yes, he was right-they *were* in it; though perhaps he would not have been sure if Malone had not removed his grasp, stridden across the room, locked the door and put the key in his pocket. Yet O'Driscoll turned at once and called out: "What are ye after, James-locking the door? Holy Michael, 'tis the fine fright ye'll be giving Mr. Tyrrell! He'll be thinking to see a Frenchman crawl from under the table itself! Come, Mr. Tyrrell, there's no need at all for alarm at Malone's pranks." He paused. It was a heavy pause; his eyebrows seemed to droop till they almost obscured his eyes, and when he spoke again his voice appeared to have descended about an octave. *"Unless ye are an English spy!"* it said.

"That I most certainly am not!" retorted the young man warmly. "It is solely concern for my sister which has brought me here. And I am not alarmed; don't think it! Mr. Malone is welcome to lock the door for all I care. We shall be the more undisturbed while you tell me where to find Gerald Roche."

Oliver O'Driscoll surveyed him not unapprovingly. " 'Tis pity that ye were not born an Irishman, Mr. Tyrrell! Maybe ye have some Irish blood in ye after all. Sit down now, and take a glass of wine with us, and tell us where ye got this crazy notion about a neutral country and a French resident-let alone that Gerry Roche was off to find one!" His tone was very pleasant, almost wheedling, and he laid his hands on the arms of his chair as though to sit down again. Malone had come back from the further side of the room.

"Why, I arrived at it by my own powers of reasoning," answered Martin lightly-but still loudly. "Is it not the sort of plan which would appeal to an Irish patriot?"

O'Driscoll shook his massive head; but he sat down again. "You have heard somebody talking!" he said, fixing Martin with his piercing grey eyes. "Who was it?"

"Then there *is* such a scheme!" said Martin triumphantly. Malone was close behind him; he had the key of the door in his possession; he might have a pistol as well, for all Martin knew. This was all insanely rash, but the adventurer was enjoying the sensation of his rashness. He kept his gaze upon the seated O'Driscoll, certain that it was he who gave the orders, and that Malone would do nothing unless he were told. Would he be told-and what would be his orders?

The tension was sharp, but it only lasted for a second or so; O'Driscoll swept it away with a wave of his hand as he sank back in his chair.

"No, Mr. Tyrrell, whatever ye've heard, there's no such ill-advised scheme afoot, and this poor afflicted country must go the way she has ever gone, I suppose, under the heel of yours. There's a deal of wild talk about, but ye'd do as well to be listening to curlews in a bog as to be taking heed of it. Come now, Mr. Tyrrell, before ye go back to Ballydare, to find your brother-in-law consoling his wife, sit down and take a glass of wine, as I bade ye just now. See, there's more glasses here." He drew the bottle at his elbow nearer and added with a chuckle: "I'm thinking that this is the best kind of 'neutral port' after all!"

So Martin sat down, and for the first time. Since they had not been expecting him the wine could not have been doctored in any way, and if he stayed a while longer who knew whether the vintage might not loosen Mr. O'Driscoll's tongue a little. Not for a moment did he put faith in his recent disclaimer.

"Thank you, sir; I will gladly take a glass with you."

Mr. Malone drew up another chair looking, Martin thought, rather askance at him. But it was Oliver O'Driscoll whom Martin watched as he poured out a fresh glass; he seemed to do much as he liked in this house and to be more the master of it than its owner. Martin wondered what Gerald's relations with him were. The lawyer's thick underlip protruded as he poured; after which, handing the glass to Martin, he remarked, "Since it's not me own wine I'm at liberty to sing its praises, Mr. Tyrrell-God bless me, what's that clawing at me leg? I declare 'tis that confounded tomcat of yours, Malone-the devil take him!"

Muttering an apology Mr. Malone stooped and picked up a very large, well-fed tabby and carrying it to the furthest of the three windows drew aside the curtain, threw up the sash, and put the cat outside. "I hope you have no objection, gentlemen," he said as he came back, "but I have left the window open, for Shan to come in again if he wishes. A little fresh air will do us no harm into the bargain; 'tis a fine night."

"But maybe Mr. Tyrrell doesn't like the air of Dublin," observed Mr. O'Driscoll. "Are ye long from England, sir?"

"No, sir," replied Martin, sipping Mr. Malone's excellent port. "I only landed a few days ago."

"And your sister is married to an Irishman? I'll warrant she's Irish enough herself by this time! 'Tis odd, now that I come to think of it: I knew a young lady once, out of Galway she was, who married a gentleman of your name —a relative of yours maybe —a Mr. Tyrrell of Alton in, I believe, the county of Hampshire. I misremember when it was-as much as twenty years ago, perhaps. She was a very pretty girl. But I remember thinking she'd be finding Hampshire a trifle different from Connemara, for instance." He smiled, sighed and put his glass reflectively to his lips.

Was it the wine, or the lowering of tension, helped by the fact that all through this parley the blurred word in Gerald Roche's letter had been subconsciously present to Martin's mind, so that even during this interlude with the wine-cup he had been busy with it again? That word sprang up before him now; he knew by heart every pen scratch which had obliterated it . . . but now those obliterations were gone, or rather, he could see through them! *Alton, Hampshire* —the conjunction of those two names had supplied him with the clue. He gave an exclamation, set down his glass, and pushed back his chair.

"Mr. O'Driscoll, I am willing to pledge you my most sacred word of honour not to meddle with the business upon which Mr. Roche is engaged, nor to mention it to any third person, if you will furnish me with an intermediate address at which I may overtake him, or with his ultimate address at —*Altona* !"

Mr. O'Driscoll too had put down his glass. He stared at the challenger; then his eyes gave a frosty twinkle. "Do ye really think that a bargain worth the offering, Mr. Tyrrell? Sure 'tis no bargain at all! And, in any case, let me tell ye, Mr. Roche has not gone to Altona."

"To Hamburg, then; 'tis the same thing!"

"No, nor to Hamburg neither."

"Mr. O'Driscoll, I am sorry to be obliged to say that I don't believe you!" retorted Martin, with the word "Altona" dancing before his eyes quite plain now, or almost plain, under its effacing marks. It *did* begin with a capital "A"; and the penultimate and antepenultimate letters *were* "n" and "o" as he had fancied; and the letter before this was a "t" —all as he had thought!

"If 'twere worth the trouble of rising," responded O'Driscoll lazily, "I'd be apt to knock ye down for that, young gentleman. However, as ye'd soon find out if ye were fool enough to go to Hamburg, or Altona either, it's God's own truth I'm speaking."

Martin got up, leaving half the "neutral port" in his glass. Hamburg (or Altona) fitted the description better. "I apologise, Mr. O'Driscoll; I should rather have said that I believed you misinformed. I will bid you and Mr. Malone good night, and again tender my regrets for intruding upon you in this way."

"If ye are thinking of acting upon this revelation which ye seem so suddenly to have received, Mr. Tyrrell, I'd strongly advise ye not to!" said O'Driscoll curtly.

"And why not? Why not, since you so positively assure me that I shall not find Mr. Roche there? Is it merely concern for my fruitless journey?"

The lawyer reared up his great bulk in the chair. "I'd strongly advise ye not to," he repeated in a very steely tone.

"I am obliged to you for the warning," returned Martin politely; bowed to him, bowed to Mr. Malone, and walked across to the door.

In his enjoyable state of exultation he was not sure whether Mr. Malone had restored the key to the lock or no, but he very shortly found, on putting his hand to the door-knob which projected from that solid mahogany, that he was still a prisoner. The two men were whispering together at the other side of the room, Malone with his mouth glued to Mr. O'Driscoll's ear. But Martin heard the latter say quite audibly (being unable no doubt through his deafness to gauge the volume of his own voice): "Tell him where Roche . . . by the Holy Virgin, no!" Then he noticed that the cat had returned to the window facing him and stood upon the ledge inside, framed between the half-drawn curtains, padding with his paws and slowly waving his tail-and quite uninterested in Hamburg or Mr. Gerald Roche.

"Will you be so kind as to unlock this door?" asked Martin, across the room.

Mr. Malone turned round from his whispered colloquy with a frown. "Only if you on your part will swear not to undertake this preposterous journey to Hamburg!"

"I might have considered abandoning it if you were not so set upon preventing me from going there!" retorted the young man impudently. After which, with his eyes fixed upon the slice of open window, he asked, "Is that the only condition upon which you will allow me to go through this door?"

"It is," replied Mr. Malone briefly. He still remained at the fireplace end of the room, not wishing, possibly, to bring his person and key any nearer than was necessary to a vigorous and, as he had already shown himself, a bold young man. The massive mahogany door was all the gaoler required.

"We will give you one minute to decide, Mr. Tyrrell!" said Oliver O'Driscoll, pointing to the heavy marble clock on the chimneypiece. His face was flushed and ugly; the strong, prominent underlip stuck out.

"I shall not take so long," declared Martin cheerfully. (He could not, of course, expect to emulate the climbing powers of a cat, but there would only at worst be an area outside that open ground-floor window; he could surely drop into that!) "I cannot, as an Englishman," he went on, "submit to arrest without a warrant . . . so I shall attempt another route!"

He was across the room before he had finished speaking and had flung the curtains wider. The cat, alarmed by his rush, had jumped to the floor; Mr. Malone sprang forward. The best use for the animal occurred at once to Martin. Exclaiming, "Poor Puss, I'm sorry!" he stooped, gathered up the heavy tabby and hurled it with all his force at its master's head; then, without waiting to see the effect of this novel missile, clambered over the windowsill, took one look below (he could not see much), hung a second by his hands, and dropped. The window was slammed savagely down above him just too late to catch his fingers.

"I wonder was that the fat O'Driscoll bestirring himself?" thought Martin as he picked himself up, grimacing, from his hands and knees, for the area stones were hard. "I wish I could see the results of my . . . catapult!" Elated by this questionable pun, he ran up the steps, found the gate at the top, as he had hoped, unfastened, and walked very quickly away from Mr. James Malone's dwelling just as a door was flung open in the dark area and affrighted female voices were heard asking each other in the name of the Blessed Mother what was that come shwooping down and they saying the holy rosary too . . .

The square, luckily, was deserted, yet Martin judged it wiser not to run. Moreover, why should he run? They would not chase him —O'Driscoll certainly couldn't; conspirators themselves, they dared not invoke the law against him either. On the contrary, it was he who had a case against them for refusing him lawful exit. He hoped that Shan had thoroughly scratched Mr. Malone; and when he got back, rather late, to the "Green Stag," slept the sleep of the successful and ingenious, dreaming only that no vessel was allowed to enter the port of Hamburg unless every passenger were provided with a tabby cat as a means of defence against any United Irishmen who might be there.

(6)

If the aphorism about morning bringing reflection means anything, it means that a man takes a soberer view of his overnight enthusiasms, and sometimes of his intentions. The rosy light has faded to grey, and there is a cool, often a chilly wind blowing from the land of commonsense. So when Martin Tyrrell awoke next day in his not over-comfortable bed at the "Green Stag" he was immediately conscious of this change of mental atmosphere, and lay for a while staring at the festoon of faded yellow fringe hanging half detached from the dusty crimson tester, and weighing his next move on Lucy's behalf with some hesitation.

The exhilaration of last night had certainly dropped from him, and the prospect of setting off for the free city of Hamburg after Gerald Roche seemed neither so inevitable nor so easy as it had done in Mr. Malone's library last night. To begin with, it was the devil of a long way to go; for he would presumably have first to cross the Irish Sea by the usual route to Holyhead, then traverse England to Yarmouth, the regular port for the Continent now that there was no traffic to France, and take the Cuxhaven packet thence. And he knew of no address in Hamburg or its neighbour Altona at which to find his brother-in-law when he should get there. Moreover, if he did succeed in tracking him, surely the mischief would be handsomely done already. He could hardly then expect to induce a man whom he knew so little to abandon his part in a scheme, however disloyal, into which he had probably been persuaded by stronger minds than his own. To follow Roche to Hamburg (or Altona) was, if one looked at it in cold daylight, a move both extravagant and useless.

And yet... Lucy's pitiful face seemed to swim between Martin and those crimson billowings above him. He had promised her to see Gerald and argue with him. Of course it was open to him to return to Ballydare and say that he could not in reason be expected to go pursuing after her rebel husband into the Hanseatic towns of the Empire, even though she had-almost, it seemed, in anticipation of some such emergency-furnished him with far more money than he needed for the expedition to Dublin. But he did not very much like the prospect of that unfruitful return. Besides-why were those two damned Irishmen so eager to prevent him from going to Hamburg? O'Driscoll's face replaced Lucy's. Had not he, Martin Tyrrell, put a heavy cat to a most unwonted use and made an unconventional and somewhat dangerous exit from a gentleman's house rather than pledge himself not to go to Hamburg? And back came, in full flood, every obstinate instinct which the attempt to exact that pledge had roused last night, and something of the exhilaration too with which he had faced it. Martin jumped out of bed and rang the decrepit bell for hot water.

* * * * *

A curious and rather disturbing incident befell Martin on his way to George's Quay. A man (addressed as Dan Heffernan) produced by Mr. Murphy to carry his valise, seemed extraordinarily ill-informed about the way to the Liffey, and involved him in a maze of dirty by-streets which even Martin, with his scanty knowledge of Dublin, that city where stateliness and noisy squalor exist side by side, felt could not afford the most direct route. Rescued from these aberrations Dan Heffernan next found that the weight of the portmanteau caused him such lamentable shortness of breath as to necessitate setting down his burden at frequent intervals and wiping a brow which bore no visible traces of over-exertion. Martin was beginning to be nervous about missing the English packet altogether when Dan suddenly bolted with the valise into a narrow alley, followed instantly by the indignant Martin, and by a half-naked urchin who for some time had been pestering him for pennies.

Martin's shouts of "Stop, thief!" brought no assistance, but he was favoured by luck, for the dishonest porter had not gone far down this unsavoury passage before he tripped and fell headlong, with Martin so close upon his heels that the dropped portmanteau had scarcely ceased rolling away before its owner had pounced upon it. Refraining with difficulty from giving the treacherous Dan a kick, he raised it to his own shoulder and made off as fast as he could out to the street again, the indefatigable urchin now offering to show him the quickest way to George's Quay for sixpence.

"Go on, then!" said Martin, still very angry, and wondering whether it was merely his wrath which had conjured up a vision of two or three villainous-looking heads peeping round a further corner of the alley-heads suggestive of men in ambush.

He reached the side of the *Hillsborough* packet breathless and with only five minutes to spare. It was not until the packet was sailing in the May sunshine out of Dublin Bay and he was staring at that panorama, that he began to speculate whether Dan Heffernan was merely a common thief who had hoped by swiftness of foot to deprive him of his property, or whether, just possibly, he had meant to decoy the valise's owner, by running off with it, into the clutch of accomplices in the pay of someone else. Was it conceivable that Messrs. O'Driscoll and Malone had resorted to this method of stopping him from going to Hamburg?

If so, he could snap his fingers at them. Looking at the hill of Howth, he did so.

(7)

The slight fog of the morning had lifted, but the packet-boat seemed to Martin to be proceeding very slowly up the windings of the Elbe, now considerably narrowed from the great breadth of its mouth, where no shores were to be seen. It was with some impatience that he viewed upon his right hand a succession of church steeples, unfamiliarly coloured red or blue, and group after group of thatched or tiled houses with little gardens, and once a village spilt about the side of a hill. But for the most part the shores on either side were flat, and owing to this fact he thought, or at least hoped, that he could already discern, a long way ahead across the watery loops, the spires of Hamburg-or more probably of Danish Altona; and none too soon either, for this was the third day after leaving Yarmouth, since on reaching Cuxhaven last night, they had anchored there until morning.

Leaning against the packet's side, divided between wondering if he had been a fool to come all this way on a mere speculation, and a certain youthful excitement about what he should see and find in Hamburg (since, owing to the war, he had never set foot on the Continent before) Martin found himself observing a gentleman who was sitting not far away reading a letter. This gentleman had only one arm, his left sleeve being pinned to his breast, and the young man could not help thinking how awkward, in these circumstances, must be the reading of a letter of two sheets (for he could see that there were two) in a breezy spot like the deck of a ship.

The gentleman-he might have been between thirty-five and forty-appeared to be enjoying the perusal of his long letter, for the corner of his mouth was crooked in a smile. Martin could not see his full face. Presently, reading in a leisurely way as he was, he came to the end of the first sheet and endeavoured, putting his hand down upon his knee, to change the relative positions of the first and second sheets. In a twinkling the breeze had seized its opportunity, and the second half of the letter went fluttering along the deck. Cramming the remaining sheet into his pocket, the reader sprang up, but Martin, already on his feet and half apprehensive of some such mishap, was even quicker, and, chasing the missive, just saved it from being blown overboard. Raising his hat, he returned it to its owner, already at his elbow-not, however, before he had quite involuntarily seen that it was signed with a woman's name —"Raymonde."

"My dear sir," said the letter's owner, as he took it, "I am infinitely obliged to you! I would not willingly have lost that letter. But, as you observe, I am sadly clumsy, for it is less than a year since I parted with that useful object, a second hand, and I have not yet replaced it by some device. I see that it is time I did so."

"It must indeed be uncommon awkward at first," murmured Martin, somewhat embarrassed by this frank reference to such a disability.

"Only," said the other cheerfully, "because we are born with two arms-doubtless as a precaution in case of having to part with one of them. Unfortunately we cannot, in that case, grow another unaided, like the lobster."

His excellent English was not free from a trace of foreign accent, and his rolled "r's" confirmed Martin in the belief that he had to do with a Frenchman. The thought at once darted into his mind that if he were driven, as he might be, into seeking a personal interview with the representative of the French Republic at Hamburg in order to get upon Roche's track, this gentleman might perhaps furnish him with an introduction to his compatriot. Moreover he was in some indefinable way attracted by his fellow-passenger's lean and humorous face, where an old scar upon one cheek suggested a possibly adventurous past. And presently he found himself standing by him in the bows remarking upon the vessel's slow progress, though by now the spires and towers of the twin towns were undoubtedly beginning to prick up in the distance over the river bends.

"Yes, we shall arrive at Altona-we disembark there-before long," said Martin's companion. "We are lucky in not having had more fog —'tis the curse of wide river mouths such as this and the Scheldt."

"You know Hamburg perhaps, sir?" hazarded Martin.

"I have never been in Hamburg before, though it is full of my compatriots."

"I had already guessed you to be French, sir. And that emboldens me to ask whether you can tell me anything about the French minister to the Hanseatic towns?"

The Frenchman looked amused. "My dear sir, how can you suppose that I know anything of the minister of the French Republic to the Hanseatic or any other towns? I am a Royalist *émigré*, like the compatriots to whom I referred. Otherwise, how the devil should I find myself travelling on the Yarmouth packet-boat, *muni d'ailleurs d'un passeport britannique* ?"

"No, of course not! I am very stupid," said Martin, half laughing, half annoyed with himself. "It must be the sea air."

"I cannot tell you anything about the citizen Reinhardt, for such, I believe, is his name," continued the *émigré*, "but I can tell you that you will find Hamburg very crowded and lodgings not too easy to obtain. But perhaps, sir, you are not making a long stay?"

Since this man owed no allegiance to the English government, and yet was no enemy to England, Martin felt that he could speak to him more freely than he would have done to a fellow-countryman of his own-for to those on board he had preserved an almost morbid discretion as to his errand. He replied therefore that he hoped to return by the next packet, as he only wished to have an interview with a relative of his in Hamburg of whose address there he was unfortunately ignorant.

"*Eh bien* , you can probably obtain that without difficulty from the English consul," suggested his new acquaintance; and Martin, opening his mouth to say that he could not possibly visit the English consul with that object, realised that it was better not to make this admission, and shut it again.

Not much more conversation indeed passed between the two, for Altona was at last coming nearer; but before parting they acquainted each other with their names, by which exchange Martin learnt that the Frenchman to whom he had done the small service-not that the Frenchman appeared to think it a small one-was called the Chevalier Fortuné de la Vireville.

(8)

In the crowded street outside the residence of the French minister to the Hanseatic towns there walked to and fro next afternoon a rather bothered young gentleman named Martin Tyrrell. From time to time he glanced distastefully at the doorway over which drooped the new and still (to him) unfamiliar flag of France, the tricolour. And he who in his callow youth (about five years ago) had written verses to the oriflamme of liberty now felt his patriotic soul rise at the sight of it.

He was hanging about thus outside the residence in the hopes of seeing Gerald Roche either enter or leave, though he had been driven to watching this doorway only because he could obtain no news of his brother-in-law anywhere else in Hamburg. He had visited with equal unsuccess the "Obergesellschaft," the "Bœuf d'Or," the "Kayserhof," the "Aigle Noir" and the "Kramer-Amthaus." In the end he might even be driven to entering this abhorrent building on that same errand. The consulate of his own native country, the natural place to make enquiries after a fellow-countryman in a foreign town, he still considered closed to him as a source of information, since he might well compromise Roche by such enquiries, the Irishman's errand and possibly even his presence being, he hoped, unknown to the British authorities. But, even assuming that M. Reinhardt was actually in communication with Roche, how was one to be sure that he would give an English enquirer his present address? He might very well think Martin an agent of the British Government come to spy upon the Irish malcontents, and more or less politely show him the door, in which case Martin would have bowed himself in the house of Rimmon to no purpose.

This seemed a very popular street, and what a crowded, busy, noisy, dirty place Hamburg was! People of all ranks hurried by; now and again a soldier in an enormous cocked hat, here and there a woman of the lower classes in her white cap with its stiff goffered edges and long ribbon lappets, or a more outlandish one in an immense flat-crowned straw bonnet, as large as a small umbrella. There came unmistakably a couple of French Royalist exiles, one with the cross of St. Louis on his shabby coat. Martin had by this time realised that Hamburg was, in fact, the headquarters of the emigration, as Coblentz had earlier been; the refugees were everywhere in Hamburg and Altona, earning their living as best they could in all sorts of capacities, like the duke and his cook who had gone into successful partnership in a restaurant.

Martin saw these two elderly Frenchmen glance up, just as he had done, at the billowing tricolour, which at that moment, as if in derision, was stirred by a gust into flapping life; and he saw, too, that one pulled the other off the rough pavement into the street in order to avoid passing under it.

"Yes, I should feel like that, if my country's flag were to be changed against my will and convictions," reflected Martin; and further considered, half inconsequently, but with a good measure of irritation, that he could not visit his own consulate, where he should have the satisfaction of seeing it flying, because of this damned affair of Roche's. As he watched the two *émigrés* he became conscious that a tall man who had already passed him in the press had abruptly stopped and turned back, and was now standing in front of him-more, that it was, oddly enough, the one *émigré* whom he knew, his yesterday's acquaintance of the packet-boat.

"*Bonjour, monsieur*," said the Frenchman, lifting his hat. "I did not think to meet you again so soon. But is it possible that I find Mr. Tyrrell admiring the new standard of my unfortunate country?"

"Indeed, no, I was far enough from admiring it," said Martin as he returned his salutation. "I was looking at your two compatriots there, monsieur, who have risked getting knocked down by some vehicle rather than walk beneath its folds."

M. de la Vireville's gaze followed them, too. "*Pauvres vieux!* I knew one of them once, in happier days, when I was *aspirant de la marine* and he *lieutenant de vaisseau*."

"You have been in the navy, sir?"

"Among other places," returned the *émigré* cheerfully. "Yes, I served under Suffren . . . centuries ago. I am thinking of returning to the sea, but to the merchant navy this time. That, indeed, is why I am in Hamburg at the moment. —And that reminds me, Mr. Tyrrell, what of your quest in this place? Have you found your friend yet?"

"No, and I am beginning to despair of doing so," answered Martin. "There are more English here, a great many more, than I had anticipated. Not, indeed, that the man I seek is English, for he is Irish; nevertheless— —"

The Frenchman, with a little exclamation, cut in: "Irish, you say? Have you by chance been to the Schildtstrasse in Altona? There is an Irish milord lodging there, opposite an acquaintance of mine."

"Indeed!" said Martin eagerly. "You do not, I suppose, happen to know whether his name is Roche?"

The Chevalier de la Vireville shook his head. "That was not the name which my friend mentioned. I think you have in Ireland the name 'Gerald,' have you not?"

"Yes—and that *is* his name—Gerald Roche! It must be he—how fortunate!"

" 'Gerald Roche?' " repeated the Frenchman doubtfully. "*Eh bien* , in that case my young friend heard but the half of it. You see, monsieur, this young compatriot of mine lodges with a Frau Meyer in the Schildtstrasse at Altona, and from what he tells me there has recently come to lodge in the house opposite a very handsome couple, of whom the lady in particular is so *divinement belle* that he— —"

"A lady!" exclaimed Martin in a tone of disappointment "Ah, then it cannot be the man I seek, for his wife is not with him." He sighed. "I thank you, Monsieur le Chevalier, but I must set about my quest anew."

But the Chevalier was looking at him a trifle oddly. "*Pardonnez-moi* , Monsieur," he said after a moment, "but do you not perhaps too swiftly leap to a conclusion? This gentleman is Irish, and he is certainly 'Gerald' something or other, for my young friend, being susceptible, took the step of going to the door of the house opposite which enshrined this beautiful young lady in order to make enquiries. 'Herr von Gerald,' the landlady called the gentleman, and told my friend that the goddess was his wife; but since an Irish milord is probably human, just as a Frenchman is . . . and possibly an Englishman, too . . . it may be that she is not his wife, and that M. Gerald Roche amuses himself in Hamburg?"

To his quizzical expression Martin opposed a thunderous brow. "That is quite impossible!" he said shortly. "Mr. Roche is my brother-in-law, but two years married to my sister, from whom I have just parted in Ireland, and I'll not believe such a thing of him!"

The Frenchman's smile vanished and he slightly stiffened. "I beg your pardon most sincerely! I had, of course, no idea that the gentleman in question was your *beau-frère* , or I should not have made such a suggestion. I beg you to believe, Monsieur, that I intended no offence. Perhaps you will allow me to say that I hope I have been, not indiscreet, but misinformed." And, raising his hat, he turned away again into the stream of passers-by.

Martin stood there a second or two biting his lip, and then, hurrying after him, caught him by the arm. "Pray, sir, do not take offence, or imagine that I have taken it! I will, on the contrary, ask you to be so good as to give me some direction how to find this house at Altona, for since this 'Herr von Gerald' is Irish it may be possible for him to give me some news of my brother-in-law."

"But with pleasure," replied M. de la Vireville who had instantly stopped; adding, with the twinkle back in his eye: "You may get a glimpse of the divinity of 'Herr von Gerald' also. The street, Monsieur, as I said, is the Schildtstrasse at Altona, to which anyone there will direct you; and nineteen is the number of the house at which my informant lodges; the Irish milord is just opposite. I am ignorant of the number, but you can find the house by its situation. *Au revoir* , Mr. Tyrrell; I do not know whether to wish you success or failure!"

And with that he was gone once more, having exactly stated the dilemma upon which Martin stood impaled in the streets of the free town of Hamburg. For if this "milord" —why "milord"? —really were Gerald Roche. . . . No, it could not be! And yet, after all, it was not impossible. Oh, if this were the true explanation of Roche's non-return, if it was for this that he had left Ireland, it would deal Lucy a far more mortal blow than any political entanglement. His own immediate course, at any rate, was clear; to go at once to Altona and find out the truth.

To Altona he went then, striding oblivious under the pleasant alleys of new-leafed trees which led thither, with one thought only in his head. He found the Schildtstrasse without difficulty, a short, narrow thoroughfare with the air of being troubled by but little traffic between its cheerful and miniature dwellings, all of mellowed red brick, and so small as almost to suggest dolls' houses. Here was number nineteen, and opposite, the brass of its door shining with a Danish zest, and a couple of window-boxes on the first floor crammed with sturdy cherub-cheeked tulips, red and pink, was *the* house.

Martin's German was fragmentary, and he had been fain since his arrival to help it out with French and English. In this mixture he now enquired at the door under the tulips for Herr Gerald Roche, an Irish gentleman. "*Ach ,*" said the smiling woman who opened, "*der Herr meint ohne Zweifel den Herrn Grafen von Gerald!* " Martin, following her up the trim stairway, could not imagine why Roche should now be styling himself a count, which he believed was the equivalent of "Graf," nor why he should have dropped his surname. The two odd circumstances together served to make him still more suspicious of an intrigue which was not political . . . . though in that case-in either case, in fact-why not have taken a different name altogether?

He was soon to discover the answer to that question-to all his questions. In another moment he heard himself announced as "Herr Tirol," and found himself in a larger room than he had anticipated, where, on a sofa by the china stove, sat sewing the most beautiful girl he had ever seen, with a young man almost equally handsome reading aloud to her. This gentleman put down the book and rose as Martin came in; and he was not Gerald Roche.

Relief came first, and then disappointment-but for widely different reasons. "I beg your pardon," said Martin, embarrassed. "There has been a misunderstanding. I am searching for a Mr. Gerald Roche from County Cork, and, being told that there was an Irish gentleman staying here . . . I must apologise."

"There is no need, sir," said the young man pleasantly. "There *is* an Irish gentleman staying here-myself; and perhaps I can help you to find the other. I am Edward Fitzgerald, at your service. Let me present you, sir . . . I am not sure that the good Frau had your name correctly . . . ?"

"It is Tyrrell," interpolated the bewildered Martin.

" —Mr. Tyrrell, to my wife."

Martin all but gasped. Recovering himself, he bowed to the dark-haired nymph upon the sofa-for nymph was the epithet which came instantly into his mind. So this was the celebrated, the lovely Pamela, the adopted daughter of Mme. de Genlis (from which phrase all the world removed the word "adopted"); and this gentleman was the famous Lord Edward Fitzgerald, the rebel son of the Duke of Leinster. He saw how the confusion of name had arisen, and realised that even a Frenchman like the Chevalier de la Vireville, who probably knew about *la belle Paméla* in the days before the Revolution, when she was a part of the Duc d'Orléans' household in the Palais Royal, had not perhaps remembered or even known that she had since married an Irishman, nor that Irishman's name. In any case, it was not M. de la Vireville who was lodging opposite.

And now Lord Edward was asking him to sit down. "Pam, we must do what we can, must we not, to help Mr. Tyrrell to find his friend. —Has this Mr. Roche been long in Hamburg, sir?"

"No, my lord. I am not even certain that he is here. If he is, then I am afraid-that is, I believe, that his errand is political." He paused, not quite knowing whether to go on in the young wife's presence. How much of this mad business did she know?

Pamela herself solved his difficulty. Turning her great soft eyes upon her husband, she said gently: "If you intend to talk politics, Eddy, I think I will go to my room for a while."

"Do, my love, if you feel fatigued," said her husband, hastening to open the other door of the room. As she rose and walked languidly towards it Martin saw that at no very distant date she would bear a child.

"Now, sir," said Lord Edward, returning, "if I can be of service to you, pray command me."

Martin had almost the sensation of pulling himself together to remember why he had come, so astray was he all at once from the groove wherein his thoughts had run with such uniformity for the past week or so. "As I said, my lord, I am searching for my brother-in-law, Mr. Gerald Roche, of Ballydare, who, I have reason to believe, is in Hamburg, and"—he was inspired to add—"on the same errand, if I mistake not, as yourself!"

"You know my errand then, Mr. Tyrrell?"

"I can guess it, my lord—I am sorry to say."

"You are *sorry*! Faith, then, you think that one should neglect the ties of kindred when to cultivate them costs a little time and inconvenience?" Lord Edward was smiling his delightful smile, and as Martin groped after his meaning, he added: "My wife has come to Hamburg to visit her adoptive mother, Mme. de Genlis, whose name is doubtless familiar to you, and to attend the wedding of Mlle. de Sercey, Mme. de Genlis' niece; and I could not allow her to travel alone, for, as you see, she is near her confinement."

All the more extraordinary to have chosen such a date for a visit to the Continent, thought Martin. Then, resolving to force the pace a little, he said: "I have indeed the honour to know of Lady Edward Fitzgerald's connection with the celebrated Mme. de Genlis. But-forgive me, my lord, if I am impertinent-from what I know of the sentiments and movements of my brother-in-law, it would rather seem as if the French minister were the attraction at Hamburg!"

He half expected the young Irishman to fly out at him and tell him to go to the devil. But Lord Edward did nothing of the kind. "Mr. Roche of Ballydare, I think you said, and he is your brother-in-law? I do not know him personally. And you, sir, are a sympathiser-yet you sound and look like an Englishman!"

"I am an Englishman," answered Martin; "nor, my lord, do I wish to sail under false colours with you. I am not a sympathiser; I have come to try to dissuade my brother-in-law, if I can find him, from a course of conduct which I believe to be most fatally misguided."

"Let us hope, then, that you will find him," said his host courteously. "Is it permitted to enquire in what this reprehensible course of conduct of Mr. Roche's consists?"

"I think I am informing your lordship of what you know already. His first aim is to obtain an interview on behalf of the Society of United Irishmen with M. Reinhardt, the French minister to the Hanse towns."

Lord Edward looked amused. "I can assure you he won't do that, Mr. Tyrrell. Only two persons are likely to cross M. Reinhardt's contaminating threshold on the errand which you suspect-myself and one other.—But sit down, sir; you stand all this while!"

Martin complied. "And that other, on your honour, my lord, is not Gerald Roche?"

"On my honour, Mr. Tyrrell, it is not. And as far as I know-remember, I am not personally acquainted with Mr. Roche-he is not in Hamburg at all; he has not left Ireland. My colleague who, I think, does know him personally, may be able to tell you more. He is coming to see me very shortly. He could probably give you some information on the subject of Mr. Roche's whereabouts. Only . . ."

"Yes, my lord?"

"Only, since you are not one of us, I do not think that I am justified in allowing you to meet him without some pledge that-you understand, sir-that you will not use your knowledge of his presence here, or your *suspicions* of his errand, in any way that would harm him with the English Government?"

"You have not, Lord Edward, exacted any such pledge with regard to yourself, I observe."

"Oh," said the high-born young rebel lightly, "the English Government probably knows my movements perfectly well! But it also knows that Mme. de Genlis is in Hamburg, and that there is a wedding toward in the family."

Was he serious in thinking that event a sufficient cloak for his questionable activities, or was he jesting? He seemed to take conspiracy in a remarkably care-free spirit, at any rate as far as he himself was concerned. After all, perhaps, thought Martin, the whole thing was but play, in which case *he* might have saved himself his journey from Dublin to Hamburg.

"I will give you that pledge, Lord Edward," he said, "upon my most sacred word of honour, if you will allow me to see this gentleman. My undertaking shall apply to you also-that is, I shall remember only that you and Lady Edward Fitzgerald are visiting Mme. de Genlis, as is but natural."

The blue Fitzgerald eyes smiled at him again. Good Heavens, how attractive he was, this young nobleman who, in spite of his title, had been cashiered from the British Army for his presence at that dinner in Paris in the autumn of 1792 where, with French deputies and generals and Tom Paine and other Englishmen in love with Republican theories, he had drunk success to the French arms and proposed the abolition of hereditary titles in his native land. He had the sweet air of a high-spirited child playing at some dangerous game which it only half understands; though he was actually some seven or eight years older than Martin, Martin himself felt him younger. What a pity! the pair of them too, that exquisite young wife in there as well. . . .

"You are looking very grave, Mr. Tyrrell!"

"Forgive me," said Martin earnestly, "but . . . is this not a very serious business for you, my lord, with your position, your connections and prospects? . . . I am afraid you must think me impertinent for venturing to say this!"

"No, Mr. Tyrrell, I do not think you in the least impertinent." His voice had the same sweetness as his look. "I could not expect you to see the matter otherwise. But we who have vowed everything to Ireland only lament that we have so little to give her. For my part ——"

He broke off, as there came a rat-tat on the knocker below. "That must be my visitor. Will you excuse me, sir?" And he was gone from the room.

Martin sat upon the sofa, waiting. This was, it seemed, the end of his chase after Roche, that totally unnecessary chase. The fox had never broken covert after all! Yet perhaps this other plotter would not confirm Lord Edward's belief that Gerald had remained in Ireland. . . . It did not appear to matter much either way; what did matter was, whether he, Martin, would have to leave this house without another sight of that nymph-like creature now gone from the room, illegitimate daughter, some held, of a French prince of the blood-or of an obscure Hampshire sea-captain and a laundress.

Lying on the floor, almost under the sofa, was a tiny bit of fine cambric. Martin picked it up, and found that it was the minute sleeve of some little garment in course of making, with gathers fine as gossamer. For a moment he held it as a Catholic might hold a reliquary, then, reddening slightly, restored it to its former position and rose, as footsteps sounded outside the door, and Lord Edward entered with his arm through that of a taller man.

"This, Arthur, is the gentleman who was enquiring for Mr. Roche of Ballydare. —Mr. Tyrrell, Mr. O'Connor."

Martin bowed. He remembered instantly that it was from Mr. Arthur O'Connor's lips-though O'Connor was doubtless unaware of it-that Lucy had gained the information which was the virtual cause of his own presence here.

Lord Edward brought his visitor to the neighbourhood of the stove. "I have told Mr. O'Connor about you and your quest, Mr. Tyrrell," he said, still with that peculiar sunny grace of manner, "and the guarantee of silence which you have given as to our mission here. I find that he can furnish you with news of Mr. Roche."

But would he do it? Martin asked himself, for Mr. Arthur O'Connor was looking at him critically out of his dark eyes. An older man than the Geraldine, he gave at once the impression of being also much abler-as a plotter, at all events.

"Mr. Gerald Roche is not in Hamburg, sir," he said at length; "he never has been in Hamburg. There was no question of his coming abroad-for any reason-and I am at a loss to imagine how such an idea can have occurred to you."

The dry, severe tone made Martin feel almost like a schoolboy in a scrape who is invited to explain his conduct, which, seeing that the speaker was a rebel seeking foreign aid, and he a loyal citizen, was ridiculous. Yet the situation was not without its thorns, since he did not wish to betray that Lucy was the source of this idea, lest he should brand her either as an eavesdropper or as a wife who wormed out her husband's secrets. So he decided to leave Mr. O'Connor still at a loss on this subject, and said nothing.

This evasion, however, did not content the United Irishman, for he went on with the same air of reproof: "If you would be good enough to satisfy me on that point, Mr. Tyrrell, I might be able to tell you, for your further information, where Mr. Roche did go-though, faith, he must be back at Ballydare by now."

"That, then, is all that matters," replied Martin, deciding, in spite of the curiosity aroused by this offer, not to close with it. "I accept your assurance, sir, that Mr. Roche is not in Hamburg."

Mr. O'Connor, however, was not disposed to be a party to this pact. "I should like to know, sir," he repeated, still very stiffly, "what induced you to take this journey?"

"I have already had the honour of informing Lord Edward Fitzgerald," answered the young Englishman, beginning to be nettled by this insistence, "that I was moved solely by anxiety upon my sister's behalf."

Mr. O'Connor made a slight gesture of impatience. "And was Hamburg revealed to you in a vision, then, as a likely place in which to assuage this anxiety?"

"No," said Martin, suddenly resolved to give this conspirator a probably unpleasant surprise, "not in a vision. It came to me in the course of a conversation with Mr. Oliver O'Driscoll and Mr. James Malone in Dublin."

He had evidently succeeded in administering the surprise. "What!" ejaculated O'Connor, frowning, and Lord Edward exclaimed in an incredulous tone: "O'Driscoll told you that Mr. Roche had set out for Hamburg?" A second later O'Connor, recovering himself, asked coldly: "May I ask how you came to speak with either Mr. O'Driscoll or Mr. Malone?"

Martin chose to reply to Lord Edward. "I never said," he explained, "that Mr. O'Driscoll told me that in so many words. But it was his insistence that I should *not* go to Hamburg, which convinced me-wrongly, as I am now to understand-that Hamburg was Mr. Roche's destination."

"You have not answered my original question, Mr. Tyrrell," said the inquisitor, throwing his head back. "What was it that caused you in the first instance to think that Mr. Roche might have gone abroad at all?"

If he goes on much longer, thought Martin, I shall say: "Because you talked too loud at Ballydare," but he was denied the indiscreet pleasure of this retort, for at that moment the door at the side of the room opened, and Lady Edward's charming head was put in. "I thought I heard your voice, dear Arthur," she said. "Good afternoon, and welcome to Altona!" And holding out both hands she came towards Mr. O'Connor, looking to Martin's instantly riveted eyes, so young, so innocent, so kind, in her loose dress of palest yellow. And why should this stiff, inquisitorial Arthur O'Connor be thus blest with her friendship?

At any rate, Pamela's entrance had quite put an end to Mr. O'Connor's examination of him, and also, apparently, to the chance of his hearing anything further about Gerald Roche's real movements. However, he had already made up his mind to do without that information; it did not affect his futile quest. He must take his leave; he could not further intrude upon what had become almost a family party. Mr. O'Connor had not indeed probed the source of the idea which had sent Martin to Hamburg, but he seemed now to have lost interest in the subject, for Pamela was talking to him in her soft, gay, half-wistful voice, not at all about politics, but of "little Eddy," whom she had left with his grandmother, the Duchess, at Ealing, before quitting England, and how adorable the rogue was. But in those few minutes Martin looked and looked again at that enchanting face-whose only fault, if it were one, was the slight fulness of the underlip, at which, too, Pamela had a little trick of catching with what were surely the prettiest teeth in the world. She had very little colour; she was like a blush rose in all its fresh fragrance.

And her great dark eyes-but were they so dark? If only he were as near as Arthur O'Connor at this moment and could look into them! But her expression, like an angel's, one could see that across the room . . . and remember it across the world!

He began to make his farewell, an exile from Eden. Mr. O'Connor accepted it curtly, Lady Edward with a charming natural grace, though Martin at that moment was neither natural nor graceful, for at last he had seen her eyes; they were brown, with golden lights in them. Then, somehow, he was outside the room with Lord Edward, going down the stairs with him, at the street door. . . .

"You must forgive Mr. O'Connor for trying to cross-examine you about coming to Hamburg, Mr. Tyrrell."

"I was not at all surprised at that, my lord," returned Martin. (Must he still talk about that stupid business of Gerald's?) "It was only natural. But you may both rely upon my promise of silence." (Yes, indeed; was not this *her* husband?)

"I am sure of it," replied that fortunate young man. "And you on your part rely, I perceive, on Mr. O'Connor's assurance that Mr. Roche did not come here, and you are right in doing so. He would not tell you a lie. But I don't think, Mr. Tyrrell, that you have obtained quite your fair share of the bargain, and so I will tell you what no doubt Arthur would have told you (as he had just told me outside) had not my wife come into the room. It was *Athlone* to which Mr. Roche was sent, on business which would only have occupied him a few days. So he is undoubtedly back at Ballydare by this time. I am sorry you should have taken this long journey to no purpose."

With a smile he held out his hand, and a moment later Martin stood alone in the street of dolls' houses.

Just by the doorstep lay two red petals fallen from the window-box above. After a moment's hesitation Martin picked one up. Surely Pamela bent over those flowers sometimes, perhaps watered them. The street was empty; he slipped the cool, satiny thing into his pocket. Up there, behind them, she was talking in that delicious voice to those two men; but he could hear nothing.

(9)

The Martin who retraced his steps along the avenues to Hamburg ignored the spring verdure just as completely as that Martin had done who less than a couple of hours before had made his way beneath it to Altona. But this Martin walked much more slowly. Yes, he had been a fool all through. He had thought himself so clever in his dealings with O'Driscoll and Malone; so clever in guessing the obliterated word in Roche's letter, so clever in what he had deduced from the Irishmen's unwillingness for him to go to Hamburg. Now he saw only too clearly the real reason for that reluctance: they were afraid that he might come upon the tracks of the two important rebels who really had gone thither upon a treasonable mission! And the obliterated word was not *Altona* after all-it was *Athlone* —Roche had never left Ireland. He had been a double fool; and nobody had fooled him; he had fooled himself!

Nothing now remained but to return to England-or Ireland-with his tail between his legs.

At any rate, his brother-in-law was not, perhaps, so deeply committed as he had feared; though Lord Edward had used the word "sent" of his visit to Athlone, whatever his business were there. And Lucy's anxiety was, no doubt, more or less assuaged by this time. He himself need not go back to Ballydare. Yet he had scarcely seen Lucy, had not had his conversation with Gerald-not that in his present humiliated frame of mind he felt capable of dissuading anybody from anything. Still, as he had sufficient money-Lucy's money-he might as well return and finish his much-curtailed visit.

Inquiries later in the day revealed the fact that the Yarmouth packet sailed only twice a week, and had just left, so that he had another three days in Hamburg, whether he wished it or no. And Martin was blind enough to wonder why, upon receipt of this news, he was conscious not of disappointment, but of a sensation of reprieve. Before he went to sleep he knew the reason, and saw himself not as a double, but as a triple fool. For what could Pamela Fitzgerald be to him?

Alas, ere the night was through she seemed to be everything-sun, moon and stars in a newly minted universe.

He spent the next three days in feverish attempts to get another glimpse of her, cursing the fate which had installed not his *émigré* acquaintance La Vireville himself, but only that acquaintance's acquaintance, in the house opposite the Fitzgeralds'. Otherwise he might have visited him there, and found it a convenient point of vantage. But he could not present himself again at the little house with the tulips, nor could he decently walk up and down in front of it all day as he desired, though he could, and did, contrive to pass through the Schildtstrasse every four hours or so. He also loitered in it after dark one evening; but only one, for Hamburg, always suspicious of her Danish neighbours, closed her gates soon after sunset, and Martin was shut out for the night on that occasion, a performance which he judged it wiser not to repeat. Twice during that vigil did he see a figure which he took to be Lord Edward come out, and once go in; but of the face which had so suddenly crazed him there was never, by day or by night, a sign.

So Martin changed his tactics and bent his efforts towards getting an introduction to Mme. de Genlis, in the hope that he might meet her "adopted" daughter in her drawing-room. But, knowing no one in Hamburg society, he failed to procure this. Devoutly did he wish that he might come across M. de la Vireville once more, since he might have been of use in this respect, though even that was not certain. For Martin had gathered in the course of his enquiries that the more irreconcilable of the French Royalist exiles would not recognise this *émigrée* who had been 'governor' to the children of the Duc d'Orléans and had stood, so they said (for all her care in disguising it), in a relation to the dead prince more intimate still. But their censure was not at all on account of what scandal hinted of the lady's past, but because of Egalité's own republicanism and his having voted for the execution of the King, his cousin.

In despair Martin then made up his mind to obtain admission, by some means or other, to the great fête which was to follow the wedding of Mme. de Genlis's niece to the rich Hamburg merchant, M. Matthiesen, of which Lord Edward had told him, and of which indeed the whole city was talking. At that reception Lady Edward Fitzgerald, who had-nominally at least-come to Hamburg for the wedding, would certainly be present. By waiting over the nineteenth of May, the date of this event, Martin would miss yet another packet-boat, for the next sailed on the eighteenth . . . but a thousand packets might sail without him in view of such a chance.

* * * * *

But it was not because he could not gain admittance that Martin never attended the wedding fête, for when the hour came all desire to attend it had flown. Only in the press outside the bridegroom's mansion did he learn the news, running from mouth to mouth that "*die reizende Tochter der Genlis*" would not grace the scene with her presence. She had given birth, prematurely, to her child the day before.

So all was over with any chance of seeing her again. To no purpose had Martin lingered in Hamburg, and written after all to Lucy saying he should not return to her. Next day he was lucky enough to find a merchant vessel on the point of sailing for Hull, and went down the Elbe in her without once looking back at the spires of Altona, that fortunate town. In any case he would not have seen much, for the fog was already creeping up the Elbe, which, before the vessel reached Cuxhaven, forced her to drop anchor, and still further delayed Martin's return. But to this he was indifferent, not having the faintest premonition of what was awaiting him on his native shores, nor how his delay in Hamburg and his latest proceedings there had every one helped to pile up a very pretty count against him.

(10)

During the voyage Martin changed his mind once more about Ballydare, but decided, since he was landing at Hull, to make for Liverpool rather than for Holyhead. Two fellow-passengers, merchants returning to Manchester, assured him that packets ran almost daily to Dublin from that port also.

Arrived at Hull, he was, with these two chance acquaintances, awaiting the examination of baggage for contraband in the Customs House, when he became aware of a couple of men, decently dressed, powerful, unattractive fellows, who seemed much interested in him, he could not conceive for what reason. They did not accost him, but he clearly saw one give the other a violent nudge, and then whisper in his ear, when, the official happening to ask him, Martin, where he wanted his baggage taken, he answered: "The Liverpool, or rather, the York stage-coach." But, a few moments later, while he was fastening up his valise, Mr. Parkinson, one of the merchants, came up to him and proposed that he should share their postchaise as far as Manchester, since they intended to take the shorter way by Pontefract and Huddersfield, instead of the longer mail route. This offer Martin willingly accepted, and thought no more about the burly, staring strangers.

He parted next day with Mr. Parkinson and his companion at Manchester, and himself spent the night there, meaning to continue his journey next day by stage-coach, for his money was beginning to run rather low, and he still had to get to County Cork. So, with his head much fuller of Pamela Fitzgerald than of Lucy Roche, he rattled with a good many other people over the Irwell, skirted the dreary waste of Chat Moss, passed outside Warrington a fifty-foot gibbet decorated with the remains of a man hanged in chains the year before for robbing the mail-coach, admired the smooth, hard surface of the road thence to Prescot (composed, so he learnt, of slag, the refuse of the now discontinued copper mines of Warrington and Liverpool), obtained above Prescot a fine view of the Welsh hills; and finally drove into what a fellow-traveller described as "the extensive and opulent" town of Liverpool, whose storehouses were the largest in Britain, and whose docks exceeded all description. The war, however, admitted the encomiast, had affected her trade.

The Manchester coach came down Shaw's Brow to the *Golden Lion* at the top of Dale Street, and instantly all was a confusion of disembarkation. Martin was for pushing on at once to the waterside and trying his luck in the matter of a packet for Dublin, and having secured a man to carry his valise, he was giving him instructions, when, without warning, each of his elbows was seized from behind, and a gruff voice said in his ear:

"You've been to Dublin once too often; you're not going there again! Now you come along peaceable-like, young man, and then there'll be no call for rough 'andling!" Turning his head, Martin recognised one of the men who had so stared at him in the Customs House at Hull.

"What the—let go my arms at once!" he stuttered. "How dare you! Let me go!"

He made violent efforts to throw off the hold of one or the other, but, by keeping somewhat in his rear, and almost bringing his elbows together behind his back, his assailants had rendered him helpless, turn and twist as he might. A gentleman passing at the moment, catching sight of what was going on, came to Martin's assistance; that is to say, he pushed towards the struggling trio, and with some indignation asked the meaning of this treatment. And on Martin's stunned ears fell the incredible reply of those who gripped him: "We're Bow Street runners, sir, with a warrant for this young man's arrest."

"Have you shown your warrant?" asked Martin's ally. "And where are your badges? —I believe you are impostors! Let this gentleman go at once, or I shall summon assistance!"

One of the men, removing a hand for a moment, and plunging it into a pocket, pulled out and contrived to flap open a paper which he presented (still in that one hand) to the stupefied eyes of the person most interested, who caught therein phantasmagoric glimpses of the Royal name, of his own, and of quite inconceivable phrases about "treasonable proceedings."

"But that's absurd!" he heard himself say in a voice of mild astonishment. "In God's name, what proceedings? I am as innocent of——"

"Then you come peaceably!" admonished the man with the warrant. "If you're innocent, you'll be able to prove it, whatever you 'ave been a-doin' of at 'Amburg, and for whatever reason you was on the point of sneakin' back to Ireland. (Bill, see that 'ackney coach yonder—'twill just serve!) I takes it, young man, that you don't want to be marched all down this here street, so you'll not object to payin' for a coach. Come along now!"

"Where are you taking me?" asked Martin, standing quite still, and conscious of a kind of sick void at the pit of his stomach. *Treasonable proceedings!* And since the recent Act, almost anything could be construed as treason!

"To the Tower in Water Street for the night; start for London early to-morrow. Come along now, sharp; there's a crowd a-gatherin', and it may be nasty to you."

"But I... good God!" exclaimed Martin helplessly. This was a thing impossible, preposterous! *Treasonable proceedings*—when he had been doing his best to prevent another man from engaging in them!

There seemed nothing for it, however. The gentleman who had intervened on his behalf, after one glance at the warrant, had walked away with a look of disgust. And Martin, moving automatically, though hurried by his captors, went meekly with them to the coach which they had indicated. He had been quite oblivious of the crowd which was forming, a rough-looking crowd such as collects easily in the streets of a seaport town. Round the coach it became quite thick, and even menacing; some ugly names were thrown at Martin and a dirty fist shaken in his very face. But the runners hustled him safely into the vehicle, congratulating themselves on the small amount of trouble which their quarry had actually given them. He hadn't shown much fight after the first, and now sat quiet in the corner, looking as white as his shirt-just as it should be! Amid jeers and groans the coach started down Dale Street.

"We should 'a' nabbed you at 'Ull," said the spokesman after a moment, "if you'd not slipped away by postchaise. We was waiting for you by the York coach, thinkin' it best not to 'urt the feelings of them friends you was with in the Customs House." He laughed as a man laughs who gives a humorously false reason for an action.

"I did not 'slip away'!" said Martin tonelessly. "I knew nothing about you."

"Ho, didn't you! Any'ow, you got a start on us by that, and when we found it out we 'ad to post, too. Got here afore you though; and all's been for the best, 'cos now we've got what we 'ad instructions to get if possible, corr*obor*ative evidence. You was goin' back to Dublin—'eard it with our own ears, which we shouldn't 'a done at 'Ull."

The man "Bill" appeared to concur, but Martin paid no more attention to their mutual congratulations. A horrible clarity which was beginning now to flood his half-paralysed brain showed glimpses of sense in this fantastic rubbish. His conduct could be made to look very suspicious; not a doubt of it! He had had one interview in Dublin with a couple of doubtful characters; in Altona he had sought out and obtained another interview with two known rebels. It could easily be argued that he had gone to Hamburg from Dublin for that purpose. Had he not made enquiries all over the twin towns for "an Irish gentleman," and hung about outside the residence of the French minister? But how had these facts become known in England so long before his own arrival there that already the runners were waiting to take him at Hull? ... Only, he began to fear, through his own foolishness, through his having stayed on in Hamburg, using every available means to get into touch again with the Fitzgeralds, lurking outside the house which contained not only Pamela, but her rebel husband also. Heavens, what a blind and innocent fool he had been!

Well, however it had been brought about, this arrest would break his old father's heart. He was absolutely guiltless, yes; but he would have to prove it, and that might be a long and costly business. How could he afford a good lawyer? Meanwhile, innocent or guilty, the mere fact of his lying in prison awaiting trial would be enough for his father. (It would indeed be more than enough for Martin himself.) And even when he was cleared his reputation might be sullied, particularly among such of his contemporaries at the University who remembered, if any did, that extremely foolish revolutionary phase of his at Oxford. But no one, surely, could remember that; it was a lamentable episode of youth which had left no traces.

But Martin suddenly clenched his hands on the edge of the seat. *No traces!* Somewhere at home, in some untidy drawer of his, among the relics of his Oxford days, were poems, scraps of verse, drafts of speeches, even some stanzas in print. Despite the gulf which separated him from the callow undergraduate who had written these things he had not destroyed them, though he had several times intended to find them and do so. Now they would be discovered, to witness against him, for he knew that the authorities in this time of national stress would not leave a stone unturned in their search for evidence.

If only he could escape gaol, could apply at once to someone who knew him and would vouch for his character-someone in authority and with influence! But to whom? (For the first time he regretted the family feud with Sir Sumner Tyrrell.) Or if he could at least get to Selham St. Peter, see his father and assure him of the entire wrongfulness of the charge, explain everything, and destroy those damning papers before the runners could follow him there!

All this while (though it was not long) they were trundling down Dale Street. Completely unfamiliar as Martin was with Liverpool, he realised that they were approaching its wide river and its docks. If he could once give his captors the slip, surely, in a port like this, there were many little narrow streets down which he could dive and twist, and in which a seafaring population would probably not be eager to deliver him up to the law? When, in front of the Exchange, they had to pull up for a moment, he distinctly saw masts at the end of a wide street on the left—a dock, perhaps, so they could not be going much further. Indeed, ahead on the right he caught a glimpse of the upper storeys of a red sandstone building (formerly, though this he did not know, the town house of the great Stanley family), and from its appearance guessed it to be the "Tower" to which he was being taken. There was not then much time left! But it would be futile to jump out here, in the busy street in front of the Exchange-even if he *could* jump out.

The coach started again with a jerk, which dislodged some unperceived object stuck in the corner of the seat between him and the side, for it fell forward against his right arm, and when he slightly shifted this member, subsided on to the seat itself. His thoughts still fixed upon the chances of making a bolt for it; he let his fingers quietly stray in search of this object, whatever it was. They encountered first a short loop of leather, then something slender and stick-like terminating in a heavy knob, the whole thing being only about fifteen inches long.

But this was fantastic! Martin knew by touch alone what this was—a life-preserver, a short cudgel with a loaded head such as travellers sometimes carried for protection, and which could be slipped into a deep pocket. Some former occupant of this hackney coach had left it behind, where, wedged upright in the corner, it had been overlooked, now, by an incredible chance, to fall almost into his hand! Martin glanced warily at his guardians, who were quite ignorant of what he had acquired, the man with the warrant sitting beside him, and "Bill" opposite, talking to each other, and not troubling overmuch about their quiescent prisoner.

And then, before he expected it, the coach stopped-in the street, not in any gaol-yard. "Out you come, sir!" said the warrant-bearer, opening the left-hand door, that nearest to himself. "Bill" naturally did not move, intending to bring up the rear. It was now or never. Martin slipped the thong of the life-preserver over his right wrist, slid a little forward on his seat as though to obey, but instead very quickly opened the right-hand door and was half out of the coach on that side before "Bill" precipitated himself upon him, grabbing him by the left arm and shoulder, and shouting: "Ah, would ye indeed!"

Clutched thus, Martin had no room to strike, but he thrust the knobbed end of his unexpected weapon as hard as he could into the man's face. "Bill" with an oath loosed his hold and fell back, and Martin, who already had one foot on the high step, tumbled rather than descended from the vehicle. Bill's first shout had, of course, warned his colleague, who darted round the back of the coach. Him Martin smote with all his strength; heard a horrid crack as the loaded knob met his skull, saw with mingled exultation and dismay the runner fall in a heap upon the muddy stones, had an impression of the other man, with a hand to his mouth, jumping clumsily from the coach, and of various people running towards the scene-all this in one flashing second of time before he himself plunged round the horses' heads towards the opening of an alley which seemed to hold out his best chance of eluding pursuit.

He ran as he had never run in his life down this very dirty alley, unconscious that no one was pursuing him, for the sufficient reason, as he learnt afterwards, that it was a place of such ill-repute, so full of crimps and bad characters, that no respectable citizen would venture down it, still less a solitary Bow Street runner-and it was quite certain that "Bill" was the only specimen of that class now able to use his legs. Seamen, old and young, hairy, bronzed and ear-ringed, lounged in doorways, but made no effort to stay him, turning to look after him without removing their pipes from their mouths. Down the centre trickled a most uninviting little gutter, and it was the slime upon the edge of this drain which brought Martin's career to a check, for, his foot slipping in his haste, he slithered and all but fell, bringing himself up by clutching at the arm of a man standing near.

"I beg your pardon!" panted the fugitive. And as the man seemed to be desirous of retaining him, he added, somewhat unnecessarily: "I am in haste; pray allow me ——"

"I see as you're in haste, sir," responded a gruff voice, impeded by a quid. "But there's no one a-chasing of ye. And what's that in yer 'and, if I may make free to ask?"

Martin had forgotten what he was holding. "I . . . I got away from them," he explained. "I had been arrested-unjustly . . . for debt," he added, feeling a sudden conviction that this avowal would not at all prejudice him in the eyes of an inhabitant of this place.

"Ah," said the seaman, looking shrewdly at him out of little blue, crease-surrounded eyes. "Nasty thing that-might 'appen to anyone! Best come in 'ere then; no one'll come arrestin' of ye in 'ere!"

Martin looked and beheld himself almost on the threshold of some kind of dingy tavern with a painted anchor swinging overhead for sign. A couple of men-also, evidently, mariners, like his friend of the gutter-were standing in the entrance. It was true; he could not have a better temporary refuge, and he went towards the door. The others made way for him. "Young gentleman's running from arrest-debt!" whispered the hoarse voice behind.

"Come in, sir," said one of the men benevolently, and in a moment Martin found himself in a sort of tap-room thick with tobacco smoke and smelling strongly of ale and spirits, uproarious with snatches of song and the banging of pewter pots upon the long table round which sat about a dozen hard-bitten sea-farers.

The man who had brought Martin in spoke in a low voice to the two others, who nodded; then he addressed the fugitive: "Just in case there was to be a hue and cry after you down Belker's Alley, sir, you'd better slip on some of our togs and sit down there in the corner among us, like, if you've no objection. All respectable privateersmen we are, sir," he continued, stripping off his own blue frieze coat and holding it out —"here, someone give the gentleman a weskit too-brig *Fair Penitent*, sailing with letters of marque to-morrow morning. You can see her out there in the river —a beauty, she is! Now, sir" —as he crammed a woollen cap on the refugee's head —"if you was to be sitting there in the corner with a pipe and a mug of ale your own mother wouldn't find ye!"

Bewildered, but conscious that this benefactor was talking sound sense, Martin took his place in the corner against the boarded wall, the drinkers making way for him. He was still somewhat out of breath, but he was beginning to realise what he had done to an officer of the Law up there by the Tower. . . . The life-preserver was no longer on his wrist: he had slipped it off when he exchanged his coat. Best so, no doubt; it was incriminating evidence. The weapon was, in fact, in the hand of his first acquaintance, who was examining it with some minuteness. In another moment he had come round and bent towards Martin.

"You used this, and no mistake, sir-there's blood on it!"

Martin suppressed a slight shiver. "Yes, I did use it, I am afraid."

"That'll likely be awk'ard for ye," observed his friend after a pause, during which all eyes were fastened with redoubled interest upon the newcomer.

"Yes, I fear that it may," murmured Martin, becoming momentarily more convinced of that fact.

The large bearded man looked round and cleared his throat. "Now a gentleman what's done that sort of thing when runnin' away from arrest," he observed to the assembly, " 'ud need to lay quiet for a bit, I takes it."

Half a dozen voices assented; the speaker then addressed Martin himself. "You wouldn't think now, sir"—he seemed to be trying to render his hoarse tones coaxing, "you wouldn't think of signing on, I suppose, for a cruise in the finest letter o' marque as ever sailed out of Liverpool, with a share of the prize money?"

"Sign on for a cruise-as a member of the crew, no," answered Martin. "I want to return to-to my home," he added more cautiously. "But if," he went on, a modification of the sailor's proposal having occurred to him, "if your captain would agree to take me as a passenger and land me on the English coast somewhere, it might be the best way of eluding pursuit."

"Ay, ay, that's a good notion," came from the assembly. "Suppose the gentleman was to do that, Jemmy!"

"Why, you thick-headed sons of——" the large seaman was beginning, when he checked himself, and said in a different tone, "Ay, indeed, sir, that's a good notion; but you must go aboard same as all o' we, in those togs, or mebbe ye might be reckernised. Well now, my hearties, I'm sure we're all glad to do a good turn to a young gentleman in a difficulty, and he'll be glad, I expect, for us to drink his health."

Martin took the hint, and fresh drinks were served, of which he partook himself, and was not sorry to. He had escaped; and seemed likely, if he boarded the *Fair Penitent* as a passenger, to have found a very useful and unobtrusive method of leaving Liverpool. But how much damage had he done to the runner? . . . That was the black shadow. He tried, like not a few before him, to drown it, but a shadow cannot be drowned for long. The room was hot and frowsty, his companions not too well washed, and these unpleasant atmospheric conditions became accentuated when, with the falling of dusk in the tavern room, lights were brought. Martin's head was aching a good deal by now with the heat and noise, and he was beginning to wonder if he had been too confiding; really the faces of these hearties, seen by candlelight, looked much like the visages of carousing pirates. He tried to guess what would be the habits of privateers in this war; was it for instance probable that such a vessel, cruising about for prey, would trouble to make the coast on purpose to land an odd civilian, particularly if, as he had by this time gathered from the talk, she had been yesterday rendered short of several hands through the inconsiderate action of the pressgang of His Majesty's Navy?

Finding his first friend now sitting beside him, he confided to him this doubt, adding that, after all, grateful as he was to him and his comrades for their protection, and for the disguise which they had contributed-which by this time he was beginning to be rather anxious to discard-he did not think that he would go on board the *Fair Penitent* with them; it seemed so unlikely that the captain would meet his views. The stout seaman said little, but soon afterwards announced that he would confer with the bo'sun of the privateer, who had just joined the gathering; and made his way through the clouds of tobacco smoke to a swarthy-looking mariner by the door, to whom he spoke long and earnestly; and presently the black-avised one himself was standing at Martin's elbow, assuring him that it could all be arranged, and inviting him, apparently as a sort of earnest of the bargain, to drink the health of the brig *Fair Penitent* in a little good Jamaica rum. Martin complied, for the glass was already in the bo'sun's hand. It was strong stuff. . . . Very soon he realised that he had been foolish not to stick to ale, for the smoke-laden, candle-lit, noisy scene was beginning to sway to and fro before him, tilting sideways with a rhythmical swing almost as though he were already aboard the privateer. . . .

*****

And when next he opened his eyes that was just where he was; and the scene *was* slightly tilted, for "the finest letter of marque that ever sailed out of Liverpool" was lying over to a fresh morning breeze off Formby Point, having sailed, garlanded and glorious, down the Mersey, accompanied by such smaller craft as could keep up with her until she hoisted her topsails, and began to plough the waters of the Irish Sea, on her way to fight the French and Dutch.

But Martin Tyrrell, lying sick and sorry in her fo'c'sle had not, as he was soon to discover, been shipped as a passenger.

III
SANCTUARY

"But beecause the poor Boy is somewhat stiffe, with the hurt of his legge, I beseech you let me have a Chamber, and a bed for him, and not of the woorst."

   Nicholas Breton.
The Miseries of Mavillia.

III
SANCTUARY

(1)

"And that," finished Martin, "is my story. It is very good of you to have listened to it, Miss Meredith, and I hope that I have not wearied you with my troubles?"

But he could not possibly have thought that the girl sitting engrossed and horrified on the turf a little above him was suffering from boredom. Apart from its subject matter, which was scarcely to be termed dull, his recital had not lasted long enough to fatigue, for he had naturally not reported conversations verbatim, nor entered into every detail of his doings . . . while of Lady Edward Fitzgerald he had made but the briefest and most colourless mention. Nor, ending his narrative where he did, had he said a word of his distasteful experiences on board the *Fair Penitent*, an ordeal of rough lying, hard words, ready blows and bad food, when indeed he had sometimes wondered if he could possibly be the same individual who, at the beginning of that month of May, had been boredly supervising the studies of the "young cub" Heseltine in Northamptonshire. The fight with the French brig, despite the wound which it had brought him, had really been the sole pleasurable episode.

The stream dripped down to the rocks, the sea sighed below; a jackdaw walked mincingly about at a little distance, and out in St. Bride's Bay a sloop, probably laden with culm from Milford, was making her almost becalmed way towards Solva Harbour. All this was so familiar to Nest that it was difficult for her to believe that the young man of her own class with whom she talked was accused-ridiculously, of course, but still with some shadow of justification-of treason and possibly of murder. Yet he was undoubtedly an almost penniless outcast in seaman's garb, and she was having what amounted to a clandestine interview with a gentleman whose bare ankles-and some inches of his shins too-were exposed to the light of day. This had never happened to her before.

"Oh, sir," she breathed at length, "what *is* to be done!"

"I wish I knew," returned Martin, staring at the distant sloop. "It is not a very cheerful tale to convey to my poor father-if indeed, madam, you are still disposed to undertake the task."

"Indeed it is not," assented his listener. "All the more reason, I suppose, that he should hear it. But you must help me, sir, to compose a letter which will not convey too much-will not compromise you, I mean. First, however, should we not discuss a little what you are going to do next?"

"The first thing is to find some more work, for two reasons: I must support myself, and I shall be less likely to attract suspicion if I have some kind of occupation."

"Yet, with that lameness, for which I am responsible," mused Nest with a sigh, "you cannot undertake farm work. . . . Is your leg very painful, Mr. Tyrrell?" she inquired, casting a rather bashful glance at that limb, where the bandage was no longer visible save as a bulge beneath the blue fustian. And, not waiting for the answer which did not seem to be forthcoming, she continued, "Indeed, sir, you must consult a doctor about it!"

"No, that I dare not do," returned the fugitive bluntly. "It would lead to my identification. I see now that it was unwise of me ever to have admitted to a dog-bite. It was on the spur of the moment that I did it that evening in the ruins; I caught at an excuse for not having found shelter in a farm."

It seemed impossible to say in so many words how grateful she was to him for not having attributed the dog-bite to its real source. "I have often wondered since-that is, I have wondered," murmured Nest, trying hastily to correct an impression that she had given the matter constant thought, "what you were doing in the ruins that evening?"

"Exactly what I told your father, Miss Meredith. I was meaning to pass the night there. It seemed best to sever, if I could, any possible connection between myself and the deserter from the *Vrijheid* (in case anyone should be aware that there had been a deserter) and I decided for that reason to postpone my search for work until the next morning, and to make as though I had come to St. David's from quite a different direction. So I remained hiding in the neighbourhood of the hayfield until it was becoming dusk, and then left it, proposing to skirt round the town — I beg your pardon, I presume it is a city! —but when I got near the Cathedral and saw those ruins below me, I thought I would snatch some sleep there, going on before it was light again."

"It was most unfortunate that we should have come there that evening," lamented Nest. "But indeed you startled me, sir-that must be my excuse for giving the alarm as I did. . . . And are you really intending to go on to Solva now?"

"I had thought of it," replied the adventurer, a shade wearily. "Do you consider, madam, that it would be a good place in which to find work? The harbour is very small, is it not?"

But Nest was looking at him so intently that she hardly seemed to have heard his question. Her pretty forehead was wrinkled into a frown; yet there was a new light in her eyes.

"I think you said, Mr. Tyrrell," —there was also a ring of excitement in her voice —"that you had been at the University?"

"Yes," answered Martin, somewhat surprised. "I took my degree in Arts three years ago at Oxford . . . Haymaking, however, was unfortunately not included in the curriculum."

"But you are well educated . . . you doubtless know about all sorts of learned things, and you write a good hand?"

"Tolerably good, I believe," answered the young man, more and more surprised.

"You could act as secretary, then, to a man of letters, a scholar who writes about the history of Pembrokeshire and such matters?"

"Not if by that you mean your father, Miss Meredith," replied Martin hastily. "I could not expect him— —"

"No, no," said the Precentor's daughter, with equal haste. "Papa is not in need of a secretary. Moreover, he would have to know your story, and he might think it his duty . . . I mean, I would prefer that he were not put in a position where . . ." She did not seem quite sure how to end the sentence.

"I perfectly understand," said her hearer quietly. "Yet you yourself, madam, do not shrink from that position!"

"But I am a woman, and not expected to do what is required of a man in such circumstances," explained Nest with complete conviction. "Mr. Salt, the gentleman of whom I was thinking, is extremely independent, and goes his own way; he cares very little, I think, for authority of any kind. And he said the other day, so I was told, that he needed an amanuensis-is not that the word? —and it has just occurred to me that you might apply for the post."

"But, Miss Meredith, I have no one to recommend me, no one to vouch either for my character or my attainments-that is to say, there are such persons, but I cannot apply to them! This gentleman would certainly require testimonials."

"Mr. Salt is what is called an eccentric," declared Nest seriously. "He might very well be induced to overlook the want of testimonials, especially if he were told a little about you first. I mean," she went on, while Martin stared at her, "that, as he has always been very kind to me, if I were to go and ask him he might (indeed I am almost sure he would) consent to see you. And I could go to see him," she considered for a moment, "yes, I could quite well go to-morrow —quite well," she reiterated, having suddenly and joyfully remembered that to-morrow her father and Jane proposed to pay a visit to Haverfordwest, and that she would be left to her own devices from morn till eve.

"Miss Meredith, you are really too— —"

"But it is so simple," broke in his companion excitedly. "For I am sure that I can persuade Mr. Salt to see you, and then you can do the rest."

Martin smiled a little; it would not be so simple as all that! He laid the objection before her. "And what if, having seen me and heard my story-or some part of it-this Mr. Salt feels that, far from employing me, he must hand me over to the authorities?"

"He would never do that!" affirmed Nest with confidence. "I would procure his promise that, whether he engaged you or no, he would respect your secret. I dare say that he would not even insist on learning what it was, if he took a fancy to you. And he has never been known to go back upon his word. Then, you see, Mr. Tyrrell, you could appear in St. David's as a totally different person; you would have no connection with the privateer or with haymaking. You might even be supposed to have been engaged by letter, and to have come straight from England!"

Martin smiled again-he could not help it-at her swift-flying plans. "Your kind and ingenious scheme, Miss Meredith, might perhaps be successful-always granted that this Mr. Salt is open to persuasion and willing to take a certain risk-but what of these clothes of mine? If I am seen approaching his door in them, and have moreover no others to wear afterwards, I am still recognisable as the man who was working for Griffiths, perhaps even as the sailor from the *Vrijheid*."

Nest's face fell. "Yes, I am afraid that is true. You must somehow be provided with other clothes, then. But how?"

"Perhaps I could buy some," suggested Martin, not very confidently.

"Yes, but where? You could not do so in St. David's without exciting remark, and Haverfordwest is so far away. . . . Oh!" She suddenly sat erect. "I wonder!"

She looked very pretty, "wondering" thus, but Mr. Tyrrell, though he was gazing at her, was not aware of it. He too was pondering the subject of a possible change of clothes. If she could by hook or by crook arrange for his employment by this eccentric Mr. Salt, what an unspeakable boon it would be to have some occupation which did not involve using his leg, the condition of which, as he knew very well, was not improving-far from it. He did not wish to allow Miss Meredith to learn how increasingly painful it had become the last couple of days. Nor did he wish to confess that his week's wages were totally insufficient to procure a suit of clothes such as should be worn by the secretary even of an eccentric.

"Mr. Tyrrell," said Nest, suddenly leaning forward, "I have thought of a plan! If you could come to the Precentory to-morrow— —"

He could not help breaking in . . . "But if the Precentor were to see me— —"

"The Precentor, sir," explained Miss Meredith in a curiously hurried voice, "will not be there. He and my sister are to spend the day in Haverfordwest." She smoothed down her besprigged flounces with a somewhat nervous hand, and went on: "So that if you were to come . . . perhaps saying that I had met you seeking work, and had promised you some better clothes (I am afraid that it would be wiser for you in that case to present yourself at the back door) I would have some ready for you which I think would fit you—a suit of my brother William's. He is away from home . . . since he is in the Navy."

A gull flying by here gave a loud squawk; and really it was not inappropriate that some comment should be made from an impartial source on the conduct of a young lady who proposed thus to take advantage of the absence from home alike of her father and her brother. In spite of his own serious situation and the pain in his leg Martin had to bite his lips to keep back a laugh . . . or possibly a squawk like the gull's. He lowered his eyes that amusement might not look out of them. But it was with real feeling that he said, "You overwhelm me, Miss Meredith; and I do not think that I ought to-that I can accept."

"But indeed you must!" exclaimed his benefactress; and giving him no more time for refusal went on eagerly, "I would much prefer not to put you to the trouble of coming to the Precentory, but I could not bring or even send the suit to you here without exciting comment and suspicion."

"No, indeed; I beg you will not think of such a course!"

"And in any case," went on the strategist, "you will be obliged to come back nearly as far as St. David's in order to reach Mr. Salt's house, which stands on the high ground between the city and St. Non's Bay. You must also hear the result of the talk which I hope to have with Mr.

Salt to-morrow. All this indeed must take place to-morrow, because to-day . . . circumstances would not be so favourable to-day." This phrase was vague enough decently to wrap up the freedom from paternal oversight which would be hers to-morrow. "Yet . . . where will you spend the time meanwhile, sir?" she asked anxiously.

"Here or hereabouts," answered the fugitive with a smile. "The weather is fine, and I have been a privateersman, you must remember, sleeping on deck before now; and there is food in this bundle." (He did not specify how little.) "Should it turn wet I can find shelter somewhere, though I shall not go to a farm again if I can avoid it, since in accordance with your excellent plan Mark Thompson must now disappear from the neighbourhood. There is no need to trouble about my welfare, Miss Meredith, I assure you!"

And on that assurance Miss Meredith got to her feet, and so did her accomplice, though not so easily as she.

"You agree to this arrangement, then, sir?" she asked, with a sudden sense of her boldness and her loquacity.

"How can I refuse?" asked the young man. "I should be the most ungrateful of wretches if I did. As it is," he added in a lower voice, "I can scarcely believe that there exists anyone so kind and compassionate. . . . And yet I ought not to accept what you propose, for the debt can never be repaid."

"But it is I who owe you repayment," answered Nest with a touch of shyness. "My dog——"

"Oh, pray, Miss Meredith," he exclaimed, "pray cease to think of that!"

She half held out her hand, then drew it back. "But we are forgetting the letter to your father!"

"Let us leave that for the moment," he suggested, "until we see what your plan for the morrow brings forth. We neither of us have writing materials here-at least I have not-and one would need, I think, to make a rough draft of the letter first."

"Yes; and perhaps Mr. Salt would help us!"

He smiled, thinking again, from the height of his own five additional years of experience, how young and optimistic she was. There were a few more words of arrangement, of explanation of the exact position of Mr. Salt's house, of instructions as to what Martin was to say when he presented himself at the Precentory, and at what time she would expect him there-the hour being fixed to allow of her seeing Mr. Salt first-and then he was watching the little figure in its beflowered yellow dress go up the path again. At the top it paused, and Nest Meredith gave a fleeting glance at the young man standing looking up at her from the green lip of the combe above the sea.

And that young man was thinking. A yellow dress again! *She*, so different, of the other yellow dress, would have done as much for him, no doubt, married as she was to a rebel. But this child from the uttermost corner of Wales was not versed in the demands of conspiracy; she could not be used to deceit, yet here she was embarking upon it without a tremor, for his sake. Bless her heart!

But when Miss Meredith had completely vanished from sight, Martin Tyrrell, sinking down once more upon the sweet-smelling turf, put his hands round the calf of his right leg as if the action would still the throbbing there, and bit his lip hard. He only wished it were to-day that the Precentor was going to pay his convenient visit to Haverfordwest, and that there were not still thirty hours or so to get through before he had the chance of assistance and shelter at the hands of the eccentric Mr. Salt. And even then it would only be a chance . . .

There was a gull again overhead; and this time a series of chuckles came down to the wingless human below; they sounded almost derisive. Throwing himself back, his hands behind his head, the latter looked up at the snowy creature carried along so serenely by its mere balancing on those strong pinions. "All very well for you, my fine fellow," he thought; "but shall I be able even to hobble by to-morrow?" And all at once, in the warm, still sunshine, an involuntary shiver ran through him.

(2)

Even though some of his peculiarities were but legendary, there could be small doubt that Mr. Jerome Salt was slightly eccentric. In an age of snuff-taking he denounced the practice as a filthy habit, and smoking as "breathing the chimneys of hell"; yet, though it might be thought from these objections to snuff and tobacco that he was of a prim as well as of a studious disposition, he could set a sail and haul on a rope with any seaman, and, for all his melancholy blue eyes, was credited with more than the usual seaman's power of invective and a surprisingly volcanic temper. Although he was translating and editing the *Itinerarium Cambriae* of Giraldus Cambrensis and other matters, and haunted the Cathedral archives, yet he never appeared there at any service save the Commination on Ash Wednesday. In the same way, though engaged upon a history of Pembrokeshire, he had not a drop of Welsh blood in his veins; on the contrary, he exulted in airing his very uncomplimentary opinions of that race, and in telling any member of it to his face what he thought of him. Nevertheless he was not at all unpopular in St. David's; for he could be very open-handed, and in the course of years the inhabitants of Dewisland had come to be proud of him, and to cherish the (quite mistaken) belief that his diatribes were but a cloak for his affection. Else why should he choose to live, so solitary yet apparently so contented, in the house up on the cliffs above St. Non's Bay, where one felt the full force of the wind, and where the trees which old Captain Bowen had planted in the middle of the century were all warped and bent —a house which had already acquired the name of Bowen's Folly before Mr. Salt bought and repaired it. That was twenty or more years ago now.

Through the gateposts severally crowned by the old mariner Joseph Bowen with the terrestrial and celestial globes, on whose stony surface continents and constellations alike were scaled over by the grey-green lichen, Nest Meredith next afternoon passed to the house, observing that Mr. Salt, as was his pious custom, had recently restored with lively paint the twin figureheads which flanked the entrance door of the house. On the right was stationed a staring and impassive female in a helmet who might have been Minerva, Bellona or the genius of Britain; on the left an equally staring native partaking of the traits both of a Polynesian and an African negro, and wearing the tall coronal of feathers proper to a Central American cacique. Nautical opinion in St. David's assigned these figureheads respectively to a ship of Sir Francis Drake's and to one of Captain Cook's, being wrong in both attributions.

Miss Meredith was shown by Mrs. Morris, Mr. Salt's housekeeper and sole resident domestic, into the library, which at the moment was empty, though it bore the signs of recent toil, for though Mr. Salt was very orderly, the big table in the centre was strewn with open books and sheets of paper. Long windows, and a glass door too, gave on to a terrace very different in its vegetation from the sheltered slopes of the Precentory, for here even arbutus and veronica hedges showed traces of the wind which came straight off the sea, though actually the house was a good half mile from the cliff edge. But it stood high, and quite unsheltered-hence its name.

Mr. Salt came in so quietly that Nest jumped when she heard his gentle, half mocking voice behind her.

"Who inhabits that bonnet? Turn round, young lady, that I may see if it is really Princess Nesta, as I was told?"

Nest laughed, and held out her hand. Exquisitely neat as usual in his trim blue coat with gilt buttons, Mr. Salt put his hand under hers as if to royalty's, and sketched a kiss upon it. "Come and sit down, my dear, and tell me why this pleasure is bestowed upon me to-day? Is it because the Precentor and your sister have gone to Haverfordwest-yes, you see I know that! You were lonely, perhaps, Princess, and bethought you of your subject up at the Folly?"

"May I sit here?" inquired Nest a trifle nervously, and sank on to a window seat. "No, sir, that is not why I have come to see you. It is because I want to ask you a favour . . . a very great favour." Suddenly the pattern of the carpet became most absorbing. How could she tell him what she wanted!

79

Mr. Salt drew up a chair as if to sit near her; then he went off and consulted a calendar upon the mantelpiece. "Friday, July the 15th," he said, returning, "a day I must remember, a memorable day. I am asked a favour by Miss Nest Meredith."

Miss Nest Meredith made a little uncertain sound. "It . . . I am afraid it is a very great favour. When you hear what it is, sir . . ." She looked at him, then down again at the comfortable hues of the carpet. What she was going to propose was no doubt absurd. "I don't think that I can ask it after all," she concluded.

"I never alter the records in my diary," said Mr. Salt in a precise tone. Stretching out a hand he annexed a little volume from the table, wrote therein in pencil, and showed her the entry. "*Miss N. M. asked me a favour, which I naturally gave myself the pleasure of granting.*" Then he looked at her expectantly.

If the carpet had been wild thyme and grass it would have been easier to speak; or if that footstool near the table had been a bundle tied up in a handkerchief and representing all the present worldly goods of an unfortunate man driven from his employment and refuge through her. But they were not. Nest looked out of the window for assistance. There the sea at least was the same, blue and full of light. She screwed herself up to the plunge; it surely should not be so difficult to take, with Mr. Salt so kind-as always to her.

"Papa mentioned the other day," she began haltingly, "that you had said you would soon have to employ somebody as secretary."

Mr. Salt leant forward. "My dear Nest, what a delightful notion! But almost too overwhelming for me! When will you come?"

"Oh, no, no," said the supplicant, blushing. "I do not mean that *I* . . . for I should not be clever enough. 'Tis somebody I heard of . . . somebody who would . . . that is, if you really need such a person?"

"My need is most genuine," replied the man of letters. "For, upon my word, I am getting so crabbed a handwriting that I cannot sometimes read it myself! But what a disappointment that it is not you who are offering yourself for the post!" He looked at her a moment whimsically and added, "No, it would be too much like having a skylark in a cage, a thing I could never tolerate the notion of. Who is the individual proposed, eh? Is he a protégé of the Precentor's? I warn you that I will not employ some half intelligible Welsh curate!"

"No, it is not a Welshman," answered Nest thankfully, "nor a curate. It is a young Englishman from the University of Oxford, where he has taken a degree."

"Ah, that's better," said Mr. Salt, who was an Oxford man himself. "Do you know how long he has left the University; and how did your father come to hear of him?"

Nest blinked a moment. "Papa . . . it is not Papa who is recommending him, Mr. Salt. Papa does not know about him-that is to say——" She broke off; Papa did know something, unfortunately! "I told you that I was asking a very great favour; and perhaps it . . ." The words died away.

Mr. Salt rose in obvious astonishment from his chair. "Am I understanding you aright, Princess Nesta? *You* recommend this young Oxford man to me? He could not have a better sponsor, but I should not object to hearing a trifle more about him!"

But it was just that desire which it was difficult to gratify. Nest had been sure that she would never know exactly how much or how little to say about Martin Tyrrell, for something she must say, even though she left the bulk of revelation or explanation to be done by the applicant himself. She turned and, once more looking out of the window, began to fidget with the curtain fringe. "It has been so very unfortunate," she murmured. "Mr. Thompson was in difficulties . . . not his own fault at all . . . and then my dog Bran bit him . . . and Farmer Griffiths of Tan-y-bach dismissed him . . ."

"Bran bit him?" inquired Mr. Salt with interest. "The deuce he did! But what has Griffiths of Tan-y-bach to do with it? Surely *he* hasn't taken to employing a secretary? And where, my dear Nest, did you first meet this fellow *alumnus* of mine?"

Nest was not certain what an *alumnus* might be, but the word did not seem to accord very well either with life on board a privateer or a hiding place in a hayfield. She decided not to answer the question which contained it, but to explain the previous conundrum. "Mr. T . . . Thompson had found work as a farm labourer at Tan-y-bach; he helped with the haymaking, but he was so lame, owing to Bran's bite, that Griffiths discharged him. So I thought that if I, who am really responsible for his dismissal, could find him some work of a quite different kind, where he would not need to use his leg . . . and then I suddenly remembered what Papa had said. If you would only consent just to see this young man, Mr. Salt . . . I do beg of you to do so-just to see him and let him speak for himself."

"I will certainly see him, if only from curiosity," answered Mr. Salt with promptitude. "Where is he now-at the Precentory?"

"Oh, no. But he will be coming there when I return-at least I hope so. Then I will send him on to you, sir . . . if you will really be so very good as to do this for me?"

"I'll do more, if you like, Nesta; I will come down to the Precentory with you and interview your candidate there, as he is so lame."

"Oh, no!" said Nest hastily. "I mean, pray do not give yourself the trouble! It is not wise for Mr. Thompson, if he becomes your secretary, to be connected in any way with the Precentory, or even to be seen with you beforehand. He is only to come there so that when I have told him that you have kindly consented to see him, I can give him some more appropriate clothes to visit you in; for he is at present dressed as a seaman."

"And why, pray? Why as a seaman? I thought you said he had been helping with the hay at Tan-y-bach?"

"Yes; but he had been . . . on board a privateer before that," admitted Nest unwillingly. "And coming to apply here at your house for a— —"

"On board a privateer! But, my dear Nest, you are evidently foisting Proteus himself upon me! After licensed piracy-which is what privateering amounts to-haymaking and secretarial work, what will be the young man's next incarnation, I wonder? And in whose clothes are you going to fit him out—a suit of the Precentor's?"

"No," answered Nest, wishing he would not quiz her quite so much, "some clothes of William's—not uniform, of course. Then he can come here looking less-looking more like a secretary; and it could appear, perhaps, as though he had arrived to apply for the post straight from Oxford-or London."

Rubbing his chin Mr. Salt studied his visitor. "You have a most masterly mind for details, Princess Nesta. I should never have expected it in you."

Nest coloured. "But you see, sir, Mr. Tyrrell is in trouble-great trouble and danger-but quite honourable trouble, and when he has told you something about it, I do hope, Mr. Salt, that you will be able to keep his secret?" She looked at the antiquary wistfully, longing to extract a promise to that effect, as she had announced so confidently to the fugitive that she would; but she saw now that in this she had been too optimistic.

"You mean," interpreted Mr. Salt after a moment, "that your Protean acquaintance's 'trouble' is likely to land him in gaol?" And as she unwillingly nodded he asked, "Have you consulted your father about it, and Mrs. Pennefather as to this rather high-handed disposal of your brother's wardrobe?"

"No," admitted the benefactress, casting down her eyes. "That . . . would not do at all. I have reasons, most particular reasons, for not wishing Papa or Aunt Gwenllian to know anything about it. I expect Mr. Thompson will tell you why."

Compressing his fine, thin lips, Mr. Salt stood gazing down upon her with a very odd expression. Finally he began to smile. "My dear child, I am old enough to be your great-uncle, and for that reason—'tis quite a good one—I must use my judgment about respecting that wish of yours. When I have seen the young man I shall know better my duty on that score-not that I distrust you, my dear little princess, but because you are not very old, you know, and have not seen much of the world."

"But indeed," said Nest with the trace of a sigh, "I have been feeling quite old lately—I am twenty, Mr. Salt! And I assure you" (she had a quaint little tippet of dignity about her shoulders now) "that there is nothing, *nothing*, whatever in this matter of the kind of thing which I think you imagine. It is entirely for Mr. Thompson's own sake that I ask you to say nothing to Papa, because Papa has already had a rather unfortunate encounter with him-only, luckily, it took place in the dark!"

"Which is where you wish Dr. Meredith to remain?"

Nest hung her head. "I am afraid so, sir. It is so very important, if you should take Mr. Thompson to be your secretary for a while, that nobody here should know anything about him."

"Not even," suggested Mr. Salt with a smile, "that his name is really Tyrrell?"

Nest sat up, catching her underlip with her teeth. "Oh, did I say so? How careless! I am not a very good conspirator, I fear. Yes, that is his true name."

"I consider you, on the contrary, a most accomplished one," Mr. Salt assured her. "You have also the gift of making an old bookworm quite ready to conspire with you, if . . . if . . . Well, I will see the young man, at any rate, and if it seems at all possible I will take him on trial. Moreover, should I consider it my unpleasant duty to tell your father anything about him, I will candidly give you warning first. Now I shall ring for Mrs. Morris to bring in the cowslip wine, and we will pledge our compact."

But Nest had seen the hands of the clock. She jumped up. "I must run home, Mr. Salt. Mr. T . . . Thompson will be coming-to the kitchen door, and I fear lest the servants may send him away. I am afraid that you must think me crazy," she said apologetically, "but you see that it was all my fault! I should have kept better hold of Bran."

Mr. Salt went to open the door, not seeking to detain her nor to learn details of the scene in which she should have kept better hold of Bran, its date or whereabouts. But he did remark: "All your fault, Nesta? But surely your privateersman's trouble is of older date than Bran's onslaught? He was in a scrape before that, was he not?"

"Yes, yes, indeed; a bad scrape, a dangerous scrape . . . but nothing dishonourable, dear Mr. Salt-and not his fault! I am sure you will be able to believe him when he tells you about it."

"I hope that I shall," replied Mr. Jerome Salt. "For your sake, my dear, I will try to subdue any incredulity. God bless you!" And this time he did kiss her little fingers before he took her out across the hall to the rejuvenated figureheads.

When he found himself in the library again he stood looking down abstractedly at the scattered sheets of his notes. After a moment he said softly, drawing his finger across his chin: "So the Precentor is not to know! I hope, 'most grave Brabantio,' that *your* Desdemona has not been beguiled by some smooth-tongued adventurer?"

(3)

"So far, so good," thought Nest to herself, as she sped down Folly Lane towards the Precentory. "I hope that Mr. Tyrrell has not arrived in my absence."

He had not-at least there was no sign of his advent. Nest instructed the maids-Dixon was indisposed-to inform her at once if a man should present himself at the kitchen door saying that Miss Meredith had told him to do so, and had promised him a suit of old clothes. These clothes, not old, either-of whose unauthorised disposal brother William would not learn until his next leave-were already fastened up into a parcel. Where Mr. Tyrrell meant to assume them she did not know; perhaps in the ruins of the Palace. The only difficulty which she had to fear, apart from the premature return of her father and sister, was that Aunt Gwenllian might raise some objection to the proceeding; but Mrs. Pennefather proved to be so absorbed in the cult of her great-nephew that evening that a regiment of beggars could probably have come and gone unrebuked, and Lieutenant Meredith's entire wardrobe be given away without remonstrance. It was wonderful what Aunt Gwenllian did not observe when she was abstracted or immersed in some concern. But there was Bran too, who was not at all given to abstraction, and might resent his enemy's coming to the house; so it was necessary to see that he was shut up.

Time went on, and still Mr. Martin Tyrrell did not appear. It was getting towards dusk-though that was rather an advantage than otherwise. Had he changed his mind, or found other employment? If he left it too late her father and Jane would be back! Nest began to feel quite feverishly anxious, sitting alone in the drawing-room with her eyes on the clock. For though she fully intended to go down in order to signify to the applicant that Mr. Salt was willing to interview him, she meant to give to this action the appearance of an afterthought.

At last! "The man you did speak of is here, Miss Nest."

The conspiratress turned her head with a very tolerable assumption of calm. "I am glad of that, Mary. The clothes I promised him are tied up in a parcel in the hall. Will you give it to him?" Then, just as the door was shutting, she jumped up. "Wait a moment; I think I had better see him."

"He" was not in the kitchen, but standing humbly at the back door, leaning in fact against the jamb; but at the sight of the young lady, followed by her maid, advancing towards him, he stood upright and touched his old hat with the gesture of that day in the lane. The hat itself was crushed down upon his forehead, and as he was standing in the dusky entry, where it happened that no light from within shone upon him, Nest could not clearly see his face.

"Here are the clothes I promised you," she said in a voice which she, at least, knew to be unlike her usual one. "Thank you, Mary." She took the parcel from her handmaid. But how to get rid of her; for Mary seemed deeply interested in the recipient of this bounty, and she herself must have a word alone with him. Nest turned her head as one suddenly listening-alas, how quickly one slid down the road of deceit! "Was that Mrs. Pennefather's bell ringing, Mary? I think you had better go and see." On which Mary, reluctantly, no doubt, withdrew.

Nest held out her brother's second-best suit in its wrappings. "Go to the Folly at once!" she breathed. "He has consented to see you. I have not told him anything about you-save that your misfortunes were not of your own making. You will not come in and have something to eat?"

Martin Tyrrell shook his head without a word. He had the bundle, but he also had by the wrist one of the hands which held it out to him. Equally without a word did he press a kiss upon the back of that hand, pick up the staff leaning against the door, and limp slowly away into the twilight. Nest stood a moment looking after him, stirred with a further vague apprehension. How terribly lame he was-and how strangely silent! —while the lips whose pressure she could still feel upon her hand had seemed as hot as fire.

(4)

Mrs. Morris, Mr. Jerome Salt's housekeeper, was one of those rapid, darting little women to whom the more ordinary methods of locomotion seem to have been denied, for she never walked if it was possible to run. She could traverse Bowen's Folly, whose architecture tended to the rambling, from garret to cellar in the time a more sober-gaited servant would have taken to answer a summons from the kitchen to the dining-room. Accordingly when Mr. Salt, who was pacing about his garden in the dusk, heard feet pelting down the steps and a rushing sound coming over the grass, he did not thereby conclude that the house was afire or that the French had landed, for on such an occasion Mrs. Morris would probably have acquired some still swifter mode of transit, such as flying.

Moreover Mr. Salt was awaiting such an irruption. His first impulse, when Nest left him, had been to tell Mrs. Morris that he was shortly expecting a gentleman to see him, but he had almost instantly decided against this, lest haply it should result in connecting the visitor in some way with Miss Meredith. For her sake, if not for his own, it was better to seem to know nothing beforehand of the applicant, this young fellow in trouble.

"There's a man asking to see you, sir," gasped the voice of his housekeeper behind him.

"A man to see me?" Mild surprise informed Mr. Salt's tone. "A gentleman?"

"No, sir," panted Mrs. Morris. " 'Tis not a gentleman, sir. A seafaring man, I should think . . . and he do seem strange in his manner whatever. I have put him in the long room, sir."

A seafaring man! Now how had she deduced that, when Nest, the little conspiratress, was to have given the fellow her brother's suit? Perhaps there had been some hitch over this part of her plan.

"Send him to me in the library," commanded Mr. Salt, starting towards the house.

"Begging your pardon, sir," trilled Mrs. Morris, skimming after him, "but indeed it might be that the young man is too drunk to come so far—begging your pardon again, sir; and I doubt if I could get him to move, now that he's sat down at the table there."

"Drunk?" queried her master; and to himself, " 'Tis fully possible, Nest being so innocent . . . I'll see him in the long room, then."

For what the late Captain Bowen, when he built the Folly, had designed the room so called remained unknown, but at least it deserved its name. Hardly used now, save as a receptacle for a certain amount of lumber, very neatly disposed, and as a store-room for fruit if there was any, its chief piece of furniture was an extensive table, one end of which bore a few rows of apples. But the other, the further end, supported at this moment a quite different burden, the outspread arms, the shoulders and the dark, untidy head of a man fallen forward upon it from the chair in which he sat. The upper portion of this man's body, which was all that Mr. Salt could see upon entering, was clothed in a garment which had certainly never belonged to William Meredith, even though he too followed the sea—a dirty white flannel waistcoat with a black binding. Rather taken aback, Mr. Salt began to wonder whether this were Nest's protégé after all.

The visitor had not moved at the sound of his footsteps on the flagged floor, so, after studying him for a moment (and glancing over his shoulder to be sure that Mrs. Morris had not followed him in) Mr. Salt asked smartly, "Are you the man whom Miss Meredith was to send to me?"

Slowly the huddled figure pulled itself up and raised its head, revealing a young, flushed, unshaven face with somewhat glazed eyes, which looked up at the questioner stupidly. "Miss M . . . Meredith?" repeated their owner after a moment, and not without a check, almost a stumble, at the name. "Miss . . . Yes. She told me . . . come here."

Mr. Salt went nearer; for although he had distrusted Mrs. Morris's diagnosis, he did think now that the man might be drunk. But there was no aroma of spirits or the like about him. He did not, however, attempt to rise.

"I am given to understand," said the owner of Bowen's Folly with some severity, "that you have taken your degree at the University of Oxford. Is this true?"

The alleged graduate of that seat of learning put a hand over his eyes. The hand had recently known hard work; but it was not the hand of a labourer. "Degree?" queried the voice below the hand. "Degree of lati . . . tude or longi . . . long . . . longitude? But . . . in any case . . . I don't know it."

"Come, come, young man," admonished the antiquary, "think what you are saying! If you have been drinking, tell me so frankly. And what have you done with the clothes which Miss Meredith was to give you?"

The hand, removing itself, merely pointed to the floor, where Mr. Salt observed a neat bundle. And the visitor shivered and caught his breath as though in sudden pain. "Drinking! . . . I have not tasted food or drink . . . since yesterday!"

Somehow the tone carried conviction; and certainly the accents, now less thick, were those of an educated man. Mr. Salt looked hard at his guest; if he had not been drinking, why was his face so flushed, his eyes so half-seeing? Mr. Salt slipped a hand round his wrist, and gave an exclamation. It was burning hot.

"Are you ill?" he asked, bending nearer.

"I . . . I think I must be," answered the young man with a little gasp. "Ought not . . . to have troubled you . . . cannot fill any post in this state . . . had better be going." He appeared to contemplate rising from his chair, but not to be anxious to do so.

"Have you any notion what is wrong with you?" asked the elder man, concerned. The young fellow, whatever were the nature of his original "scrape," was clearly a gentleman.

The visitor propped his head on his fists, looked down at the table, and did not answer for a moment. Then he said in an almost inaudible tone, "If you could let me have . . . a glass of water . . . I could tell you . . . what it is *not* ."

The last words were so low that Mr. Salt, already hastening into the adjacent kitchen for the water, barely caught them. "Here you are," he said, returning. "But would you not like a drop of something stronger?"

Nest's protégé shook his head and, seizing the glass in a hand so shaky that he was obliged to bring the other to its aid, drank the water off thirstily. Then, putting down the glass, he covered his face with his hands for a brief moment, removed them, and said with a sigh of deep relief, " 'Tis not *that* , then, thank God!"

"Not what?" queried Mr. Salt, still quite at sea.

"Cannot you guess, sir?" A very wan smile appeared for a moment. "I was bitten by a dog last week."

"My dear boy!" exclaimed the antiquary, shocked into this unwontedly paternal form of address, "you have not, surely, been fearing hydrophobia? But Miss Meredith's dog is not mad! What a damnable old fool I am, I had forgotten all about that bite, although she told me of it. Probably indeed it is the cause of your present indisposition, but for God's sake put away all thought of hydrophobia! Let me have a look at the wound; I know a little both of medicine and surgery."

The young man half demurred. "No, I could not allow you, sir, to trouble . . . 'Tis not a pretty sight."

"All the more reason for looking at it, then," quoth the editor of Giraldus Cambrensis. "Come along-where is it?"

Five minutes later Mrs. Morris, who had returned to the kitchen, was considerably astonished by being told to make up a bed in the spare bedroom without delay, and to provide there hot water, linen for bandages and a nightshirt of her master's. These amenities could not be intended for anyone but the drunken seaman, or whatever he was, in the long room, the whole proceeding being to her mind so outrageous as almost to cause her to think that Mr. Salt was a good deal more than eccentric. However, if he had really taken leave of his senses it would be even more dangerous than usual to remonstrate with him. Mrs. Morris shut her lips tightly, and raced forthwith to the linen press.

Like many of her class and nation she was extremely inquisitive, yet of what occurred in that bedroom after Mr. Salt had helped the seaman up the stairs to it she could learn nothing, although lurking with attentive ears upon the same stairs. Perhaps even the vagabond himself did not know overmuch of the happenings there, save for one very unpleasant episode. Some twenty minutes later, however, after the ease of the comfortable bed and the coolness of its sheets had had time to penetrate to his consciousness, and even the horrible pain in his leg had abated a little, he was aware that his host had seated himself by his bedside.

"Listen, young man," said he. "The wound in your leg has become poisoned—but not from any venom in the bite, that's clear, or the inflammation would have shown itself earlier. Some dirt or other obnoxious substance has probably entered it. I have done what I could by lancing the place. If by to-morrow both it and you are not showing signs of improvement, then I shall be obliged to send for the doctor; but I imagine that you would prefer not to have one if possible. No"—as Martin tried to say something—"I don't want to hear your story now. You may be an arrant impostor—I dare say you are-but I could not turn you away in this condition, if only for Miss Meredith's sake and that of the undertaking I gave her. Now I shall have some soup sent up to you; after you have taken it, try to sleep. One word of warning however; don't go talking to my housekeeper; she is the most infernal gossip in Pembrokeshire. But she can cook . . . I will look in again myself after a while."

* * * * *

All night long did the fever, whose course Mr. Salt's surgery had at least checked, swing Martin Tyrrell to and fro upon its infected tide. Often he had no idea of his whereabouts, scarcely of his own identity; but at other moments, finding himself in the trough between two waves of that hot, grinding sea, he was conscious to the full, and most thankfully conscious, that he lay in a bed and not in a windy nook on the cliffs, and that a period had been put to what seemed, in retrospect, the year-long endurance and apprehensions of the past twenty-four hours, during which his physical condition had altered so alarmingly for the worse.

He hardly knew how he had dragged himself all the way back to the Precentory, but he was determined not to let Miss Meredith become aware of his condition; so he settled to say as little as possible there, and in the end never realised that he had said nothing at all. And when he turned away, clutching the bundle of clothes, so important for the plan, he had all at once felt too ill to face the struggle of changing into them. Moreover, where was he going to do this? His head was too giddy to look for a convenient spot . . . It was ironical that he should not be able to put on Lieutenant Meredith's suit after all the trouble taken about the matter; he felt this. Or rather, he felt that there was something wrong about carrying the bundle thus unopened with him to the Folly; but by the time that, shivering and burning in turns, he stumbled in between Mr. Salt's gateposts even that impression had been obliterated.

Well, here he was, thank God, in a bed; though with a leg on fire, a throat full of sand and a head which seemed actually to open and shut, it ached with such vehemence behind hot eyes. But at least he need make no more exertions; if pigs and hayforks, sails which would not furl and reef-points which would not tie were all blended into discomfortable dreams, there was sometimes the sensation too of the nearness of a lovely face which he never clearly saw, but which, when he did, would surely be compassionate as well as lovely. Yet it was not Miss Meredith's.

And the face which he actually did see in the night-thrice, had he been able to count-was not a woman's at all, and was surmounted by a nightcap with a tasselled end.

(5)

"If you please, sir," announced Mrs. Morris, appearing in her employer's study one morning a few days later, "the young man upstairs is wishful for to come down and see you, if you will allow him."

Mr. Salt raised his handsome grey head sharply from his writing. "I never gave him leave to rise!"

"But I thought you was of opinion, sir, that he had been long enough abed, and — —"

"Confound you, woman!" flashed her master. "Why do you degrade the word 'think' by applying it to the process which goes on inside that skull of yours-and how dare you undertake to interpret what goes on inside mine? Did you give him to understand that I wished to turn him out of his bed?" Emitting sparks, he got up and started for the door. "I am a fool to put up with you for the sake of my — — Come in!"

A knock had cut short his tirade. The door thereupon opened and revealed, standing somewhat hesitatingly upon the threshold, a pale young man decently attired in a nearly new bottle-green suit.

"Come in, come in!" repeated Mr. Salt. "Do you require an arm?"

"No, thank you, sir," answered Martin, attempting a smile. "I can walk quite well." Endeavouring to subdue his limp, he advanced into the pleasant, book-lined room.

"*Go!*" said Mr. Salt savagely to his housekeeper. "And for Heaven's sake try not to 'think'!" And, Mrs. Morris flitting with haste through the door, he put his hand under the invalid's arm, piloted him to a high-backed chair, sat him down in it, and looked at him for a moment. "Why did you get out of your bed and come downstairs?" he then demanded with some asperity. "I suppose that meddling old succubus gave you to understand that I wished it? If she did, she lied-as she generally does."

"I have got up, sir," replied Martin, without offering any remarks upon the succubus, "because I feel that I ought no longer to be enjoying your extraordinarily generous hospitality when you do not know my story. I must tell it to you without more delay, and then, if you wish, relieve you of my presence. You have already done, sir, what not one man in a hundred would do for . . . a vagabond who came — —"

"But not one vagabond in a hundred has Miss Nest Meredith to speak for him," returned Mr. Salt significantly. "Is that not so?"

"Yes, sir; but I dare say that you think I imposed upon Miss Meredith, who is young and inexperienced, and, above all, was distressed because her dog had attacked me."

"I admit I think the imposture quite likely. And that is why I declined to promise the young lady not to acquaint her father with the affair. So you see, Mr. Tyrrell or Thompson," —it was the first time he had addressed his quasi-patient by any name —"that even after hearing your narrative, I may yet hand you over to the authorities. You run a risk in telling me anything at all; you understand that?"

"Yes, sir, perfectly. And if, on the other hand," observed Martin, "when you have heard my tale, you should decide not to surrender me to the law, but even perhaps, as Miss Meredith hoped, to give me some employment, you too run a risk of being, I understand, considered an accessory after the fact. For the position in which I find myself is a very serious one-you can imagine how serious when I tell you that if your recent skill and kindness has saved my life, as I believe it has, the day may come when I shall wish it had not been exercised."

"This indeed piques my curiosity!" said Mr. Salt, drawing forward another chair. "I must certainly hear your adventures. And of course," he went on with his peculiarly subtle smile, "if I have indeed saved your life-many thanks for the compliment! —I shall be the less likely to wish to see that existence taken away or even threatened by the law-if that is your meaning. . . . A glass of wine first, however; and I will get it myself, in order not to admit that inquisitive female." With the alacrity which characterised all his movements he left the room.

Martin leant his head against the back of the chair and closed his eyes. Rest and food had done wonders for him; the poison was gone from his wound and the fever from his body, though his leg was still stiff and weak. To his great relief it had not proved necessary to call in a doctor, though Mr. Salt had several times been upon the point of doing so. The "eccentric" had made no effort to question the patient about his situation; had indeed silenced him on the one or two occasions when he had attempted to broach the subject. Yet Martin himself, more and more annoyed at having willy nilly presented himself at Bowen's Folly in such a collapsed condition, felt somehow that he would be making less appeal to pity-of which appeal there had, he considered, been quite enough already-and more to a considered judgment, if he could manage to rise and interview his putative employer on his legs and in the proper place and clothes. (And indeed he had no choice of raiment, for when he struggled out of bed this morning he found that all his seafaring garments had vanished; and so at last he endued himself in the outer habiliments of Lieutenant William Meredith, wondering what the doubtless gallant officer would say if he could see him.)

"Drink that," commanded Mr. Salt, returning with a glass of port. "You are too young, I fear, to have the palate to appreciate it, but it is of a very famous vintage."

Obeying gratefully, Martin found himself recalling a certain "neutral port." But this was even better than Mr. O'Driscoll's wine, or else he needed it more urgently.

"I understand that you were at Oxford," observed Mr. Salt when he had finished. "At what college?"

"I was at Brasenose, sir." But even as he said it Martin wondered if he ever had been; it seemed so long ago.

"Ah. They had not much of a cellar there in my day-which was a century or so before yours . . . for Brasenose is my college also, as it happens. But perhaps you knew that, Mr. 'Thompson,' and-chose yours accordingly?"

Oddly enough, Martin did not resent this rather cynical frankness; on the contrary, he welcomed an astringency which braced him. "You might well think that, sir," he returned, "save that you will agree that I had not much opportunity, when haymaking at Tan-y-bach, of learning what your college was."

"There is always Miss Meredith!"

"That is true," admitted Martin as he put down his glass; "but have you not found, sir, that to ladies one college-at either of the Universities-is much the same as another? But I can, I hope, prove to you that I know things about Brasenose College with which an impostor could not be familiar, such as the custom of invading Lincoln College every Ascension Day morning through that little door in the quadrangle, and demanding ale; and the habit which the present Principal, Bishop Cleaver, has of wearing purple gloves and always walking with his hands upon his breast. I can describe to you the manner in which that door opens, and ―――"

"Enough," said Mr. Salt. "I accept your University and college-the more so as you are undoubtedly a man of education. Now, tell me what you told Miss Meredith-and more, if it bears upon the subject."

* * * * *

It took Martin much longer to relate his story to Mr. Salt, for the latter, unlike Miss Nest Meredith, asked questions and insisted upon details, and his questions were probing, so that in the end Martin had to confess the real reason of his lingering in Hamburg after finding that his brother-in-law was not there. He hated making this avowal, but it was best, for his own sake, to be frank.

For some time after he had finished Mr. Salt sat looking at him, his fingertips pressed together, his lips too; his blue eyes narrowed and furrows upon his brow.

"Yes," he said at length, "there's no denying that you are in a pretty mess, Mr. Martin Tyrrell. But at least you became involved in it through no actual fault of your own, save a certain rashness which is proper to youth. Indeed you seem to have embarked upon this sea of misfortune for a much more creditable reason than actuates most young men who get into scrapes-affection for your sister. . . . It was, undeniably, an act of pure folly to strike that runner-but I believe I should have done the same. (By the way, it should be easy to make discreet enquiries in Liverpool—I have a correspondent there-and ascertain if the man did actually expire of the blow; which I very much doubt. Those Bow Street gentry have heads like cannon-balls, both inside and out.) Then there is your father; we must devise a means by which news of your safety if not of your actual whereabouts can be conveyed to him-in someone else's handwriting. That reminds me, I should like to see in what sort of hand you are going to copy my illegible fist-but it is not fair to ask for a specimen now. Another point: do you happen to know anything of Giraldus Cambrensis-Gerald de Barri?"

Martin did not answer; the relief was so intense that for a moment he put his elbow on his knee and shaded his eyes with his hand.

"Humph!" observed Mr. Salt, surveying him. "You need not think, young man —I suppose you must have a new name, neither Thompson nor Tyrrell-you needn't think that your post with me will be a bed of roses. I can exhibit the devil's own temper at times, and I like to have my own way-and always do have it, even with that accursed Welshwoman of mine. You might do well to think twice before you accept the post of amanuensis. How much salary do you consider yourself worth?"

Martin raised a rather haggard face. "As if I wanted any money at all, sir! Shelter . . . your silence. . . . Indeed I cannot quite believe that you are going to do this for me . . . and I cannot ever thank you adequately!"

"Then oblige me by not trying to do so," retorted Mr. Salt briskly. "But naturally I am going to pay you a salary. Moreover, I shall not be without my own reward. The day when I see you and Dr. Meredith making polite conversation to one another, the knowledge that you punched him in the ribs and that he doesn't know it ——"

"But I cannot ever meet Dr. Meredith, sir!" protested Martin in great alarm.

"Not even to please me? I do not think much of your gratitude, then," quoth Mr. Salt, chuckling. "But you will be certain to meet him sooner or later; besides, what of little Nest-to whom I shall have to present you as a stranger? Do you not wish to show your gratitude even to her? And that old bore Doctor Jenkins, who would have apoplexy if he knew your history, but who, when he hears that you are assisting me with Giraldus, will discourse to you by the hour-as I shall too, only I am not a bore-about Gerald of Windsor and the Lady Nest, too romantic and even improper a story for that dusty old divine to handle . . . the Helen of Wales. But I see that you have no idea what I am talking about!"

"I hope that I may learn, sir," replied Martin humbly, thinking it odd that he should have escaped from the Geralds and Fitzgeralds who in the present life had proved so disastrous to him, only to fall among those of the past. For, like the tones of the ancient mariner upon whose story Mr. Coleridge was even then engaged under the shadow of the Quantock Hills, a story which Martin, if he remained unhanged, would be able to read in about two years' time, the voice of Mr. Salt then descanted upon the Norman-Welsh conquest of Ireland, informing him that this Princess Nesta ("Nest," too), the daughter of Rhys ap Tewdwr Mawr, was the ancestress of all the Geraldines down to this last disloyal young scion of the house of Leinster, with whom Martin had talked in the room behind the tulips at Altona, and in addition the grandmother of Gerald de Barri, the same Giraldus Cambrensis who would soon become more than a name to him.

"But there," finished Mr. Salt, suddenly breaking off, "that's enough. I will take you for a little turn in the garden, if you can get so far, and, like Adam with the beasts in a similar locality, assign you a name. (Forgive me; I'm afraid that's hardly a civil way of putting it!) You can also consider what information about yourself you would wish to be conveyed to your father. Come along!"

On his new employer's arm Martin hobbled out through the long window into the sunshine. "I cannot conceive, sir, why ——" he was beginning, when Mr. Salt cut him short.

"Partly," he replied, "because you voluntarily abandoned your position of vantage in bed, which you must have known I should never have thrown you out of, to come down, with difficulty, as I guess, in order to have the situation out with me. That pleased me."

(6)

"The smiling babe upon my knee,"

wrote Mrs. Pennefather poetically, perhaps, but inaccurately; since the babe in question lay at present on her niece's lap in the nursery, and was also, had Mrs. Pennefather but known, most certainly not smiling.

"The smiling babe upon my knee,
What does it know of life,
Of passion's (here she left a blank) *mystery,*
And (an extended blank) *strife?"*

"What can the infant's lisping tongue

"Do you want anything, Nest?"

"I am very sorry to interrupt you, Aunt," said her younger niece, seeing by the quill and paper that the afflatus was upon Mrs. Pennefather, "but neither Jane nor Nurse can find the soothing syrup, and baby is crying so incessantly, in fact almost yelling — —"

The poetess instantly rose; and indeed through the open door came at this moment unmistakable evidence that the lisping tongue was endeavouring to interpret its owner's sensations of strife of some order or another, probably internal. Both ladies thereupon ran from the room.

With such domestic interests were Nest's days now pleasantly occupied, and, save that there was an as yet undiscovered gap in her brother's wardrobe, the episode of the ex-privateersman might almost never have been. About ten days ago, it is true, Mr. Salt had sent her a discreet and ingenious little note, expressing his thanks for the *volume* that she had been good enough to recommend to him, which volume he was keeping for the present and hoped to find of use, although at first it had been badly in need of repair. And she had heard also from her father that Mr. Salt was said to have engaged an amanuensis to copy out his translation of the *Itinerarium Cambriae* —some young man, Dr. Meredith believed, from Oxford or Cambridge. He must get Salt to bring him to the Precentory.

That, reflected Nest, would be a difficult meeting to carry off when it came; meantime she caught nowhere any glimpse of the young man from Oxford or Cambridge-and the *Fair Penitent*. She supposed that Mr. Salt was either keeping him hard at work, or considered it better that he should not show his face until that of "Mark Thompson" had passed from the immediate memories of any who had chanced to set eyes upon it. But she longed to know how her protégé was faring. What had Mr. Salt meant by "in need of repair"? Presumably he had been referring to poor Mr. Tyrrell's lameness . . . which, of course, now she came to think of it, was another reason why one did not see him about. Secretly she hoped that she might somehow chance upon Mr. Tyrrell by himself, and have a first word with him alone. It would be so much less embarrassing.

It pleased Fate, however, that the meeting should be neither one nor the other. For a few days later Nest, returning homewards from the further side of the Alan, saw, as she crossed the tiny bridge near the Cathedral and St. Mary's College, two gentlemen surveying the scaffolded west front, where Mr. Nash's restoration was still in progress.

If Nest had not recognised them by sight she could have done so by hearing, for as, somewhat hesitatingly, she approached (since she must pass them to reach the Precentory) she overheard, in Mr. Salt's cool, clear tones:

". . . what possessed the man to deface it with this galaxy of pepper-pots only the devil knows! Probably it was Lucifer himself who drew the plans! You can see what a ludicrous and loathsome commixture of styles will confront us when this scaffolding is removed. I could wish it might remain in place. Better a ruin than a laughing-stock! How the Chapter——" Here he was aware of a light footfall, and turned.

"Ah, my dear Nest, you arrive in the nick of time to save me from a possible fit of apoplexy! Here is my new secretary-did you know that I had engaged one?" (His eyes twinkled.) "I want to present him to you, so that you may become better acquainted with each other. — Mr. Towers."

Nest's privateersman advanced and bowed. How different he looked! He was not wearing William's green suit after all; he was in very dark grey.

"You may not recognise in him the volume which you sent me a little while ago," pursued Mr. Salt, the twinkle more pronounced still. "As you perceive, it has been recovered; the binding in which it first appeared was unsuitable, as you had guessed. Now that the damage to the *calf* has been repaired, the tome is proving most useful. You did me a good turn in procuring it for me."

Nest looked at him helplessly; she was not good at repartee, and to respond to Mr. Salt's elaboration of his quip in the same spirit was beyond her. The "volume," too, at first seemed disconcerted and coloured a little; then he recovered himself.

"And what of the good turn which Miss Meredith has done me, sir?" he asked, looking from one to the other. "Shall nothing be said of that?" There was much feeling in his tone.

"I suppose, my dear Towers," responded his employer, "that if you once began upon that topic you might enlarge upon it as long as the Alan there continues to run to the sea! But," he turned to Nest, "as I wish to take him now to see the tomb of Gerald de Barri in the south choir aisle there, I shall not allow him to embark upon it. If you will accompany us, Nest, it will be very pleasant. But first let me impress upon you the new name of this gentleman. He now calls himself 'Mr. Towers'; pray do not forget it."

Martin could not help smiling to himself as he reflected how little voice he had had in the choosing of his fresh alias. For Mr. Salt at the outset had declared that his Christian name recalled to him the Norman filibuster Martin de Turribus who, landing in Fishguard Bay in the last year of William the Conqueror, had established himself successfully in a lordship at Nevern. "Martin of the Towers he was-Martin of Tours, like his sainted namesake. And by the way, you have taken a few tours lately! I shall call you Towers!" And Towers Martin had to be.

Mr. Salt had already made for the south door, and probably from design passed in first, so that Martin, holding the door open for Miss Meredith, was able to say in a low voice: "He is quite right; I should never cease thanking you if once I began."

It was not the first time that Martin had entered the Cathedral, yet, used chiefly as he was to his father's little church at Selham, he was struck anew into an admiring silence by the space, the great piers with their slender flanking shafts, their noble sweeping arches with one band of moulding, the rich effect of clerestory and triforium (this despite the coat of whitewash first inaugurated by Laud's successor in the See, Bishop Field) and the magnificent timber roof. Not indeed that there was silence in the great church, since it was the custom to use the lower part of the nave, between the north and south doors, as a thoroughfare, and on Sundays the dogs of the congregation were assembled there during service under the charge of a man with a whip.

Mr. Salt led the way through the transept out into the south choir aisle. Like its sister aisle on the north, it was roofless and completely exposed to the weather, for which reason the arcades of the choir had had to be filled up, thus completely cutting off the unsheltered aisle itself. Grass-grown, strewn with fallen stones, the windows in the outer wall roughly blocked up, the wall itself crumbling at the top and crowned with snapdragon, valerian and small shrubs, it was, like so much at St. David's, a sad vestige of former glory.

Under the first arcade of the choir, in a niche of the newer masonry with a wooden beam across to keep the stones of this in place, lay the weather-worn figure of a vested priest, his head on a cushion supported by angels, his hands clasped on his breast, a lion or a dog at his feet. The three stood looking down at it.

"As you know, Nest," said Mr. Salt after a moment, "—or as you should know-he who lies here (for though there is nothing to show that this is his tomb, tradition has always pointed it out as his) was the nephew of Bishop David Fitzgerald, and hoped for years to wear the mitre himself. It is interesting to think that our friend Mr. Towers, as you may have heard, recently made a not very fortunate acquaintance with a later member of the Fitzgerald family, the husband of the lady who — —"

"Excuse me, sir," broke in "Mr. Towers," with really unmannerly haste, "but did you tell me this morning that this aisle has been roofless since the Reformation or since the Civil Wars?"

Nest could not imagine why Mr. Salt, usually so quick-tempered, not only suffered this interruption with placidity, but even smiled as if amused, ere he answered: "I said that some assign the beginning of the decay to one upheaval, some to the other, the difference of a hundred years or so in the process not being discernible now. It is but twenty-one years since the roof of the Lady Chapel fell in, but in another twenty-one, alas, the ruin there may be as advanced as here. But, as I was saying outside, there is a nobility in decay not always to be seen in restoration. —Well, young people, having paid this pious visit to the tomb of Gerald the Welshman—who was only half Welsh—I must return to my translation of a portion of those remarkable writings of his which survive his own mouldering dust by well-nigh six centuries." Yet he still lingered, looking down at the nameless effigy, and then added meditatively: "To think that the man who fought all his life for the prestige of the great See of St. David's against a Norman sovereign, and whose election to it might have changed the whole course of its history, was in the end basely abandoned by his compatriots of the chapter. Put not your trust in clerics nor in any son of Wales!"

It was Martin's turn to feel uncomfortable-on Miss Meredith's account. There was no trace of banter now in Mr. Salt's tone, which was, on the contrary, quite fiery. Had he forgotten that the young lady's father was both a cleric and a Welshman? But perhaps Miss Meredith was inured to these denunciations; at any rate, she did not show any discomfiture, as they went in again and proceeded down the nave. 'Down' was certainly the word for it, thought Martin, so perceptible was the slope. He could fancy a ball rolling all the way to the west door without a check.

On the way Mr. Salt recovered his more usual self and remarked in a low tone to Nest: "You expected to find our hero attired in green, did you not? But he only wore your brother's clothes for a day or two; these are the product of Haverfordwest."

"I had thought," Martin, on the other side of the speaker, was beginning, when hurrying steps behind caused him for prudence' sake to break off. It was one of the Canons, intent upon catching Mr. Salt, whom he bore off, not too willingly, out of earshot.

"I was about to observe, Miss Meredith," began Martin again, "or rather to ask, whether I should not at once return the suit of your brother's, which has indeed scarcely been worn. Will not its absence perhaps cause you embarrassment in the future?"

"It would perhaps be better," admitted Nest, thinking what a remarkable difference clothes could make. No one could suspect Mr. Tyrrell-Towers-of being a runaway seaman now! "It was not my original intention, but . . . yes, when my brother comes and misses his suit. . . ."

"I will bring it this afternoon."

"No, I do not think that would do very well. There might be enquiries . . . or the servants might suspect. . . . I think it would be better if you waited until I communicated with you about the best method of returning it unobserved. There is no hurry; my brother William will not be able to get leave for months."

Martin said that he quite understood the need of circumspection in the matter. He was rather glad to have this conversation out of hearing of Mr. Salt, for he did not want Miss Meredith to learn that, for all her trouble and planning, he had never worn the clothes on the occasion for which they were chiefly intended, a fact which he feared that his employer might have revealed. And Nest, too, was not sorry. For she had time to hazard, with a glance at Mr. Tyrrell's knee, the remark: "Your lameness, sir; I am glad to observe that you do not appear to suffer from it any longer?"

"No," answered Bran's victim, "the wound is quite healed, and I feel no ill effects whatever."

"I am indeed thankful. You were obliged to have a doctor, I fear?"

"Fortunately, owing to Mr. Salt's skill, I was enabled to avoid it."

"I wish," said that gentleman, rejoining them at that moment, "that Mr. Salt's skill had sufficed to avoid Dr. Jenkins. That man is a pest! Your father, Nest, should arrange for a pinnacle-one of Mr. Nash's for preference-to fall upon his head . . . save that I fear 'tis the pinnacle which would be shattered!"

(7)

"A very charming young lady, don't you think so, Towers?" observed his employer, as, having parted from the young lady in question outside the south porch of the Cathedral, they made their way towards the long flight of steps which led up from the precincts to the Tower gate, the only remaining one of the four entrances.

"More than charming," responded the young man warmly. "I have not words to express what I think her besides."

"Useful, in fact, in addition to being ornamental," commented Mr. Salt, with that humour which his secretary was already beginning to find a little disconcerting.

Martin had, in fact, discovered that there might be more truth than he had at first realised in the description of Mr. Salt as an eccentric. The historian had indeed displayed towards him the most extraordinary benevolence, which nothing could ever cancel or efface; but he certainly was irritable, and could, Martin fancied, be a good deal more than irritable. Those blue eyes of his, sometimes mirthful and sometimes melancholy, had nevertheless the choleric possibilities of most blue eyes. Had not the freakishness of his humour been tempered by an obviously genuine kindness, and had Miss Meredith not assured him that Mr. Salt had never been known to go back upon his word, Martin might have felt that his position at Bowen's Folly was very precarious. Mrs. Morris, the housekeeper, though fair spoken enough and to spare, regarded him, he was sure, with the utmost disfavour, and the secretary, remembering his host's warning, strove to have as little to do with her as possible.

However, if his bed was not altogether of roses he was profoundly thankful for a bed of any kind, and did his best, not only from self-interest, but also from gratitude, to satisfy his employer, though, to tell truth, he found the copying of Mr. Salt's crabbed handwriting for hours on end very tedious work. He was no mediævalist, and though to transcribe Mr. Salt's rendering of Gerald de Barri's *Itinerarium* was not too dull, since that twelfth-century ecclesiastic had a lively mind and was full of curious and often amusing anecdote, the pages of Mr. Salt's own compilation, the *History of Dyfed or Pembrokeshire*, proved most trying, being sometimes not more than notes which required expansion, and always replete with Llewelyns, Griffiths, Merediths, Rhyses, Angharads and Anarawds who were all one to the English scribe. That same afternoon, in fact, there was to be an explosion over *Dyfed* for that very reason.

Mr. Salt was occupied with the *History of Pembrokeshire* at his big table in the middle of the library, while Martin copied away at the translation of Giraldus Cambrensis at the smaller table set apart for him at right angles to the windows. At the moment the amanuensis was interested and even entertained by de Barri's journalistic talents; could he really have been as credulous as he seemed? This story about the toads which he was copying, for instance.

> "In our time a young man, native of this country, during a severe illness, suffered as violent a persecution from toads, as if the reptiles of the whole province had come to him by agreement; and though destroyed by his nurses and friends, they increased again on all sides in infinite numbers, like hydras' heads. His attendants, both friends and strangers, being wearied out, he was drawn up in a kind of bag, into a high tree, stripped of its leaves, and shred; nor was he there secure from his venomous enemies, for they crept up the tree in great numbers, and consumed him even to the very bones. The young man's name was Sisillus Esceir-hir, that is, Sisillus Long Leg. It is also recorded that by the hidden but never unjust will of God, another man suffered a similar persecution from rats."

Martin, smiling to himself, had just reached the end of this singular passage, when he heard from behind him an exclamation of a flavour and intensity which carried him back for a moment to the decks of the *Fair Penitent*. He turned round in alarm, and beheld Mr. Salt springing from his chair spouting expletives.

"You really are too — — — — careless, sir!" he exclaimed furiously. "All this page which you have copied" —he smote the MS. before him on the table —"refers to Llewelyn the Second; by omitting a sentence —a whole sentence-you have made it appear as though I meant Llewelyn the Great, his grandfather! Because you are a blockhead and an ignoramus that is no reason why I should be made to look one too!"

A few weeks of privateering had fortunately accustomed Martin to abuse. Still, he did not like it.

"I am very sorry indeed, sir, that I was so careless," he said humbly, yet with a certain stiffness.

"The standard of education at the University must very much have declined since I was up at Oxford," continued Mr. Salt, still very angry, "or else you were never there at all, in spite of the local detail you showered upon me!"

The floor of the library seemed to give a slight lurch under Martin's feet-for by this time he was standing too. If, after all, Mr. Salt were going to have doubts of his veracity! Then he, also, was angry.

"I gave you my word, sir," he said, throwing his head back.

"I know that," snapped his employer. "And I do not say that you deliberately deceived me. But I think that a man who can make an omission so vital in a work of scholarship and not perceive what he has done, is capable of having imagined that he went to the University, though he received in truth no further education than the dame school!"

This was so outrageous that Martin did not reply to it. But he said-he felt bound to say —"If I am so incompetent, sir, I had better resign the employment which you were good enough to give me."

"And what would become of you then?" enquired Mr. Salt. "Your privateer would not take you back again-though indeed I think you would be better employed in scrubbing out her fo'c'sle than in — —"

At this moment, doubtless fortunately, there was a thud, and something was seen to fall past one of the windows.

"That's a bird dashed itself against the glass again!" exclaimed Mr. Salt, instantly diverted; and, abandoning his tirade, he ran to the long glass door and let himself out into the garden. In a few seconds he reappeared, carrying carefully in his two hands something very soft and brown.

"Most extraordinary! 'Tis a young owl! Poor creature, I hope it is only stunned! Look here, Towers; do you think that it is really hurt, for if so I shall have to kill it . . ."

He stood looking down upon the inert feathery thing with tenderness. Martin came over to him and looked too.

"I don't know much about birds, sir, but from what I have seen of owls they appear so covered with feathers that I should think even a knock like that could not hurt one. In fact, I believe it is reviving."

And indeed the great eyes had opened, and the creature suddenly fluffed up its feathers in a protesting manner. "Must put it outside again at once," said the historian, hurrying again to the glass door. He deposited the owl on a window-ledge outside and stood watching it. The bird, blinking, unfolded first one wing and then the other; and then was gone from the ledge with the noiseless flight of its kind. Mr. Salt came in again with a satisfied air.

"All's well that ends well. . . . I apologise, Towers, for rating you so just now! I told you I had a bad temper, though I believe that people say of me, in their usual senseless way, that my bark is worse than my bite . . . unlike Miss Meredith's dog, egad! But you annoyed me greatly!"

"I am afraid I gave you good reason, sir," replied Martin, this time with real penitence. "I will try to be more careful in future, especially as I find so many identical Welsh names, joined to the absence of surnames, confusing. Pray let me have the page to recopy!"

His employer gave it to him. "Yes, the great paucity of names is, I consider, one of the many signs of the low intelligence of the Cambrian race. I should have warned you to be upon your guard. Now, however, that Minerva's bird has visited us, you will doubtless exercise more care; and I shall learn to be less peppery."

(8)

After this outburst things went smoothly again, for ordinarily Mr. Salt was quite easy to get on with, and, even had he not been, Martin would have put up with a great deal on account of the extra risks which, out of pure kind-heartedness, that gentleman had taken upon his shoulders in the last few days. For, entirely with a view to setting old Mr. Tyrrell's mind at rest, he had engaged in proceedings which, if discovered, could not fail to prove his knowledge of what his secretary was charged with. He had first of all written a cautious letter to a correspondent in Liverpool giving some excuse or other for his curiosity, but requesting him to find out if he could what had been the ultimate result of a fracas in May between two Bow Street runners and a prisoner whom they were escorting to the gaol. Had one of the runners, as was rumoured, died of his injuries? Secondly, after consultation with Martin and an enquiry whether his father could read Greek-to which Martin was able to reply that, for a country parson, he had always kept it up wonderfully well-Mr. Salt wrote a letter to Mr. Tyrrell, senior, as one old Oxford man to another, saying that he believed the reverend gentleman was interested in the study of Homer, and that he was therefore taking the liberty of enclosing a passage in Greek from the twelfth-century commentary on the Odyssey by Eustathius, Bishop of Thessalonica, with which Mr. Tyrrell might possibly not be familiar.

"The passage," wrote Mr. Salt, thoroughly enjoying himself, "deals with the well-known episode, in the Fifth Book, of Odysseus' arrival shipwrecked at Phæacia, his swimming up the river, landing and making himself a bed of leaves." ("Hay," he observed in an aside to Martin, "is not mentioned in the text, but you will admit that the word ἐπεχεύατο" —he put his finger on it in the Homer open before him —"does imply that your prototype heaped the leaves over his body, even as I understand that you heaped the hay.")

His pen proceeded. "You will also remember, reverend sir, Odysseus' finding by the maiden Nausicaa, who answers him kindly, supplies his wants, especially in the matter of clothing, brings him to the city, but bids him enter it alone; and you will not have forgotten how, upon his staying his steps in the grove of Athena, Athena herself, in the form of a young girl, directs him to the house of Alcinous. —Pray, sir, attend particularly to the remarks of the learned Eustathius upon the whole of this incident."

Mr. Salt then took a fresh sheet of paper and proceeded to turn into Greek a passage, already drafted in English, which the learned Eustathius would certainly not have recognised, but which, owing to its appearing in a dead language with the further advantage of a script that only a Greek scholar could read, might be assumed to be unintelligible to any eye which should nowadays pry into the Reverend Mr. Tyrrell's correspondence. The gist of Mr. Salt's forged passage of commentary was, of course, that he was himself playing the part of Alcinous to the recipient's son, aided by a damsel who, even as Nausicaa, had come upon the latter hidden not far from the shore (for the coincidence was too neat for the writer to omit this, even though the parallel did not extend to Nausicaa's being his daughter, as she was Alcinous's in the original), and that, after various nautical adventures, this modern Odysseus was safe and well, implored his father to believe that he was innocent of the wiles which the Trojans laid to his charge, and was prepared and wishful to return to Ithaca should his father desire it; otherwise Alcinous, with whom he had found employment, was ready to keep him "until the sky was cleared of tempest".

"I shall be glad, sir," concluded Mr. Salt, "of your opinion upon this gloss; perhaps you will be good enough to send me in return the comments of one of the older scholars, *exempla gratia* Aristarchus of Samothrace."

"And I hope, Towers —I should say, Odysseus," remarked the commentator as he sealed letter and enclosure, "that your respected father will realise that he must write anything which concerns you in Greek or Latin. I really do not think that anyone else can possibly guess what is meant by all this rigmarole, which I propose to send under cover to a friend in London to frank for me, in order that no one at Selham St. Peter can remember having seen the St. David's postmark upon it."

Pleased and even struck with admiration as Martin was, he wished there might have been a little less about the young lady in this communication-not that he in the least desired to minimise the part she had played in his affairs, or was anything but profoundly grateful to her. But-his father might entertain ideas which were quite without foundation.

(9)

A couple of days after the meeting with Miss Meredith outside the Cathedral, there came an invitation to Mr. Salt to dine at the Precentory the following afternoon, and to bring with him his secretary, whose acquaintance Dr. Meredith professed himself anxious to make. This communication was read out by its recipient with an undisguised chuckle.

"I was hoping for this," he remarked. "But you will not, I trust, inaugurate your second acquaintance with your host, Towers, by punching the precentorial waistcoat?"

"I am sure I had better not accompany you, sir," returned the unhappy Martin. "It is very kind of Dr. Meredith, but —I will feign some excuse not to go; it would really be better."

"Short of saying that you are ill, or that I keep you at your work without intermission for meals, I do not see what excuse you can feign," returned his employer, with enjoyment. "Moreover, it is extremely unlikely that the Precentor will know you again, seen as you were that evening in the dark and having then a passably villainous aspect. And do you not wish to see your Nausicaa?"

Martin replied that he did naturally wish to see her if he could do so without implicating her in any trouble; for trouble, he imagined, must ensue if Dr. Meredith should discover the assistance which she had, unknown to him, been rendering to his unworthy self.

"You are quite right," agreed Mr. Salt. "The Precentor is easy-going in some ways, and very fond of his daughter, but he has a great notion of his own authority. Yet I think that if you seemed to avoid him-and you must meet him some day-it would afford a more fertile ground for suspicion to grow upon, did there chance to be a seed of it in his mind, than if you boldly accepted this invitation to dine with him, since in his wildest flights of fancy-not that he has many, good soul-he could not imagine the vagabond of that night in the ruins venturing under his roof. It will be exactly a month to-morrow since you assaulted him, so the feast to which he bids us falls most aptly."

A little before half-past three next afternoon the two set forth down to the Precentory, but from their conversation as they went, a new apprehension seized upon Martin; if Mr. Salt were in one of his freakish humours there was no knowing to what phrases of double meaning he might not give vent, which would render both his secretary and Miss Meredith most uncomfortable. And yet it was not in Martin's power to ask him to abstain from such quips. The only comfort was the knowledge that Mr. Salt had no real desire to imperil his protégé, and more than sufficient wit to restrain his tongue from actually doing so.

"Quite informal," Dr. Meredith had said in his invitation, but Martin, as he followed his employer into the drawing-room, thought that he would have preferred a larger gathering, the more formal the better, to this group of four members of one family, none of whom could he meet without secret embarrassment. In the case of the elderly lady with the large cap ("my sister, Mrs. Pennefather") and the vivacious young one with the dark ringlets ("my elder daughter, Mrs. Stalybridge") the constraint was less. Last of all Martin was presented to her to whom he needed no presentation, and wondered if she would have looked more or less shy had he really been the stranger he must affect to be-since he was unaware whether or no she had told her father of their meeting in the close the other day.

Miss Meredith falling to his share to escort to the dining-room he contrived, as they descended the stairs, to say in a low voice, "I feel that I ought not to be here," to which, not looking up at him, she replied in one lower still: "Yes, it . . . it is . . . a little awkward . . ." Then they went in and sat down to the solid good cheer for which Dr. Meredith's table was famous, to green pea soup, a fine piece of salmon, boiled chicken, hashed calf's head, roast ducks, blancmange and currant pie.

The Precentor also, as Martin knew, was an Oxford man-as a Welshman, he had been at Jesus College-and after the meal was under way he began to talk to his guest of their common University. So long as he confined his remarks or questions to this and allied topics Martin's wits were not unduly exercised, since there was no need for dissimulation. It was not, however, such plain sailing when Dr. Meredith asked him what he thought of St. David's, and how much he had seen of it since his arrival; presumably he had been shown by Mr. Salt the Cathedral and its, alas, ruined companions, the Bishop's Palace and St. Mary's College? Yes, answered the young man, Mr. Salt had kindly conducted him round the Cathedral.

"But not round the Bishop's Palace?" queried the Precentor. "That was a lapse on his part, for the Palace is unique, quite unique."

"I thought," observed Mr. Salt, with that twitch of the lips which Martin was coming to dread, "that it was not, perhaps, necessary to introduce Mr. Towers to the Bishop's Palace."

Martin grew hot; this was really too bad! He dared not look at Miss Meredith.

"My dear Salt, why not?" ejaculated his host. "I suppose you mean that Mr. Towers had already visited those sublime remains? Had you, sir?"

Whichever answer I give, thought the unfortunate Martin, I am sure to wish I had given the other! But his employer, confound his impishness, had almost forced him to admit the truth-or rather a modified version of it. This version he now put forth, saying as carelessly as he could: "Yes, sir; and Mr. Salt was aware that I had wandered in there by myself a few days previously."

"And did you not admire the Palace, Mr. Towers?"

"I thought the ruins extraordinarily fine, sir."

"Though I believe it was, unluckily, somewhat dark when you visited them, was it not, Towers?" commented Mr. Salt, still with the same secret mirth. "And by the way, Precentor, has it ever occurred to you how easily, the entrance gateway being unfenced, gipsies or the like could get in, and, perhaps, indeed do get in, and spend the night there?"

Dr. Meredith cast a curious, almost a startled glance at him; then one at his younger daughter. "That very idea," he said, compressing his lips, "has been a subject of cogitation with me lately, owing to an occurrence which was recently brought to my notice; and I am on the point of having the entrance made more secure."

Ill at ease as he was, Martin could not help sharing in his heart the secret amusement which he knew must be enlivening Mr. Salt's at this proof that Dr. Meredith had no inclination to admit his own personal encounter with a vagabond inside the ruins, presumably because his dignity had suffered therein. But a moment or two afterwards the Precentor, probably considering how strange this abstention would appear in the eyes of his younger daughter, who had shared the adventure with him, added, still in an Olympian manner: "As a matter of fact, I myself discovered a . . . a species of gipsy in the Palace about a month ago-it was when Mr. Thistleton was staying with me-and since that episode I have come to the conclusion that steps must be taken to prevent such undesirable intrusions in future."

"And what steps did you take with the intruder on that occasion, Meredith?" enquired Mr. Salt. "Strong ones, I'll be bound!"

"I summoned him to account for his presence there," replied the Precentor with majesty. "But the man, a most impertinent and disreputable fellow, who affirmed that he was merely passing the night there, made off before we could-er-detain him. He was no native of these parts, but I should know him again in an instant if ever I came upon him!"

Martin, supremely uncomfortable himself, and not daring to meet his employer's eye, knew that Miss Meredith, at his side, was only pretending to eat. In an effort to dissociate himself from the interchanges about the Palace he started to talk to her about that always safe and luxuriant topic, the weather. Soon they were agreeing that it had been wonderfully fine; that the hay had been cut and carried under the most favourable conditions, and that it was to be hoped the corn would ripen and be garnered with equal success. In fact, their conversation took so agrarian a turn that Mrs. Stalybridge remarked across the table: "Why, Nest, you are becoming quite an agriculturist! Surely that is something new! You did not appear at all anxious to watch Griffiths of Tan-y-bach getting in his hay the other evening!"

Martin saw the colour leap up under Miss Meredith's delicate skin; for an instant her whole neck was dyed with it. He groaned inwardly; not even that theme, it appeared, was innocuous. Hay had its thorns, as he ought to have remembered.

"And I am sure," pursued Jane, "that at the University Mr. Towers did not learn anything about crops and harvesting."

Martin, suddenly realising that the speaker must have been the same young lady who had been Miss Meredith's companion on that occasion at Tan-y-bach, tried not to look as apprehensive as he felt. But surely Mrs. Stalybridge could not be referring to that episode with any malicious intent; she *could* not have recognised in him that lame haymaker!

"It is true that——" he was beginning, when the turbaned head at the end of the table inclined in his direction.

"You must forgive my niece, sir," said Mrs. Pennefather apologetically; and then, addressing that niece, said in a reproachful tone: "My dear Jane, you forget the Georgics of Virgil! There the immortal Mantuan has set forth in imperishable verse all the processes of tillage and of planting, of cattle-breeding and of bee-keeping: as he says himself: '*Haec super arvorum cultu pecorumque canebam, Et super arboribus.* ' The Georgics no doubt formed part of Mr. Towers's studies at Oxford."

Heavens, thought Martin, as the Latin flowed from those feminine lips, the good lady is a blue-stocking! And he became more nervous than ever.

"Moreover," observed the Precentor from the other end of the table, "we need not assume that Mr. Towers is by upbringing totally ignorant of agriculture. He comes perhaps from a rural district."

If this were an invitation to disclose his place of origin Martin did not feel inclined to respond to it. However, Mr. Salt, for once reversing his rôle of Puck, saved him from the necessity of answering at all by suddenly asking the Precentor a question about some recent contentious happening or other at the annual Cathedral audit on St. James's Day, which immediately inaugurated a discussion, Mr. Salt upholding the views of the Chancellor and Treasurer, Dr. Meredith defending his own.

And after the ladies had withdrawn the three men discussed politics, a safe subject perhaps, but not a very cheerful one, what with the fall of the funds, the growing distress (last year's bad harvest having been the second in succession) and the continual ascendancy of the star of France on land, though not at sea. Shaking his head, Dr. Meredith at last rose from table, and they went upstairs to the drawing-room.

Immediately they arrived Mrs. Pennefather rang for tea to be brought in, and with its advent there bounded into the room, with violent waggings of the tail and the general demeanour of an escaped thrall who more than half expects to be sent back to bondage, the four-legged cause of Martin's most recent misfortune.

"Bran!" exclaimed his mistress, starting up at once. "You naughty dog, what are you doing here?" And the Precentor said in his deepest voice: "Dear, dear, we are not accustomed to this, Nesta!" Nevertheless, he emitted an encouraging noise in the direction of the intruder, who by ecstatic writhings at his daughter's feet, was visibly imploring forgiveness and perhaps also permission to remain.

And then quite suddenly, and for no perceptible cause, the dog's ears went back, his tail clamped itself between his legs, and he was crawling under the nearest sofa.

"Whatever ails the animal!" exclaimed the amazed Dr. Meredith. "Bran-Bran, come out-good dog! Why, he seemed positively terrified!"

"Perhaps," suggested Mr. Salt softly, "he has seen a ghost, as animals are said to have the power of doing when no human being can perceive anything. Is this room haunted, Precentor?"

"Not to my knowledge," replied the Precentor, still trying to see under the sofa without unduly stooping. "I think-it sounds uncomplimentary, I fear-that he must have taken a dislike to the only stranger present, who happens to be Mr. Towers; but I have never known him do such a thing before."

"The instincts of dogs *are* very strange," observed Mr. Salt in a detached manner, while Nest Meredith and her sister engaged in attempts to lure Bran from his seclusion. "You remember, Meredith, how in the Odyssey (which I have had occasion lately to re-read) it is his dog Argos which recognises Odysseus on his return to Ithaca, and that the faithful hound dies of the joy of it."

"But Bran cannot very well be recognising Mr. Towers; and he does not appear to be at all overjoyed!"

"Dogs do take the oddest dislikes," remarked Jane Stalybridge, on her knees by the sofa. "Come, Bran, do not be so foolish-come out and make friends with this gentleman!"

"No, no!" cried Nest, springing up. "He might-truly he looks under there as if he might bite. . . . Don't go near him, pray, Mr. Towers!"

"My dear," said her father reprovingly, "there is surely no need to agitate yourself so excessively! Bran has never been known to bite anybody."

"Can you swear to that?" asked Mr. Salt softly from the hearth-rug; but his query passed unanswered in the slight turmoil which accompanied the digging out of Bran from his earth, and his subsequent ejection from the room. After this Dr. Meredith, evidently feeling that as a topic of conversation Bran's sudden dislike to the guest was scarcely courteous to the latter, rather markedly put a stop to it. And whether Miss Nest Meredith thereafter purposely avoided Mr. Towers' society, or her more lively and self-assured sister purposely sought it, for the rest of the time before he and Mr. Salt took their leave Martin talked either to Mrs. Stalybridge or to the Precentor's blue-stocking sister, whom he found less alarming than he had feared.

Walking back with his employer, he admitted that he was glad the entertainment was over. "I am afraid," said Mr. Salt, with just a tinge of penitence audible in his voice, "that I ought not to have said that about your visit to the Palace, but the temptation was too great. If I had known that the dog was afterwards going to create such a to-do I would have held my tongue."

"I was not referring to either of those contretemps, sir," replied Martin, knitting his brows. "But I think I should have shown more delicacy by staying away altogether. After all I was a guest of Dr. Meredith's under false pretences; had the truth been known about my identity I should neither have been invited nor received."

"In fact, you are criticising my lack of delicacy in taking you to the Precentory," retorted Mr. Salt rather sharply. "You are an ungrateful young puppy!—But there," he added more pacifically, "you may be in the right of it; at any rate, 'tis commendable in a young man to feel a scruple by which the old man is too insensitive to be disquieted!"

(10)

Next afternoon, as Martin was wrestling with a particularly badly written paragraph of Mr. Salt's, that gentleman, whom he had not seen for some time, entered humming a little air, and coming over to him clapped him on the shoulder.

"Traitor you may be, Martin de Turribus, but murderer you evidently are not, so my roof shelters one crime the less. I have just heard from my correspondent in Liverpool. Your runner had his head broken, as the phrase goes, but recovered. You won't hang for that little affair, at any rate!"

And though he spoke with such levity, there was a good deal of feeling in the way in which he wrung Martin's hand. As for Martin himself, Mr. Salt's smiling face and the room itself looked for a moment quite strange to him, as the shadow of that rope which had dangled over him since May withdrew itself. For fancied treason the law might imprison him; it still might do so-he did not know-for attempted murder; but to hang him for actual murder was no longer in the power of any authority. The worst cloud had vanished from his sky; he could not find his voice.

"We must remove this weight from your father's mind also," said Mr. Salt kindly, perceiving this, "as soon, that is, as we hear that he has received the remarks of the learned Bishop of Thessalonica, which, unless something has gone amiss, should be any day now. I must devise some neat classical method of conveying this recent reassuring news." He went at once to his own table as if to start upon this congenial task, and then added over his shoulder: "Take a turn in the garden if you like, Towers."

Although it was raining Martin thankfully accepted this offer, and out there in the wet sea-wind thanked God not only that he had escaped a great peril, but also that he had not on his soul the death of a fellow-creature who had only been doing his duty. He realised now, more fully than before, that, to an unintentional murderer at least, there are two sides to his deed.

And yet this news did not bring any nearer the prospect of being able to clear himself of the charge of treason. He had already explained to Mr. Salt why he could not do so without involving Gerald Roche and through him Lucy, and that he would not do unless his own danger was extreme. He went over this ground again with Mr. Salt that evening, and his employer did not attempt to change his resolution; possibly, as he suggested with his whimsical smile, "from purely selfish motives. I don't want to have to procure a new secretary now that you have mastered my handwriting. And talking of handwriting, pray do not forget to buy me some fresh quills to-morrow; you can get them at the post-office."

And that was how Martin chanced to be in the little post-office next day just at the right moment to enquire if there were any letters for Mr. Salt (who generally fetched his own), and was in consequence handed the solitary letter which awaited that gentleman . . . in his own father's writing! He hurried out, omitting to gather up the change from his purchase, and almost ran back to Bowen's Folly.

He found Mr. Salt by his front door, pointing out to his gardener and general factotum a discovery which he had only just made, namely, that in repainting the figureheads on either side of it he had omitted to paint the flat portions at the back. Owen Owen, the factotum, appeared to be replying that he had received no orders to that effect, or alternatively, as lawyers say, that the back part did not show; on which his employer retorted that the omission for either reason was just of a piece with the Welsh character. Martin waited impatiently for the warfare to cease, and when their common employer sharply ordered Owen Owen to go at once and mix some paint, tendered him the letter without more ado, briefly saying: "It has come at last, sir!"

Mr. Jerome Salt took it, saw that the seal was unbroken, observed: "Why did you not open it yourself?" ran his eye over the contents, murmured: "Yes, that is satisfactory as far as it goes," gave it back to Martin and left him there, in company with the helmeted lady and the plumed cacique, to read his father's reply (in Latin, not in Greek) to the alleged comments of the learned Eustathius on the fifth book of the *Odyssey*.

The gist of the letter was that, in Mr. Tyrrell's view, Laertes, the father of Odysseus, implored his son to remain at all costs at the house of Alcinous for the present, and called down all the blessings of Olympus on that benefactor's head for his hospitality. To that son Laertes sent his blessing and his assurance that he believed none of the rumours against him, though he had been exceedingly anxious for his safety. Now, however, a heavy weight was lifted from his mind; yet he once more reiterated his entreaties that Odysseus should not return to Ithaca; the Trojans, he was sure, were keeping a watch upon his (Laertes's) dwelling, which, in fact, they had already raided, carrying off all Odysseus' writings upon which they could lay hands. (Here the figureheads might have observed the reader looking very grave indeed.) They had also paid a second visit to discover whether Laertes had received any news of his son, which at the date of their visit he could truthfully deny.

The letter concluded, in English, by thanking Mr. Salt for his great kindness in sending the writer the exceedingly interesting Homeric gloss.

The sight of his father's shaky old writing had brought tears to Martin's eyes. Into what a sea of sorrow and anxiety he had plunged him! And yet it had all come about through his endeavours to help Lucy in *her* difficulty. . . . Or at least, it had all originated in that attempt. Many times during the last few months had Martin reviewed his own conduct, and been forced to condemn it as precipitate and ill-judged. He had rushed into action when he should have hesitated, as in the case of setting off to Hamburg upon such meagre evidence, and delayed when he should have acted swiftly, for he had prolonged his stay in that city solely on the chance of catching another glimpse of that incarnation of grace and sweetness in the house with the tulips. Had he not thus fruitlessly tarried, who knew but that he might never have been arrested; and certainly if he had not been arrested he would never have assaulted a Bow Street runner.

But here the approach of Owen Owen with a sulky face, a paint-brush and a pail, sent Martin in to deliver to Mr. Salt the bundle of quills and his own reiterated thanks for his kindness and his ingenuity.

IV
THE KINGDOM BY THE SEA

"My little heart is satisfied with you;
You take up all her room, as in a cottage
Which harbours some benighted princely stranger,
Where the good man, proud of his hospitality,
Yields all his homely dwelling to his guest
And hardly keeps a corner for himself."

Nicholas Rowe, *The Fair Penitent*.

"*Rosalind*: Not true in love?

   Celia: Yes, when he is in, but I think he is not in."

As You Like It, Act ii. sc. 4.

IV
THE KINGDOM BY THE SEA

(1)

Summer was passing into autumn, but slowly, and with visible reluctance. The corn was reaped and housed; the lanes were sometimes miry instead of dusty, and other flowers bloomed in them, not so profusely; and there were fresh stars in the sky. The north wind was giving place to the south-west, and a blue sea to a grey; sometimes, even, it was leaden in hue, and came in upon the headlands in wrath and foam, though there were days, too, when it lay as fast asleep as in July.

And meanwhile the war went on, with fewer allies left to England, and her National Debt swollen by enormous subsidies to those who had proved faithless. All the Dutch colonies, which she had now seized, and colonial gains from the French both in the East and West Indies could not prevent the growth of discontent and disaffection. But for Nest Meredith this autumn began as peacefully, even as dully, as the last. Jane and her offspring had left at the end of August. She did not often see "Mr. Towers" save at Morning Prayer on Sundays, which, as the Precentor remarked with approbation, he always attended; this showed that the young man had received a proper upbringing.

So he had; moreover, Martin considered that he owed it to his father not to omit an observance which he would certainly have paid had he been at home with him at Selham St. Peter; and it was something to feel that the dear old man was using the same prayers and reading the same lessons, though amid much less space and relics of past splendour than surrounded the Welsh congregation on the south side of the nave, or the English in the choir, of the Cathedral here. And when Dr. Jenkins prosed away in the pulpit, or the saintly old Dr. Vaughan (who reminded Martin somewhat of his father) preached one of his limpidly devout sermons, the exile used to wonder which of his discourses the Vicar of Selham St. Peter was reading this Sunday-or had he perhaps written a new one? The Cathedral did make a link; besides, it attracted him for its own sake.

Moreover-though this did not occur to the Precentor-Mr. Salt's church-going secretary also appreciated the sight of Miss Nest Meredith in her Sunday bonnet of green with an edging of the fur of the beaver, whether listening so demurely to the Lessons or the sermon inside the Cathedral, or blushing slightly as he lifted his hat to her in the dispersing groups outside the south door. Not that his heart was at all engaged in these glimpses, being, he was convinced, interred at Altona (that is, if his divinity were still there; if not, sepultured in Ireland), but because his gratitude and his æsthetic sense alike demanded them. If one admired a vermeil cheek (naturally he did not, since Pamela had so little colour), Miss Meredith's had the true wild rose tint, delicate and fresh; and if brown hair with auburn lights in it had been to his taste, instead of locks much darker, what the beaver-trimmed bonnet revealed of Miss Meredith's curls was distinctly attractive . . . or would have proved so had his heart remained above ground.

For so much glamour still hung, like the lingering smell of incense in a shrine, about the memory of that one sight of Pamela Fitzgerald, that Martin could sometimes count the hardships of privateering, haymaking under difficulties and his present precarious situation no excessive payment for that hour. He could never be the same again, he told himself, and was not ill-pleased with the thought, for he was young. At these exalted moments he even went so far as to picture himself metaphorically laying his wrecked career and his threatened liberty as an offering at those slender and unconscious feet. But not always; not, for instance, in those very chill and lonely hours at Ogof-y-Ffôs, when death by hydrophobia had really seemed to him the not impossible culmination of his misfortunes; nor indeed when he reflected that he had involved the old father for whom he had so sincere and protective an affection in his own holocaust.

His romanticism might also have undergone a slight modification if he had known of the part which the stout and wily Mr. O'Driscoll had played in his arrest; how that deaf lawyer, desiring at all costs to stop him from going to Hamburg, and finding his first effort at doing so fail, had forthwith sent an anonymous letter of denunciation to the authorities at Dublin Castle. Almost from the day of his arrival in Hamburg, therefore, Martin had been under observation. But of this fact he was (perhaps fortunately) ignorant, since the gleams of romantic satisfaction which he could gain by counting the world well lost for the hopeless love he bore to Lady Edward Fitzgerald would certainly not have visited him had he realised that he had lost it much more through the malice of Mr. Oliver O'Driscoll.

Another matter of which, however, he was conscious of being in ignorance, was the present state of affairs at Ballydare. Gerald had presumably returned home long ago; but had he renounced his connection with the United Irishmen, or had he plunged more deeply into those troubled waters? And did Lucy know of the disaster which had befallen her brother in his attempt to help her? If she did, Martin feared its results in her present state of health. It was fortunate that he had written from Hamburg saying that he did not propose to return to Ireland at present; she could not know that he had later changed his mind. Possibly his arrest and escape had not found its way into the newspapers, and he supposed that his father also might have kept it from her; but in a second Latin letter which had come from him (in response to one informing him that no charge of slaying a "Trojan" could now be made against Odysseus) there had been no mention of Lucy at all.

So the weeks went by, undisturbed at Bowen's Folly by enquiries or alarms; and Martin copied and copied while Mr. Salt translated and translated, and, now that the weather was no longer so suitable for it, took to sailing his little cutter, with Martin for crew, in St. Bride's Bay, past Solva Harbour's narrow rock-hindered entrance or the long stretch of Newgale beach; and, one none too calm day, round to the further side of Ramsey Island with its pinnacled and fretted cliffs, haunts of myriads of guillemots and razor-bills. Nothing untoward happened; yet Martin was not sorry that Mr. Salt finally abandoned a projected trip to that round lump of Grassholm fifteen miles away, though Grassholm was, so Mr. Salt informed him, the fabled Gwales or Gwalia, the land of mystery, where his knights kept the head of King Bran the Blessed for four score years, till the day when Heilyn, the son of Gwynn, opened the door of the hall where they feasted and looked towards the land. . . . . And if the head of Bendigeid Vran had remained hidden under the White Tower of London, where it was then taken, no invasion could have come upon Britain; but Arthur "disclosed" the head because he chose not to hold Britain save by his own strength. And in addition to this Vortigern "disclosed" the bones of Vortimer (which had the same property) and also (seeming to have made a hobby of it) those of the dragons buried in the rocks of Snowdon. "So now you understand, my dear Towers, why we live every day in fear of a French invasion!"

(2)

But one wet afternoon something happened to break the monotony at least of Miss Nest Meredith's existence, for to her great surprise it was announced to her that young Mr. Perrot from Camrose was in the drawing-room, having come to pay his respects to Mrs. Pennefather and herself, and would she please to go thither. For a moment Nest hesitated. Mr. Perrot's defection had hurt her pride more than she knew; then she decided that if she remained in her bedroom the wound might be apparent to him, so she went.

Mr. John Perrot, of a younger branch of that old and famous Pembrokeshire family, was alone in the drawing-room —a good-looking, rather self-confident young man upon whose attentions any maiden who received them might quite justifiably plume herself. Nest, surprised, swept him her most formal curtsy.

"Is my aunt not here? I believe she has been informed of your arrival, sir."

"Very likely," responded Mr. Perrot, raising himself with swiftness from his bow, and hastening towards her. "But I trust it is permitted to hope that Mrs. Pennefather may be delayed for a few moments longer, because I wish to explain to you in particular, Miss Meredith, why you have not seen me for so long. I ——"

"Is it so long?" interrupted Nest, with an air of innocence. "I cannot indeed remember exactly when ——"

"Cruel!" ejaculated Mr. Perrot, who seemed determined to waste no time while he still had it unshared at his disposal. "You cannot then have found the months as long as I have-indeed, why should you? Yet I had hoped . . . I have been out of England," he explained, "on a voyage to Jamaica."

And, man-like, he proceeded uninvited to give an account of all that had happened to him: length of voyage-roughness of sea (not that he was ever sea-sick) —several hours' chase by a French privateer (here, detecting some slight alteration in Miss Meredith's delicate complexion, Mr. Perrot assigned a flattering but erroneous interpretation to the change) —stay in Jamaica-heat-mountains-negroes-palm trees and exotic fruits-return voyage-its conditions compared with those of the outward trip-pleasure at seeing shores of old England again-more than pleasure at thought of revisiting St. Davids, and particularly the Precentory. All this he was able to rattle off before the entrance of Mrs. Pennefather-and then had the gratification of relating it over again to that lady.

Now that Mr. Perrot was back in Pembrokeshire it was obvious that his sojourn in the West Indies had heightened his appreciation of a Welsh girl's charm, and that he wished to make up for lost time. But Nest, who in the spring had not been able to make up her mind about him and his attentions, now surprisingly discovered that she had. She found them a trifle tiresome, and would rather have been without them-unless, of course, they should haply serve to produce a stimulating effect in another quarter. But she never went so far as to formulate this coquettish thought, even in her own mind. Besides, she hardly ever saw Mr. Tyrrell, so how could he know that Mr. Perrot was paying court to her; and even if he did know, why should he care? He was always entirely courteous and charming to her if ever they exchanged greetings after Morning Prayer, but she felt bound to discount a good deal of this on the score of his obligation to her; for, little as Nest was accustomed to pride herself on any doing of hers, she could not avoid knowing that the young man was most deeply in her debt.

It was true that this obligation, still more the knowledge which they shared of his past, linked them, together with Mr. Salt, into a kind of little secret fellowship; and Nest had a feeling that Mr. Salt was quite willing-perhaps even a little more than willing-that she and his secretary should see something more of each other, for he had several times invited Mrs. Pennefather and her to drink tea at Bowen's Folly before the afternoon when Aunt Gwenllian at last accepted. On the day, however, the poetess developed a severe headache, and could not go; yet, not wishing to deprive her niece, as she said, of the benefit of Mr. Salt's erudite conversation, she proclaimed that in view of his age and long acquaintance with the Precentor it would be perfectly proper for Nest to go alone, even though he had a young man staying with him. Nest was not sure whether she was glad or sorry that matters had turned out thus, for Aunt Gwenllian would probably have talked most of the time to Mr. Salt, thus affording her a chance of a *tête-à-tête* with Mr. Salt's amanuensis, a privilege which had never come her way since their long and momentous interview on the cliffs, and which was now unlikely to be hers this afternoon.

Nevertheless, she enjoyed herself. She declined to preside over the tea-table, partly from shyness and partly because she guessed that an old bachelor like her host preferred his own methods of making and dispensing that beverage to those of any woman. He was not in so quizzing a vein as sometimes, and prevailed upon Mr. Tyrrell to tell of his adventures in the *Fair Penitent*—it seemed a long, long time since Nest had first heard in that honeysuckled lane of the fight with the French brig. In that pleasant voice of his Mr. Tyrrell talked, too, of his home, of his father and of his married sister in Ireland. (And yet somehow Nest felt much shyer of him than that day at Ogof-y-Ffôs.) She heard also the good news about the runner's recovery from his injury; and further that Mr. Salt was considering the advisability of approaching his acquaintance Lord Cawdor, or even possibly Lord Milford, the Lord Lieutenant, who was an old friend, upon his secretary's behalf.

Nest was also informed by Mr. Salt, somewhat to her confusion, why he had christened her Nausicaa; indeed, for the first time in her life she heard the immortal story told in full-told well and vividly, the scraps of sonorous if unintelligible Greek somehow heightening the effect. In the course of his narrative Mr. Salt could not refrain from pointing out to his guest the close resemblance, which he declared had only recently struck him, between Dewisland and Phæacia, that country so dear to the gods that it had no need to fear an enemy. And he quoted some Greek. "That means," he explained: " '*Far apart we live, in the wash of the waves, the outermost of men*' —just like you and me and all of us, Nesta." Phæacia, he told her further, had like St. David's a haven on either side of the town, and "a goodly temple" —"though only, I must admit, to the heathen god Poseidon." And picking up the *Odyssey* he translated for her especial benefit Odysseus' comment to the queen on his interview with her daughter Nausicaa. " '*To her I made my supplication, and she shewed no lack of a good understanding*' —that was certainly so, was it not, Towers? —'*behaving as thou couldst not hope for in chancing upon one so young, for the younger folk lack wisdom always*.' " Then, turning over the leaves, he began to translate another passage: " '*Who is this that goes with Nausicaa, this tall and goodly stranger? Where found she him?*' ". But at this point Mr. Salt very abruptly stopped, gave a chuckle, and passing the book to his secretary, with his finger on a line, said: "Shall I read that, Towers? Better not, perhaps, eh?"

"No," said the young man, colouring as the Greek met his eye; and he firmly shut the *Odyssey* and laid it out of Mr. Salt's reach. Nest felt dreadfully embarrassed, as she instantly supposed that Mr. Salt had been upon the brink of reading out in English one of the many improprieties of which she understood the classics were full; for she could not know that the line from which Martin Tyrrell had saved her-and himself-was merely this: "*Her husband will he be, her very own* ." And yet no impropriety would have made Miss Meredith blush more hotly.

And the *tête-à-tête* was vouchsafed after all. Just before her departure the question of the return of the borrowed suit came up (since it had only been worn for a day or two), and Nest, explaining that she did not wish it left at the door of the Precentory lest this should give rise to enquiries, offered to take it back herself. This of course neither gentleman would hear of her doing, and the matter ended by Mr. Tyrrell asking to be allowed to escort her home bearing the parcel, which he would transfer to her charge at the last moment.

And thus Nest found herself alone again with her privateersman, walking away from the old sea-captain's residence pursued by a damp wind which had already stripped some of the leaves from its huddled oaks. The pity was that the distance home was so short. . . . unless she took the longer way, down beneath the terrace wall, and went in at the lower gate opposite the Cathedral. Would Mr. Tyrrell think it strange if she did this?

He was asking if the winters at St. David's were severe. She told him, no, not in the way of frost or snow, but there was wind from the two seas, and wrecks came ashore sometimes, for it was a very dangerous coast, as Mr. Tyrrell could see.

"Yes, I can imagine that," he said. And then, as if to himself: "I wonder if I shall still be here when winter comes."

Nest's heart said very secretly: "I hope you will," but her lips made answer-and not, indeed, quite insincerely: "I trust that by Christmas Day you may be back with your father, Mr. Tyrrell. I am so glad that you have been able to communicate with him-even in a dead language. How useful 'tis to know Latin and Greek!" And she remembered how just before their first encounter she had been thinking that it behoved her to study one of these . . . because of Mr. Perrot's defection. Now she had Mr. Perrot back-but there might still be need of the consolations of the classics.

Then she in her turn made enquiries, somewhat timidly, about his relations with Mr. Salt, and whether he found him difficult to live with, and having been reassured on that score, came more timidly still to a question which took its origin from something that gentleman had said at tea.

"Mr. Tyr-Towers, did Mr. Salt mean that you were too ill to put on those clothes of my brother's before you went to Bowen's Folly?"

"I wish he had never mentioned the matter," answered her companion, with pardonable irritation. "I must confess that it was so-but I did not wish you to know it, after all the trouble to which you had put yourself to provide them."

"I thought after you had gone away that evening," said Nest unhappily, "that there was something amiss. It was that wretched bite of Bran's, I suppose?"

"There are no ill effects now, Miss Meredith," responded Bran's victim, "so let us forget all about it. . . . How sweetly the Alan runs through the meadows here; the Vale of Roses is the old name, is it not? You have a pleasant prospect from the windows of the Precentory."

"Yes indeed. Another name for it is the Merry Vale," said Nest, blushing a little, and hoping that Mr. Tyrrell would not realise that she had caused him almost completely to circumnavigate the Precentory in order to make the voyage longer.

But now they had arrived at the lower gate of her home, and the sloping path up through the garden. And here she asked her escort for the parcel.

Since they were still some way from the house chivalry forbade Martin to comply. "I will give it to you in the porch," he said, and they advanced up to that goal between the grass borders and the low lavender hedge. And it was this chivalry which brought about the failure of the whole scheme, for just as they reached the latitude of the upper gate, but were still some yards from the front door, there suddenly appeared through this gate, from the direction of the town, the Precentor himself.

"Ah, Mr. Towers!" he exclaimed. "Escorting my daughter home-that is very kind of you!"

Under Dr. Meredith's eyes a package of some size could not possibly be transferred to his daughter's arms without his commenting upon it and probably enquiring as to its contents, and Nest only hoped that Mr. Tyrrell would not attempt the feat. Yet she dared not say so, nor even give him some negative sign. Her father was now talking to him affably about Mr. Salt. Perhaps he would ask the young man into the house, in which case it would be quite natural for him to deposit his burden in the hall, where she could surely get possession of it unobserved.

But no; the Precentor was saying: "Well, I must not keep you, Mr. Towers, for I take it," here he glanced at the parcel, "that you are going on elsewhere. I thank you once more for seeing my daughter home."

It was practically a dismissal, and Nest could find no way of intimating her desire that her escort should enter, for, since Papa had not bidden him to do so, it would have been unprecedented for her, in his presence, to issue such an invitation.

She observed the borrower of the suit to make one wavering and uncertain movement as though to give her the parcel; but, if that had been his intention, he very quickly thought better of it, and translated the gesture into a mere shifting of his burden to his other hand. "Good night, sir. Good night, Miss Meredith." Raising his hat, he turned away; and thus William's suit, which had so nearly reached port, had to return whence it came.

"A gentlemanly young fellow, that secretary of Salt's," observed Dr. Meredith, opening his front door. "But where, by the way, is your aunt? Did she not accompany you?"

"She is suffering from a headache, Papa, but she allowed me to go without her, seeing that Mr. Salt is so old a friend of yours."

"Yes, yes, that is quite right and proper. By the way, I met young Perrot this afternoon, and he desired his compliments to you. Ah, this, methinks, is a letter from Thistleton!" He took it up and opened it. "H'm, all about some recent discoveries of Roman remains in York, I fancy." He turned over three closely written pages, but the fourth and last drew from him a species of snort. "Here's a postscript asking if I ever came across any further signs of 'that irreverent gipsy,' as he calls him, in the Bishop's Palace? I should think not, indeed; though I have sometimes wondered where he went to."

Nest shivered.

(3)

It was a day like late summer, and Martin Tyrrell, strolling along the cliffs, found it almost impossible to believe that October had run half its course. Over the blue floor below was spread a wash of mother-of-pearl; beyond the handle of the sickle-sweep of St. Bride's Bay-Skomer Island-the sky ocean was navigated by a fleet of cloud three-deckers in full sail. The flowers were gone now, though here and there the dry bladders of the campion rattled gently in the breeze, and every clump of gorse showed a few flecks of its adventurous bloom.

Mr. Salt, telling his secretary that there was nothing ready for him to transcribe this afternoon, had bidden him go for a walk, and Martin had gladly obeyed. Yet, conscious as he was of the surprising beauty of the day, his heart could not soar with the late lark which was singing above his head like the fount of all imaginable joy. How much longer was he to remain here, an outlaw dependent on the good will of an eccentric man of letters, still liable, for all the undisturbed security of the last three months, to be unmasked at any moment, and feeling himself an impostor when he accepted invitations, as he was now beginning to do, and especially an impostor at the Precentory? This situation could not be indefinitely prolonged; and yet (supposing some catastrophe did not end it for him) he was afraid to end it for himself, either by risking a return home, or by allowing Mr. Salt to refer his case to Lord Milford or Lord Cawdor, since not even Mr. Salt could foresee what view either of these noblemen would take of it. So at present it seemed as if matters must go on as they were; though uneasy, Martin was not unhappy here, and his father was still begging him to remain.

No, he was not unhappy, and the country which he had begun by disliking, with its wide treeless spaces, its extraordinary natural fastnesses of crag rearing themselves up, not only on the hill-tops but quite suddenly out of field or marsh, he now saw with different eyes. And though he hardly shared Mr. Salt's passion for the past history of Pembrokeshire he did find its sharp division into a "Welshery" and an "Englishry" of interest. For St. David's was as Welsh as any Welsh shire; but Haverfordwest and the country round and beyond it —"Little England beyond Wales"—as English as his own Northamptonshire.

He walked on now, looking down at a wall of cliff intersected with columns of that purplish stone which rain or the receding tide left nearly as red as blood, and was almost within sight of Porthclais, the miniature harbour of St. David's, when he became aware of a seated female figure with its head bent. This figure was clad in something blue —a blue sufficiently resembling that of the thousands of little scabious which used to deck the cliffs in July for him to have the thought, "There is a flower in bloom here after all!" For he recognised the wearer of this blue redingote, or thought he did; and he must always feel a peculiar tenderness for little Miss Meredith. He wondered what she was doing, sitting there so still and absorbed.

As he came nearer he saw; she was evidently making a sketch in water-colours of the coast away towards Solva, its headlands and little islands. Then she heard approaching feet, looked up and recognised him.

"Oh, Mr. Tyr-Towers! Pray don't look —'tis very ill done indeed!" And she laid her production down upon the grass.

"I will certainly not look if you do not wish it," returned Martin smiling. "But I am not Sir Joshua, you know, Miss Meredith, that you need fear my opinion. I was not aware that you painted."

"My attempts hardly deserve that title," said Nest seriously; and added with apparent inconsequence, "but it is such a fine day!"

Martin looked at her, still smiling. He had never before seen her bareheaded in the sunshine, and had not therefore guessed how much gold lurked in the brown of her curls. She had a darling little head . . . and he wished that she would not put her bonnet on again, as some instinct was apparently moving her to do, for she had reached out a hand to it where it lay on the turf by her side.

"Don't —" began the young man; and then, thinking better of it, changed his protest into a query. "Don't you ever bring your dog Bran out with you now, Miss Meredith?"

There was a moment's pause, while the bonnet strings were tied. "He would not lie still while I drew," replied Bran's mistress. "And besides," she added after a further second or two, "I do not like to take him anywhere near Bowen's Folly, in case he should see you and either attack you again or . . . or behave as he did that day after dinner. Papa thought that so odd, and it was difficult to explain."

For perhaps the first time Martin was visited by a stab of remorse on account of Nausicaa, obliged to invent excuses, to resort to shifts, perhaps even to lie outright on his behalf. "May I interrupt your sketching for a moment?" he asked and, without waiting for the permission which would certainly not have been refused, sat down by the little heap of stones upon which she had perched herself.

"I am afraid, Miss Meredith," he began gravely, "that your extraordinary-your really heroic kindness to me has often placed you in somewhat difficult situations at home. I cannot say how much I deplore it. I had already been thinking," he went on, plucking at a tuft of grass, "that the time has come for me to consider some means of removing myself from this neighbourhood; and if my remaining is likely to cause you more of this particular kind of distress it is certainly what I ought to do."

There was at any rate no doubt of the distress in the eyes which Miss Meredith turned upon him at that. "Oh, no, Mr. Tyrrell! No, you must not go away-for that reason! It would be wrong, very wrong. Think of your poor father! I . . . have to be a little careful in what I say, that is all. Pray, *pray* do not think of going away upon my account!"

"I believe that I ought to go," repeated Martin.

"Then you throw away all that . . . all that Mr. Salt and I have arranged for you!" And Martin almost believed that she turned away her head because the tears were coming into her eyes.

"That is true," he said slowly. "And I would not wish to do that."

"Why should you suddenly speak of the necessity of going-unless your circumstances are changed for the better?" she questioned, and having taken up her sketch was now holding it upside down upon her knee. "You are now settled and accepted here, sir; nobody thinks you anything else than what, in fact, you are —a graduate of the University of Oxford who is assisting Mr. Salt in his literary work. If you were only pretending to be that it might be different; for it would be possible, perhaps, to trip you up in some way; but you know that even Papa, who was at Oxford too, must accept you for what you say you are-because you *are* that!"

"And, in Dr. Meredith's case, I am sorry to say, something else as well," commented Martin in a rueful tone.

"He will forget about that incident in time," said Nest consolingly. "And as he has never had the slightest reason to connect you with the man in the ruins, why should he suddenly do so now? I really do not anticipate any more difficulties of that sort. Pray promise me, Mr. Tyrrell-no, I must not call you that-pray promise me that you will not leave Bowen's Folly upon my account!"

"As things are at present, then, I promise," replied Martin, and not too unwillingly. "Nevertheless you are over-generous, Miss Meredith." And then, feeling a desire to turn the talk into a lighter channel, more suitable to the day and to the extremely pretty picture which his Nausicaa made, sitting there, he said, "Be more generous still, and allow me to see your sketch, for even as you are now holding it, it looks charming."

Nest righted her effort and held it for his inspection. Alas, as one who himself drew a little, Martin could not truthfully say either that the perspective was irreproachable or the colour remarkable for the method of its application. But, after all, it is not everyone who can depict the sea convincingly . . . "I think, Miss Meredith, that you ——" he was beginning, not quite sure even then to what extent he was about to perjure himself, when a man's voice suddenly said, "Good afternoon, Miss Meredith!" Both, startled, looked up and beheld before them, in the act of raising his hat, a young gentleman who must have approached from the direction of Porthclais.

"Oh, good afternoon, Mr. Perrot," returned Miss Meredith, the ready colour tingeing her face. "I did not see you coming."

"Evidently not," remarked Mr. Perrot in a tone not devoid of significance, and he looked at Martin, who got up from the turf in a leisurely manner. And as Nest, a little flurried, also got up, nearly dropping her sketch and completely dropping two brushes which had secreted themselves in her lap, he added stiffly, "I think I have not the pleasure of this gentleman's acquaintance?"

Martin, picking up the brushes, heard Miss Meredith say, "This is Mr. T . . . Towers, from Oxford, who is helping Mr. Salt of Bowen's Folly with his literary work. He was kindly going to criticise my drawing for me. Mr. Perrot-Mr. Towers."

The young men bowed to each other in a reserved manner. "So you studied drawing also, at Oxford, sir?" inquired Mr. Perrot. "That, I think, must be something new in the curriculum of the University."

"It certainly would be, did it form part of it," replied Martin coldly. "No, I have no real qualifications, I fear, as a critic of art. Are these all the brushes you were using, Miss Meredith?"

"I think the rest are in my paintbox," answered the artist.

"Then," said Mr. Perrot, "if you will allow me I will escort you back to the Precentory for dinner, of which Dr. Meredith has been kind enough to ask me to partake. It was he who told me that I should find you here, though he did not tell me that you were receiving . . . instruction in your art."

"Naturally not," returned Nest Meredith with a spirit which Martin would not have expected in her. "How should Papa know that Mr. Towers would be walking this way? I hope that we shall soon see you at the Precentory again, sir," she finished, offering Martin her hand, "I should like to show you my sketch when it is finished."

And thus, not without the honours of war, she went away with her escort on the path which led landwards above the inlet of Porthclais. Half amused, half annoyed, Martin strolled further and looked down from the verge into that little fairy harbour of Nature's making, all save the green, half-breached breakwater which human hands had set and reset-even, it was said, from Roman times-to guard its narrow entrance, and which seemed now as much of natural growth as the rocks on which it had been reared and the verdure-clad wall of rock towards which it stretched. . . . Who was this Mr. Perrot? Martin had by now imbibed enough of Pembrokeshire history from Mr. Salt to know that the name was one of the most famous in the county, though the direct line had died out, and the old seat at Haroldston was fallen into decay. Was he a suitor for Miss Meredith's hand? It looked like it, and it was quite probable that the Precentor approved of his suit. Did Miss Meredith?

(4)

It is safe to assert that Nest Meredith remembered every detail of her interrupted interview with Martin Tyrrell on the cliffs-everything at least which *he* had done or said in that short space of time; particularly how he had "so nobly," as she put it to herself, offered to go away to spare her further embarrassment.

Less vivid were her remembrances of her walk home with Mr. Perrot, though she was aware that that young gentleman had asked who "that fellow up there was," to which she had replied, repressively, for her, that she had already told him; so that before they reached the Precentory, Mr. Perrot had got it into his head that she was vexed at having been taken away from "that fellow's" society, which, though it was true, Nest was too sweet-tempered ever to have let him see if he had not made some slightly disparaging remarks about her late companion. That there was anything of an understanding between them (in the only sense in which Mr. Perrot conceived such a thing) was to his eyes disproved by Miss Meredith's informing her father in his presence that Mr. Towers had come upon her sketching, which news the Precentor had received with equanimity, and observed that Salt must soon bring him to see them again. Of course (so reflected Mr. John Perrot as he rode homewards) she might have made this announcement merely to forestall his mentioning the fact, but it was equally certain that the Precentor had not been perturbed by it, so there was probably nothing in it. Indeed, why should there be-an unknown man named-what was it, Towers —a secretary? But their heads had been very close together over that sketch!

Before she got into bed that night Nest stood a moment, her bare feet peeping out beneath her nightdress, surveying with a critical and humble gaze the unfinished water-colour which she had propped up on the dressing-table. By candlelight it looked quite different, and did not in any way approach the standard held up by her late drawing-master at Haverfordwest, though that, indeed, she had never hoped to attain. She stood there wondering what Mr. Tyrrell had really thought of her production. Now she would probably never know, for if Mr. Salt did bring him to the house again she doubted if she would have the courage to raise the subject. There was always the possibility that he might; but no, he would probably have forgotten all about it. She sighed and, putting the sketch away, slipped into bed.

Lying there she began to think of that problematical meeting. If she had the opportunity of a few words alone with Mr. Tyrrell she would certainly assure him again that there was nothing in her situation for him to distress himself about, for it would be terrible if that idea of going away into fresh danger in order to save her embarrassment should take root in his head! Briefly reviewing any possible occasions of difficulty she could find none to presage; they were past, like reefs which a ship has avoided.

Except one-and a very crucial one! With a catch at the heart Nest sat up in bed, her curls bouncing on her shoulders. William's suit! She still had not got it back! And when Admiral Thompson's squadron, in which William was cruising off Brest, was relieved by Admiral Colpoys', which she knew, from a letter of her brother's, was due to happen some time in November, William would be given leave-at least, she hoped with all her heart that he would. She must therefore secure the return of his clothes within the next couple of weeks. How indeed could she have forgotten the necessity? And to think that, owing to Mr. Perrot's inopportune appearance this morning, she had missed the inestimable chance of discussing with Mr. Tyrrell in person the best way of solving the slight but teasing problem of the method of their return! Well, she must give her mind to it to-morrow.

The result of this operation was that next day she suggested to her father that, if he had any intention of soon asking the two gentlemen from Bowen's Folly to the house, he should add them to the small evening gathering which he and Aunt Pennefather were planning for next week; and, the Precentor declaring that this was an excellent notion, its originator resolved that she would meanwhile write to Mr. Salt and ask him, if he accepted the invitation, to arrange that Mr. "Towers" should once more convey the fateful parcel with him to the Precentory on that evening, and she would somehow arrange for its discreet reception. It had occurred to her that the more people who were coming the easier this reception might be. Later in the day, finding that the invitation had already gone, she decided that the best way of despatching her note to the Folly was to take it herself.

As sometimes after a very fine day in autumn this day was wet and windy. Nest waited until the rain had quite ceased, which it did about two o'clock; then, sitting down at the little escritoire in her bedroom under the sampler, her own childish handiwork, wherein the ranked letters of the alphabet preceded an adjuration in cross-stitch to "Remember now thy Creator in the Days of thy Youth!" she wrote her request to Mr. Salt, and sealed the note with the cornelian seal which her father had given her on her eighteenth birthday. Afterwards she sat looking at the impression on the wax —a dove flying with a letter suspended from its beak-and the half-thought came to her of the convenience it would be if William's troublesome garments could be conveyed to her by some such aerial messenger, arriving in just the best way possible, through her window. Then, armed with an umbrella, and with Bran-lest the purpose of her sally on such an unpropitious afternoon should be questioned by Papa or by her aunt, she went forth. Neither of these authorities, apparently, saw her go, and once out of the gate she called the disillusioned Bran to her and put him on a leash.

Before she reached Bowen's Folly she had decided to ask if Mr. Salt could see her for a moment. It would so greatly simplify matters if she could know at once that the arrangement which she proposed could be carried out. But alas, Mrs. Morris, arriving at the door like a second Atalanta, told her that both gentlemen were out, having started for a walk even before the rain had stopped. This was unexpected and disappointing-for more than one reason. In a sense, it seemed foolish not to be able to ask Mrs. Morris to give her the parcel, no doubt still in readiness, and to take it home herself and be done with it, but she dared not touch on the matter with a woman whom she fancied Mr. Tyrrell did not trust, and who might know a little too much already. So she gave her the note for her master, Mrs. Morris peering in a sidelong way at Bran, who, seeing a cat cross the hall, made an instant and whole-hearted effort to do the same.

"*Yr anwyl fo'n gwarchod!*" exclaimed Mrs. Morris, appealing to heaven to protect her. "Oh, Miss, 'ouldn't that dog of yours be nasty tempered if he wass loose! I declare he 'ould be biting someone!"

Nest loyally replied that Bran was the best-tempered dog upon earth, though he did enjoy chasing cats; but as she walked away she wondered how much the housekeeper knew, and what exactly she had meant by that remark?

It had begun to rain again, and Bran, excited by his glimpse of a forbidden delight, displayed unwonted indocility, so that between his assaults upon the leash, and those of the wind upon her umbrella, Nest, by the time she arrived home, was a little breathless. There was luckily no one in the hall to ask her where she had been, and she was glad to cast herself down for a moment on the settle in the corner.

But almost at once she jumped up again. What could it be that she was sitting upon-something exceedingly hard, concealed under what she had taken in the gloom to be a rug of some kind lying on the settle? Upon one portion of it, which hung down towards the chequered black and red stonework of the floor, there gleamed, as she now saw, a strip of something bright and golden ... A sudden suspicion, at once joyful and stupefying, seized Nest; she flung aside the rug which had become an overcoat, and pulled out from beneath it a long scabbarded object not unfamiliar to her-her brother's sword. William had come home before he was expected!

(5)

Nest stood a moment staring at the weapon in her hand, and then was aware of flying feet and Mary's excited voice: —"Oh, Miss Nest, Miss Nest, the lieutenant's come home-Mr. William is back-he's in the library with — —"

"No, he is not-he's here!" exclaimed a young, cheerful and rather loud voice. "Nest, my little darling, how are you?" Before she could speak Nest was in those uniformed arms, receiving and giving fervent kisses; then, amid the ecstatic yelping and leaping of Bran, she was lifted off her feet and, greatly to the admiration of Mary, carried bodily to the threshold of the library, in whose open doorway Aunt Pennefather was standing with clasped hands and a rapt, creative smile ("The Sailor's Return," Verses by Camilla) and there set down, laughing and remonstrating. "What a little heroine it is, braving the weather on a day like this! I declare, Nest, that you shall be made captain of a sloop! . . . I found her in the hall, sir," continued Lieutenant Meredith, addressing his father, "holding my sword as if she had never seen it before!"

"I sat down upon it . . . that was how I knew you must be here," murmured Nest, half crying, and clinging very closely to her brother. "Oh, William, how sorry I am that I was not at home when you arrived! How long have you been here . . . and why have you returned so much sooner than we expected?"

"Because the *Serapis* started a plank, and as the weather has not been very propitious-no joke, my little sister, cruising about day and night upon an enemy coast with no port to put into-she was sent back to Lord Bridport's squadron at Spithead, and he gave all the officers ten days' leave, which you may guess I was not slow to take advantage of. I have only been here a few minutes-arrived by the Haverford coach. So you sat down upon my sword out there, did you, Nesta-deuced hard it was, no doubt! Gad, it will be something of a relief to exchange this uniform with all its appendages for something more comfortable."

"But I like to see you in uniform, my boy," protested the Precentor, looking upon him with fond pride.

"So do I," chimed in Nest, quite truthfully, but with a horrid sensation of deceitfulness nevertheless. "Are you not going to wear it for a day or two at least, to please us and St. David's?"

"I'll undertake to wear it on Sunday," quoth William, "but I won't promise anything more. Come now, I want to hear all the news. How does Jane, and the infant of which I hear I am the uncle?" And sitting down he pulled his sister upon his knee.

Yet, through all the eager talk which followed, Nest's brain was working hard, though she lost scarcely a word which fell from William's lips. And when the conference at last broke up, she had made up her mind what to do. If her brother should at once miss his bottle-green suit-which was possible, though she believed it was neither his newest nor his only civilian one-she would say that she had taken it away for a slight repair which she had not yet completed, but that he should have it back to-morrow. Meanwhile she would take immediate and frenzied steps to get the said suit into her possession again that evening. These involved scribbling a second note to Mr. Salt, slipping out secretly into the garden, finding the gardener's boy, taking him from his task of sweeping up fallen leaves (which labour he was performing at the rate of about two leaves a minute, and left with the utmost alacrity) and despatching him at once up to Bowen's Folly. Since it was probable that Mr. Salt had not yet returned home she could not safely instruct her messenger to wait for the parcel. Her letter, after apprising Mr. Salt of William's return, said: "I think it would be best if you could contrive to have the clothes sent to the Precentory this evening, directly it is dark, and placed somewhere just outside the porch where no person entering would be likely to see them, but where I could easily find them if I slipped out unobserved. I am still afraid to have them handed in at the door to Dixon or one of the maidservants."

In that regard, indeed, the position was still unchanged, except perhaps slightly for the worse. Nest's present plan, though open to several objections, yet seemed to her the best she could devise. No doubt Mr. Tyrrell himself would bring the parcel, and would place it in a suitable spot; but she dare not attempt to see him. She did not volunteer to William the explanation which she had decided upon, because it was just as likely that he would not make his discovery yet awhile.

But he did make it, and a further one too, which Nest had not anticipated. For she had not long been back in her own room after her expedition to the garden when there was a knock, and her brother's head was put in.

"Nest, you little sinner, where's that green suit of mine-not that you can answer that question with any degree of accuracy *now*, I fear!"

Nest's heart jumped. But she brought out her lie quite naturally. "Oh, yes, William, I can. I took it out of your room a few days ago —a buttonhole needed repairing; you shall have — —"

"That's all right," returned William with an air of relief. "But when I asked Mary just now what had become of it, she said she thought you had given it away to a tramp in the summer; and as I was intending to wear it I am glad to hear that she was mistaken."

"Yes," said Nest, turning away to hide the flush which she could feel upon her cheeks, "Mary was mistaken. I will try to let you have the suit to-morrow. You do not specially wish to wear it this evening, do you, William, particularly as Papa likes to see you in uniform?"

"No, no," returned Lieutenant Meredith, easily. "Spend as long as you like caulking the buttonhole, kind sister. I only wondered where the suit had gone to." He made for the door, and then a thought appeared to strike him. "What suit *did* you give the tramp, then? I have not missed any other."

"It was not a complete suit," replied Nest rather desperately. "Just some odds and ends which I thought you did not require any more. Mary did not see what was in the parcel."

"Well, child, I am not accusing you of a crime!" protested her brother, "Though I admit I should have thought a tramp too well dressed in my bottle-green. Carry on!" He waved his hand and shut the door behind him.

Nest sat down on the nearest chair and pressed her hands to her hot face. How dreadful, dreadful this was! She had been brought up to regard lying with great horror and the ultimate destination of liars as a certainty. Two direct lies in the space of a minute, since one lie had not sufficed! How could she say her prayers to-night? The only chance of condonation lay in a possibility that God would regard with a little leniency lies told for the safety of someone else, but she did not feel at all sure about this, especially as the lies tended to shield herself too. Nevertheless they *were*, fundamentally, for Mr. Tyrrell's sake, lest somehow too searching enquiries about that unlucky suit of clothes should lead to the discovery of the "tramp's" identity. Yet in any case, the Bible nowhere *said* that you might tell a lie for the sake of another person; she could not remember the smallest fragment of a text to that effect. And, looking at her large Bible where it lay upon the table by her bed, she felt unworthy even to open it. . . . Perhaps some day, when Mr. Tyrrell was pardoned and reinstated, she would be able to confess all her deceit, and Papa would say a prayer over her, and she would no longer feel as though in the next thunderstorm the lightning would search her out. . . .

Half an hour later, darting in once more through the hall door after a hasty but fruitless search round the porch in the darkness-the wet darkness-which had now fallen, she ran into her brother's arms.

"Here, my female sloop-captain, that's not the rig to go confronting the weather in!" he exclaimed, laying hold of her thin jacconet dress. " 'Tis raining, child! What on earth were you doing out there? —and supper just coming upon the table!" For that repast had been considerably advanced, upon his account.

"I . . . I only looked out for a moment," faltered Nest, "and then I found that it was raining . . ."

"Come along, come along!" admonished the Precentor jovially, appearing at the foot of the stairs. "Our mariner is hungry, and we must dispense with formality. Where is your aunt, Nest? —ah, here she is! You have brought up the port from the far bin, Dixon-that is right."

And a moment later he was launching into the Latin grace which he reserved for special occasions.

At intervals during the meal, while William, doing ample justice to roast leveret and damson pudding, talked cheerfully of his maritime experiences, Nest could forget the worrying fact that the parcel had not yet been placed outside the front door, and cease for a few minutes to wonder whether it was now on its way thither, whether it was going to be sent at all (since she had received no assurance to that effect), or, thirdly, whether it had already been sent, but removed again by some person unknown. How horrid it was to have these speculations going on in her head when she wanted to listen intently to every word that William was saying!

"No, the first squadron is commanded by Rear-Admiral Sir Roger Curtis in the *Formidable* ," he was now replying between two mouthfuls. "But, as I think you know, sir, the bulk of any of the three squadrons is usually at Spithead, while only eight or nine ships cruise about, keeping an eye upon the enemy-the cat watching the mouse-hole. —Aunt Gwenllian, your bottled damsons are better, I declare, than fresh!" And a moment after, in reply to another question, she heard: "But, sir, the destination of the French fleet preparing at Brest is just what we don't know —I wish we did! Ireland, Portugal, or Gibraltar-it might be any or none of these, but the best authorities think Gibraltar the most probable object of attack. Anyhow, we poor sailors have to be prepared for anything when the French do come out."

"Ireland," said his father reflectively, "Ireland is in a highly disaffected condition since the recall of Lord Fitzwilliam, and there are rumours that those scoundrelly United Irishmen, as they call themselves, have invited French intervention. A most dastardly and treasonable act! If the French should be so daring and so misguided as to comply, I presume they would make for the North of Ireland, where, as I gather, the discontent is most rife."

"Wherever they make for," announced William cheerfully, "I'll engage they never get there! We shall —I hope-sink 'em all first!"

"Provided, dear William, that they do not evade you on the way," observed Aunt Pennefather, with more attention to the subject in hand than she usually displayed.

"Exactly," agreed Dr. Meredith. "But we must not insult our glorious tars by suggesting that their watchfulness is not all-embracing!"

"All the same," observed his son thoughtfully, " 'tis a deuced wide area to keep a watch upon."

Mrs. Pennefather was so full of William and his doings when she and Nest left the two gentlemen to their port, that Nest could not break away from her before going up to the drawing-room, as she had intended, and search once more for the missing parcel outside. And Aunt Gwenllian continued to be equally talkative even when they had sat down in that apartment; but no doubt in a few moments the chance would come; if not she would break into the conversation by pretending that she had dropped her handkerchief downstairs. How hot and uncomfortable that reference at dinner to the United Irishmen had made her!

"Aunt," she said at last, getting up, "I think I ———" And there she stopped, for she heard her father's step outside the door. He and William had finished their wine much sooner than she had anticipated-very much sooner.

"William is just coming," announced the Precentor, entering. He was in a mellow and proudly paternal mood. "The boy is just taking a turn outside to see what the weather is like —a true sailor! I went to the door with him and observed that the rain had stopped, but it was a little too damp without for my fancy." Sitting down by Nest, he pinched her cheek. "Well, my dear child? You look a thought pensive. Surely this should not be on the night when we have our William amongst us again!"

"Oh no, Papa, I am not pensive," replied Nest, trying to rouse herself from an alarmed vision of what William might possibly be discovering outside the front door. (But no, he would have no reason to search the ground; he would be looking at the heavens, observing the direction of the wind. . . .) "Are there any stars out, Papa?"

"I do not think so, my dear; and as I say, it is still very damp."

"To steer by the stars!" observed Mrs. Pennefather suddenly, dropping her fancy-work, "what a poetical idea! And to think that our dear William——"

"I fancy that he steers by the less poetical compass and sextant," said her brother, smiling. "However, the first mariners——"

The door opened. "I say, look what I have just found outside the porch!" exclaimed dear William, coming in. And he held up a largish parcel. "It was leaning against the wall of the house by the old vine. 'Tis fairly heavy, and has no name or direction upon it. Shall I open it and see what it is?"

Oh, William, William, if you had not been such a true sailor . . . if I had not tried to get it back . . . if I had never given it away! But she must do something, *something*, quickly! Actually scarce aware of what she was doing, his sister had given a little cry and had come forward. "Oh, William, I am afraid that it must be that green suit of yours-and it will be so wet! Let me take it and have it dried!"

"Yes, but, dash it all!" protested William, "how did my green suit come to be outside the front door in the rain?" Hearing of the identity of the contents of the parcel, he was already tearing off the sodden paper. Sure enough, green cloth, darkened with wet, came into view.

"Dear me," said his father, coming to look, "this is highly mysterious!"

"It is all my carelessness, I am afraid," declared Nest, inspired by desperation. "I placed the suit on my window-seat—I told you, William, that I had taken it to repair-somebody must have opened the window, and it blew down into the garden. . . . Oh dear, it *is* wet!"

"Somebody threw it down, more likely," corrected William, examining his damp apparel with a certain rueful curiosity. "There is certainly not enough wind to-day to blow a heavyish parcel round the house and prop it up by the front door!"

"It must have been found by someone, John Parry, perhaps, before it began to rain, and placed where you found it," hazarded Nest. "I am so sorry about it, William! Give it to me, and I will have it set to dry at once." And, gathering up the suit, she fled from the room, feeling sure, from the very promptitude with which this explanation-preposterous though it might be-had come to her, that the Father of Lies was now her sworn associate, and that she would be delivered over to him for ever!

William teased her, of course, on her return, about her ideas of meteorology, about the force and direction of a non-existent wind which must, nevertheless, have had the characteristics of a typhoon if it could suck up a fairly weighty packet from a seat below the level of the window and whirl it round to the other side of the house. And a casual remark on the secure manner in which the suit had been wrapped and tied up having elicited a faint rejoinder from his sister about moths, he laughed at her again, and said that her precautions rather suggested fear of rats or white ants. But the subject was sooner dropped than Nest had dared to hope, again no doubt through the good offices of the Evil One, now enlisted on her side, and the rest of the evening passed without a cloud, save for that upon Nest's own conscience.

Next day, in some attempt to placate this troublesome mentor, she laboriously unpicked a buttonhole of the green suit and buttonholed it up again-deception to salve deception-and was immensely relieved to find a genuine little rent in the lining of one of the pockets. This she mended, and then unobtrusively replaced the suit in one of her brother's drawers.

(6)

The proposed entertainment at the Precentory being a somewhat staid affair, it was decided to postpone it until William's short leave was over. Nest was immensely relieved, for she felt it much better that the true owner of the bottle-green suit and its latest wearer should not meet. But on the second morning of his stay her brother announced his intention of paying a call upon "old Salt," and asked his sister if she would care to accompany him. In vain Nest attempted to dissuade William from the visit, suggesting that Mr. Salt would be busy with his literary work in the forenoon. But William replied that the old fellow would realise that a sailor's leave was short, and that Salt himself could sail a cutter-rig as well as any man he knew, the bearing of which argument was a little hard to follow, though it evidently appeared to William to justify a morning call. In the end Nest decided to go with him, because, as she told herself, she might thereby be able to exercise some small control upon the conversation if William showed signs of directing it into dangerous channels. If there were another reason, too, she did not acknowledge it.

They were admitted by the smiling Mrs. Morris, full of "So you are home again, sir . . . and looking so well, I declare!" ("She'll tell me in a minute that I have grown!" growled William in Nest's ear.) But brother and sister found themselves entering a room which contained only Martin Tyrrell, rising from a writing-table near the window. The big table in the centre was unoccupied.

Mr. "Towers" came forward, looking faintly surprised. "Good morning, Miss Meredith. Mr. Salt has only gone into the garden, I think; I will fetch him."

"Introduce me first, Nest," said William; and when his sister had murmured some words of presentation the young sailor observed: "Don't be in too much of a hurry, pray, Mr. Towers; tell us first how you get on with old Jerome? I suppose that when he is annoyed with you-for we all know that he has a queer temper-he throws one of these deuced great books of his at your head instead of a marlinspike?"

"I do not know why you should fancy that Mr. Towers needs to have anything thrown at him," interposed Nest, half laughing, "neither books nor marlinspikes, whatever they may be."

"Mr. Salt has not thrown even a duodecimo at me," said Martin, smiling, and thinking that the young lady in her soft green winter tippet with the brown beaver edging looked very charming, sitting there against a background of the "deuced great books." "He is a very kind employer."

The young naval officer was meanwhile strolling about the room. "Don't you find this an odd corner of the world to fetch up in, sir?" he suddenly enquired. "I mean, after the University, and so forth?"

"I find the people of these parts exceedingly hospitable to a stranger," replied Martin. Something about William Meredith made him fear that in another moment he would ask him outright what had brought him to Bowen's Folly, so he hastened to add: "I think that I had better go and find Mr. Salt, for he will wish to know that you are here." As he unfastened the long window and stepped out on to the windblown terrace it occurred to him to wish, for quite another reason, that Miss Meredith were not accompanied by her brother. Had she been alone he would not, he thought, have troubled about finding Mr. Salt just yet awhile.

Meanwhile William continued to wander round the room and to justify Martin's apprehension by saying: "This Towers is a younger fellow than I had imagined. I wonder what made him take employment with Salt; I should really like to know."

"But you cannot possibly ask him that, William," said Nest reprovingly. "Sit down, you restless creature! —No, you really must not examine Mr. Towers' writing-table!"

"Why, he is only copying out some of old Jerome's boring stuff, I'll be bound!" replied William, glancing from a distance at the sheets upon the table. But to Nest's relief (for she thought it just possible that Mr. Tyrrell might have been writing some compromising letter) he did not approach to verify this conjecture, and at that moment Martin himself returned,

121

announcing that he could not find Mr. Salt anywhere in the garden, and thought that, as it was a windy day, he might have gone for a walk along the cliffs. Perhaps Miss Meredith and her brother might care to follow on the chance of overtaking him?

"In a moment, sir," replied the latter. "Do you know if Mr. Salt has a copy of Dampier's *Voyage Round the World* ? I should like to consult it, if I may?"

Martin went to a shelf. "It would be there, sir, if he possessed it, but I am pretty certain that he does not. No; but here is Dampier's *Discourse of Winds* , though I suppose that will not serve your purpose?"

"*Discourse of Piracy* would be more to the point, since that was really the old fellow's calling," returned William. "No, thanks, I do not want it. I wonder Mr. Salt admits him to his shelves."

"Why not? Mr. Salt is not, so far as I have found, squeamish."

"No, that he is not," confessed the sailor. "But, as I have heard him give vent to the absurd opinion that privateering is only a form of piracy, I imagine that he must have a bee in his bonnet on the subject of piracy. . . . By the way, I hear that there was a Liverpool privateer put into Ramsey Sound this summer for water. What did Salt say to that?"

"I do not know. I was not in his employment then. But I have heard," added Martin, "that it was a prize which put in, not the privateer herself."

"I believe you are right. And did not the crew desert or something of the sort? Perhaps," suggested William, with a laugh, "old Salt had incited them to do so?"

"One man deserted, I believe," answered Martin steadily, replacing the *Discourse of Winds* on the shelf, while almost at the same moment Nest's voice, somewhat hurried, was heard from behind: "Ought we not to be going, William, if we wish to overtake Mr. Salt?" She had risen from her chair.

"We are more like to meet him returning, I should think," said her brother, and with that went to the window. Here he surveyed the weather for a second or two. "It looks uncommon boisterous out there for a lady, Nest, and as you can't, I suppose, take any reefs in that fur-trimmed affair of yours, you may find you are carrying too much sail for comfort. I think you had better stay here, and I will pick you up when I put in again. I shall probably fall in with Salt almost at once."

"Very well," agreed his sister, sitting down again. "It . . . does appear to be windy out there."

So William, cramming his hat upon his head, put out from harbour leaving his consort behind.

"I was a little afraid that my brother would get on to some uncomfortable subject or other," said Nest after a moment, sighing. "To tell the truth, I did not want him to come here at all. But you answered his questions about the privateer and the deserter with such wonderful readiness, Mr. Towers!"

"If my guilty eyes can survive the sight of that green coat upon its rightful owner, Miss Meredith," returned Martin gaily, "my tongue ought to be able to make response to an awkward remark or so. But tell me, did you have trouble the other night over its restitution-did you find the parcel easily? I obeyed your instructions to the letter."

Nest cast down her eyes. "The matter was a little difficult," she admitted, "because unfortunately it was not I, but William himself, who found it, and I . . . I had to invent some lame explanation of its being in such a place at that time, and . . . and I have a horror of lies," she added rather pitifully.

"You poor little thing!" was on Martin's lips; it nearly came out. He sat down by her. "Dear Miss Meredith, then you have made yet another sacrifice for my sake! How can I ever repay it? I cannot, I see that! I have involved the innocent in deceit; believe me, that is the heaviest weight yet upon my conscience! Would you prefer me to ——"

"I do not wish you to do anything," said Nest, without waiting to hear what he might be going to propose. "It does not matter . . . I hope you have good news of your father?"

"Thank you, I have good news; at least, my father keeps well, which is the best news I can hope for. And I hear from him that my sister Lucy, who expects to be a mother by Christmas, is well too, and happy in the prospect. Yet she expresses wonder, my father says, that I do not write to her-for he has succeeded in keeping from her the fact that I never returned home after my visit to Ireland."

"And your brother-in-law?"

"He is back at Ballydare," answered Martin, "that is all I know. I only trust that he has broken for good and all with the United Irishmen, but as my sister was keeping his connection with them a secret from my father (even as he is keeping my misfortune a secret from her) there is nothing to tell me whether that is so."

"It has often been in my mind lately-though I dare say the notion is but foolish," said Nest, with some hesitation, "that it is, after all, within your power to clear yourself without much difficulty of the false charge against you. For that, have you not merely to explain the real reason of your journey to Hamburg, and of your interview with Lord Edward Fitzgerald and the other man-to say that you only undertook the journey in order to dissuade ——" She stopped, for her hearer was shaking his head with a smile.

"Dear Miss Meredith, I cannot do that without revealing my brother-in-law's connection with them, which may, for aught I know, be continuing still, and without calling my sister as a witness-as the sole witness, in fact-of my purpose in going to Hamburg. Unless I were absolutely driven to it I could not do such a thing-especially at this time. The distress of it might kill her."

"Yes, I see," said Nest. Her eyes shone. Mrs. Lucy Roche was a person to be envied, the object of a brotherly love so unselfish. "Yet if your sister knew your plight, she would surely choose that you should clear yourself, even at her expense!"

"If it were really at her expense, yes, I am certain that she would. But you see, Miss Meredith, it would at bottom be at her husband's . . . and she loves him. Besides, you know, one has one's pride. In her extremity Lucy appealed to me to assist her. I failed, chiefly, I fear, through my own fault; but at least I need not, from a would-be helper, make myself a means of actual injury! 'Tis bad enough to be a broken reed, but at least you need not pierce the hand which has grasped you!"

But, seeing an admiration which he could hardly misread in his hearer's eyes, he added, with a touch of shame-facedness lest she should think him more heroic than he was: "If I were in the dock I should be obliged to have recourse to Lucy's evidence, but as long as I can keep out of that place I will not do so."

And Nest concurred. "The dock"—how awful that sounded. Presently she said:

"I am sure that you must be longing to be home again!"

"I am-and yet I am not," answered Martin; and Nest's heart moved like a bird in her breast as he thus qualified his assent. "Think, Miss Meredith, how much Welsh history I am acquiring! I know all about your namesake, Princess Nesta, now."

"But you will forget it all when you go away," prophesied the present Nesta rather sadly.

"Yes, most of it, no doubt. But the story of Gerald de Windsor's wife I shall always remember, and that more tragic tale, too, of poor Nest of Kidwelly. . . . I think you can probably guess why, Miss Meredith?"

He looked at her with the smile which she always found so attractive. The riddle was not indeed very difficult to guess, but Miss Meredith, as became a modest young lady, must make shift to pretend to find it insoluble at first sight. And before she could with propriety admit to some faint notion of the correct answer, Mr. Salt-alas, too soon encountered! —was opening the glass door with William behind him, and the brief *tête-à-tête* was over.

(7)

With William's return, a few days later, to Spithead and the *Serapis* the autumn seemed to settle down with its face towards winter, and one day slid past much like another, both for Nest Meredith at the Precentory and for Martin Tyrrell up at Bowen's Folly. There were times, it is true, when Martin felt that it must end in his giving himself up and facing a trial. But there was another obstacle in the way of his attempting to clear himself besides that which he had mentioned to Miss Meredith; the fact that she also would undoubtedly be brought into the business. How could he drag that gentle child into court to be questioned, to hear titters and innuendoes? Even if her personal testimony were not required her name would recur over and over again in the evidence, on account of her connection with his present employment. All St. David's would hear what she had done for him, and draw the same conclusions. No, he must go on living with Mr. Salt and all his Llewelyns and Rhyses, and with Gerald the Welshman. For the translation of de Barri's *Itinerary* being now concluded, Mr. Salt had started work upon the same writer's *Description of Wales*.

So the weeks drew on towards Christmas-an anxious time for England. She was almost alone in Europe, for Spain had declared war against her in October; and since Naples had come to terms with France, the British fleet was compelled in November to withdraw from the Mediterranean. Austria, her only effective remaining ally, was nearly exhausted. Invasion was daily expected, and the militia was greatly augmented in consequence. Once more Pitt made overtures for peace, to include England's allies, offering to restore all her French conquests if France would return the Austrian Netherlands to the Emperor; but he had his terms flung back in his face, and Lord Malmesbury, the British Envoy, was ordered, on December 19th, to leave Paris within twenty-four hours. Indeed the darkest days of all were not far off, when Austria should make peace without her ally, the Bank of England be obliged to suspend cash payments, and British sailors be driven by their grievances to mutiny when a Dutch fleet was preparing to descend upon their native country.

But those black hours did not come until the spring. And meanwhile there was plenty of corn in Western Pembrokeshire-Dewisland had always been a granary-and St. David's was remote from war's alarms. Martin, though he ached to be fighting the French in any capacity, was aware that his country would not accept the sword of an alleged traitor, and had to resign himself to military inactivity-though not to social. He had by now several acquaintances, both young and old, in the little Cathedral city-or village, for it was no more-and was occasionally invited to certain mild festivities; but for the larger gatherings the place was Haverfordwest, sixteen miles away, where the county families had their town houses and whither they repaired in the winter season for balls; but these Mr. Salt's secretary naturally did not attend.

By now he was familiar, too, with the fabric of the partly ruined Cathedral and on terms of salutation at least with the rest of its dignitaries —a depleted band-with the Treasurer and Chancellor and canons and vicars choral as well as with the Precentor. From the tedious Dr. Jenkins he had more than once suffered, as Mr. Salt had predicted, but the feeling which he had had from the first for old Dr. Vaughan had led from acquaintance to something like friendship. It was from that frail old man that he learnt most of the history of the Cathedral and as much as was to be known of the almost legendary saint whose name (with that of St. Andrew) it bore, whose relics it had once sheltered, and whose empty shrine it still contained. Sometimes Martin almost fancied himself a mediæval outlaw who had taken sanctuary there, "in the house of thy servant David," as Dr. Vaughan was fond of calling it. It was a pleasure to the old man to attempt (though he never succeeded) to trace kinship with Bishop Edward Vaughan, who had built the beautiful little chapel, with fan-traceried roof, behind the high altar. To Martin he seemed more like a spiritual descendant of Bishop Ken and the old High Church party with its nonjuring tradition, whose temper was not unknown to him because it survived in his own father.

Although it was Mr. Salt who had first introduced Martin to the great church, he soon found that that gentleman's interest in it was one-sided; the owner of Bowen's Folly knew its history well, but had not Dr. Vaughan's loving acquaintance with its very stones. And indeed Martin was no nearer to solving the discrepancy between Mr. Salt's untiring interest in Welsh chronicles and his continually expressed dislike and distrust of the Welsh race. For his own part Martin found the dwellers in Dewisland, high and low, notably kind and courteous; so much so that he was increasingly visited by qualms about his own false position. Mrs. Morris he did indeed dislike and distrust; she constituted the one real problem of his life at Bowen's Folly. Those beady eyes of hers were always, he knew, upon him; and she displayed an almost morbid interest in his doings. It had been a source of considerable wonder to him that she had not immediately spread abroad tittle-tattle about the very unorthodox arrival and attire of her master's secretary, until he learnt from Mr. Salt that he had taken immediate and strict steps to prevent this extremely probable revelation. "I told her," he had informed Martin, "that the moment a syllable of such gossip came to my ears, as it assuredly would, she should leave my service that day. She knows that I always keep my word, and she evidently fears that any such disclosure would become known to me at once-though, between ourselves, I am not so sure that it would-and so, wishing to retain her place, she appears, *mirabile dictu*, to have kept a shut mouth, though I imagine that, as with the Psalmist, it must have been pain and grief to her."

(8)

At last came Christmas Day, with its tradition of over-eating. Martin's thoughts were much at Selham St. Peter; he wished he were back-the old man must be so sad and lonely. Soon he *would* return; his own unfortunate affair must be nearly blown over by now.

A few days after Christmas Mr. Salt, having perversely let pass the unusually fine and calm weather before the end of December, now selected for an expedition to St. David's Head a day at the tail end of the easterly gale which had raged on and off over Christmastide itself. So he and Martin, buffeted and sometimes quite breathless, examined the hut-circles scattered over the desolate plateau looked down upon by the strange grey rocky eminence of Carn Llidi, scrambled over most of the wind-beaten promontory itself, and ate the bread and cheese with which they had stuffed their pockets, crouching behind the mysterious stones of the prehistoric barrier which crossed it, Clawydd-y-Milwyr, the Warriors' Dyke. Finally they set off homewards by way of the sandy tract known as the Burrows, where some held that Menapia, the vanished Roman city, had its grave.

Martin received the impression that this (in the circumstances) strenuous expedition had been designed, he knew not wherefore, as a species of treat for him, since Mr. Salt was not really much concerned either with prehistoric or with Roman remains; his interests lay later. He liked to tell the young man how the peregrine falcons which bred on Ramsey Island and St. David's Head had always been famous, since the day when one had swooped down and killed King Henry II's Norwegian gerfalcon, after which that monarch would hawk with none but Pembrokeshire birds; and how the long sandy stretch of Porth Mawr had for centuries been the traditional landing-place from Ireland; on a clear summer's day, indeed, the mountains of Wicklow could be discerned from the summit of Carn Llidi. But there was not much of a summer's day about the picture which Martin carried away of that wild grey sea, churned by the off-shore wind, clutching in baffled frenzy at the tumbled lichen-clad rocks at the lower end of the Head-the snout of the crocodile.

Down by the Cathedral on their return-for the shortest way to Bowen's Folly lay across the close-it was not quite so gusty. As they approached the long flight of steps leading up from its further side to the Tower gateway they saw the fragile figure of Dr. Vaughan coming down them, holding to him a wind-snatched cloak. They met about midway on the ascent, and Mr. Salt, touching his hat, would have passed on with a "Good day, sir," but that the old man laid a hand upon his arm and said in his thread of a voice, only just audible in the commotion: "I doubt if it be a good day, Mr. Salt! Have you heard the dreadful news from Ireland?"

"No," answered the historian. "Mr. Towers and I have been since ten o'clock taking the air-and in abundance-on St. David's Head. What has happened in Ireland?"

"The French have come!" answered the old man. "They have landed in Bantry Bay, thousands strong, with I know not how many ships. On Christmas Day it was. I fear that by now they have taken Cork, and that all the south of Ireland will rise!"

"Good God!" exclaimed Mr. Salt, looking very grave. As for Martin, the blood froze in his already chilled veins. "How did the news come, sir?"

"I have but just heard it from the Precentor. I think he is still under the archway with young Mr. Perrot, who brought it in a while ago from Haverfordwest or Milford. Oh, my dear sir, where was our navy, our ships in which we put such trust-more, I fear, than in the Lord of Hosts-although vain is the help of man!"

"We must not keep you standing here in the wind, sir," said Mr. Salt to that, "but go on and find Dr. Meredith or Mr. Perrot. Towers," he added in a lower voice, as they ran up the steps together, "this, depend upon it, is the doing of your Hamburg friends!" And Martin groaned.

Under the archway, than which no draughtier place could have been selected, the Precentor, holding his hat upon his head, was talking earnestly to Mr. John Perrot and an attendant group of listeners; but, almost as Martin and Mr. Salt appeared, Nest's admirer and her father parted, young Perrot hastening off towards the town, while the Precentor, propelled, it seemed, to some degree by the wind, came at a stately trot towards them.

"Meredith, Meredith!" cried Mr. Salt, raising his voice, "what is this about the French having come to Bantry Bay? Is it true?"

"Too true, too true, I fear!" shouted the Precentor. "But come into the house and I will tell you what I know. We may have more news to-night, when Dr. Thomas returns from London. Perrot's news is a day old."

"You don't mean to say that the French have actually landed in Ireland-invaded it?"

They had reached the gate of the Precentory, which Martin, who felt incapable even of asking a question, held open for his two elders, before Dr. Meredith replied: "No, thank God, it seems that they had not yet been able to land because of the easterly gale which sprang up-the weather has been very bad in the south of Ireland, apparently, even worse than here. But that their ships are in Bantry Bay in great force is indisputable. God knows what will be the outcome of it, for I believe there are hardly any troops in Cork!"

Wind and apprehension accompanied them into the house. In the study Mr. Salt enquired what the English fleet had been about. "I thought that there was a squadron specially keeping a watch upon Brest, since it was well known that the French were meditating a descent somewhere?"

The Precentor sank heavily into a chair. "Yes, there is such a squadron; my son William is in it. . . . No, the only one of His Majesty's ships which appears to have sighted this armada at all was the sloop *Kangaroo*, which had put into Bantry Bay under stress of weather, and which, soon after she had left on the 20th, sighted a French fleet of twenty sail or so-about half the total number, it seems. Her commander, Captain Courtenay Boyle, sent an officer by land to warn Colonel Dalrymple at Cork, and himself set out, in the teeth of the gale, to carry the news to the Admiralty. As the sloop probably put into Milford-though I am not sure of this—I wonder the news did not spread to us earlier. I imagine precautions must have been used to keep it secret. But now young Perrot has brought it from those parts, and I hope we shall hear fuller details from London to-night. A pretty New Year we are like to have!"

Bantry Bay-Bantry Bay of all places! What was happening at this moment to Lucy and Gerald? Had Roche been implicated in this invasion? Or, nearly as bad, would he be considered to be implicated? So absolutely tongue-tied was Martin that he did not give vent to even the mildest expression of horror, but stood there stupidly listening to his employer and Dr. Meredith exchanging views on this catastrophe, the Precentor pointing out that only some hundred and thirty miles of sea separated St. David's Head from Cork Harbour, perhaps by this time in the possession of the French invaders. The young man was not even conscious, in his horrified absorption, of a sniffing process which, after a few minutes, began round his legs, and only became aware of an interested presence near the region of the floor when he heard a growl and, looking down, beheld Bran standing a few feet away from him, his lips drawn back and the hair erect upon his neck.

The sound drew the Precentor for a moment from his sinister predictions. "Good gracious, I did not know the dog was in here! Lie down, Bran, at once! I apologise, Mr. Towers—'tis extraordinary the dislike which that animal appears to have conceived for you!"

Still growling, Bran retreated backwards, and Martin was thankful to see him go. Shortly afterwards Mr. Salt and he took a depressed leave. There had been no sign of Nest. Martin realised, as they struggled up the hill to Bowen's Folly, that he had been hoping all the time that the study door might open and she come in.

"Yes," said Mr. Salt, unwontedly silent, "a cheery New Year we are like to have if this be true!"

And it was true. No less than seventeen ships of the line and thirteen frigates, with a number of corvettes and transports, making in all forty-three sail, and carrying about fifteen thousand soldiers, as well as a large quantity of arms and ammunition for distribution in Ireland, had left Brest on December 15th, in weather as bright and soft as May's. Hoche himself and Wolfe Tone, the Irish rebel, were on board.

But the Irishman's profound distrust of French seamanship was soon justified. Some of the vessels speedily came into collision; a ship of the line, a 74, ran on to a rock and sank; others missed their way, and the flagship, carrying the admiral, Hoche and the treasury, became separated from the rest and never rejoined them at all. Nevertheless, by the 21st thirty-five sail still remained in company, and, on the evening of December 22nd, with a favouring wind and a smooth sea, fifteen or sixteen ships, with five or six thousand troops on board, entered the mouth of the deep Bay of Bantry and anchored off Bere Island, four leagues from the spot where landing was contemplated. Nineteen or twenty remained outside the bay. But that very night a strong easterly gale arose, laden with snow and blowing directly from shore, which not only prevented all thought of a landing, but threw the ships into confusion, and for the fourth time the fleet was separated, the ships outside the bay fleeing before the storm. On the night of Christmas Eve those in the bay stood further in for Bantry; but, during that night and on the cheerless Christmas Day which followed, it blew a hurricane, and it was doubtful whether the whole squadron would not be dashed to pieces on the rocks, not to speak of being bottled up in the bay by the English fleet, should it arrive with a wind which favoured it. And still the gale continued, reinforced by a fog. Several of the French ships having repeatedly dragged their anchors, they gradually, and with thankfulness, got themselves clear of the bay. Yet even so on December 30th four large French ships and some smaller ones were reported to be making for the bay, and on New Year's Day two more. But in the end they also vanished. The French Armada was dispersed.

Yet afterwards it was clear enough to any informed observer that, had the expedition but started a few days earlier, had the French been possessed of even ordinary naval skill, and had there not been such violent and such prolonged bad weather, nothing could have prevented an army of fifteen thousand men being landed within forty-five miles of Cork, the second city in Ireland, which would almost certainly have fallen into their hands; on which rebellion would probably have broken out in Ulster, perhaps in the other provinces as well.

(9)

The descent upon Bantry might not cause the New Year to be a "cheery one" in Dewisland, but it did provide every inhabitant thereof with an inexhaustible subject of conversation, capable of being embroidered at will with the flowers of almost any emotion. It was not pleasant for Martin to be obliged to listen and respond to the pointed comments on the unspeakable wickedness and folly of the disloyal wretches who had, presumably, arranged this attempted invasion in concert with England's worst foes, though he could hardly believe in his heart that his brother-in-law had had anything to do with it. If he had, he must greatly have misjudged the temper of his own neighbourhood, since all accounts agreed in showing that the reception which would have greeted the expedition, had it succeeded in landing in County Cork, would have been anything but friendly. Indeed the display of loyal feeling evoked by the danger, especially among the Roman Catholics, was the one redeeming feature of the episode, for Cork, Galway and Limerick, the great Catholic centres, all vied with each other in spontaneous proofs of loyalty.

By the end of a few weeks, however, when the spate of alarm, speculation and anecdote had somewhat spent its force, it became apparent that it had left behind it at St. David's a kind of alluvial deposit of reassurance. Pembrokeshire felt safer now that the threatening French armada had definitely launched its attack and been so signally baffled-by the weather. After its limping and long-drawn-out return to Brest, with eight ships wanting, no second French fleet, the county inferred, was likely to venture against Britain. Mr. Salt, however, said what many others were saying throughout the kingdom, that it was strangely disconcerting to think that a great French squadron should have been able to sail unmolested to the coast of Ireland, to remain, the major half of it at least, for five whole days in an Irish bay, and then to return to France without encountering any English naval force. He told Martin that he was longing to ask the Precentor what Lieutenant William Meredith's opinion of this failure might be, and to point out what an undeniable truth the Prayer Book enshrined in the response to "Give peace in our time, O Lord!"

But Martin was glad that he refrained from these gibes. He himself felt too uneasy about the Bantry Bay attempt, almost as though he had had a hand in it, which was absurd. At any rate, it did not, somehow, seem to advance the prospects of his own eventual rehabilitation.

January blew itself out, and February came in; and Martin was aware that there was talk in Cathedral circles no longer of the insolence and discomfiture of the French, but of an unusual festivity to be held at Haverfordwest on the 8th of the month, a Subscription Ball, the proceeds to go to some charity or other. Coming rather late in the season for such doings, and being, it appeared, a masked affair, it seemed to excite the young people of St. David's and even to interest Mr. Salt himself. For one morning, as Martin was doggedly writing: "*Rhys, son of Gruffydd, son of Rhys, son of Tewdwr, son of Eineon, son of Owen, son of Howell, son of* — — " he was startled more than a little to hear from behind these words:

"Towers, why are you not going to the ball at Haverfordwest next Wednesday?" And before he had time to reply his employer went on: "You know the proverb about all work and no play? There will be some people there with whom you are acquainted-including, of course, Miss Meredith. And as I hear rumours that it is to be a *bal masqué*, that seems to make it peculiarly suitable for you!"

"I . . . to tell truth, I had never thought of it," stammered Martin. "For one thing, it would mean my absence for the night, and the procuring of a costume."

"Your absence," replied Mr. Salt, "I can easily bear with. Touching the costume, were the affair a real masquerade, which it is not, it would be a pity that I burnt your late seaman's habiliments. As it is, all you will need is ordinary gala attire, a domino and a mask. You may go over to Haverfordwest to-morrow and take steps about these requisites, and if there is any difficulty about money I will advance you what is required from your salary."

Martin was even more pleased than he allowed to appear, for after all he was only five-and-twenty, and if his work for Mr. Salt was preferable in his own eyes to tutoring, it was not of an intensely absorbing nature. He had now been at Bowen's Folly nearly seven months, during which he had only twice left St. David's for a few hours.

A journey to Haverfordwest next day, with an introduction to a tailor, resulted in his ordering himself some modest finery; after which, armed with Mr. Salt's recommendation, he was able to purchase himself a ticket for the ball; for, since the guests were to be masked, every care had to be taken that tickets should be sold only to persons of repute or those whom they could vouch for. Martin, as he bought his, felt very sure that he did not belong to the first category.

Coming back, he descended from the coach at Solva, that Porthclais on a larger scale, and strolled along the picturesque natural harbour clasped between its green heights, and with a convenient turn in it which made for good shelter. It was a pretty sight, and would make, he thought, a pleasing pencil sketch with its quantity of little craft, and that larger vessel, a small fore-and-aft schooner, at the quayside. He looked her over idly; she was old, with a battered figurehead not unlike the female figure which guarded Mr. Salt's front door. On her stern, in fresh paint, was inscribed: "*Raymonde*, St. Helier's." And Martin knitted his brows; where had he seen that name before? Why, it had been signed to the letter which he had saved for the French Royalist on board the Hamburg packet. But though its recurrence here was a curious coincidence, it was not unnatural, he supposed, that a vessel from the Channel Islands should bear a French name.

The picturesque appearance of Solva Harbour was to give Martin, as he walked on to St. David's the inspiration for which he had been seeking during most of his transit from Haverfordwest, namely, how to make some small return to Mr. Salt for his kindness. He had, as it happened, considerable aptitude for drawing (though to Miss Meredith he had denied any qualifications as a critic). What if he were to turn this gift to account, not indeed by drawing Solva Harbour, but by secretly visiting the Cathedral at the first opportunity, and seeing what he could make of the reputed tomb of Mr. Salt's hero Giraldus, and, if the result were passable, presenting it to him?

(10)

A small fern was pushing its way out of the stones in the niche where Gerald the Welshman's effigy lay, just above his folded hands—a testimony, like the turf beneath the artist's feet, and the somewhat chilly condition of those feet themselves, to the fact that the south choir aisle of the Cathedral was exposed to the weather. The artist in question, engaged the very next afternoon upon his surprise for Mr. Salt, was reflecting with a smile that, with so much greenery about, he might with profit have borrowed Miss Meredith's water-colours. No, because she might have wanted to see the results of his labours, which he could not help knowing would be a good deal better than that comical little effort of hers last autumn on the cliffs, and he would not for words hurt her feelings.

As a matter of fact, Martin was reticent about his own modest gift; he had no wish to be taken for a drawing-master. Yet he had once thought that when in the army-that goal which now seemed so unimaginably distant-it might prove very useful to be able to dash off a sketch map of a military position. But he had never then imagined himself so soberly and antiquarianly employed as this.

Egad, it was getting cold here, sitting on this heap of broken corbels and what not, and the light was now none too good! And someone had just emerged from the transept-by his slow approach, some sightseer who would probably want to accost him, and to make remarks upon his drawing. It was certainly time to leave. Before collecting his materials Martin turned his head to glance at the newcomer; and having turned it, remained thus, staring at a figure which he could not believe to be real. Indeed, he would scarcely have been more astonished if old Giraldus himself, six centuries dead, had come to life; for there at a little distance, looking at him with equal astonishment, stood his French acquaintance of the packet-boat and the street in Hamburg, the Chevalier de la Vireville. There was no mistaking him, he had far too individual a face and bearing for that. But what on earth was he doing in St. David's?

"*Mais c'est impossible!*" Martin heard him murmur to himself; and then, more loudly, in English: "Is it Mr. Tyrrell, or his ghost?"

Martin jumped up, drawing and pencils going to the sward. "Not that name here, for heaven's sake, sir!"

"What, you are incognito?" exclaimed M. de la Vireville, smiling. "Raphael, as it were, in disguise! Be assured, sir, that I will respect your wish; yet I trust that you will permit me to see that chef-d'œuvre which you treat so cavalierly-in memory of our meeting at Hamburg last year."

At that the artist caught him firmly by his sound arm. "Monsieur de la Vireville, not a word of Hamburg either, I implore you, unless you wish to ruin me!"

The Frenchman looked at him with a merry, but, it seemed, an understanding imp dancing in his eyes. "I, too, had not so long ago a *sobriquet*," he said; "*donc je m'y connais*. It served me well-for a time. *Mais enfin*, it is so astonishing—*j'ose dire si agréable*—to find you here that it is not more astonishing that I must call you . . . *eh bien, monsieur le peintre, what* must I call you?"

"Towers," answered Martin, lowering his voice. "But come with me into the chapel at the end; few people go there."

Snatching up his masterpiece and collecting his scattered pencils, he led the way almost at a run to the roofless Lady Chapel of the Cathedral. He did not exactly intend to confide in the Chevalier de la Vireville, who had thus dropped from the skies upon him, but he had at least to make quite plain to him, if he had not already done so, that if he were staying in St. David's he must keep silence about his previous acquaintance with Mr. Salt's secretary in another place and under another name.

"*Ma foi*, these seem appropriate surroundings in which to take an oath of secrecy," observed the *émigré*, gazing about him in the deserted chapel. "But on what relic do you propose that I shall swear?"

Torn between the impulse to tell him everything and a doubt whether such complete confidence were wise, Martin looked scrutinisingly at him, and now realised for the first time that he was attired in a blue coat of a cut which, to one who had served in the *Fair Penitent*, somehow suggested the upper ranks of those who followed the sea, say, the master of a ship; he also saw that the Royalist's left sleeve was no longer pinned up to his breast, and that from its cuff protruded the usual substitute for a hand, a stout steel hook.

"Will you not tell me, Monsieur le Chevalier," he began, half to gain time, "what *you* are doing in this corner of Wales? You were not more surprised to see me than I to see you!"

"*Volontiers*," said the Frenchman, seating himself on a fallen block of stone. "*Eh bien*, you now behold in me the master and owner of the schooner *Raymonde*, late the *Indian Queen*, of St. Helier's, Jersey, in the coasting trade. Did I not tell you, in-that place where we met-that I was thinking of returning to the sea? My little vessel is far from being new—I am a poor man-and coming up-Channel she had the misfortune to strain her rudder, besides losing a small spar in a squall. As the wind was not favourable for putting into Milford I found myself obliged to make for that small harbour in the Bay of St. Bride called Solva—a harbour with the devil of a great rock in the entrance! There lies my poor schooner, that these damages may be repaired. I myself, having nothing to do at the moment, walk over to the city of St. David's! I do not find a city, it is true, but I descend to view the Cathedral of which I see at first nothing but the top of a large tower. Inside I find a magnificent roof, a floor as sloping as the deck of a frigate lying over to the wind, and outside—M. Towers!"

"It is amazing!" agreed Martin. Now the schooner with the name *Raymonde* was accounted for. Sitting down beside M. de la Vireville he suddenly said: "I have learnt a good deal about the slope of a deck since I saw you last . . . and partly on account of that house to which you directed me."

"*Vous dites?*" said the Royalist, with interest. "It was not the right house-the house you wished to find-nor the right Irish milord?"

Martin shook his head. "I was upon the wrong trail altogether, and an unfortunate one for me, as it turned out. But I am not blaming you, sir. Yet" (yes, he would tell him!) "almost immediately upon my return to England, just because I had entered that house, I was arrested for treason. But I escaped from the men who took me, knocking one of them upon the head-somewhat hard. Some sailors with whom I had sought refuge drugged me and carried me on board their vessel, a Liverpool privateer. I served in her for two months, was put on board a Dutch prize which the privateer was sending into Liverpool, deserted when the prize came in here for water last July, and have been here ever since under an assumed name as the secretary of an antiquarian gentleman named Salt. And so you see——" There seemed no need to finish.

"In effect, I see," returned the Chevalier de la Vireville after a moment, during which he stared at the narrator with renewed interest. "But, Monsieur Tower-Towers?—on what possible grounds could your Government accuse you of treason? May not an Englishman go to . . . that town where we met? I saw several others there."

Martin dropped his voice. "He cannot, evidently, go there with impunity if it becomes known that he has had there an interview with well-known Irish rebels who have themselves gone to that town rather than to Paris, in order to open relations with the Republic through the French minister! That was my unwitting crime!"

"Oho!" said M. de la Vireville. "But-pardon me-you seemed yourself anxious to open relations with M. Reinhardt!"

" 'Twas really the last thing I desired to do," returned Martin warmly. "Let me explain why I appeared to have the desire." He explained.

When he had finished the Chevalier emitted a soft whistle. "And *that* was the Irish milord with the similar name in the house in the Schildtstrasse!—By the way, did you see the lady with him who so turned the head of my young friend lodging opposite?"

"Yes," admitted Martin rather unwillingly. "I saw her for a few moments."

"Was she so lovely?"

"Yes," replied the young man, turning his face aside.

"You do not sound very enthusiastic! Most men who have seen *la belle Paméla* —unhappily I am not one of them-scarcely find language to express her perfections."

Martin turned an accusing gaze upon him. "Then you knew who she was!"

La Vireville shook his head. "No, not then, or I should have told you-and you would have known that her husband was not the man you sought. I learnt it later, when all Hamburg was raving of her."

All at once Martin felt that it was hard to submit to an implied criticism on his taste which he certainly did not deserve. "I confess I, too, am in the condition of those others whom you speak of —I cannot find words to paint her charm. I should not think the world holds such another!"

And there in the roofless chapel, as he stared at an empty window mullion, she came before him again in all her sweet and natural grace . . . though, to tell truth, it was some time since she had done so.

"As I directed you to that house," the Frenchman was saying, "though, it is true, with the best intentions possible, I feel that I am in part responsible for your present situation, Mr. Towers. I wish with all my heart that I could do something to assist you. But surely your little affair has blown over by now; it is, is it not, already some nine months old?"

"You forget, sir," said Martin, with sombreness, "the formidable expedition which the French Republic lately launched against southern Ireland! That was undoubtedly arranged in concert with the United Irishmen, as they call themselves; for all I know, I may be assumed to have played some part in that arrangement. The attack only failed owing to the severity of the weather."

"And owing to the infernally bad seamanship of my degenerate countrymen!" added the master of the *Raymonde* between his teeth. "In the days when I had the honour to serve in His Majesty's Navy, the great Suffren would not immediately have allowed himself to become separated from the rest of the fleet under his command, nor would one of his ships have run on to the rocks in fair weather, nor . . . but why do I go on? You will think that I regret the failure of the attempt; naturally I do not; yet as a Frenchman, once a naval officer, I am not proud of French naval incompetence . . . *Mais je divague* . I see indeed that the fact of this so nearly successful invasion of Ireland does not improve your position. . . . And by the way, does this learned gentleman of the name of Salt —*un drôle de nom* —know the truth about you?"

"Yes," said Martin. "I felt obliged to tell him everything. I have nothing to fear from him on that score-in the way of further discovery, I mean."

"And-forgive my curiosity-is he the only person here in whom you have confided?"

Martin felt himself redden. Tell a Frenchman that the only other was a young lady? Immediately he would leap to the most untrue of conclusions!

"There is one other person," he admitted unwillingly, "the person, in fact, who acted as go-between with this Mr. Salt who employs me; but I have complete confidence in that person. . . . I believe, after all, that someone is coming here!"

This was, if timely, true as well. Voices were audible, though still at some distance. Both men got up.

"*Et cette autre personne, alors* ," remarked M. de la Vireville, with interest, "*est-ce qu'elle — —?* "

"*Elle!* " broke in Martin, colouring. "I never said it was a woman!"

"*Ni moi non plus!* " returned the Chevalier in obvious surprise. "I beg your pardon; I spoke in French without intending it . . . and in French '*personne*' is of the feminine gender, that is all!" He looked at Martin keenly for a second or two and added: "It is true, I think, that someone comes, and perhaps you would rather not be seen with me, for I know that any Frenchman is suspect at first; but let me say that if your difficulties should become pressing, I shall be at Solva with my schooner until, perhaps, Thursday or Friday in next week, and if I can help you in any way I am at your service. You would find me either on board or at the 'Ship' Inn. *Et, foi de gentilhomme, je suis vraiment une troisième personne qui saurait respecter votre secret!* "

He had lowered his voice and dropped into French again as three people entered, a commanding middle-aged ecclesiastic, a young gentleman and a professional-looking individual with a case under his arm-the Precentor, young Mr. Perrot (to Martin's astonishment) and someone whom he did not know. But, in any case, it was too late to flee.

"That is the Precentor, the highest Cathedral dignitary in St. David's," whispered Martin to his companion. "The best thing that I can do is to present you to him; he likes those who take an interest in the Cathedral. Talk English to him; that, I know, is not difficult for you."

Dr. Meredith was not for a moment aware of them. "You see, Mr. White," he was saying as they came in, "that the re-roofing of this unhappily neglected chapel —— But I think we have visitors here! Ah, it is Mr. Towers."

Martin came forward. "It is, sir. I was conducting this gentleman, a stranger, round the Cathedral. Will you allow me to present him to you-Monsieur le Chevalier de la Vireville, a French Royalist emigrant."

The Precentor and M. le Chevalier bowed to each other. And, far from finding the Frenchman suspect, Dr. Meredith's greeting was unexpectedly cordial. "I account it an honour, sir," he proclaimed, holding out his hand, "to make the acquaintance of a sufferer for religion and monarchy. I have met in London some of the excellent and devoted priests of your Church, thrust into exile and penury by the godless republicans. If you are interested in this ancient fane you have a good guide in Mr. Towers, who must now know it well. Meanwhile let me present you to Mr. Perrot, a gentleman of this neighbourhood, and Mr. White, the architect whom I am consulting about the possibility of putting a roof upon this chapel."

Martin was no less surprised by this affable welcome than by the errand upon which the Precentor had come-but still more surprised by the presence of young Perrot in the commission of survey. The re-roofing of this derelict chapel would, he imagined, be an immensely costly business, with the restoration of the west front not yet completed; what interest had that gentleman in it? Then he remembered that Mr. Perrot was well off, and reputed to have large expectations also; was it possible that he intended to put up a substantial contribution towards an object in which Martin, at least, could not believe him genuinely interested? If so, what was his motive? The answer seemed to be, that the Precentor was Nest Meredith's father. And, unknown to himself, Martin looked very blackly at Mr. Perrot, who was talking to the architect, while the Precentor continued in friendly discourse with M. de la Vireville, even, in a becomingly sympathetic voice, making an oblique reference to the patent loss of his arm.

"Yes, I parted with that after Quiberon," he heard the *émigré* respond cheerfully (which was more than Martin had elicited from him). And Dr. Meredith replied, "Quiberon! What a pity that my sailor son is not now on leave; he knows all about that unfortunate expedition, though he did not, to his regret, take part in it. —What, you must be leaving us, monsieur? Good day, then; and pray remember that I shall be pleased to see you at the Precentory at any time."

But meanwhile Mr. Perrot, turning from the architect, after staring at the Frenchman had caught sight of the sketch under Martin's arm. "Drawing, Mr. Towers?" he enquired, with the slightest trace of a sneer. "Then I was right in concluding that the subject was studied at the University of Oxford?"

"No, you were not, sir," returned Martin curtly. "I never had lessons at Oxford or anywhere else."

" 'Tis natural genius, then, I perceive, fostered no doubt, even without direct tuition, by the air of that University. I regret that I have not had the advantage of residence there."

"It is certainly a great pity," retorted Martin. After all Perrot had attacked him first. But what either of them would have said next remained unknown, for at that moment the Precentor swung round, caught sight of what was under Martin's arm, said, "What, Mr. Towers, are you also engaged in plans for the restoration of this chapel?" and Martin, not very willingly, had to explain what he had been doing. It was thus some minutes before he was able to convey himself and M. de la Vireville away.

"He is imposing, *ma foi, celui-là*!" was the Frenchman's comment when they got out of hearing. "He must be the bishop, surely-the Archbishop, perhaps?"

Outside the south porch they came face to face with no less a person than Miss Meredith, just about to enter it. But when she saw Martin she stopped, changing colour a little.

"I think my father is in the Cathedral, is he not, Mr. Towers?"

"Not exactly, Miss Meredith, but he is in St. Mary's Chapel with an architect."

"In that case I will go round outside," said Nest, who seemed in a hurry. "I have an urgent message for him." And she went quickly along the way they had just come.

"That was Miss Meredith, the Precentor's daughter," explained Martin to his companion. "I would have presented you had she not been in haste."

"*Elle est tout-à-fait charmante*," observed the Frenchman, as they began to move away from the Cathedral. "I think you have chosen your refuge with taste, Monsieur Towers, and with wisdom too, since you have as a shield your acquaintance with that dignified prelate. But I wager that you did not tell him of your little adventure-it would have shocked him too much."

"Yes," assented Martin with a sigh, "I fear that it would."

"Yet I warrant that it did not scandalise-on the contrary it greatly interested . . . *Mademoiselle sa fille*," remarked the Chevalier, darting at him a quick, half amused glance.

"How do you-what do you mean?"

"*Ne m'en voulez pas, je vous en prie!* You all but told me that the other person who knew your secret was of the fair sex. I only hazard the guess that the favoured person is the pretty daughter of the prelate!"

Martin coloured. "It was owing to an accident-to her dog's biting me," he admitted half angrily. "Miss Meredith-well, I had better tell you the whole story of my arrival here." Inwardly he was confounding the Frenchman for being so sharp. Of course, too, he would draw a totally wrong conclusion.

Whatever conclusion the Chevalier drew at the close of Martin's narrative he kept to himself, except that he rather significantly observed that his own better acquaintance with the lady who only last year became his wife had begun with an injury sustained by him. Then they parted, since the Frenchman wished to walk and view Ramsey Sound, but Martin, still marvelling at the strange coincidence of the arrival of his schooner at Solva, bore back his sketch to Bowen's Folly.

Mr. Salt was delighted with it, asked why he had kept his talent under a bushel, declared his intention of having his translation of the *Itinerary* illustrated by more drawings from the same hand, said that he would pay him for each one, in addition to his present salary, and sent him off two days later to Porthclais to see what he could make of the ruins of the little Capel-y-Pistyll or Chapel of the Spout, erected over the spring which had miraculously gushed up for the baptism of St. David.

And here, before he had quite reached the spot, Martin observed a young lady with a little basket in her hand about to cross the handbridge over the stream. He quickened his steps, raised his hat and, congratulating himself that Miss Meredith could not know what was under his arm, said, looking at this basket, "I think you must be a sorceress, Miss Meredith, to be able to find primroses so early in February!"

"I know a very sheltered, sunny place up there where they come out very early," said Nest almost apologetically. "There are only a few. —I am glad to meet you, Mr. Towers, for I wanted to say that I feared I had interrupted your conversation on Saturday with the French Royalist gentleman, as Papa afterwards told me that he was."

"It was no interruption, I assure you," said Martin. "But it may interest you to know that that French gentleman and I had already met-at Hamburg." And on that he told her of the part La Vireville had played in his adventure there, and of his having now confided his secret to him.

"But, Mr. Towers, was that wise . . . I wonder if it was wise?" She looked up at him with a wide, troubled gaze.

"Bless her," thought Martin, "still taking my cares upon her little shoulders!" Again he was conscious of an even stronger pang of remorse for ever having laid them there. "But I am sure," he said gently, "that he is to be trusted, and to take him into my confidence does not put him into any awkward position, since he is not a British subject."

"Then that makes three people altogether in these parts who know about you," said his Nausicaa, with the suspicion of a pout. (Was it possible that she was jealous of the Frenchman's sharing his secret?)

"But M. de la Vireville will not be in this neighbourhood for more than a few days," he replied. "His schooner is repairing at Solva. To change the subject, Miss Meredith, I suppose that you are going to the Subscription Ball at Haverfordwest on Wednesday?"

"Yes, I am going," said Nest without much enthusiasm. "I am to stay with Sir Henry and Lady Wogan."

"I hoped that you were going," said Martin.

"Why, sir?"

"Because I am going too."

"You!" Was she pleased? At least she was surprised. "Oh, Mr. Towers, how pleasant!"

"It is indeed-for me. This is Mr. Salt's doing; he quoted the proverb about all work and no play; and so I have bought a ticket and engaged a room in Haverfordwest for the night."

Miss Nest Meredith smiled; yes, she did look pleased, he decided. "At heart, you know, Mr. Salt is very kind. I too have sometimes thought," she continued, rearranging her primroses, "that life at Bowen's Folly must seem a trifle dull after your experiences on board the privateer."

"It is certainly much quieter," agreed Martin with a smile. "But I am afraid," he went on, still under the empire of conscience, "that I have caused you to think a great deal more than can have been agreeable about my wretched affairs. And I cannot help hoping, in spite of the recent French attempt in Ireland, that I may soon be able to quit these parts and relieve you of your share-your more than kind share-in this troublesome secret of mine."

"It . . . it is not troublesome . . . I mean to me," answered Nest, very low, and once more arranging the primroses in her basket-so ill that some fell out. Martin picked them up carefully and restored them to her.

"Do you mean that you are leaving St. David's . . . soon?" she asked as she took them.

"No, not immediately. I do not see any prospect of that. I only meant to relieve your mind," said the unperceptive young man, serenely unconscious that he had done precisely the opposite. "You will not then have to be . . . an accomplice, a confederate . . . which indeed I ought never to have made you."

"I shall . . . feel vastly strange when the confederacy is over," said Nest bravely. She looked for a moment down the narrow haven; the tide was out, and the mounds of seaweed shone golden-brown on either side of the current of the Alan, not in itself sufficient to bear a boat of any size. "But I must be going home. We shall meet then at the ball. You know, I suppose, Mr. Towers, that we are to be masked until midnight?"

"Yes, but I shall know you, I am sure. If you on your part do not recognise me when I ask you for a dance-which I venture to hope that you will give me-what password shall I use . . . *Vrijheid* ?"

"Oh, no, no! Oh pray be careful! No, I shall recognise you without any password, Mr. Towers-better, I expect than you will recognise me!"

"And how, pray?" asked Martin.

She looked for once thoroughly mischievous-and delightful thus. "One always knows persons by their voices."

"But at a masked ball one is supposed to disguise one's voice!"

"Is one? I have never been to a masked ball before. But I shall know you! . . . I must be going; good-bye, sir." And she hastened, almost flitted, over the bridge; and Martin, looking after her, wondered what was the real mark of identity which she had in her mind.

Then he saw one primrose lying forsaken at his feet. He picked it up, and looking at its sweet and fresh little face decided that it bore a happy resemblance to her who had plucked it. Putting it in his buttonhole, he proceeded to his artistic task.

" 'Pon my word, Towers," said his employer when he later scrutinised the fruit of his labours, "you have quite a pretty gift. I remember saying to little Nest the day she first came to plead your cause, that she seemed to be thrusting a very Protean individual upon me, and that I wondered what your next incarnation would be. Now I begin to see. And meanwhile you have certainly earned your jaunt to Haverfordwest on Wednesday."

And whether he had earned it or no Martin found his thoughts running upon that jaunt with pleasurable anticipation. To dance with Miss Meredith, among others, would be by no means disagreeable.

* * * * *

Wednesday came in bright and keen, with a light frost. Martin had not expected to be permitted to set off for Haverfordwest until the afternoon coach, but Mr. Salt told him that he might go by the morning one, and utilise the daylight to see more of Haverfordwest than he had done —a place with so fine a position and so long a history, with a charter given by Richard II and a never-taken castle.

So, earlier in the day than he had anticipated, Martin was slowly borne south-eastwards. As the coach toiled up the very steep hill out of Solva he remembered the Chevalier de la Vireville and resolved to find him on his return journey and bid him farewell, unless he had sailed too early. Thinking of that return it occurred to him that it would be pleasant did he happen to come back in the coach with Miss Meredith. The thin coating of ice on the puddles crackled under wheels and hoofs, and the long bank of pebbles with which the sea had fortified Newgale beach, to which the road descended, glistened frostily in the mild February sunlight. If his affair had blown over (yet how could an actual warrant "blow over"?) this was the road that he would take to go home; he might almost at this moment be on the first stages of his journey back to England and Selham St. Peter, having said farewell to the peaceful if stagnated life at St. David's, and to all the confusing personages of Welsh story into whose company Mr. Salt, so little a true lover of that race, had plunged him.

They were up on the level again, and Martin knew that if he looked back St. David's— dwindled city and great cathedral tower alike-would be vanished as though they had had no existence... Yes, surely the time was not far off when he could venture to cut-though, curiously enough, with regret-the ties which bound him to his place of exile in the land of the Phæacians, those people who dwelt "far apart in the wash of the waves, the outermost of men."

V
"CAME THE BLIND FURY——"

"He went in quest of Hudibras
To find him out where'er he was,
And, if he was above ground, vow'd

He'd ferret him, lurk where he wou'd."

Samuel Butler *Hudibras*

V
"CAME THE BLIND FURY——"

(1)

Although Martin, on the road to Haverfordwest, thus pictured himself severing, at no very distant date, his seven months old connection with St. David's, he would have been very little pleased to learn that an individual in that city of refuge had for the last three days been occupied in severing it for him, and that this male Atropos was plying the shears beneath the small but blameless roof of Miss Mathry Jones.

Mathry was not this lady's Christian name, but a cognomen drawn from her birthplace in the neighbourhood; and she let lodgings, good hotel accommodation being to seek at St. David's. In the first week in February a certain Mr. Manisty, from London, sought her hospitality for a few days, stating that he had been sent down by the Admiralty to report upon the Pembrokeshire coast in the vicinity of St. David's, more particularly on the possible shelter for shipping afforded by Ramsey Sound. And though Miss Mathry Jones had always understood that there was not shelter for so much as a rowing boat in the Sound if it came on to blow; and was aware that the Admiralty had sent a surveyor six years before to report upon the possibilities of Fishguard harbour, yet, in spite of his reporting favourably, had done nothing to improve it, she had no objection to the English indulging in these fruitless activities if they liked.

So this Mr. Manisty took his notebook and was off to Ramsey Sound or elsewhere, February or no February. Chilled, no doubt, by the wind at Porthstinian he called on his way back at the farmhouse at Rhosson to ask for a glass of ale. In the course of conversation with Mrs. Lloyd he, after duly admiring the woolwork wreck, revealed his mission, and asked a few questions about the number and fate of ships driven into the Sound by stress of weather; and very soon had advanced to the topic of those who dropped anchor here from choice rather than from necessity. Of these Mrs. Lloyd did not recall many; though she well remembered the Dutch prize which had put in there last summer for water.

"Ah," said Mr. Manisty, finishing his ale, "that would be the vessel from which a privateersman deserted. I wonder what became of him; did you ever hear, madam?"

Mrs. Lloyd replied that folks did say that a strange man had worked for a while for Mr. Griffiths of Tan-y-bach, who was afterwards thought to have been the deserter; but he only stayed there a very short time, and that was long ago, in hay harvest.

"Ah yes," said Mr. Manisty, and departed to continue his researches into the coastline of Dewisland. And he next turned up on the other shore, above the tiny bay of Caerbwdy, which by no stretch of imagination could be regarded as a possible harbour. At the farm of Tan-y-bach he made enquiries about the "elegant and unusual purple stone" which he had already observed in the fabric of the Cathedral, and which he had been told was to be found in the little inlet below. Quelling the barking of the farm dogs, Mrs. Griffiths told the enquirer that this was so, and that the stone in question was quarried in the next bay also, Caerfai, and had its name therefrom. Mr. Manisty then asked if Mr. Griffiths had any interest in the quarrying. Griffiths? Oh no; he was a farmer whatever. And how had farming prospered in the past year; had the haycrop been good, and was it easy to procure extra labour in these parts? Sometimes; but not last summer; and the only extra labour they had been able to get had not been of much use to them—a man who had come along just at hay harvest and asked for work, but who had proved so lame (besides being inexperienced) that Griffiths had in the end to dismiss him. Lame? Yes, sir, lame from a dog-bite, which it appeared afterwards had been inflicted by the dog of Miss Meredith from the Precentory, for she came enquiring after the man when he was gone.

Mr. Manisty found this most interesting. Then Miss Meredith must have met this man previously? What had been his occupation before he came to Tan-y-bach? He had never told them, but his clothes looked like a seaman's, and Miss Meredith, when she came, said that was what he had been, and agreed that Solva might be a good place for him to seek work. But whether the man-what was his name now? Thomas . . . no, Thompson-had found work at Solva, she did not know; at any rate she had never seen him again.

The Admiralty surveyor then went on to make a preliminary inspection of the little port of Solva; and among the vessels there, mostly small craft engaged in carrying limestone, culm, or corn, noticed a schooner from St. Helier's, Jersey, recently put in for repairs. No one, however, could give him any news whatever of a lame stranger, presumably a seafaring man, who had either found employment there last summer or shipped thence in any vessel.

Mr. Manisty thereupon returned to St. David's, and despite an alleged dislike of such places, assiduously frequented the inn next day, and also such gatherings of loafers round the city cross as the weather permitted, in order (as he explained) to have, for his report, the benefit of the opinions and conversations of the old salts and retired sea captains who had made their homes at St. David's. Yet the individual whose conversation appeared to give him most satisfaction was not that of a seafaring man at all, but of the young groom who was the sweetheart of Mary, the maid at the Precentory.

A conversation with Miss Mathry Jones next followed, a long and pleasant conversation, in which she had no idea that she was being pumped; nor what was the sole small item of information for the sake of which the colloquy had been begun. This morsel exactly tallied with an impression gained from those other chats with the local worthies-and that was, that the only newcomer who had settled recently in St. David's, was the young man acting as secretary to Mr. Salt up at the Folly—"Tower," or some such name; and he had come as long ago as last July or August. Discreet enquiries as to Mr. "Tower's" personal appearance (checked privately by a description which, oddly enough, Mr. Manisty appeared to have already in his possession) then led to that gentleman's taking a great deal of trouble to patrol the lanes leading to the globe-crowned portals of Bowen's Folly. Here in the afternoon of the eighth of February, the day of the Subscription Ball, his diligence was rewarded, though not, as he had hoped, by a sight of Mr. Towers himself, since Mr. Towers was already in Haverfordwest. But a small, respectably dressed woman, wearing the usual high-crowned beaver hat, and with a basket on her arm, came trotting out of those gates towards Mr. Manisty, slowly walking in her direction. Some superior domestic from the house, I warrant, he thought; on which, when she was almost abreast, he lifted his hat with great civility and enquired if a Mr. Tower or Towers was living at the house yonder, which he understood to be Mr. Jerome Salt's?

Impressed by the hat-lifting, Mrs. Morris halted in her flight and dropped a curtsy.

"Indeed yes, sir. Was you wanting him, if you please?"

Mr. Manisty intimated that he did desire speech with the gentleman.

"Dear me, and that's a pity!" commented Mrs. Morris, "for he've gone away until to-morrow, whatever."

"You are sure that he is returning to-morrow?"

"By what he did say, yes, sir; and he have not taken much with him."

"You belong to the house, I see, my good woman?"

Another curtsy. "Yes, sir; I am the housekeeper."

Mr. Manisty glanced up and down the lane; there was no one in sight. He pulled out his purse, inside whose meshes there took place an agreeable clinking. "I take a great interest in Mr. Towers, especially in the manner in which he made his first appearance at Mr. Salt's house. If you know anything about that, madam, and feel inclined to tell me of it, and also what you know about Mr. Towers in general, you will find it well worth your while."

If she is in the pay of "Towers," or for any other reason devoted to him, he thought, she can but spurn the notion, and, "Towers" being away, she will not be able to warn him that enquiries are on foot about him.

But there was nothing in Mrs. Morris' eager black eyes of the spirit of one who spurns; on the contrary.

"Mr. Salt did say that I wass not to tell anybody in St. David's whateffer," she replied; yet it was perfectly clear from her tone and her glance towards the purse that this prohibition was not a buckler to her soul, but a burden.

"But I am not of St. David's," returned Mr. Manisty. "I come from London; indeed I am sent here by the Government, and thus, if you do not tell me what you know, it might be the worse for you. Besides, there is the reward." He jingled his purse a little more, and then, seeing that the thing was as good as done, added, "Let us go a little further down the lane."

The injunction was obeyed with such speed that Mr. Manisty had some ado to keep up. And then, having attained a sufficient distance from its entrance gates, Mrs. Morris began rapidly to narrate the circumstances attending Mr. Towers' first appearance at Bowen's Folly.

(2)

"A gentleman, sir, to see you," announced old Dixon about half-past four to his master, proffering a card. "That is, he says, if you could kindly spare him a little of your valuable time."

The Precentor took the card, and was less impressed with the name thereon than with the words "Upon business connected with the Board of Admiralty," which were written in pencil below. And as it happened that he was at the moment employing his valuable time in reading the fullest account which had yet met his eyes of the Bantry Bay affair of Christmastide, his mind, filled thereby with renewed indignation, pride and apprehension, was perfectly attuned to the visit of any emissary from the Board of Admiralty. He commanded that their official should be admitted without delay to his presence, bowed with cordiality when Mr. Manisty entered, and begged him to seat himself near the excellent fire which even Bran (who was sometimes permitted the run of the study) had found a little too hot, for he had withdrawn himself therefrom to a nook of his own. Of Mr. Manisty, with whom he had no unpleasant associations, he took no notice whatever.

The Precentor saw before him a solidly built, tallish man, remarkable only for the extreme squareness of his somewhat tallow-hued face; Mr. Manisty saw and no doubt admired in Dr. Meredith his commanding presence, his handsome features, and the excellent curl of his snowy wig.

"You come on business from the Admiralty, I understand, sir?" began the Precentor. "Then, if I may say so, you arrive very opportunely, if it means that the Government is at last waking up to the defenceless state of this coast and countryside. What if such another dastardly attempt upon a large scale should be made here as has recently, under God's providence, been foiled by the weather in southern Ireland? We could not rely upon a second miracle, and what else have we to rely upon? A small fort at Fishguard, sixteen miles away, the Cardiganshire militia, the Castlemartin yeomanry-also at a distance! Meanwhile, not to speak of the city itself, here is this most venerable and famous Cathedral exposed to profanation and pillage! If you have come, sir, armed with powers to report upon possible means of protecting the sea-board of western Pembrokeshire, you may be assured of my warmest co-operation!"

Mr. Manisty, thus provided with an opening for his real business more favourable than he could have anticipated, yet hesitated a moment, unwilling to dash the hopes of this impressive cleric. "Well, sir," he said, surveying his shoes, "I am afraid that I have not come about the question of defence in precisely the sense in which you mean it; yet, in another way, my errand *is* closely connected with it. Indeed I may say that the late attempted invasion of Ireland by the French is the cause of my being in St. David's, and any assistance which you could give me in my search I should most gratefully receive."

"Search?" said the Precentor. "What search?"

"I will tell you in a moment, sir; but first I must be frank with you," replied Mr. Manisty deprecatingly. "I have not come from the Admiralty, though I *am* upon a Government errand, and one whose nature demanded that I should have some cover for my activities here."

"Not from the Admiralty!" exclaimed Dr. Meredith in a disappointed tone. "Then what, pray, are your 'activities' here?"

Mr. Manisty slightly dropped his voice. "I am in the Government secret service, and have been particularly sent to St. David's to track down a man whom there is much reason to connect with the arrangements for bringing the French fleet to Bantry Bay less than two months ago, and against whom, indeed, there has been a warrant out these nine months for treason."

"God bless my soul!" exclaimed the Precentor, exceedingly startled. "But I am certain that we harbour no such wretch at St. David's; this is the most loyal of neighbourhoods!"

"I do not doubt it, sir," returned Mr. Manisty warmly. "And though this plotter certainly came to St. David's six months ago I had, upon my arrival here, no hopes of finding him still in the vicinity. Now, however, I believe I am hot upon his trail . . . and I venture to look to you, Mr. Precentor, or to a member of your household, to confirm my suspicions in that regard."

"You look to *me*—to my household! I assure you, sir," ejaculated the Precentor with visible displeasure, "that you must be mistaken! What connection can I or mine have with a scoundrel accused of treason? I find the notion distinctly offensive!"

"My dear Mr. Precentor," said Mr. Manisty, as soothingly as he could, "I implore you to cast from you any such thought! Not for worlds would I suggest anything so abhorrent. No, the connection between you or . . . any member of your household and the man of whom I am in search is purely one of charity-fortuitous and mistaken charity! I must tell you briefly that this man, an Englishman, paid a hasty visit to Bantry Bay last May; then, after an interview with two most pernicious members of the Society of United Irishmen in Dublin, went straight to Hamburg to confer with two other rebel leaders there, Lord Edward Fitzgerald (whose name is probably familiar to you) and Mr. Arthur O'Connor. They in their turn had gone there to open relations with the French minister to the Hanse towns, which it is known that they did. This young man, Martin Tyrrell, was arrested at Liverpool, on his way back from Hamburg, just as he was on the point of re-embarking for Ireland once more; but by violently assaulting one of the Bow Street runners who carried out the arrest, he escaped, and, as was afterwards discovered, shipped on board the *Fair Penitent* privateer of Liverpool, which was just upon sailing, and so was lost to view for some time. In July the privateer sent into Liverpool a Dutch prize of which this man formed part of the temporary crew; but he, taking advantage of the prize putting into Ramsey Sound here for water, deserted, and thus disappeared again. This fact, however, did not come to the knowledge of the authorities until the *Fair Penitent* herself arrived at Liverpool, just before Christmas—I mean that it was not until then that the deserter's identity was established. Almost at the same time the frustrated French attempt in Bantry Bay decided them to make a fresh effort to execute the warrant; and I am here, Dr. Meredith, to do it!"

"But why *here*?" queried the Precentor. "It is seven months since the Dutch prize was in the Sound—I remember it quite well-and no deserter could have remained undiscovered in this neighbourhood for so long."

"I think I can prove to you, sir, that he could," replied Mr. Manisty. "A stranger whom I believe to be Tyrrell began by obtaining work in hay harvest with Mr. Griffiths of Tan-y-bach, but was dismissed on account of his lameness. That lameness, Mr. Precentor—I will ask you to mark this-seems to have been due to a dog-bite inflicted, if Mrs. Griffiths is to be believed, by a dog belonging to your daughter, Miss Nest Meredith. And that," went on Mr. Manisty quickly, entirely disregarding the Precentor's incredulous exclamation, and even his raised hand of protest, "that is no doubt why Miss Meredith, moved by feminine compassion for this man, about whose antecedents she of course knew nothing, gave him a suit of clothes, thus innocently furnishing him with a disguise which——"

But the Precentor was no longer to be disregarded. He broke in. "My daughter give an unknown man a suit of clothes—*my daughter!* Nons——" There he stopped abruptly; and but that the expression conveys a sense of vacuity, it might be said that his jaw dropped.

"The young lady being, as I say, totally unaware of the man Tyrrell's real character," reiterated Mr. Manisty apologetically. "But if it is true that her dog bit him, then that no doubt is why she——"

"But-but I know nothing about all this!" again interrupted Dr. Meredith, frowning and perplexed. "Nothing of dog-bite nor of——" Again he stopped. "And my daughter conceals nothing from me."

"Yet in this case," suggested Mr. Manisty with delicacy, "she may have thought that you would consider her foolishly charitable, and have kept silence for that reason. If I might be allowed to see the young lady herself for a moment——"

"Miss Meredith is away from home," said the Precentor sharply. "And on what grounds, pray, do you assert that she gave this villain a suit of clothes?"

"From a conversation which I happened to have with a young man betrothed to one of your maidservants, sir," replied Mr. Manisty succinctly.

Dr. Meredith's brow grew black indeed. "Do you remember the young man's name-or the maidservant's?"

"His name was Rees, and he spoke of the young female as 'Mary.'"

The Precentor rang the bell. "Send Mary Lewis to me at once, Dixon. —This is a most extraordinary business, Mr. —er-Manifold. I must get to the bottom of it."

And in a moment or two Mary Lewis with her round face and her awestruck curtsy was there to assist him in this operation.

"Mary," began the Precentor; and then, seeing that she looked scared, he added, not unkindly, "I have not sent for you to reprove you, but merely in order to ask you a question. Do you know if Miss Meredith has at any time given away a suit of clothes to a . . . to a tramp or vagabond?"

Dropping another curtsy Mary replied, in a reverent voice but without hesitation, "Yes, sir; please, sir, she did give one to a man last summer."

"Last summer? Odd that she never told me-that I did not know of it at the time! Can you remember when it was, Mary?"

Again the damsel replied without hesitation: "If you please, sir, it was the day when you and Mrs. Stalybridge was gone to Haverford."

The Precentor spent a second or two digesting this. Then he said: "This man came begging, I suppose?"

"Please, sir, no; Miss Nest had told him to come."

"*Told* him to come!"

"Yes, sir, please, sir. Miss Nest did know that he was coming; and she did come down to the kitchen door and give the clothes to him herself, sir."

"Your daughter, Mr. Precentor," interrupted Mr. Manisty, "is evidently a most compassionate young lady. But I fear . . . May I ask your domestic a question or two?" And as Dr. Meredith, obviously struggling in deep waters, made a sign which might be taken for assent, he requested some description of the recipient of this bounty. But Mary could not give one; for it was getting dark when he came and she could not see his face. Was he young? Oh yes, to be sure he was young. What was he wearing? She had not noticed, save that he had on, she thought, a white waistcoat. And from what she could see of him did he look as though he might be a sailor? Yes, that was what he looked like whatever. And then, Mr. Manisty having apparently reserved his best question, like a titbit, to the last, manœuvred to catch the Precentor's eye before he put it:

"You must have observed whether this young man was lame or no, my girl. Was he?"

Pleased at having something about which she could be definite, Mary responded with alacrity, "Yes, sir, indeed that he was! When he came he was limping very bad indeed, so bad as old Captain Matthews."

"You see, sir!" remarked the square-faced man under his breath to Dr. Meredith. And then he resumed rather more tentatively: "You did not, I suppose, Mary, hear what the man said to Miss Meredith when she gave him the clothes?"

"No, sir, because just then Miss Nest thought she did hear Mrs. Pennefather's bell ring, and I did go to answer it."

Mr. Manisty looked as if he would very much like at this point to put a supplementary question about that bell, but he had not the chance, for the Precentor intervened.

"It was, of course, quite right and proper of Miss Nesta to show charity to this man, and as I was away at the time she could not consult me on the matter; but do you know, Mary, what suit it was she bestowed upon him, for I have not missed anything of mine?"

Another curtsy. "If you please, sir, I think it was a suit of Mr. William's."

"Thank you. That is all, Mary. You can go."

"May I put just one question more to her?" pleaded Mr. Manisty. "Mary, have you ever seen this man about in St. David's since?"

Mary reflected. "No, sir, never." And being dismissed she departed to carry to the kitchen the thrilling news of her interrogatory.

"You observe, Mr. Precentor," said Mr. Manisty, turning to his host with a modest air of triumph, "that this evidently *was* the man who worked at Griffiths' farm and was turned off on account of his lameness. And if that lameness was due to a bite from Miss Meredith's dog, as Mrs. Griffiths asserts, it is easy to understand that Miss Meredith wished to do something to compensate for it. It is even possible that Tyrrell-for I assume him to be this man-frightened her into promising him some clothes."

"But I cannot conceive," the Precentor heavily mused, "under what circumstances the dog can have bitten the scoundrel. Perhaps he had already come to the house soliciting alms, or my daughter had met him while out walking, and Bran——" At this moment Bran himself, hearing his name, and also a form of the magic word "walk," emerged from his retreat, wagging his tail with an engaging air. Dr. Meredith's gaze fell upon him, and he instantly clapped his hand in an almost melodramatic manner to his forehead. A pictorial memory of quite startling vividness had shot into his mind, of Bran retreating with every sign of guilty dismay beneath the drawing-room sofa at sight of——

"Good heavens!" he exclaimed. "Can it . . . no, 'tis impossible, quite impossible!"

Mr. Manisty's pallid rectangular visage was eagerly turned towards him. "You begin to see, I think, sir, what I meant when I asserted that Tyrrell was still in St. David's!"

"Oh no, it's not credible that it could be . . . not credible at all! And yet . . ." The perturbed ecclesiastic still looked darkly upon Bran, who, thinking that he was forming the subject of discussion, redoubled his tail-wagging and gave a litlle yelp intended as an incentive to the prospective walk.

"If you would kindly share your suspicion with me, sir," suggested Mr. Manisty, "I might be able either to dissipate or to confirm it."

The Precentor looked at him. "I hope, I hope very much that you can dissipate it," he said uncomfortably, "for if confirmed it may involve an old friend of mine in unpleasantness." Still he did not disclose his suspicion, but took a turn up and down the room, watched by Bran with an anxious and speculative eye. At last, coming to a standstill, he said weightily, "If it be true that the man whom you are seeking was bitten by this dog here, my daughter's dog, then, impossible though it seems, the animal's subsequent behaviour does appear to point to the villain's being still here in St. David's, passing as-no, no, I cannot believe it!"

"Passing as the secretary of Mr. Jerome Salt the antiquarian, you were about to say, I think, sir?"

Dr. Meredith stared. "But how have *you* arrived at that conclusion?" he exclaimed.

"Because," returned Mr. Manisty, this time with an air of undisguised triumph, "that secretary made his first appearance at Mr. Salt's house suffering from a dog-bite, and wearing the clothes of a seaman, but carrying with him a package containing a better suit, procured-you can guess where, sir!"

The Precentor leant heavily on the library table. "Yet Mr. Towers is a graduate of the University of Oxford!"

Triumph still vibrated in Mr. Manisty's nod. "Martin Tyrrell *is* a graduate of that University! It was there, indeed, that he gave the first signs of his subversive ideas. The poems and essays which he then wrote, of the most violently republican sentiments, were found when his home in Northamptonshire was searched."

"But the identity of this Tyrrell and Mr. Towers is not absolutely proved," countered the Precentor, who now seemed concerned to repudiate their common deduction. "I do not at all dislike young Towers."

"Mr. Tyrrell is said to have a pleasing address-all the more dangerous! Let me remind you too, Mr. Precentor, that there is another side to him. He very nearly brained the Bow Street runner with the original warrant when he escaped from arrest in Liverpool, and has had a prodigious near shave of being wanted for murder as well as for treason."

"I cannot believe it, I cannot believe it of that young man apparently so quiet and so studious, and attending Morning Prayer with such regularity! He must be the most consummate hypocrite! ... And why, Mr. Manifold, since you are so convinced of his guilt, have you not already arrested him, or gone to a magistrate, if you are not armed with a warrant for the purpose?"

"I am armed with a warrant, sir," returned Mr. Manisty, "but in the first place Tyrrell, as I have ascertained, has gone off somewhere for the night; in the second, I wished to be sure of a doubtful link in the chain, as, thanks to you, Mr. Precentor, I now am. I shall either take him into custody upon his return or, more probably, go after him this evening, when I have seen Mr. Salt, which I propose to do now, and have ascertained Tyrrell's present whereabouts."

"I am afraid that this will be very distressing for Mr. Salt, and extremely unwelcome to him," observed the Precentor unhappily. And then he suffered another revulsion of feeling. "Really, Mr. Manifest, this cannot be true! Young Towers was undoubtedly being of real service to Mr. Salt; Mr. Salt told me so himself!"

"And why not, sir?" demanded Martin Tyrrell's pursuer. "The man is well educated, a gentleman, the son of a country parson."

"And yet a traitor, connected with this most impudent French attempt upon Ireland! ... And if that be so, he may well be in communication with the French now, may be sending them maps of the Pembrokeshire coast, details of our defenceless state!" Distinct alarm had fallen upon Dr. Meredith.

"I do not think so for a moment, sir," said his visitor reassuringly. "It is not for that purpose that he is here, but because he finds St. David's a good earth to hide in. But I am stopping it. In that you have helped me much, Mr. Precentor, and I am profoundly grateful." He took up his hat.

But the Precentor was plunged in a gloomy reverie. "Now that I come to think of it, young Towers displayed neither surprise nor horror at the news of the French fleet's being in Bantry Bay-for I witnessed his reception of the news. Yes, the sooner you can put a term to his disgraceful activities the better. Yet I trust," he added, as his visitor prepared to take his leave, "that you will spare my friend, Mr. Salt, as much as you can in the execution of your duty? It will be most mortifying for him to discover how he has been taken in; the young scoundrel evidently had forged credentials. And I may as well warn you, sir, that Mr. Jerome Salt has rather a quick temper, and seems quite to have taken a fancy to the impostor, so that he may not receive you very cordially."

Mr. Manisty had got to the door when the Precentor added, "By the way, sir, as you seem to be so well informed, can you tell me, just as a matter of curiosity, the colour of the suit which this man Towers carried with him to Bowen's Folly?"

"It was green, sir, with a waistcoat of a lighter shade."

* * * * *

Mr. Manisty had been gone quite a long time, and still Dr. Meredith sat in his library. His hands were tightly clenched round the ends of the chair-arms —knobbed, semi-ecclesiastical ends they were, carved with complicated foliage and birds-for he was wrestling with a conviction of a nature so unpleasant as to be almost shattering. It was bad enough that Salt, and through Salt, he himself, should have been taken in by this young man, but what about his own daughter-how far had she been taken in too? And-much worse-to what extent had she, his daughter, made a tool of by this scoundrel, been deceiving her own father, and for how long? That bottle-green suit of William's, its mysterious return, Nest's curious and confused explanation, not indeed much regarded by him at the time! But now! There were depths here which he could not fathom. Why, too, had Nest never told him of Bran's biting some man, whoever he was or pretended to be?

Suddenly Dr. Meredith smote one hand hard upon the unyielding wooden leafiness beneath it and rose quickly from his chair. Bran and that bite of his were the key to a further scandalous revelation. That man hiding in the Palace ruins in whom he thought at the time that he could see a likeness to one of the privateersmen . . . and had been right about it after all-that man had confessed to a dog-bite! And he had punched him, the Precentor of St. David's, in the ribs! and subsequently-Dr. Meredith clenched both his fists-subsequently had had the consummate impudence to accept an invitation to his house, had sat at his table and drunk his best port . . . and was all the time linked in some kind of confederacy with his innocent daughter!

With what in a layman might justifiably have been mistaken for a strangled oath the Precentor rushed out of his study, seized his hat, and banging the door behind him set off hot-foot up to Bowen's Folly.

(3)

" 'Pon my soul, I believe I really miss that young fellow's society," thought Mr. Jerome Salt, pausing a moment in his labours and glancing over at Martin's untenanted table in the corner. "Odd! Well I trust he will enjoy himself at the Subscription Ball . . . and I hope little Nest will do the same!" He resumed; but though his quill wrote for a while of Griffith ap Madoc and Griffith ap Gwenwynwyn, his thoughts swung round once more to his absent secretary. "Yes, I like my privateersman, and there is no doubt that Princess Nesta likes him too. Why don't he fall in love with her, when he owes her so much? There are difficulties, naturally . . . he is poor . . . Meredith would be greatly opposed to it . . . and then there is that preposterous charge hanging over him into the bargain . . . though by this time that must surely have been abandoned . . . (I *will* approach Milford or Cawdor about it one of these days!) . . . In our grandfathers' time he would have married her out of hand, or at least done his best to. Now, cold-blooded young dog, he's very civil and no more, on account of that beauty of doubtful parentage, one sight of whom bewitched him. And her he can't marry! God bless me, what utter fools young men are!"

He resumed his writing once more, to find that his pen was scratching, started to mend it, then, remembering that "Towers" was much better at that operation, threw it across on to his neatly ordered table and drew out a new one. Hardly had he dipped it into the ink when there was a knock at the door and Mrs. Morris appeared, her black eyes very bright.

"A gentleman to see you, sir, come surveying from the Admiralty, if you would please to give him a little of your time."

"I don't care where he comes from," retorted her master, waving away the proffered card. "I cannot see anybody! If he wants to survey, tell him to go and survey!"

But the visitor was already upon Mrs. Morris' heels, and undeterred by this less than luke-warm reception he advanced past her. "You must please to excuse me, sir," he said firmly. "I am here upon business of the utmost importance-Government business-which admits of no delay."

"The deuce you are!" observed Mr. Salt, just glancing up for a moment. "Take a chair, then, and forgive me if I finish this sentence." He wrote for about ten seconds more, and then, lifting his head very suddenly and observing his housekeeper still in the doorway, said acidly, "I did not invite *you*, Mrs. Morris, to take a chair, either inside the door or outside it!" Mrs. Morris vanished.

The visitor had meanwhile seated himself near the hearth, his hands folded on the head of his cane, his eyes fixed on the other writing-table almost as if its usual tenant were sitting there.

"Well, sir?" said Mr. Salt after a moment, "what can I do for the Board of Admiralty? Does it wish to mount a carronade upon my terrace, or a semaphore on my roof?"

"It is not, in point of fact, the Admiralty which asks anything of you, sir," responded Mr. Manisty, "but the secret service of His Majesty's Government." He paused, but whatever unpleasant shock these words may have conveyed to Mr. Salt's intelligence no ripple of it was transmitted to his face. He merely shook his head with a little smile.

"I am too old, sir; willing as I am to serve my country in these perilous times ——"

"You misunderstand me, sir. Your country asks no *personal* service from you."

"Then what, pray, does it ask?" enquired Mr. Salt, leaning back in his chair. (But he knew. What a mercy that he had sent "Towers" off to Haverfordwest!)

Mr. Manisty pointed with his cane to the vacant table. "Last July, sir, I believe you engaged the services of a secretary-in ignorance, I am sure, of what sort of man you were taking into your employment. If you are really willing to serve your country, as you say, you will give him up with all readiness to that country's representative."

"You mean by that, I suppose, to yourself?" queried Mr. Salt, bethinking himself of the spectacles which he so seldom used, and putting them on in order better to sustain the part of a learned fool. "But surely, sir, His Majesty's Government cannot rate my secretary's abilities so highly as to wish to monopolise them, and deprive of assistance a loyal citizen who, as you may guess, is beginning to feel the onslaughts of old age?"

Mr. Manisty could not be sure whether he were being jested with or no, since after all he had not yet told this loyal but ageing citizen why the Government desired to deprive him of his secretary. Briefly and clearly he now gave him this information, ending by rising and laying before him on the table the warrant authorising him, James Philip Manisty, to secure the person of Martin Tyrrell, gentleman, and requiring all to whom he showed it to assist him in that operation.

At this document Mr. Salt sat staring as one who cannot believe his eyes. During the recital he had at reasonable intervals ejaculated "Impossible!" or, "I should never have thought it of him!" that being the line it seemed on the whole wisest to take in this crisis. His own fearless and combative temperament, never averse from a conflict with authority, was really urging him to admit frankly that he had known all along of "Towers' " past, but was so sure of his innocence that he had engaged him nevertheless. But to do this might, it seemed to him, involve little "Nausicaa" in trouble. So he kept on averring that he could not believe in the truth of these dreadful charges against his amanuensis, of which he was now hearing for the first time; and so managed to receive them with all the naturally horrified surprise of a guileless and unsuspicious man of letters.

And indeed he had need of all his assumed guilelessness and his spectacles when Mr. Manisty referred, in a half accusing manner, to "the man Tyrrell's" first arrival at Bowen's Folly, ill, lame, and clad in a fashion little calculated to recommend him as a secretary-in seaman's slops and flannel waistcoat. Surely, he suggested, Mr. Salt must have felt *some* qualms about taking in so disreputable-looking an individual, let alone about employing him in a literary capacity! Did he not know that the Dutch prize had gone off short of a man by desertion, and did it never occur to him ——?

"But I had never even heard of any Dutch prize!" broke in Mr. Salt, blinking through his glasses as no one had ever seen him blink before, his heart meanwhile a perfect cauldron of wrath against Mrs. Morris, whose treacherous tongue must have supplied these details of Tyrrell's appearance. "I live a very secluded life here. And I had naturally no thought of making the young man my secretary *then*! It was common humanity alone which dictated my course of action that evening. The poor fellow was ill, almost dangerously ill, with a poisoned leg; I could not turn him away. When he was better he told me how, having incautiously gone into some seamen's haunts in Liverpool, he had been drugged and carried on board a privateer which was on the point of sailing, and forced to work as a member of her crew, and not unnaturally had taken the first chance which offered of escaping from her. Being almost penniless, he had sought employment as a farm labourer, had been turned off on account of his lameness, saw this house of mine here on the cliffs, and in his extremity came seeking shelter. I then found that he was well educated, took, I admit, a fancy to him, and having for some time felt the need of a secretary, engaged him in that capacity to assist me in my historical work, which he has done to my satisfaction-or almost so-ever since. I have never enquired about his family, nor do I know any more about his private affairs than what he told me at the beginning. And I have never heard him express a single sentiment which was other than truly patriotic. Surely, Mr. Manisty, there is some grievous mistake!"

Martin's pursuer shrugged his shoulders. "If there is, it will come out fast enough at his trial. At any rate I have some cause to be grateful to you for keeping Tyrrell here at St. David's, and thereby saving me from following a six months' old trail to I know not where . . . But did it *never* occur to you, Mr. Salt, that a young man who took a false name ——"

"But I didn't know that it was false!" expostulated Mr. Salt. "How the dev —— how should I?"

"Well, sir, did it not at least occur to you that a young man so anxious to lie hidden and to cover up his antecedents must have committed at the least some misdemeanour, some crime other than that of having suffered drugging and kidnapping?" There was more than a trace of sarcastic pity for the blindness of the learned in Mr. Manisty's voice. "The misdemeanour there was not on *his* side!"

Mr. Salt blinked faster. "But he had deserted from the privateer's crew!" he objected. "He feared justice on that account."

"My dear sir-when he was (as he alleged) entrapped on board her!"

"But pressed men——" begin Mr. Salt.

"If they are pressed for His Majesty's Navy-that's a very different matter! However, I am not blaming you, sir. Tyrrell evidently knew what he was about when he chose his refuge-and would be careful not to confide his real doings to you! . . . Can you tell me, did he ever receive or write any letters?"

The "eccentric" appeared to be trying to remember. "Not to the best of my knowledge," he replied at length.

"He would not, naturally, have allowed you to become aware of it," observed Mr. Manisty almost in the tone in which one explains things to a child.

As Mr. Jerome Salt, the originator of the classical correspondence with Mr. Tyrrell senior, here felt a premonition that he could not much longer suppress a smile, he turned his facial muscles to the task of calling up a melancholy look instead, and his lips to the task of saying, "It is very sad, very sad indeed, to find that I have apparently been so mistaken about the young man's true character. I liked him, Mr. Manisty, and he was quite useful to me." Unknown to himself he was almost echoing the Precentor's words.

Martin's pursuer made sympathetic reply: "I can understand your feelings, sir, and I will therefore endeavour that Tyrrell's arrest shall be carried out with as little annoyance to yourself as possible. If you will furnish me with his present direction-since I understand that he is away for the night—I will, if he be not too far away, follow him and spare you an unwelcome scene in this quiet retreat of yours when he returns."

"That is extremely obliging of you," replied Mr. Salt—a trifle between his teeth, but that Mr. Manisty did not observe. "It was my housekeeper, I presume, who gave you that information. She did not tell you then *where* Mr. Towers had gone?"

It was with real trepidation that he waited for the answer, since he was not sure whether the infernal woman knew or did not know that "Mr. Towers" had gone to Haverfordwest. He for his part had not told her; but had she got it out of the young man himself? Much hung on that; for if she did not, he already had a vision of where, with some plausibility, he would locate the fugitive.

"No, sir," returned Mr. Manisty, "she did not tell me, for she was ignorant of his destination."

Thank Heaven for that at least! But it would be of no use pretending that Tyrrell had left for good, since some of his effects must still be in his bedroom, and the succubus would be aware of that. If only he could have prevented her having speech with this bloodhound! She should leave to-night, if he had to do his own cooking!

"Mr. Towers has gone," he proclaimed, "on a little errand for me." Here he leant back, joined his fingertips together, and began to amble along in a leisurely manner. "I do not know, sir, whether you have heard that I am writing a history of Pembrokeshire, in some ways the most unique shire in Great Britain. For Pembrokeshire, though in Wales, is in part purely English . . . It consists, indeed, of two quite distinct portions-or more, accurately, as you will see, of three-and was conquered as to its southern and northern districts by the Normans, but in totally different manners. In the southern half, what has been sometimes called 'Little England beyond Wales,' whose boundary line (so to speak), Mr. Manisty, is not very far from here, it was Arnulph Montgomery and Gerald of Windsor, the husband of——"

Mr. Manisty broke in. "But that is ancient history sir," he said, rather impatiently. "At least, by the style of the names, I suppose it to be. If you will tell me where——"

"Ah yes," said Mr. Salt with a smile, "you are right to recall me to the point. I must not be led off into the story of the *Earldom* of Pembroke. It is of the *Lordship Marcher* of North Pembroke that I wish to speak to you. No, no," as Mr. Manisty showed signs of jibbing, "it *is* relevant, I assure you! For it was in Fishguard harbour, in the year 1087, that Martin de Turribus ——"

"Another ancient person," murmured his chafing visitor. "But his name too was Martin?" he added with a flicker of interest.

"Yes, a not uncommon Norman name; it survives for instance in Castlemartin, whence Lord Cawdor derives his title. Well, sir, this Norman leader, setting up his headquarters at Nevern, beyond Fishguard, built himself a castle there and made himself lord of Kemes-though the castle at Newport, of which the ruins remain, was built by his son. The most interesting fact about this occupation is the peaceable ——"

"Mr. Salt," interrupted Mr. Manisty with firmness, "it may be interesting, but not, I assure you, to me. Time is going on" (a fact of which Mr. Salt was well aware) "and you have not yet told me where I am to find Tyrrell."

"I will tell you then," responded Mr. Salt amiably, "so that you can start at once; for I should certainly prefer that his arrest, if it must take place, should not be carried out here. In the old churchyard, then, at Nevern in Kemes, beyond Fishguard-beyond Newport, in fact-there is an extremely fine specimen of an ancient Celtic cross, with-but probably you occupy yourself but little with such things. I have long wished to possess a drawing of this cross, and as I have recently found that Mr. Towers is not unskilled with the pencil——"

Mr. Manisty got up. "I am to understand then that you have sent him to this place, Nevern, to make a drawing of some old cross or other in the churchyard-is that it?"

"Yes," admitted Mr. Salt. "And I also suggested that if he had time, he should make a sketch of the ruins of Newport Castle. Newport lying this side of Nevern, he has possibly gone there first; but whether he intended to stay the night at Newport or at Nevern I cannot undertake to say."

"I thank you," said Mr. Manisty somewhat grimly, moving with speed towards the door. "And the road to Newport? —No," he added hurriedly, fearing to let loose a history of its making, "I shall easily find it. Good day, sir, and thank you."

"I'll see you to the entrance," quoth Mr. Salt, determined that he should have no further conference with Mrs. Morris. Then, Mr. Manisty departing with briskness, the avenger went, straight as a hawk swoops, to the kitchen.

(4)

A quarter of an hour later he was back at his writing-table inditing a careful Latin note to the reveller at Haverfordwest, telling him what had occurred and adjuring him on no account to come near St. David's at present. As he turned his periods he was considering by whom he should despatch this warning, which must go off as soon as possible. By no chattering Welshman, it was certain, or the fact would be all over St. David's to-morrow—or at least Mr. Salt chose to anticipate such a result. There was however a certain Scottish lad of nineteen or so to whom he had shown kindness since his father, a Scot settled in St. David's, had been drowned one squally night off the Bishop and Clerks in the Dewisland coasting vessel of which he was part owner. Young Macalister, Mr. Salt believed, had the knack of keeping his mouth shut; the warning should go by him. When he took him the letter he would call at the dwelling of Ellen Hughes, the tongue-tied, almost dumb woman whom he designed to employ in the place of the dismissed Mrs. Morris, already (he hoped) packing up her effects, since she had been ordered to leave the house at once. "I warned you what would happen if you gossiped about my private affairs," he had just sternly told her. "Kindly leave your kitchen tidy!"

Mr. Salt was just applying the sealing wax to the candle flame when there came a vehement tapping on the glass of the garden door behind him, and looking round he was aware of a large dark form standing outside in the dusk. "Oh Lord!" he thought, recognising it, "and just when I want to get off to Macalister with this. And why has he chosen to come in this way . . . I suppose Mrs. Morris is too sulky to let him in at the front door?" He rose, and unwillingly admitted the Precentor, the latter obviously in no placid frame of mind.

"What has happened to you, Salt?" he demanded severely, "that you are barricaded away like this? I have been knocking for quite a long time at your front door; no one opened it, so I came round by the garden. And that scoundrel, where is he?"

"Which one?"

"Which one?" fumed Dr. Meredith. "Are there so many in St. David's? Which one, indeed!"

"My theory, Meredith, as you know," returned Mr. Salt with much blandness, "is that every Welshman is a potential scamp-except yourself, of course!"

"The scoundrel I mean is not Welsh," retorted the Precentor angrily. "In plainer words then, where is that secretary of yours?"

"Gone to Nevern," replied Mr. Salt. "Won't you sit down?" Meredith was not the sort of man to lay a trap, and if he asked where Tyrrell was, it was because he did not know, any more than Manisty had done, that the culprit was in Haverfordwest.

Dr. Meredith did not sit down. "To Nevern! For what purpose?"

"To make a drawing of the old cross in the churchyard for me."

"To make a drawing of the old cross for you!" repeated the Precentor with scorn. "To make a drawing of the coast for the French, more likely! Do you know what sort of man you have been harbouring here? No, you cannot-unless you have recently had a visit from a person called Mannering or something of the sort."

"Manisty," corrected Mr. Salt with an appearance of languor. "Yes, he has not long left me. A most tiresome individual!"

"*Tiresome!* Is that the epithet you apply to a man who——"

"Yes, yes," reiterated Mr. Salt, this time with a show of impatience. "I do call a man tiresome who intends to rob me of my secretary on some preposterous charge or other. Am I to gather that he has been disturbing your peace of mind also?"

"Do you mean to tell me that he has not disturbed yours? Yours of all people, I might say, when he told you of the disgraceful antecedents of this protégé of yours? I must say that I think you might at least display some regret for the humiliation which you have brought upon us here at St. David's! Under your ægis this young villain, this traitorous impostor, has been received in our houses, and made free of our local society, has associated with our daughters——"

"And very nearly danced with them too," murmured Mr. Salt under his breath.

"What's that you say? Now I can see, Salt, that you are not taking this seriously! You antiquarians, living in a world of books — —"

"Not taking it seriously!" ejaculated the culprit, giving the fire a vigorous poke. "Absurd! Who should take it more seriously than I, for the very reason that I do-or so you say-live in a world of books, and am like to lose my secretary, in whom I have just discovered a very useful gift with the pencil also? But I am trying to practise a precept which I might recall to your memory, Precentor. According to the testimony of, I believe, St. Paul, 'charity thinketh no evil.' "

"Do not quote Scripture to me!" exclaimed his visitor, almost passionately, "you who never attend Divine Service! And don't continue to evade the point, or I shall begin to think — I know not what!"

Now as Mr. Salt emphatically did not desire Dr. Meredith to embark on any logical train of thought whatever, he hastened to say mildly, again indicating a chair: "I do not wish to evade any point of yours, my dear Meredith, I assure you. But *my* point is that I am convinced that Towers is entirely innocent, and that that meddling tipstaff is upon a fool's errand, chasing after him along the road to Cardigan."

"If Towers were innocent there would be no question of chasing, for he would not run from arrest. I wish to Heaven that Man-what is his name? —or some other of his breed had done some chasing before ever that young ruffian came here last July! For I am afraid that you and I are not the only ones to have been taken in by him." He sank at last into a chair and sat glowering at the fire, while Mr. Salt, still preserving as best he could his air of the simple scholar, put about merely by the overthrow of his own convenience, thought: "That is obvious. But what does he know about little Nest, I wonder? I must walk as warily as though I were after gannets' eggs on Grassholm!"

Suddenly Dr. Meredith fixed his eyes upon him. " 'Tis a very curious coincidence," he remarked, "that this Towers or Tyrrell, who has been at St. David's so continuously for the last six months, should be absent just when the warrant comes for his arrest!"

"It is," agreed Mr. Salt instantly. "And I cannot pretend that I am sorry it has happened so. But for all that, Meredith, I did not send him off expressly (if that is what you are hinting at), since I had no more idea of this Manisty's pestilential activities than the proverbial babe unborn."

It was pleasant and even sustaining in this business to find oneself speaking the untrammelled truth now and then.

"Then you never had any inkling, any suspicion whatever, that something of the sort might happen one day?"

(This would not be so untrammelled!) "My dear Meredith, how should I? Who am I to know a felon (if he is one) by sight-any more than you do?"

"Well, you cannot pretend," retorted the Precentor, "that the rascal first arrived here in the garb and with the appearance which you would naturally expect in a candidate for the post of secretary!"

("Oho," thought Mr. Salt, "he knows that, does he? From Manisty, I suppose. Then Manisty must have seen that cursed woman before he went to the Precentory! But if it is from Nest, then he knows everything. Yet Nest, fortunately, is away at Haverfordwest.") "Why, what have you heard about his arrival here?" he asked placidly.

"The man Manisty told me that he came dressed as a seaman-and lame." Dr. Meredith's face darkened a good deal as he uttered this word.

"Manisty? Ah, yes, he has been pumping my housekeeper on the sly, so you are indebted for that piece of information to servants' gossip," observed Mr. Salt, planting this small sting with relish. "But it happens for once to be perfectly true, and the whole business turns upon that lameness, caused as it was by a neglected dog-bite." And with that Mr. Salt embarked upon much the same account which he had given to Mr. Manisty, finishing by saying: "But I do not believe in Towers' identity with this man Tyrrell-or at least, if he be Tyrrell, then I do not believe that Tyrrell is what he is accused of being, a potential traitor. That's my case; 'tis perfectly clear."

"Only because you are wilfully shutting your eyes to facts. But," said the Precentor ponderously, and as one making up his mind to an unpleasant plunge, "here is a fact connected with him to which you cannot blind yourself. When Tyrrell or Towers threw himself upon your hospitality he brought with him in a parcel, as I have good reason to know, a bottle-green suit with a waistcoat of a lighter colour, exactly resembling one belonging to my son William. Whether he ever wore it here you can best say; but he naturally never appeared in it at the Precentory. Yet on the night of William's unexpected return on leave it was found, fastened up in paper, outside the front door in the rain. Now, how do you account for that?"

This, thought Mr. Salt, is the Pass of Thermopylae. But I will not merely defend it; I will attack the Persians. "What do you mean by saying 'exactly resembling my son William's suit?'" he demanded briskly. "Am I to understand that it was William's?"

"Yes, it was William's."

"Then why in the name of Cadwallader did you not say so? But perhaps you are not quite sure of it?"

"Of course I am sure of it," said Dr. Meredith, irritated. "William himself found the package and instantly recognised the contents as his own clothes. Some explanation of the extraordinary situation in which the suit was found being required ——"

"I should think so!"

"My daughter Nesta asserted that it must have fallen or been blown out of her bedchamber window, she having taken it into her room to repair."

"Well?" said Mr. Salt enquiringly.

The Precentorial brow darkened again. "It is not at all 'well,' and requires more explanation than that!"

"But *I* can't give it, Meredith! I neither put William's suit outside your front door nor in your daughter Nesta's room, nor am I in league with Boreas to waft it from her chamber window. Why are you not satisfied with her explanation?"

Dr. Meredith snorted. "Satisfied! Satisfied now that I have learnt that she herself, unknown to me, gave it to this criminal, this outlaw! Satisfied!"

Mr. Salt burst out laughing. "She gave it to him, little Nest? But how-and when? Anyhow, 'pon my soul, Meredith, here's charity again in the more usual sense of the word! As a Christian and a Church dignitary you ought to be delighted!"

"I am not delighted! And I know of no man-not the veriest heathen-who would be delighted to discover such deceit, such dissimulation in his daughter. More than a single act of dissimulation indeed —a course of deception, I very much fear, a protracted course!"

It seemed to Mr. Salt, metaphorically avoiding gannets' eggs, that it would be no help to Nest-rather the reverse-to admit complicity with her, which he would very greatly have preferred to do. He was also beginning to get fidgety about the despatch of the warning in his pocket, for it was now rapidly growing dark; in fact, it was chiefly by the firelight that the Precentor's troubled and angry face was visible to him. Yet he saw no means of getting rid of his visitor until this matter had been thrashed out.

"Oh, surely not deception," he protested. "I agree that Nest ought not to have given away her brother's good clothes without permission, but such charitable feelings ——"

"Charitable feelings, as you call them, do not cover a plot to recover the suit unknown to anyone and then to tell lies about the proceeding! Charitable feelings do not cover concealing from me and from Mrs. Pennefather the fact that quite a week before she gave away William's suit-choosing for the purpose a day when I was absent from St. David's —she must already have had an encounter with this criminal young man, and had not breathed a word of it to anybody . . . except, I begin to suspect, to *you*!"

"To me! My dear Meredith, why the devil ——"

"This dog-bite, now," swept on the Precentor, like a foaming tide, "this confessed dog-bite on the impostor's leg—I am informed that it was inflicted by her dog Bran. Now, be frank, Salt-was it?"

"My dear Meredith, I do not know the configuration of Bran's teeth sufficiently well to recognise their imprints-especially more than a week afterwards! I cannot possibly tell you."

"You are enough to try the patience of a saint! Of course I do not mean that! But that abandoned young man must have given you some account of the episode. What was it?"

"That he had been set upon by a farm dog somewhere or other."

"Yes, I have heard that before," said the Precentor grimly. "It *was* Bran, I am convinced of it. Look at the animal's behaviour on the afternoon you first brought the impudent rogue to the Precentory-and again the day when we learnt the news of the Bantry Bay affair!"

Mr. Salt shrugged his shoulders as though to say: "Have it your own way, then!"

"That it should be Bran, and that Nesta should never tell me of the episode! It is quite clear that your 'Towers' was the vagrant whom I encountered and called to book in the Bishop's Palace last July. I was half convinced at the time that the fellow was one of the boat's crew which I had seen land from the Dutch prize that very morning. He had the dog-bite then-confessed to it; so that he and Nesta had already met and entered into some understanding, horrifying and incredible as that is! Nesta, trained under my own eye in all the principles of upright and womanly conduct-Nesta to behave thus!"

For the first time Mr. Salt felt sorry for the Precentor. He said so, but added: "However, I am sure that you will find the business not so bad as it looks, when you go into it further."

"How can I?" asked Dr. Meredith. "How can I find palliation for a long concatenation of deceitful actions and speeches . . . and she at this moment," he glanced at the clock, "preparing for thoughtless gaiety when she ought to be bewailing herself on bread and water."

"I can only repeat that I am very sorry," said Mr. Salt again. "But I can really give you no assistance, Meredith. Moreover," and he, too, looked at the clock, "I have a piece of work which I very much desire to finish this evening."

The Precentor surveyed him in the firelight. "It is absurd to repeat that you can give me no assistance," he responded, with much warmth. "You have harboured this young man for months; he has certainly confided in you———"

"Why should you suppose that? Mr. Manisty told me that he obviously would not do so."

"I know better!" said the Precentor; and now he rose, in wrath. "I am perfectly convinced that you know a great deal more than you will tell me. *You* to pretend that you are such a simpleton, such a gull, so ready to accept whatever unlikely story a disreputable outlaw chooses to hoodwink you with! Bah!—However, if you refuse to be frank with me, and I am keeping you, to no purpose, from some *magnum opus* which I doubt if anyone will read, I will leave at once-at once!"

"Don't, at any rate, leave by the way you came!" said Mr. Salt hastily, for the Precentorial form was making in the firelight for the glass door, "or you will certainly fall down the terrace. Let me at least escort you to the front door."

"Understand me, Salt," said his visitor, looking larger and more imposing than ever in the dim light, "I shall not rest until my misguided daughter has told me the whole truth about this affair, from first to last. And I shall be greatly surprised if your name does not occur in her confession. As for the viper whom you have been harbouring———"

"I have dismissed her," said Mr. Salt like lightning. "The too-communicative Mrs. Morris leaves to-night—or has perhaps already left. That is why the door was not answered."

"Your levity, sir, is disgusting!" was all the answer he received, and Dr. Meredith, at that moment marching out of the study, got half-way across the unlit hall before he collided with the newel post of the stairs and said something under his breath.

"If you had only waited until I got a light!" protested Mr. Salt. "I do not ask you to break a limb-or one of the commandments-in consequence of my levity, as you call it!" The flame of the candle he was lighting sprang up, and he preceded the angry ecclesiastic to the front door, through which the latter strode without another word save a curt "Good night."

The candle guttering furiously, Nest's accomplice stood there on the threshold of his presumably empty house and thought, "Poor, poor little Nausicaa to come back to-morrow from her jaunt to the chambers of the Inquisition! But I've got to bestir myself for Tyrrell now." Hastening back to his study he took out his unsealed letter, added a postscript in the same useful dead language as the rest, to the effect that the Precentor had just been to see him and that he feared the game was up as far as Miss Meredith was concerned, and that the recipient had better prepare her for this if he had the opportunity, and also tell her that he, Jerome Salt, had, purely for her sake, denied any knowledge of or complicity in this affair, but that he was ready to come to her assistance at any time. And he repeated his injunction to Martin to disappear as best he could, and instantly.

Then without further delay he set off on his twenty minutes' walk to the little farm on the way to Dowrog Pool, where young Macalister lived with his mother and sister, found that the boy had a horse capable of carrying him the sixteen miles to Haverfordwest at a moderate speed, gave him his instructions and saw him depart, himself turning homewards fortified by the knowledge that, short of an earthquake or assassination, the young Scot would deliver the letter to "Mr. Towers" wherever he might be, and keep a shut mouth about the whole business.

Mr. Salt then visited the abode of the providentially afflicted Ellen Hughes, engaged her to come on the morrow (though he was more than doubtful about her cooking) and returned to the dark and deserted Bowen's Folly thinking of young Macalister urging his rustic steed up and down that succession of declivities between St. David's and Haverfordwest, and-with much more satisfaction-of Mr. Manisty at right angles to him on the road to Newport-nearly there, perhaps, by this time; and of his search to-morrow at Newport and Nevern for an artist who had never been near the ruined hillside castle of the one nor the yew-shaded little churchyard of the other.

VI
THE END OF THE MASQUERADE

"And Nausicaa, dowered with beauty by the gods, stood by the pillar . . . and marvelled at Odysseus, beholding him before her eyes, and she . . . spake to him winged words: 'Farewell, stranger, and even in thine own country bethink thee of me upon a time, for that to me first thou owest the ransom of life.'"

Odyssey VIII.

VI
THE END OF THE MASQUERADE

(1)

How strange it seemed to be preparing for a ball; it was long enough now since he had been to any sort of junketing! Martin Tyrrell, carefully arranging his lace cravat in front of the dulled greenish glass of his candle-lit mirror in the inn bedroom at Haverfordwest, thought, "After all, I am not such an ill-looking fellow, for a man charged with treason!" Smiling, he gave a final twitch and turned away to slip into his new striped cinnamon coat, idly wondering who, among the few young ladies whose acquaintance he had made at St. David's, would be at the ball, and whether it would prove difficult to secure more than one dance with Miss Meredith. That fellow Perrot would be sure to be dangling about her, and a good many young bloods of this neighbourhood as well.

As he pulled out his ruffles it suddenly occurred to the reveller that the very last time he had arrayed himself for any festivity was in that fatal May last year at Hamburg-for the wedding feast which he had never attended. He stood a moment to conjure up for the hundredth time that lovely once-seen face which had drawn him to M. Matthiesen's house that day, an uninvited guest. But to-night the image did not tremble before him with the earlier vividness. He had to recreate it by an effort of will where once he had possessed it like a miniature.

Martin gave vent to something between a sigh and an exclamation of impatience, and taking up his mask from the dressing-table adjusted it. A featureless and inky blank replaced his own previous image in the glass. That disguise would be tolerably impenetrable. And as he tied it tighter he wondered why Miss Meredith was so sure that she should know him masked.

Shrouding his finery in the plain black domino lying ready on the bed, he blew out the dressing-table lights and descended the creaking stairs. Pamela Fitzgerald would not go with him to the Subscription Ball.

The Assembly Rooms, only a few minutes' walk under the February stars from Martin's inn, though the centre of the winter gaiety of the county, were in themselves neither beautiful nor even particularly well kept up. Within and without the paint was a little dingy, and the building seemed possessed of an unnecessary number of draughty passages. To-night illumination and bustle served in a measure to disguise these drawbacks, but as yet the impression lacked colour and sheen, and not till after midnight would one catch more than an occasional glimpse of bright silks and satins when a domino chanced to swing aside for a moment over the shimmer beneath.

When Martin arrived at the Rooms, ladies were still being borne up the steep street in sedan chairs, a method of conveyance which lingered long in Haverfordwest. He watched one or two of these as the roof was raised, the door opened, and the fair but masked occupant stepped forth; then he reflected that Miss Meredith, staying as she was with the Wogans at a little distance, would probably arrive in their chaise. Feeling for the moment an almost boyish access of shyness, Martin presented his ticket at the entrance to the ballroom. This was already fairly full, but since the ball was masked no introductions could take place, and he was consequently left to his own devices, and not altogether pleased at it. He had, it is true, the privilege of approaching any of the disguised ladies and requesting the honour of leading her out; but he wished to ask Miss Meredith before anyone else, and her it was extremely difficult to identify among these moving, chattering, black-visaged groups, so that when the fiddles in the gallery struck up a preliminary note or two he had not succeeded. However, he captured without difficulty a lady whom he was fairly certain was the niece of that bore of St. David's Cathedral society, Dr. Jenkins, a lady not free from the same deadly taint and inclined to be arch into the bargain. "I do so vastly wonder who you are, sir-you dance so well!" was the theme of her whispered comments as they went together through the customary evolutions.

The next was a country dance; he resolved to secure Miss Meredith for that.... In the end he had to dance it with a tall, thin young lady whose hair, imperfectly powdered, was evidently by nature not far removed from the carroty; in any case not the hair (nor the stature) of Nest Meredith. After that he found himself involved with a sprightly dowager.

The young man was beginning to get annoyed and did now quite definitely condemn the wearing of masks. At midnight, when they were to come off, he would of course be able to recognise Miss Meredith at once-but by that time she might well have promised every subsequent dance, since, for all her little retiring ways, she must be perfectly well known in this society. And in a pause after his gyrations with the dowager, Martin, standing somewhat retired in the lee of a preposterous statue of a Triton, painted green and reared upon an enormous pedestal (which, he could not imagine why, encumbered this corner of the room), started once again to scrutinise every bedominoed lady within his field of vision.

Certainly Miss Meredith was not that dumpy female over there, talking to the tall man whose peach-coloured stockings showed beneath the hem of his disguise; nor was she the young lady now sitting down by her (presumable) duenna on the other side of the room; nor that one squired by a gentleman whose domino came down to his heels; nor that damsel on the further side of this very pedestal, whose cavalier seemed to have abandoned her and whose fan had fallen from her hand and now lay, apparently unnoticed, at her feet, for she was looking up at the lustily blowing sea-god above her, her face of course concealed by the black silk and lace of her mask. A moment more and she would have moved away, leaving her fan on the floor, had not Martin come quickly round the pedestal and picked it up.

"Madam," he said behind her, "I think this is your fan."

The masked lady turned and put out her hand. "I thank you very much, Mr.... Thompson."

The owner of that all but forgotten name nearly jumped; certainly his heart did so-but not, after all, with alarm. "It *is* you, Miss Meredith!" he exclaimed, and continued reproachfully, "I have been trying to find you ever since I came!"

"You have been very unsuccessful then," replied the sweet little voice-she had forgotten to disguise it, and he would have known it anywhere. Besides, who else would call him "Thompson"? "When I saw you taking Miss Jenkins for me——"

"But indeed I did not!"

"——I decided to help you if I had an opportunity, so when I saw you standing there ... though I fear it was terribly forward of me." The voice was suddenly demure. "Thank you again for picking up my fan."

"You dropped it on purpose?" exclaimed the enlightened Martin. "But how did you know that it was I who was standing there?"

A laugh came through the fringe of the mask, a small laugh and a trifle shy. "That is my secret," said the young lady.

"Miss Meredith," Martin was very near her now, "are you promised for this next dance? No? What good fortune! Then may I have the honour-no, 'tis too late to take our places. You shall give me another presently if you will be so generous. Let us find a spot where we can talk; see, others are doing the same!"

"But I ought to go back to Lady Wogan," objected Miss Meredith doubtfully, turning her head in the direction of the group of dowagers on the red plush benches at the other side of the room.

"Ah no; it is not obligatory at a masked ball, and not after ... dropping your fan! Come with me behind this ocean monstrosity; there may be some seats and 'twill be a little more private ... Why, here's an open door and a little room-empty too!"

The person responsible for the arrangement of this little room seemed to have been in two minds as to the purpose which it was to serve this evening. A number of bare pegs protruding from the walls suggested a cloakroom: yet there were several chairs disposed in it, and even an old sofa of pink brocade. But, however unattractive in itself, it had the advantage of being empty.

"What an odd assemblage of chairs!" observed Martin. "Still, they *are* chairs! Shall we sit down?"

But this Miss Meredith did not seem disposed to do. Martin had the impression that her little feet, in the green shoes which looked so incongruously gay beneath the sable domino, longed to be moving to the sound of the fiddles without. A moment more and he was proved right, for she suddenly held out domino and skirt and sketched the first steps of the first figure of the minuet. Martin instantly did the same; she sank in a curtsy and he inclined in a deep bow. But when she came up again she said demurely, "How exceedingly foolish we are, Mr. Towers!" and her feet were still.

But Martin had gained an appetite for further foolishness. "I saw a glimpse of a most charming dress just now," he averred. "Would it be permissible for me to see yet a little more of it-in order that I may claim you after midnight with the least possible delay?"

"But, sir," protested his masked Nausicaa, "that is forbidden-at least I suppose so-for if one may remove mask or domino before the hour what is the use of them at all?"

"Why, that is just what I have been asking myself, ever since I hunted for you with such ill success! Some amends should surely be made to me for my pains!" And as she hesitated, tempted, he thought (but her face being invisible it was impossible to be sure), he added, " 'Tis surely a very minor offence, which nobody will know of . . . and we are already linked in crime, are we not?"

He pushed the door more nearly shut-he dared not shut it entirely, lest he should give occasion for gossip. Nest said softly, "Yes, we are already very wicked," and her hands went slowly up to the strings of her mask. Then they came down again. "But you too must take off your disguises, Mr. Towers-both of them!" He obeyed; and next moment was face to face with a Nest Meredith whom he had never seen. Her dress, soft and narrow after the newer mode, and high-waisted, flowered round the bosom into an upstanding frill. And the dress was pale green, the green of a primrose stalk; the ruff pale yellow. There was-he noticed it now —a narrow green fillet wound among the powdered curls which gave her that unwonted, but delightful resemblance to a figure in porcelain, and round her white throat a little chain of pale, sparkling topazes which made it seem whiter still. Martin was charmed.

"Titania must have given you that gown-or Flora, who helped you to find the primroses at Porthclais!" he exclaimed.

"Does it please you, sir?" she asked, smiling radiantly. But she was not even glancing at herself; she was surveying him, with his shrouding domino thrown back; and perhaps Martin wished that he had a finer costume than this, so hastily procured, perhaps he felt a little reassured by the remembrance that he had this very evening thought himself not so ill-looking. There was no time for him to know certainly what he felt, for Nest, looking in alarm at the door, ejaculated, "Someone is coming!"

Like guilty children they pulled their half discarded dominoes over their finery, and tied on their masks with nervous fingers; then Martin, offering his arm, led Miss Meredith with outward sedateness forth into the music, and almost into the arms of a tall mask, who evidently knew her in spite of her disguise, and who asked angrily, in the voice of John Perrot:

"Miss Meredith, where have you been hiding this long while?"

"Miss Meredith has not been hiding anywhere!" responded Martin, in one equally angry. "Shall I take you back to Lady Wogan?" he enquired of the little figure upon his arm.

"I . . . I think I have promised the next dance to . . . this gentleman," replied Nest, slipping her hand from its support.

"I do not see any . . . *gentleman* ," remarked Martin as offensively as he possibly could in the direction of Mr. Perrot, but as Mr. Perrot was saying at that moment to his recovered partner, "I am gratified to observe, madam, that that undertaking has not been forgotten!" he did not hear this comment, and bore off Miss Meredith, leaving Martin with a violent regret that he could not in these circumstances aid his going with a kick.

Mr. Salt's secretary then turned rather crossly to forage for another partner for himself. But he had the promise of the second dance after midnight with his associate in crime. How delicious she had looked in that flowerlike dress! He did not believe that there was anyone in the room who at the midnight unmasking would look more charming.

More dances followed with fortuitous companions, but on the whole luck served Martin not ill, and the fact of his being so little known in the neighbourhood gave converse with the daughters of the South Pembrokeshire squires a (to them) welcome spice of mystification. Near midnight, for instance, Martin was engaged in interchanges with a partner who said that she was convinced that he was one of the Lorts, though she was not sure which, but that as a Lort he must know quite well who *she* was. He was just disclaiming the honour of belonging to that well-known local family when he heard one of his other names proceeding from a little group near him, in which he saw the purple domino of the master of ceremonies. Letting his partner chatter on, he lent a receptive ear to this individual and heard:

"None of you gentlemen then is Mr. Towers?"

"Faith, no . . . Are you going round, sir, to every man in the company to ask that question?"

"Excuse me for a moment, madam!" said Martin hastily, and followed the purple domino as he disengaged himself from the group. "I think I overheard you asking for me, sir; my name is Towers."

The master of ceremonies turned. "Egad, that's a piece of luck! There's a lad from St. David's outside with a message for you, Mr. Towers —a verbal message, I presume, since he asks to see you personally. It appears to be urgent."

An urgent message from St. David's? It could only be from Mr. Salt. Had he met with an accident, or was he taken ill? "Where is the lad, sir? I'll go at once."

"He is waiting in the passage leading in from Castle Street. I am sorry that I must give you the trouble of going to him, Mr. Towers, but I could not well have him admitted in here."

Making a second apology to his deserted partner, Martin hurried out of the ballroom, sincerely anxious about his employer, but cherishing a hope none the less that the news of him was not so serious, but that he himself could at least return and have his promised dance with Miss Meredith. Yet the news *must* be serious, or a messenger would never arrive at that time and place.

Why the said messenger, even though not admitted to the ballroom, should wait in the dark and draughty passage from the street in which he finally found him, Martin could not imagine, for he was not by any means disreputable, but on the contrary a decently-clad, redheaded youth about eighteen, whom he could not remember ever having seen before.

Martin removed his mask. "I am Mr. Towers. I believe you have a message for me?"

The youth looked carefully at him. "Aye, ye'll be the gentleman I hae whiles seen wi' himself-wi' Mr. Salt. He's after sendin' ye this." And at that he pulled a letter out of his pocket and handed it to him.

Standing in the draught under a guttering sconce Martin opened it; it was in his employer's handwriting and couched in Latin.

Mr. Salt, for once, had taken pains with his calligraphy, and after a little the meaning of the note was clear enough-much too clear. Perhaps the veil of Latin served a merciful purpose, since the shock of the news which it conveyed did not leap with such speed from paper to brain as if that news had been conveyed in the medium of English. But it arrived there none the less surely. . . . And yet Martin could scarcely believe it. That all was discovered, that the Government had not after all relinquished its pursuit, that "Canidia ilia," in which Horatian tag Martin easily recognised the "witch," Mrs. Morris, had betrayed him to their agent, that the Precentor knew the truth, and that little Miss Meredith's part had come out. . . .

And it was certainly to Martin's credit that after the initial cold pang of incredulity and revolt his first concern should have been for her. Dr. Meredith could probably be very stern. . . .

"Will I be takin' any answer to Mr. Salt, sirr?"

Dazed, Martin looked up. Slow gouts of tallow were falling from above on to the sleeve of his domino, but he was unconscious of them.

"Tell him that I thank him for his message and will"—yes, he supposed he must; it would be crazy to fly in the face of this warning—"will follow his instructions. That is all."

The sandy-haired youth-surely he was not a Welshman? said, "Verra gude, sirr," and was gone. With him went Martin's farewell to his fancied security.

In that gust-haunted passage, where the chill night air of February made him shiver after the heated Assembly Room, the young man felt a kind of spiritual unprotectedness as well, the blow had been so unlooked-for. He was once more an outlaw, once more uprooted, the ties violently sundered between him and that safe peaceful life which he had led between Bride's Bay and St. David's shrine-he who only this morning had been thinking that he would soon cut those bonds himself, and travel that same hilly road to England and his home. What irony!

Yes, it was irony, but out of that memory of his morning's journey there suddenly flashed an answer to the question he had scarce had time to formulate as yet-the question of where to go next. For M. de la Vireville's schooner would still be in Solva harbour, and on the point of sailing, and her owner had offered him asylum on board should he ever need it-an offer, it is true, which he had dismissed into a corner of his mind as unlikely ever to be claimed. But it came out now from its seclusion and held out its hands to him. Perhaps Fate had not such a personal grudge against him after all! He thought rapidly: "If the Chevalier really meant what he said . . . if I can reach the schooner untraced . . . what more satisfactory way of leaving the neighbourhood . . . a complete disappearance . . ."

He began to walk up and down the dark passage, his brain working more easily now. He must not wait till daylight to reach Solva, lest he should be tracked there, or, possibly, meet his pursuer upon the road. Provided that encounter did not happen, it would even be an advantage to thus double back again, almost into the lion's mouth, for if this man with the warrant traced him, as he probably would in the end, to Haverfordwest (though Mr. Salt hinted that he had sent him in a northerly direction) he would hardly imagine that his quarry had returned to within three miles of St. David's. He would picture him fleeing from Haverfordwest to any quarter but that.

Martin began to think out more immediate details. He must go to Solva on foot: he had the rest of the long February night for the journey, about thirteen miles. To hire a horse so late would be difficult, and would attract notice; moreover if he did he must leave the animal somewhere, and that would afford too good a clue to his whereabouts. He must return at once to the inn, shed these festive clothes, and, leaving them behind, either say that he had been summoned away or merely slip out unperceived, leaving enough money for his bill.

Yes, that was the best he could do for himself. But first-Miss Meredith. He must find her at once, take some farewell of her before vanishing, and warn her that her father apparently knew everything, and that she must go back alone to face the Precentorial wrath on account of what she had done for *him*! Poor child-and yet he was helpless to save her from it!

He was so helpless, in fact, that a cowardly suggestion seized the opportunity to uncoil and raise its ugly head. Why, in that case, need he go back and warn her at all? She would find out soon enough. Who knew what obstacles he was putting in the way of his own safety by lingering and appearing once more in the Assembly Room . . . and all to no purpose whatever!

The young man gave an exclamation of disgust that so mean a thought should have had power even to formulate itself, and instantly hurried back along the ill-lit passage, fastening on his mask again as he went. The silence of the violins and the buzz of voices told him ere he re-entered that no dance was at present in progress; better so, perhaps. He pushed open the swing door, went through and found himself in a scene so different from that which he had left that it almost took away his breath. The room was now a shifting, shining medley of colours in place of all those black cloaks, and bodies once more had faces in place of masks. It was a kind of general resurrection.

The moment of unmasking had, as Martin instantly realised, come and gone while he had been out in the passage with the messenger of destiny; his next realisation was that his entry, still in mask and domino, was likely to draw upon him the last thing he desired, public notice. He whipped off both, but not before several men near him had cried, "Unmask, unmask, sir!" With a laughing apology he slid as quickly as possible from the region of the door, and could not avoid thinking, "It is, or it will be, a real case of "Unmask!" unless I am lucky!"

And where *was* Nest Meredith? Even though he now knew her dress it took him a moment or so to find her, standing under a lustre in converse with no less than three swains, none of whom, however, Martin rejoiced to see, was the egregious Perrot. How happy the child looked there rosy and sparkling, pleased with her charming dress, pleased with everything! It was a brutal task to break that young enjoyment, and a task all the more repellent because of his own prospective flight. And there was no time to lose over the business, for already the musicians in the gallery were putting their fiddles up to their chins. How unbelievably everything had changed in the last quarter of an hour!

Martin appeared beside the group. "I believe that I have the honour of claiming this lady," he announced with a masterful air-though he was not sure whether this really were the second dance after midnight.

It was plain from Miss Meredith's look that he was right. The swains melted away with commendable rapidity. He offered the little figure his arm, smitten with very sharp compunction as he met her smile.

"I must speak to you in private, Miss Meredith," he said in a low voice. "I fear we cannot have our dance after all. I have just received some rather disturbing news."

It was pitiful to see how the roses of a moment ago faded from her cheeks—a good proof that it was not the rouge pot which had planted them there. "Oh, my dear!" thought Martin remorsefully, as he marked that wilting.

"Could you not . . . tell me here?" she asked after a second or two.

"No, I fear not; we might be overheard. Would you object to our returning to that little room behind the statue?"

"I saw . . . other people using it," she answered, her voice unsteady.

Martin looked searchingly round. The dance was forming which he and she would not tread together after all. The last thing he wished was to make her conspicuous or to create even the mildest scandal. He could not possibly take her out into the passage whence he had just come, nor to any other outlying region, without instantly doing this.

"I fear that we must go into that little room again," he said. "Perhaps now that dancing has begun again it will be empty. And let us pretend, as we go there, that we are conversing on some cheerful subject."

Instantly she tried to smile; and then he found that for all his just-made recommendation he could not think of a single thing to say-the more so that as he guided his little fellow-conspirator round the outskirts of the various sets of dancers, who did not observe them, and past the dowagers on the plush benches, who did, he was rapidly coming to the conclusion that he could not possibly allow her to return alone to bear the brunt of her father's displeasure. He too must go back to St. David's and face Dr. Meredith-even though it would probably involve arrest.

They arrived at last at the towering pea-green figure, and walked, quite silently, towards the door behind it. This was ajar, as before; Martin pushed it open, to find to his immense relief that though the place was now full of cast-off dominoes hanging from the pegs, heaped on the chairs and even cast upon the floor, it contained no human being. Again he did not dare entirely to shut the door; again he pushed it nearly to, and then he drew his partner to the furthest corner of the small apartment, now a gloomy as well as a disorderly sight with so many discarded black garments. Almost unconsciously he took both Nest's hands and held them while he told her, with scarcely a preamble, the news which had just come to him, suppressing the fact that Mr. Salt had urged him to disappear at once-and that five minutes ago he had fully intended to do so.

The roses were entirely gone now. Martin's heart sank; but he was going to make the only reparation in his power.

"Does . . . anyone but Mr. Salt know that you are here?" was the first thing she said.

"No one, so far as I am aware. Miss Meredith, are you returning to St. David's to-morrow?"

Nest nodded mutely, still holding his hands as he was holding hers-and more tightly, no doubt, than she knew.

"At what time of day-for I should wish to be sure of seeing Dr. Meredith before you do?"

Nest loosed his hands; astonishment and then horror dawned upon her little white face.

"See my father—*you*! Mr. Tyrrell, you cannot know what you are saying! You are not going back to St. David's now that by such good fortune you are here in Haverfordwest, and that no one knows it! You cannot mean that!"

"But I do," said Martin firmly. "I am not going to allow you to return alone to face what I am afraid will be your father's grave displeasure. I cannot!"

"What is my father's displeasure against your liberty-your life perhaps! Mr. Tyrrell, you cannot, you cannot be going to do this mad thing upon my account!"

"It is not mad," urged Martin. "How can I leave you to bear the brunt of all this? All you did was for me-am I to run away and leave you to pay? I must at least see your father and explain; that does not necessarily mean that I shall be . . . captured."

"If you do," said his Nausicaa, with a fire which he would never have suspected in her, "you will break my heart-you will indeed!" And she clutched his hands again and went on breathlessly, gazing up at him with eyes little short of anguished, "Why did Mr. Salt send this warning in such haste if it were not that you should take advantage of it-if it were not to give you the best chance of getting away? Why did he lie, and send this man who is pursuing you off somewhere else, but with that object? Oh, do you not see what you will bring on Mr. Salt if you return and are arrested? It will come out that he knew all the time where you were, and that he tried to defeat the ends of justice . . . I suppose that is how it would be put. Did he not in that letter urge you to escape? I am sure he did!"

Martin kept his eyes down and did not answer.

"Besides," went on the childish voice, but with a note of heartbreak which was not childish, "if all that has been done comes to naught like this, it might as well never have been done at all! Oh, Mr. Tyrrell, I implore you to take the chance of safety which Heaven has put within your reach! It is noble of you to wish to return for my sake, but indeed, indeed it would do no good. I think it would make matters worse! Why should Papa be a jot less angry with me because you came back to St. David's and were . . . perhaps . . . arrested there-which he would very greatly dislike? He is more likely to forgive my deceiving of him if he . . . never sees you again." Her voice faltered noticeably for a moment, then it revived. "It is noble and generous of you beyond words to have the intention, but I beg you, I beseech you not to carry it out-for Mr. Salt's sake, for my own!" She was shaking; and her clasped hands of entreaty came suddenly apart and went up to her face.

No, he could not insist, if that was how his resolve appeared to her. It was true, he must consider Mr. Salt also, who might be involved with the law. Yet the more the child urged him not to return and stand by her side, the more reluctant he was to abandon the idea, recent though its birth had been. Nest's hands were down again now; how pale she was! "Promise me!" she whispered. Martin bowed his head without answering, and, in the momentary silence, the music for the first time was audible to both of them through the half-open door.

"You must not stay here," came Nest's voice again, as altered as her face. "Have you any plan?—you must be quick!"

"I might," said Martin almost sullenly, "accept the offer of my French acquaintance M. de la Vireville and get off in his schooner, which was still at Solva when I passed, and sails, I believe, to-morrow—that is, to-day."

"Do you know her destination?"

"It is Jersey, I suppose. But whatever it is, I should, unless I were tracked to Solva, get clear of this neighbourhood without leaving a clue."

"Then go, go!" said Nest eagerly. "I shall never let them know in St. David's that you were here to-night. And I am sure that Mr. Salt will stand by me to the best of his power."

"Yes, indeed; for I was to give you a message to that effect. It is true; he will be a better ally than I could ever be. But I cannot endure to think of you ——"

"I do appreciate that!" she said. "I shall never forget it! But your arrest would be much harder for me to bear even than papa's displeasure. . . . The music is stopping, I think-go, go!"

"I feel," began Martin, and experienced difficulty in expressing what he felt. "Oh, Miss Meredith, I shall ever remember what you have done for me! I am grateful to the very bottom of my soul . . . and ashamed, deeply ashamed, that you should pay, and I leave you to pay alone!"

He had her hands in his now, but he was conscious of a vehement desire to take her in his arms and kiss her face, so changed and sorrowful; but he was sure that she would be deeply affronted, and an affront was the last memory he desired to leave with the little Nausicaa who had done everything for him and whom he was now deserting in her need. Besides, at any moment someone might push open the door. He pressed both her hands to his lips; but even so that was not to be their actual parting, since he could not rush out and leave her stranded among that population of limp dominoes. He offered his arm again to conduct her back into the ballroom, and thus they emerged to the back view of the Triton and the animated scene beyond.

"I shall contrive to communicate with Mr. Salt at the first opportunity," said Martin in a low voice, forcing a smile-he felt that it was a grin-on to his face. And that was all that passed between them before he delivered over his charge with a bow to Lady Wogan, after which, watching his chance, he slipped quietly out of the Assembly Rooms, and muffling himself in the domino which, as though in absentmindedness, he had retained upon his arm, set off quickly to his inn. Abrupt indeed was the end which had come to his own seven months' masquerade.

(2)

It was still dark when Martin came down the hill to the level of Newgale beach, but not so dark as it had been, and the stars which had cheered him on his long walk had vanished. There was hardly any wind, yet on the other side of the great pebble barrier he could hear the waves arriving and withdrawing with a disheartening sound; and just about the time that he knew himself, having crossed the brook which ran out there, to be back in the "Welshery" of Pembroke, he became aware of sea-mist as the probable reason why he could no longer see the stars.

The long pull up again from Newgale beach found him beginning to feel tired; he had already walked more than nine miles and had another three to cover. Yet he was not sure but that he should arrive in Solva too early-for he did not wish to attract attention by too matutinal an appearance. On the other hand he much desired to gain the shelter of the *Raymonde* before the inhabitants were about. It was difficult to hold the balance between these two aims.

By the time he got to the top of the very steep descent by which the road threw itself anew into Solva he was aware that the village below-or at least the upper part, where it clung along the wooded side of its little river-was shrouded in mist, so that mist would certainly cover the harbour also. It did, making it difficult to locate the *Raymonde*, which was not now to be found at the quayside, though out in the harbour Martin saw a shape which from its bulk might be the schooner, for it loomed large among these little coasting vessels. There was not a soul about; the white silence was almost ghostly. He found a boat tied up at the quay, and, working one oar quietly over the stern, approached the unknown ship and shouted.

His voice went ringing in the thin mist, but there was no response from the schooner. He shouted again; heard a movement on deck, and witnessed the uprising over the side of a head in a red cap, which emitted remarks in a language that sounded like French as he knew it, but was not.

"Is this the schooner *Raymonde*, of St. Helier's?" he next shouted up. The head nodded.

"He understands English, at any rate," thought Martin. "I want," he resumed aloud, "to speak to the owner if he is on board-the Chevalier de la Vireville."

At that the head informed him in English that the Chevalier was not on board, but at the "Ship Inn" in the village; after which it disappeared again.

This was a nuisance. Martin could not insist upon going on board, nor could he well knock up the inn folks so early without, perhaps, raising curiosity in their minds. He pulled back to the quay, tied up the borrowed boat again, and, to pass the time, started to walk out past some lime-kilns up the headland which, like a wall, separated the harbour on its eastern side from the marshy valley made by another stream. Here indeed one seemed out of the world entirely.

It was certainly chilly, and he shivered as he stood there. The grass was bedewed with fog; yet in a sheltered pocket he saw a little galaxy of primrose faces looking up at him with their innocent and cheerful gaze. But the sight did not hearten him; it reminded him of poor little Nest, who, later in this day, must pass through Solva on her return to St. David's and retribution. For a while he walked despondently to and fro on the side of the ridge; then seeing that it was nearly six o'clock, made his way back to the village.

The door of the "Ship Inn," to his relief, was open, and a maid was busy there with a mop. Martin asked whether the French gentleman from the schooner in the harbour were staying there. The girl, who seemed friendly (and fortunately could speak English), said that he was, and added that she had just taken him his shaving water, for he was always early afoot and would be going back to his ship as soon as he had breakfasted. This being of excellent augury, Martin next enquired if she would ask the Chevalier whether he would see him at once, as he had brought him an important letter upon affairs. He was even going to add a further explanation about the whereabouts of his non-existent horse, when he perceived that his lying words would fall upon empty air, so fast had the damsel sped away. "Do all Welshwomen run like Mrs. Morris?" he asked himself.

In a very short time the girl was back, announcing that "the French gentleman"—Martin had felt sure that she would not venture upon his name-would see him at once, and he found himself entering a low-ceiled bedroom where, by candlelight, a half-dressed figure in which he recognised M. de la Vireville was being shaved, presumably by some underling of the inn. This was not so excellent, for he had counted upon seeing the *émigré* alone. Murmuring some apology, he tried to withdraw; but it was too late, for though M. de la Vireville could not turn his head, the operator continuing to scrape, he called out in English, "Come in, sir; this good fellow will have finished with me in a moment. I make my excuses for receiving you thus; but I gathered that your business was urgent."

"Yes, sir," replied Martin, hoping that he would not recognise his voice, and come out with either his real or his assumed name. "But I can well wait until you have finished dressing. I have been sent post-haste by your agents in Jersey with a letter; something, I believe about cargo or ports of call. I will await your leisure downstairs."

"No, pray do not do that!" said the Frenchman, and, seizing an opportunity, did turn his head. He took a pretty long look at his visitor. "That will do, John; quite close enough for a dark morning." And he rose, looking very tall in the low room (for he was a tall man), unwrapped the towel from about his neck, and while "John" was gathering together his materials said, in the most natural manner, "I was expecting to hear from Lefebvre Brothers, but not quite so soon. Are you the clerk I saw in their office last time I was there?"

"Yes, sir," replied Martin, thinking what a mercy it was that M. de la Vireville was so quick-witted, and so ready to assist him to his suddenly assumed alias, all for the sake of the stupid-looking and now departing "John." The moment the door was closed the Chevalier strode up to him and laid his only hand upon his shoulder.

"What are you doing here, *monsieur le commis des frères Lefebvre* ? Are you in difficulties again?"

Martin nodded ruefully. "There is a man come to St. David's with a warrant. By great good fortune I was away at Haverfordwest for the Subscription Ball, and he did not discover that, for Mr. Salt despatched him on a false trail in the Fishguard direction and sent me a warning. I . . . remembered what you said the other day . . . and I thought that your vessel would now be upon the point of sailing." He looked the Royalist straight in the face. "But perhaps I ask too much; in which case, I can go as I came, a clerk from Lefebvre Brothers."

"I never make an offer which I am not prepared to carry out," returned the owner of the *Raymonde* , dropping into his native tongue. "You know French, do you not, and it is natural that I should speak it to a Jerseyman. Nevertheless"—he went to the door, opened it and came back satisfied. "I am flattered that you should have taken me at my word. Will you come as supercargo or as one of the crew? But first I must tell you that I shall not be able to sail until to-morrow evening, whereas you had probably hoped to get away at once?"

"If you are good enough to take me, Monsieur de la Vireville," responded Martin gratefully, "I shall naturally be ready to fall in with your arrangements."

"You have not boarded the schooner yet?"

"No; and the man who saw me in the half-darkness and the mist would scarcely be able to recognise me again."

The Chevalier put on his coat. "Then, if you have no objection, I think you had best ship as a member of the crew. My men are not particularly rough; you have had, no doubt, sufficient experience in your privateer to be able to sustain the part, and you will be less conspicuous before we sail, *n'est-ce pas* , as a deck hand than in those clothes and in the character of a clerk or supercargo. If the men are at all inclined to gossip, a stranger of that sort arriving unexpectedly would make their tongues wag much more freely than my engaging another hand would do. Do you agree?"

"Entirely," responded Martin.

"You cannot, by chance, cook, I suppose?"

"After a fashion. That is to say, I helped in the galley of the *Fair Penitent* for a week or two, and when the cook scalded himself I took his place altogether for a few days."

"And were, evidently, not thrown overboard! I could put you in the galley, then, for a while at least. It might be a safer place for you, too, while we are still in harbour . . . Seaman's clothes, now; you must procure some at once-or rather I must, for you should not go in person to buy them."

"This is putting you to too much trouble and perhaps risk, Chevalier," protested Martin. "I think I had better not——"

La Vireville laughed. "I enjoy it; it is like the old days-that is to say, the year before last, when I was a Chouan and carried my life always in my hand."

"You were a Chouan, sir!"

"But certainly, with a price on my head. So you see I know well what it feels like to be hunted-even being put against a wall and shot, as happened to me after Quiberon. I will tell you about it some day . . . Let me reflect a little more on your clothes and appearance."

"If only I had the seaman's garb in which I first came to St. David's," said Martin regretfully. "But Mr. Salt long ago made away with it, and even if he had not I could not come at it now."

"And a very good thing too! You want indeed to look like a seaman, but not the same seaman. Describe those clothes to me."

Martin did so.

"No white flannel waistcoat for you this time then, but something quite different. I will charge myself with all that. My suggestion is this: You shall come down and breakfast with me now-if you have walked from Haverfordwest you must be famishing-still posing as the clerk from Jersey. Then you will start back along the Haverfordwest road, double back again and make your way into the nearest thicket up the stream here. As soon as I can I will join you there with a bundle of clothes; these you will put on, retaining your others if you like, in a bundle, and you will return with me to the schooner as the new hand whom I have engaged somewhere in Solva. And in case anyone should come on board to peer into the faces of my crew, I shall shave that hair of yours as close as is possible. You might wear ear-rings, too," said the Chevalier, displaying a certain gusto over these details. "A beard will take some time to produce. I fear these little alterations would not commend you to *la belle personne* who was your first accomplice, but they may make a vast difference to your chance of being recognised before we leave the neighbourhood."

"My first accomplice," said Martin with a sigh, "goes back to-day from Haverfordwest to St. David's to face her father's wrath . . . and I can do nothing to avert it."

"*Parbleu!* " exclaimed the Frenchman. "Then *M. le*—what is he—*M. l'archiprélat* knows everything?"

"I fear so. If only I could take it upon my own shoulders!" But all that was laid there was the Chevalier's hand once again.

"Impossible, my friend. But console yourself; who knows whether after all the young lady may not wring some consolation out of her sufferings on your behalf. Come, and I will order a good breakfast for us both!"

(3)

"*If anything,*" read Mr. Salt two days later, "*if anything could add to the satisfaction which the poor man now enjoyed, he received this addition by the arrival of an excellent shoulder of mutton, that at this instant came smoking to the table; on which, having both plentifully feasted, they again mounted their horses, and set forward for London.* "

Arriving, with these words, at the end of Book Twelve, chapter thirteen, and of the dialogue at St. Alban's between the hero and Partridge, Mr. Salt closed *Tom Jones* and gave himself up to reflection. For this the time and place were suitable, since it was after eleven o'clock at night, and he was in bed, comfortably propped up with pillows. A lamp burnt at his side, and he had been reading Fielding's masterpiece for relaxation after the labours of the day. As a matter of fact, however, this particular day had seen little progress made with either the *Description of Wales* or the *History of Dyfed*, for much of it had been spent in cogitation, and cogitation of a far from peaceful sort, which had caused the antiquarian to rumple up his thick grey hair and to alarm his new handmaid, Ellen Hughes, by firing out upon space-not upon her—a string of the most questionable expressions. Part of it had also been taken up in an extremely trying visit to the Precentory, and the whole punctuated with the constant though unrealised expectation of receiving a visit, which would be equally trying, from the indignant Mr. Manisty. Small wonder that Mr. Salt upon retiring to his couch had invoked the aid of fiction as a soporific.

Being an "eccentric" the owner of Bowen's Folly lay in a small fourposter from which all the cosy, stuffy, draught-hindering curtains had long ago been removed, though the breeze from the slightly opened window now and again caused the lamp flame to jump a little-an open bedroom window in February, even in a warm February, being, of course, especially in the case of an elderly man, the sign of something approaching nearer to madness than to mere eccentricity. But he did wear a nightcap; and under this headgear a frown was now visible as Mr. Salt surveyed the day's unsatisfactory doings.

The non-appearance of an empty-handed Manisty from Nevern to pick up the real trail left him much more in the dark about Martin Tyrrell's position than a visit from the disappointed pursuer, however unwelcome, would have done. Again, if he could have seen Nest when he went this afternoon to beard the Precentor he might have learnt something; but to interview Nest was, alas, forbidden. On the other hand he could still see Dr. Meredith, majestically reprobatory, still hear him saying with all the fervour of denunciation of which his rich voice was capable, "I should never have believed it of you, Salt, never!" No, he had not got much comfort out of his visit to the Precentory; nor had Nest, on whose behalf he had chiefly paid it.

Jerome Salt was himself surprised that he missed his secretary so much, and felt such anxiety concerning his present plight. He thought: "If I had shut my heart to Nausicaa's pleading that day, or been unmoved by pity for her Odysseus' lamentable condition when he appeared; or even turned him out in a few days when he was fit to leave, I should not be feeling so harassed as I do, silly old fool that I am!" And in an irritated manner he took up *Tom Jones* once more from the bedclothes, read a page or two of the next chapter, then shut the book with a bang, thrust it under his pillow, and turned down the lamp. And, in spite of teasing thoughts, he was asleep almost as soon as the expiring flame had jumped itself into extinction.

Some time later he woke rather suddenly with the impression that he was chilly, that there was not enough on the bed, and that he would consequently have to emerge from it in order to seek another covering. Disinclined to take this step, he lay trying to persuade himself that he was in reality perfectly warm; and, as he so lay, came suddenly to the conclusion that his wakening was not due to his having felt cold, but to quite another sense. For his ears now told him that the bottom sash of his unfastened window was being gently pushed up, presumably from outside.

Mr. Salt waited until he was quite sure of this fact, waited indeed until a slightly different noise told him that the intruder, whoever he might be, was scrambling as quietly as possible over the sill; and then, instead of calling out, like the average householder, "Who's there?" or "Stay where you are, or I fire!" he coolly observed to the unseen intruder:

"There is nothing worth stealing in this house, for the only valuables are of an intellectual order, so I advise you to climb down again. And kindly close the bottom of the window after you!"

The only answer was a continuance of the scramble, a little laugh, and then the words, "You cannot think how pleasant 'tis to hear your voice again, sir!"

"Good God!" exclaimed Mr. Salt, and sat bolt upright in the darkness. "What in the devil's name are you doing here?"

Yet he, too, was glad-though astounded-to hear *that* voice again. Martin seemed to arrive upon the floor in the vicinity of the window. "I had to come to find out ——"

"Wait a moment," interrupted his late employer, "while I light the lamp. Perhaps you had better pull the curtains together first, so as not to be seen . . . and I should like the bottom of the window shut."

Dimly, very dimly, he could now make out a form against the window, and waited, with the flint and steel in his hand, until he heard the curtain rings rattle forward and saw the form disappear. The lamplight, slowly springing to maturity, showed him an individual in a blue jersey with a close-cropped, almost shaven head, and rings in his ears. At this apparition he sat staring and then began to laugh.

"Great Neptune-gone to sea *again*! But you look like a convict!"

"That is M. de la Vireville's fault," said Martin ruefully, passing a hand over his denuded poll. "I told you about his having turned up at Solva, sir. In order to get away, I have shipped as cook in his schooner."

"Cook? But if you wanted to cook, Towers, as well as draw, you could have applied for Canidia's place here. I dare say you would do at least as well as the successor to the Borgias who now presides in my kitchen!"

"It is not that I want to cook, sir, but that the Chevalier thought it wiser for me to be in the galley-at least while we lay at Solva. However, the *Raymonde* is sailing to-night, not indeed for Jersey, as I had concluded, but for the Isle of Man and perhaps Fleetwood."

"Then why the deuce are you not on board her? Surely the suffering crew have not already kicked you out?"

"No. I am rejoining her to-night, off Porthclais; meanwhile I walked here from Solva along the cliffs. La Vireville will send a boat to take me off about one o'clock. I do indeed apologise for breaking in upon you like this, sir, but I could not gain admittance any other way, and I knew that you generally slept with your window open."

"Do not apologise, Romeo," said Mr. Salt, lying down again. "As a matter of fact, I have been thinking a great deal about you to-day, you and that infernal tipstaff of yours, of whom I have heard nothing. By the way, how did you ascend this blank wall?"

"I knew where the gardener's ladder was."

"Humph! And you were not afraid that I might shoot you, bursting in on my slumbers like a housebreaker?"

"I did not think that you had any firearms, sir, though I was not sure. In any case I had to risk it."

"And to risk the fact that, for all you knew, the house might be occupied by a posse of Manisty's raising, waiting for you to walk back into it-and to risk being nabbed at Porthclais now when you go off! If your motive was merely a longing to see me-which I can scarcely believe —I am vastly flattered! —I wish you would sit down."

Martin complied. "I must confess, sir, that it was not entirely or even chiefly to see you that I have come. Mr. Salt, I am terribly distressed about Miss Meredith and the trouble in which I feel sure she has involved herself on my account!"

"A very right and proper feeling," observed the occupant of the bed. "And your prognostication, I regret to say, is perfectly correct."

"You mean that Miss Meredith is . . . under her father's displeasure?"

The nightcap nodded. "One could hardly expect otherwise. I wish that plaguey Manisty had fallen into St. Non's Bay before ever he set foot in the Precentory!"

Martin leant forward, looking extremely piratical in the lamplight. "Have you been able to see her since her return, sir?"

"No; I was not permitted to. But I have seen the Precentor—a compound of Jeremiah and a raging lion."

"Raging against you too, sir, I am afraid," said Martin unhappily.

"Yes, but fortunately he cannot lock *me* up."

"You cannot mean to say that Miss Meredith is *locked up*!" exclaimed the pirate in horrified tones.

"But I do-like Miss Sophia Western in this work." He held up *Tom Jones*. "Locked up on bread and water in her room. I pleaded to have a word with her-as an accomplice-but the Precentor was adamant."

There was a moment's silence while the cook of the *Raymonde* digested this information. "For how long is he going to practise this barbarity?" he asked indignantly.

"I believe until he has completed his arrangements for sending Nest away."

Martin leapt up from his chair. "Away? *Away?* Where?"

"I wish I knew. Oh, not to the plantations!" said Mr. Salt, half laughing at the expression on his visitor's face. "Somewhere out of St. David's. Exile in disgrace for a while. It appears that she confessed everything, except, I fancy, the fact that you were at the ball at Haverfordwest."

"She said that she would keep that to herself-the little heroine! But, sir, were you not able to explain to Dr. Meredith——"

"That I originated the whole plan? As a member of the supposedly stronger sex, I felt bound to tell that lie. But it was too late; Meredith knew the real facts from her. (I had tried to see him before she came back, to forestall this, but I did not succeed.) I did my best, I assure you, to shoulder as much of the blame as I could. But it had no effect . . . by which I mean no good effect; and your little heroine will, I fear, remain in durance, eating the bread of affliction and drinking the water of affliction—I think her sire actually used those words-until she goes into banishment."

"Mr. Salt, did you get rid of my sheath knife as well as of the clothes in which I first came here?" asked Martin rather fiercely.

"No, I did not. I thought it would be useful for pruning my arbutus hedge and so forth. But you are not intending to poniard the Precentor, Towers? I really cannot countenance that!"

"I shall not return to the *Raymonde*," replied the young man, still more fiercely, "and I think therefore that I had better have some weapon about me, merely for the sake of being able to threaten violence. I swear I will not do more than that. But I am going to see Miss Meredith at whatever cost, and her father too. May I know where my knife is?"

The next moment Mr. Salt was standing before him in his nightshirt. "Martin" (never had he called him that before), "Martin, you are going to do no such thing! Do you wish to make your arrest doubly certain?"

"I don't care a rap about my arrest," asserted Martin. "I only want to defer it until I have had speech with Miss Meredith and her father. It is I who am responsible for all this, and do you think that I am going to sail away and leave a girl to pay like that for the whole affair?"

"If I am to listen to heroics," quoth Mr. Salt, "I will put on my dressing-gown. No"—he caught himself up quickly—"no, in theory I am entirely with you, young man, and if you could accomplish anything, I would say, Go, at whatever personal cost, and do it! But you can do nothing-except possibly to make matters worse. Suppose you turn up at the Precentory to-morrow—for you cannot think that to fetch Meredith out of bed at midnight would placate him much-what would be the result? Merely to confirm him in a possible conviction that you had been making love to his daughter under cover of seeking her assistance-which was the last idea in your mind, was it not?" And he looked at Martin with a somewhat inscrutable expression, going on, after a moment, gravely, "I hope I need not point out that should you be crazy enough to go anywhere near her window to-night the Precentor would be justified in thinking that you had a design of actually seducing her."

"If he found out," said Martin truculently.

"Of course he would find out!" retorted Mr. Salt, slightly shivering. "In any case, do you want to heap more deception on the child's head-create more for her to conceal? If I know Nest, her sole consolation now is that she has at least confessed her past misdeeds. Yes, she is probably regarding her present punishment (which after all is only what might have been expected) as a just expiation for her faults." Mr. Salt, quickly assuming his dressing-gown, looked at him whom he had recently characterised as "a cold-blooded young dog" a trifle apprehensively, for after all one may rouse indignation to a pitch higher than one intended, and have some difficulty in damping down to a safe incandescence the fire thus lighted.

"You mean that I am tamely to go back to the schooner and sail away and not lift a finger?" asked Martin between his teeth.

"It is your only course. But when Nest returns, as in due time she will, from her place of banishment-perhaps her sister's house in Lincolnshire —I will give her any message you please; or you can write a short letter and I will give it to her, or even send it to her when I discover her place of exile . . . if I think it wise to do so. And I shall see to it that she learns how you risked your liberty and endangered my night's rest by returning to ask news of her, and that I had difficulty in restraining you from more headstrong proceedings. You will find a pen and ink on the table yonder, and meanwhile I will fetch you your sheath knife-if you will undertake not to use it against any of the *genus homo*, not even against that quite superfluous specimen of it, James Philip Manisty?"

Martin nodded gloomily, and Mr. Salt, candle in hand, went in his slippers out of the bedroom. After a moment the ear-ringed intruder sat down at the table and seized a sheet of paper and a pen.

Dear Miss Meredith, I—(what was he to say?) —*I have just learnt to my great distress* —*I cannot express to you* —*I hear* — —" He ceased, gnawing the feathers of the quill, and before he had got any further there was Mr. Salt's voice behind him.

" 'Tis later than I thought. You had better leave that, my boy, unless your Frenchman's shore-boat intends to stand by till morning." He had his watch in his hand. "Here is your knife. Perhaps it would be as well to put the ladder back in its place. Be careful of the cliff edge in the dark and if you value Miss Meredith's good name keep clear of the Cathedral close! God bless you!"

"And God bless you, sir-for everything!" responded Martin, wringing his hand hard.

"Send me news of yourself if you can contrive it, Odysseus!" were Mr. Salt's last whispered words as Martin's head sank from the level of the window sill.

Having cautiously replaced the ladder in Owen Owen's shed, the travesty of Romeo stood upon Mr. Salt's terrace beneath the sharply twinkling February stars and thought: So, after all, I am going to abandon her! And, though he knew Mr. Salt's prudent counsels to be right, he very nearly set his face towards the slumbering Cathedral close, and felt himself to be a hateful coward as he made his way back to the cliff path. If he fell in with any who were searching for him it would at least solve the question "To flee or not to flee" —though how, in the case of capture, he should have assisted Miss Meredith by not fleeing remained unelucidated.

There was also the chance of falling into St. Non's Bay. In some places on this piece of coast, as Martin knew, the cliff edge, fretted and fantastic, was sharply and unexpectedly indented, and it was now darker than when he had walked the much longer stretch from Solva. But he was acquainted with the dangerous spots, and contrived to give them a wide berth, though often at the cost of stumbling painfully through gorse. He had brought with him a small lantern in case of real emergency, but he did not light it, for besides possible searchers after himself, the coast, a favourable one for smugglers, was occasionally patrolled by preventive men. However, he met nobody, and before long came to the cleft which was the tiny harbour, and through the sharp stillness of the winter night, through the slow heave and splash of the tide against the base of the cliffs below, could detect, he thought, the creak of oars in row-locks and the sound of subdued voices. What the men manning the boat now coming for him thought of these proceedings on the part of their newly shipped cook, and of the captain's indulgence towards him, he could not imagine. Nearly all Jerseymen, except the mate, Challacombe, who came from North Devon, they had so far displayed no undue curiosity about him and his sudden appearance among them, while his previous experience before the mast, brief though it had been, had taught him the expected lines of his own behaviour.

The tide was low; the boat, he knew, would come just up to the half-ruined breakwater. And when he got to the edge above he could tell that it was already there. Scrambling recklessly down the rough path, hardly seeing where to put his feet, Martin gave the three low whistles agreed upon as a signal, heard them answered, smelt seaweed, made out the boat with dim forms in her, climbed over the blocks of tumbled stone against which the tide chuckled and gurgled, was adjured to "Look lively now, mate!" and in another minute was being carried on the swell away from his sanctuary of more than half a year and his now helpless little confederate. Coward-coward!

(4)

"No, I wish *you* to go and tell her, Gwenllian," said the Precentor. "I do not desire to see her again at present. Here is the key of her bedchamber." Looking like Jove delegating a thunderbolt he held it out.

The coffee urn still steamed faintly on the breakfast table from which he and his sister had just risen. But there were only two covers laid there.

"*Must* you send her away, brother?" asked Mrs. Pennefather, reluctantly accepting the key.

"I have already said so," returned Dr. Meredith, still Olympian. "Considerations of discipline apart, I much fear that the man Manisty, if he were to return here-as he may, if unsuccessful-would make efforts to procure an interview with Nesta. I should greatly dislike such a possibility."

Mrs. Pennefather sighed. Her cap was more awry than was usual so early. "And you have arranged with Mr. Mortimer for her to go to-day?"

"At one o'clock. Mortimer is coming himself in his gig, and will take her to Trehowell. I have laid stress upon Nesta's being in need of a change of air, for I do not wish him or his daughter to guess that she is in disgrace."

"That was kind," murmured Aunt Gwenllian, still looking with distaste at the key which she held. The full story of her niece's continued reticence, deceit and untruthfulness had deeply shocked her, and yet . . . the child had now been locked up in her room for two days! All through history males had been so terribly prone to the imprisonment of females! Had or had not Mary Wollstonecraft in that marvellous book of hers touched upon this point? "As you desire it I will tell her of your decision," she resumed unhappily; yet at the door she made one more protest. "You do not think, Robert, that you are perhaps a trifle hard upon the child, now that you know how Mr. Salt — —"

"Jerome Salt," interrupted Jupiter in his deepest voice, "Jerome Salt, disgracefully as he has behaved, did not originate this incredible plot, although he did his best to make me believe so. His compliance and collusion are indeed beyond the terms of any vocabulary rightly to characterise; yet they do not absolve Nesta. That the abandoned young scoundrel himself should have worked upon her in the beginning is possible, though she denies it; but, as I have already said, Gwenllian, were an archangel to argue with me I should still be of the same mind. Nothing can alter the fact that my daughter had it in her power to be open with me, to seek my assistance-our assistance-in order to free herself from the toils which this villain had wound about her . . . and that she did not! She preferred to aid and abet him-with Salt's assistance-and to lie to me, to lie repeatedly. There is no more to be said."

Indeed there was not, and so Mrs. Pennefather went sadly from the presence. Four days of storm had blown the sails of her mental bark first in one direction, then in another. She had liked that quiet and well-mannered young man; all the greater had been the shock of learning of his antecedents. Yet, even as she mounted the stairs to her niece's room, wisps of romantic tales were floating in and out of her poetical mind, stories of various heroines of history or legend incarcerated-usually on account of a love affair-in some high castle tower by father or husband. Probably these heroines too had not always spoken the truth.

Compared with these lofty prisons, Nest's place of captivity was humdrum, being merely her own bedchamber. Yet it had its rigours. No domestic possessing a key to it, the morning's supply of bread and water was standing unadmitted upon a table outside. The soft-hearted and (in theory) partly emancipated Aunt Gwenllian stood looking at that meagre fare. It was right, of course, that this and a locked door should be the girl's portion; in Aunt Gwenllian's own youth misdemeanours of a much paler shade of guilt had been visited upon her with the like discipline, and Nest had been astoundingly wicked. She fitted the key into the lock and entered, bearing the penitential diet with her.

It was the first time that she had been allowed to visit the culprit, and she did not know what she would find-probably an extremely woe-begone damsel in a scene of desolation. But there were no signs of disorder; the bed was already neatly made, and the captive, with a shawl round her shoulders, was setting her simple dressing-table to rights. Mrs. Pennefather was touched, she knew not why.

Duster in hand, Nest had turned at the sound of her aunt's entrance. She looked white and pinched, and her eyes were still red from yesterday's, if not from more recent weeping. Mrs. Pennefather's first words were not of reprobation. They were: "It is too cold for you here without a fire, niece; I did not know that you had none!"

Nest flushed at the first sympathetic words which had fallen on her ears since her return. She shook her head, however, and replied in a low voice: "Thank you very much, Aunt, but I am only a little cold."

Putting down the bread and water, Mrs. Pennefather went to her and caught hold of a hand. It was certainly not warm. "I shall ask your father if I may have a fire lit here. You have most deeply shocked and grieved him, Nest; but he would not wish to see you ill."

Nest clutched the duster rather harder in her other hand and said nothing, her eyes upon the floor.

"If the fire were but laid I would put a light to it myself," continued the good poetess. "Meanwhile sit down and take your . . . breakfast, and I will tell you what your father has decided about you."

Nest lifted her eyes. "He spoke yesterday of sending me away from St. David's. Is he going to do that?"

"Yes; but not very far away. —Come, eat some of this bread!" Mrs. Pennefather went and fetched the little tray. As a breakfast beverage in winter the glass of water lacked attractions, and indeed Nest did not attempt to drink any. But she nibbled obediently at a bit of bread, looking at her visitor meanwhile with that patient and half heart-broken gaze.

"Do you know where Papa is sending me, Aunt Gwenllian?" she asked after a moment.

"You are to go and stay with good Mr. Mortimer of Trehowell, in Pencaer, and his daughter, whom you know. Your father in his kindness has arranged it with them on the score of your requiring a change of air; and indeed it is high and healthy there, and you will have the advantage of their excellent farm produce. He does not wish it to get about that you are being sent away as a punishment for your behaviour; but that, as I hope you realise, Nest," concluded Mrs. Pennefather, making an effort to be duly severe, "is the true reason for your banishment."

"Yes," replied the culprit in humble tones, "I do realise that; and I more than deserve such a punishment. Papa is very good to have put the matter on those grounds to Mr. and Miss Mortimer."

And despite the fact that she gave the impression of having in the past forty-eight hours cried so much that she could cry no more, two long tears rolled slowly down her face and on to her little shawl.

Mrs. Pennefather went over to the window. It seemed to her that there must have been some very strong incentive for Nest's amazing course of behaviour, and most probably that which is the strongest incentive of all in the case of two young people of opposite sexes, a motive which, oddly enough, her brother never appeared to have investigated, perhaps because he thought it best ignored. He seemed to have concentrated on the fact of Nest's long-drawn transgression rather than enquired into its springs. Aunt Gwenllian would have liked to know more. But since she had grown up Nest had never much confided in her aunt, which was often a grief to the good lady. Mrs. Pennefather contemplated the Cathedral tower for some moments, and then brought out, void of preparation, the question which she had meant to approach in a more roundabout manner.

"Tell me, Nest, did this abandoned young man never make love to you in any way? —He must have done so!"

At this unexpected frontal attack the colour flared up in her niece's pinched face. "Oh, never, never! Never in any way!" And though, for all her leanings to romance, Mrs. Pennefather did not catch the forlorn undertone of, "I only wish he had!" she did hear the unmistakable ring of truth in the reply, and was relieved, if unenlightened.

"Then why, child, did you ——?"

"Because, as I told Papa, I was so sorry for him," answered Nest, with a deep sigh. "And because Bran bit him . . . I do not think that I want any more breakfast, Aunt Gwenllian. At what time am I to be ready to start for Trehowell?"

"At one o'clock," said Mrs. Pennefather, abandoning the window and her attempt at eliciting a confidence. "I shall send a maid to light a fire and to pack your clothes, and you shall have a hot meal before you set out upon the long drive to Trehowell-with your father's permission, of course."

"Oh, Aunt Gwenllian," faltered Nest, "you are good to me . . . truly I do not deserve it!" Another pair of tears seemed about to well from their almost depleted reservoir when she caught up the duster by mistake for a pocket handkerchief and checked them.

"It is not, child, as though your father also were not good to you," said her aunt, with a tinge of reproof. "But-there must be punishment for misbehaviour so grave and so prolonged as yours!" (On which account she could not put her arms round the meek little sinner as she had a sudden wish to do.)

"Indeed, I am glad to be punished," averred Nest in tones of humble sincerity, "because I know that I deserve it, many times over! As I tried to say to Papa, it was so dreadful to me to deceive him, that all the time the knowledge of what I was doing was itself a punishment."

"And yet you went on deceiving him, Nest! That is hard to understand!"

"Mr. . . . Towers had had such ill-fortune, and he was innocent! Oh, Aunt, I am sure that he is innocent," asseverated Nest most earnestly. "Innocent, in spite of all that dreadful man seems to have said! Is there," she put the question timidly enough, "is there any news of him-of Mr. Towers, I mean?"

Mrs. Pennefather shook her head reprovingly. "None at all, I am glad to say."

"Perhaps," hazarded Nest in a very small voice, busying herself with some trinket on her dressing-table, "perhaps Mr. Salt knows something?"

To this her aunt responded with real stiffness: "Your father is not likely to hold any communication on that subject with *Mr. Salt*! You must put all thoughts of that misguided young man out of your head, Nest, and at once; it does not indeed become you to need reminding of that duty! Pray and read your Bible instead of letting your mind dwell upon him! —I am glad, however," she added in a softer tone, "to see that you are at least in a penitent frame of mind, and that you acknowledge the justice of your punishment."

It was as she was leaving the room that her niece said, still in the same humble and patient tones: "Do you know how long I am to stay with the Mortimers, Aunt Gwenllian?"

"No; your father did not mention it. I imagine, until he returns from Bath, at least. You know that he goes there at the end of the week, and is to preach in the Abbey?"

"Yes, Aunt. He once spoke of taking me with him, perhaps. I . . . I had been greatly looking forward to it."

"So he did —I had forgotten. But you were not, surely, thinking that he would still take you!"

Nest mutely shook her head.

"I will see about your fire," said her aunt, with a final half compassionate look at her, and went out.

When the key had turned behind Mrs. Pennefather the captive, wrapping her shawl closer about her, went and sat upon the window-seat, staring out for a long time into the bright windy morning, full of buffeted rooks and snowdrops, and of romping sunlight which rushed like an engulfing wave over the great rock of the Cathedral and fell back again, only to chase itself, over the landscape, gleam after gleam, as far as Carn Llidi's craggy height. Papa's just wrath, the dreadful sense of estrangement, her consciousness of her own wickedness, that wickedness which was not yet fully purged, for not a word had she said of Martin's having been at the ball (though, fortunately, she had not had to lie about it, merely to keep silence), the deprivation of this delightful half-promised visit to Bath-all these various pangs together were nothing in sharpness to the pain of knowing that she would never see Martin again. Even the knowledge of the revived danger in which he now stood had not afflicted her with the hemlock bitterness and finality of that draught. Once it had been his peril which had loomed so large; now it was her own loss. It little mattered to her where she was, whether she sat in this chilly bedroom with the Palace ruins beneath her eyes, and the Cathedral porch outside which she had been used to see him, and sometimes to exchange a word with him, or whether she were exiled to that high rocky plateau of Pencaer, among the little isolated farms where he had never been and never would be-all was one to her now.

When she was a silver-haired old maid, knowing Latin and perhaps a little Greek, and interesting herself a great deal in the poor, how would she remember him best-as he had looked at her last sight of him in the Assembly Rooms, so debonair and handsome in his cinnamon coat, and then so distressed and heroically desirous of rushing into peril for her sake; or at her first, her very first, sitting on the thwart of the boat in the little landing-place at Porthstinian, with his sun burnt hands resting on the oar and the blue waters of the Sound behind him?

The glass against which she leant her cheek was icy, but Nest was too miserable to feel cold. And when a scratching and a whining outside the door told her that Bran had once again succeeded in slipping upstairs and was trying to penetrate to his mistress, she did not go and speak to him through the crack as she had done yesterday. Yet, with the exception of poor Mr. Salt, whom she had involved in this affair, Bran was the last link-if an unfortunate one-which she had with Martin Tyrrell, and even to hear him snuffling out there brought back that hayfield and the lane flaunting with honeysuckle and snapdragon. Memories she had-but she had nothing else.

VII
"DANGER'S TROUBLED NIGHT"

"And as they sat thus, they beheld thirteen ships coming from the south of Ireland, and making towards them . . . 'I see ships afar,' said the king, 'coming swiftly towards the land. Command the men of the Court, that they equip themselves, and go and learn their intent.'"

Branwen the Daughter of Llyr

(THE MABINOGION)

"Since my Love went, I have been frighted so."
Dryden, *The Indian Emperor*.

VII
"DANGER'S TROUBLED NIGHT"

(1)

A grey, ill-tempered sea leapt round the schooner *Raymonde*, a grey sky curved low above her, as she laboured close-reefed down St. George's Channel against a south-west wind which was half a gale already. On her lee stretched the cruel, iron-bound coast of Cardigan, in her hold was ballast in some danger of shifting, and in her stuffy little galley a young man known as Jem Gregson, who strove valiantly not only with pans that suddenly fell over with a clatter and liquid which sprang unexpectedly from its receptacles but also with occasional feelings of nausea. For the experiences of a previous nautical incarnation on board the *Fair Penitent* had not been very prolonged, and he had soon discovered that summer voyaging in a large and well-found brig was by no means the same thing as a winter cruise in a small and ancient schooner.

Only yesterday had they left Peel Harbour, in the Isle of Man, with a pleasant north-westerly breeze, the *Raymonde's* prospective further trip to Fleetwood having been abandoned for the sufficient reason that the Manxmen had bought up practically the whole of her general cargo. Finding himself unable to ship another of any kind in the island the Chevalier de la Vireville was obliged to come away in ballast, having, however, conceived the idea-due to what he had observed during his stay at Solva-of putting in at Milford for a cargo of lime and carrying it to Bideford, where, on the mate Challacombe's authority, he would be sure to find a ready market for it. La Vireville had imparted this information to his cook rather apologetically, since this plan entailed a return to Pembrokeshire, though to a different district of it; but Mr. Gregson's reception of the news had led the Frenchman, a keen observer and, like most of his countrymen, not uninterested in the relations of the sexes, to say to himself: "Aha! one sees that it does not displease Mr. Tyrrell to revisit the county inhabited by Miss Meredith!"

Yet he had been a trifle too clever in this deduction, for Martin now thought of Miss Meredith as an exile in the fens of Lincolnshire, with the width of England and Wales between her and St. David's twin shores. She was often in his mind indeed, the poor little banished heroine, with all the Precentorial wrath upon her brown head. If ever he was in hers, he hoped that her thoughts of him were not too unkindly, although he was the cause of all her tribulation.

Heavens, how the schooner was rolling and groaning, and how she shivered when a wave dealt her one of those resounding thumps! Cardigan and northern Pembrokeshire formed an extremely unpleasant coast to have upon one's lee, and Martin, with his recently gained smattering of nautical knowledge, had once or twice wondered whether the *Raymonde* had enough sea room. He stumbled out of the galley and glanced about; the weather looked uglier than ever, and less sail was being carried than an hour ago. The atmosphere was too thick for him to see the pitiless, rocky reception awaiting the *Raymonde* at this moment, but he knew it was there—a shore, so he had been told, not only without a harbour, but without even a beach of any kind-nothing but implacable cliff and snarling reef. Having received a shower of spray he went back to the galley.

Five minutes later the door was opened, and the master of the *Raymonde* himself stood there in wet oilskins.

"*Mon cher ami*, a word to tell you that since it is clear that we shall never make Strumble Head, not to speak of St. David's Head, against this wind, we must run for the only harbour on this *côte d'enfer* which can shelter us from it, and that is Fishguard. You must not go ashore there, that is all. *Dieu*, I hope that ballast has not begun to shift!" And, as the schooner suddenly heeled over to an angle which almost gave colour to this view, La Vireville vanished again.

The *Raymonde's* ballast did not shift, or she would not have fought her way successfully into Fishguard's bay and harbour as she did late that afternoon. Nor did her cook listen to the voice of prudence, but, alternating as he now did between short fits of nervous caution and long stretches of recklessness, went ashore to do his marketing next morning as though he did not know that Mr. Manisty had been sent by Mr. Salt into that very neighbourhood. For, after all, as he told himself, no one in Fishguard knew him, and it was now nearly a fortnight since the bloodhound had pursued in this region a false trail which he must long ago have abandoned.

And so, in upper Fishguard-for the town itself was poised high above its secluded harbour-fat and obliging Mrs. Powell, in her general shop, observed that morning with one corner of her eye the entrance of a young seaman in a jersey, with a basket over his arm. But she was engaged just then in serving an esteemed female customer, and the young fellow would have to wait; which he did with respectful patience.

"Yes, Miss Mortimer, yes, surely; the boy shall take the sugar and the other things to the "Royal Oak," and they shall be there before you do start back-yes, have no fear whatever! But the tea, now; was you saying you wished something out of the common good, Miss Mortimer?"

"Yes," replied the customer, "for, as I daresay you know, Mrs. Powell, we have Miss Nesta Meredith from St. David's paying us a visit for her health; and I should desire, since I must buy more tea, to have some really superior, such as she is no doubt accustomed to drink at home."

"Indeed to goodness now!" exclaimed Mrs. Powell, impressed. "A sweet young lady by all accounts, and his Reverence the Precentor could not do better, I'm sure, than to send her to the good air of Pencaer. Now this is the best tea I have, Miss Mortimer; I'm told it's what the Lord Lieutenant himself drinks, but I'm sure he do pay more for it in London or Haverford than what I sell it for. You'll take a pound of it, Miss Mortimer *bach*? And is there anything else Miss Meredith would be likely to fancy? No? Well, the tea shall be sent with the rest, indeed. Good day, ma'am, good day to you. —Now, young man, what might you be wanting?"

Leaning upon the counter, under its canopy of hams, boots, saucepans and onions, the young man asked eagerly: "Who is that lady just gone out?"

"Why, Miss Mortimer of Trehowell, to be sure," replied Mrs. Powell. "Trehowell Farm, out Strumble Head way. Well, now, what is it you do be wanting?" she added, with a hint of impatience, for several other customers had now entered.

It was a good thing that Martin had armed himself with a list of requirements, since otherwise the crew of the *Raymonde* might not have had the adjuncts to their salt pork and biscuit which he intended. Mrs. Powell was in a hurry to finish with him lest her other clients should go away; but he reflected that he could easily obtain elsewhere more precise directions about the whereabouts of this Trehowell Farm which so astoundingly housed his Nausicaa. He *must* see her!

Having cooked the midday meal and washed up-hateful task! —in a species of frenzy, he hurried to the captain's little cabin. The Chevalier was writing a letter.

"You have no objection, I suppose, to my going ashore for some time this afternoon?" quoth Martin.

"As master of this vessel, none," responded the *émigré* promptly. "*Mais* —are you wise in doing so, my dear friend? It was to these parts, was it not, that your pursuer was directed? You ought indeed to have sent one of the crew to do your marketing for you this morning."

"I am very glad that I did not, for I learnt the most surprising fact; that Miss Meredith's place of exile is not far from here —a farm called Trehowell, on the way to Strumble Head."

Fortuné de la Vireville looked at the young man with a sort of amused interest. "And you intend to visit Trehowell? I do not need to point out to you that if the young lady's father —*ce prélat magnifique* —has acquainted the farmer with the situation he will undoubtedly hand you over to justice!"

"I had thought of that. But I shall not actually present myself at the farmhouse. I shall cruise about in the offing," announced Martin nautically, "on the chance of Miss Meredith's taking a walk, or of my somehow obtaining a sight of her."

"*Eh bien*," said the Frenchman, "*faites ce qui vous semble bon. Mais prenez garde que le chien de la demoiselle ne vous morde pas de nouveau!*"

"I don't suppose that she has been allowed to bring the animal with her," replied Martin.

Between Fishguard and Goodwick was a long stretch of firm sand, separated from the marshy ground behind by a bank of pebbles where sedge and dog-rose had rooted. Martin had to traverse this level and then to mount again to the plateau of Pencaer; and the hill which took him to the latter was so long and formidable that his heart was going at double pace before he reached the top. But then it had undoubtedly been working at an accelerated speed ever since his visit to Mrs. Powell's shop this morning. That Miss Meredith should be up here, and not in Lincolnshire, was surely, he told himself, one of the most extraordinary coincidences upon record, and it must certainly be intended that he and his little accomplice should meet yet once again. And he would tell her how, after all, he had returned to St. David's by night, and how hardly he had been restrained by Mr. Salt from bearding her father, and of a letter begun in haste and never finished. (But perhaps Mr. Salt himself had contrived to inform her of these facts.)

Once up, he walked quickly along the indifferent road which seemed to run on a sort of spine, for it afforded immense sweeping views of the fields stretching down to the cliffs, and of a vast expanse of sea. At last this road brought him to a moderate-sized white house flanked by outbuildings, standing at a slightly lower level, and with a short avenue leading down to it; and this, from directions which had been given to him, he knew to be Trehowell.

At first he walked discreetly past its gate a number of times-with no memories of similar manœuvres in the Schildtstrasse at Altona to plague him. Afterwards he ventured to stand a moment leaning upon this gate. Neither move brought him any sign of the presence of Miss Meredith. Then he wondered whether she might not be taking a walk, and, since she loved cliffs, upon these of Pencaer perhaps, either in the direction of Goodwick or of Strumble Head. The spin of a coin indicated the former. Going a little back along the lane Martin climbed the bank into a field, crossed some cultivated land, then stretches of rough grass and furze, and found himself at last on the edge of a pleasant promontory looking at the great azure expanse of Cardigan Bay.

He thought, having seen no sign of Nest's figure, "Perhaps she is down here," and began to descend the headland, for it was not as steep as it first seemed; and it was clothed with green to the rocks at its base, and even had primroses in the hollows. There was no young lady anywhere, but there was an amazingly fine view. Immediately to the right there ran inland a long and very narrow combe, so thickly clothed with trees that the bottom was invisible; on the other side of it jutted out a long pale finger of a reef. Beyond the opening of Fishguard Bay (which he could not distinguish) the great up-ended bluff of Dinas Head defied the waves, and much further away on the Cardigan coast ran out yet another bold cape. Some effect of light and colouring gave Martin the idea that the seas over which his prototype Odysseus had wandered must have been like this. Surely it was the sort of view which might attract a young lady with a taste (however misguided) for rendering the ocean in water-colour. And, not pausing to consider that one did not usually indulge this taste in February, nor, probably, when one was in exile, he staged in his mind a pleasing scene to be played to-morrow afternoon, following the lines of that in which he had come upon Miss Meredith plying her art above Porthclais last October. No interruption was likely here; and perhaps not much sketching would be done either. But if it were a day as fine as this they would sit in one of the lower hollows of this headland, where even the light breeze would not visit her, and gaze at the clear blue-green water at its base, lightly curling into surf, where surely Nereids and dolphins should sport together in the sun. (It will be remembered that Martin had written verse at Oxford.)

At any rate, Miss Meredith was not here to-day, and Martin did not analyse his conviction that she would be here to-morrow. He roused himself, walked up the slopes again, and thereafter steered towards a hamlet which he observed set under a rocky outcrop like those round St. David's. He saw a little grey church; and passing a man in the lane asked the name of the place, and was told it was Llanwnda. The name seemed familiar; and after a moment he remembered why; it was because Giraldus Cambrensis, who was now a real person to him, had once (pluralist as he was) held the living. Martin went up the steep ascent to it—a strange little church standing in a strange little churchyard, with miniature walled gardens set apart for the sepulture of different families. The chief marvel was the magnificent view of the ocean, and indeed of much of this windy tableland. Not very far away below was Trehowell among its trees, and the headland whence he had just come. Catching hold of an ancient man, he pointed to the latter, and, though they could not speak each other's tongue, gathered from him that it was called Careg Gwastad.

Martin trudged back down to Goodwick and on across the bay to Fishguard disappointed, and yet expectant, to find that La Vireville had arranged to go off next morning to Cardigan, some fifteen miles away, to interview a merchant, and that half the crew had been promised a day's holiday (which one man indeed appeared to have anticipated, for he had gone ashore and had not returned). So there would be nothing to keep "Jem Gregson" from spending most of to-morrow hanging about Trehowell and the adjacent cliffs, in the fine weather which the cloudless sunset seemed to promise.

"'Tis not nearly so windy as last night," observed Miss Mortimer that same Tuesday evening, looking up from her sewing; and Nest remembered how last night the chimney of the big hearth before which they sat had howled with melancholy fury behind its slung fowling-pieces and row of bright copper vessels.

"No, indeed; and I think to-morrow will be fine whatever," replied her father cheerfully, shutting up the backgammon board. "Thank you, Miss Meredith, for a very pleasant game!"

And Nest smiled at the good farmer. Even with a lacerated heart she could smile now, for the Mortimers were the kindest of hosts, and, so far from feeling a disgraced outcast, she was made to know herself a welcome and even an honoured guest. If there had been any gossip in St. David's it had not penetrated to the ears of this estimable and well-to-do yeoman farmer, the most considerable of his class in the windy sea-bordered upland of Pencaer, nor to those of his handsome capable daughter, who at thirty or thereabouts seemed to prefer her independence and the overseeing of her father's house and dairy to marriage and the overseeing of a husband's.

"Well, well, now, we must not keep you from your bed, Miss Meredith," continued Mr. Mortimer, glancing at the grandfather clock in the corner. "Otherwise, look you, we shall not be fulfilling our promise to his Reverence to put the roses back in those cheeks of yours. Myfanwy, my dear, where have you put Miss Meredith's candle?"

There was a small wood fire burning away in Nest's little bedroom immediately at the top of the stairs, all old-fashioned furniture, dimity and pink bows; and after she had brushed out her hair she sat by it a little, watching the lively spurts of flame and thinking of a certain person, who was safe in Jersey by now-or so she must hope. For, unromantically enough, Miss Meredith's Cymric blood had not informed her that that same person, urgent to see her, had actually this afternoon been prowling round the very house in which she was. This was perhaps because the Celtic gift of susceptibility to warnings and premonitions had encountered a force sufficient to impede any such spiritual communications. In other words, Nest had caught a cold.

At least it seemed to her sadly probable that she had, although so far she had contrived to disguise this probability from Miss Mortimer; and Nest herself still hoped that the prickling soreness in her throat was not the preliminary onslaught of the army of occupation. And, since she sat musing by the fire instead of getting quickly into bed, she must either have been reckless or sceptical about the threatened affliction.

Next morning she felt rather flushed and heavy, but so divine a day was in the making that she decided to say nothing of her sensations, lest she should be kept indoors. But she did not get far from the house, for Miss Mortimer, detecting her surreptitiously using her pocket handkerchief, made a searching enquiry as to the reason of its employment. Nest, however, contended that the air of so lovely a day could not hurt her, and walked to and fro in the little avenue; for the air was warm and serene and moved sweetly, and was full of the notes of the first bird-songs. And so she stood at the gate under the bare sycamore boughs; a brave chance that would have been for Mr. Martin Tyrrell, who less than twenty hours before had leant upon its further side thinking of her. But to-day, unfortunately, he was miles away.

After dinner, which the Mortimers took at midday, not in the afternoon, she was persuaded to retire to rest awhile; but she had not been long in her own chamber before Miss Mortimer came to her looking very animated.

"Here's a piece of news, Miss Meredith!" she exclaimed. "We have just heard that there are four men-o'-war coming up-Channel from St. David's, and making, it is clear, for Fishguard! Nothing will serve my father but to provide a great supper for the officers, or for such of them as care to come out here; and I am going to set about preparations at once."

"You must let me help you!" exclaimed Nest, springing up. "How vastly exciting! What ships are they?"

"Nobody knows yet, save that they are British. Two frigates, they say, and some smaller vessels. My father would like to feed all the men too, I believe, as well as the officers. But

I cannot accept your help, dear Miss Meredith, when you should be in your chamber nursing your cold."

"I have no cold!" cried Nest gaily. " 'Twas indeed but to please you that I came up here. Pray, pray allow me to assist you!"

In the end Miss Mortimer gave way, and the two plunged, with the aid of everyone in the house, into preparations which would, thought Nest, have sufficed for the officers of an entire fleet. They boiled, they baked, they rolled pastry; they brought out elderberry wine, home-made cordials, and-with more prospect of its consumption perhaps-home-brewed ale, *cwrw dda* , and numerous bottles of claret. Mr. Mortimer likewise broached a pipe of that port, untaxed and unpaid for, with which the recent fortunate wreck of a Portuguese ship had furnished practically every farmhouse on Pencaer. Nest enjoyed it all very much, and it was only when all was ready that a thought loomed up like a sudden dark thunder-cloud.

The Mortimers had taken it for granted that she would appear at this mighty supper, for they did not know, kind souls, that she was here in disgrace. But, in the circumstances, Papa would never approve of such a thing, and it would be like defying him outright to banquet with all the naval officers-for banqueting it would be, no less-when she was in spirit, if not in the letter, still confined to the penitential fare which had been her lot at home. No; gradually the great cloud grew and grew; and Nest knew that she must not share this feast. She would have to seclude herself in her own room while those enormous pies, those noble hams, that array of capons and geese, and that multitude of tarts were consumed.

But how, on what plea? Was she to say that she felt too shy to descend, or all at once to reveal to the Mortimers what Papa had so generously concealed from them? No! But suddenly, very suddenly, her repudiated cold would have to come upon her once more.

The distress, self-reproach and disappointment of poor Miss Mortimer, when that pocket handkerchief came out again, were almost too much for Nest. "I should never have let you help with the preparations! Oh dear me, dear me-you feel that you cannot appear at the supper? And I just driving over to Fishguard with my father . . . no, I will stay with you, and he shall go alone!"

But Nest would none of this. She had gathered that Mr. Mortimer was driving down to invite the officers (since otherwise they could not know of the feast awaiting them up on the heights of Pencaer), and it was plain that though Miss Mortimer did wish to purchase a few extra dainties for the banquet, she was also desirous of sharing in the excitement at Fishguard when the men-of-war came into port. Such an event was rare there. No, declared Nest, Miss Mortimer must go with her father; yes, she herself would submit to be tucked up on her bed and to accept a posset which Miss Mortimer now wished that she had given her earlier; and if, on Miss Mortimer's return, the patient still felt unable to descend, some supper should be sent up to her. And so it was decided.

The posset was warm and comforting, for Nest had really a touch of cold. She heard the horse's hoofs and the wheels of Mr. Mortimer's gig pass up the little avenue as she lay well tucked up on her bed-for into her bed she had refused to get. She had banished herself for conscience' sake, but she was not going to forego the very minor pleasure of later looking out of the window and seeing what she could of the naval guests. And, thinking how odd it would be if William chanced to be among them (though she knew that to be impossible, for the *Serapis* was not in English waters), she sank into a heavy sleep. . . .

It was so startling to have gone to sleep in daylight-just for a few minutes, so it seemed-and to wake up in a room full of dusky shadows, with the fire burnt low, that Nest lay for a moment with her heart beating, wondering, as one does so readily in a strange bed, where she was. But she soon remembered.

Yet, how extraordinary to have been asleep for so long-hours, it must have been-and that neither Miss Mortimer nor one of the domestics should have been near her! For-her next thought-Miss Mortimer and her father must certainly be back, and the feast have begun; the amount of noise coming up from below told her that. Indeed, it might well have been those sounds which had wakened her. The naval officers must be doing full justice to Mr. Mortimer's great supper; they must be absolutely carousing. And, as occasional bursts of laughter came up to her, and a shout or two, Nest felt for the first time glad that she had elected to stay in her room. Yet it still remained strange that no supper had been brought to her as arranged, for she could not imagine Miss Mortimer forgetting her. Perhaps it had been brought and taken away again, as the posset had thrown her into so sound and prolonged a sleep.

Strangely puzzled nevertheless, Nest crept out from under the patchwork quilt and groped her way to the window. It was not so dark outside but that she could distinguish, down below, the figures of a quantity of men moving about. They must, she supposed, be sailors from the frigates come up with the officers; a sort of bodyguard, perhaps. Then, a couple of them happening to cross a stream of light from one of the uncurtained ground-floor windows, Nest saw clearly that they were not sailors, for they wore some kind of military uniform, and-though surely this was a mere trick of eyesight due to the dusk and the lamplight from within-she received an impression that the uniform was not red, but brown. Whoever heard of English-or indeed of any soldiers-in brown uniform . . . and what were soldiers doing here at all? It must be a dream!

And as, not wishing to be seen, she drew back from the window, a fresh outburst of mirth from below made Nest wonder if William's brother officers usually made such noisy guests? Surely not with their host and his daughter present! . . . It almost seemed as if the Mortimers had *not* yet returned. In that case. . . . But surely British naval officers would never behave otherwise than as gentlemen. Yet, if they should become drunk . . . She had better lock her door.

At that moment a considerable racket outside penetrated the shut window-mingled laughter, shouts like imprecations and loud quacking as of terrified ducks or geese. Nest ran to the window again. Down below shadowy figures were dodging about after a number of vociferous white patches; and it came to Nest that they must be trying to capture Mr. Mortimer's geese. And with that a cold trickle of fear slid into her heart. This was much more like a nightmare than a dream. . . . Who *could* these people be?

The question, put at last, so numbed her faculties that for a moment she forgot her unlocked door. And-horror-was that feet running up the stairs just outside it? She hurried across the room, but stumbled in the dark over a chair, upsetting it and nearly falling herself. Next instant the door was flung open and a man looked in, a lantern swinging from his hand.

"Aha!" he exclaimed, holding it up, "then there *is* someone left in the house after all!"

"And, by good luck, a pretty girl, too!" chimed in a second, peering over his shoulder.

Nest gave one long, piercing scream and fled into the remotest corner of the little room, squeezing herself into the space between the wall and the side of the old press which held her gowns. It was not so much the actual words which terrified her as the language of their utterance. These men were French!

(3)

The promise of the sunset had not been belied, as Martin observed with satisfaction when he turned out of his hammock that morning to go whistling about his work. " 'Twill be even finer than yesterday," he thought. "This time I shall go straight to the cliffs and wait for her."

But as inns contain hosts whose idea of the reckoning may differ from that of the customer, so do ships contain mates. Later in the morning, as Martin was peeling potatoes outside the galley door, he was sent for by Challacombe, and found him in the bows mixing with his own hands a pot of blue paint for the embellishment, presumably, of the *Raymonde's* dingy figurehead.

"Yu knaw, Gregson, that that there dratted Dumaresq niver come back last night?"

"Yes, sir."

"Since the cap'n left this marning," pursued the mate, "I've heerd that some of the hands thinks the fule has follered a maid he were seen talking tu yesterday, a maid that simingly du belong tu a farm called Pen-y-coed, up to a place called St. Dogwells — 'bout eight miles south of here 'twill be."

"I suppose that is possible," agreed Martin, who had no views on the matter.

"Howsomever," declared Challacombe, stirring with renewed vigour, "I'm gwyne to have Dumaresq back aboard this schooner afore the cap'n returns this evening, or my name bain't Jonas Challacombe; and so yu and Tom Pelley be to go arter him to this St. Dogwells and find him if so be he'm to be found, and bring him back wi' ye if ye has to carry him!"

"Go after . . . go to St. Dogwells!" stammered Martin, thunder-struck. "But that's ridi —I mean, I have no notion how to get there, and it is not in the least certain, sir, that Dumaresq has gone to this farm! To run over the countryside looking for him would be like — —"

The mate had ceased to mix the paint. "I don't care what yu think 'tis like, Jem Gregson!" he retorted, his red beard glowing menacingly in the sun. "The pint is yu'm to goo and look for Dumaresq wi' Tom Pelley, what's bin in these parts afore; and seein' as yu'm an intalligent young fellow, and cap'n thinks so much of 'ee, I've put he under thy orders. So off 'ee goes, my lad, and look lively about et!"

But Martin's stupefaction was turning to rebellion. "What of the crew's dinner?" he asked in a very sulky tone.

"Yu'm not the only man on board as can cook!" declared Challacombe angrily. "Most of 'em can cook a mort better, too! Off wi' ee!"

This was preposterous; he was not going to be sent on a sixteen-mile wild-goose chase; he was going to Careg Gwastad to meet his Nausicaa . . . and watch dolphins playing in the sun. "But, Mr. Challacombe," he began, deeply annoyed.

The compatriot of Drake and Raleigh let out a roar. "Don't 'ee 'but' me! If I have to come arter 'ee wi' a rope's end thou'lt be sorry for it!"

It was highly probable. The mate was a very big, powerful man, and had authority as an ally, too. Martin had not sailed before the mast in a privateer without gaining a wholesome respect for mates, and there was no captain to appeal to this morning. He turned upon his heel and went in search of Tom Pelley.

And about this time, or a little earlier, a certain retired mariner, Captain Williams of Trelithin, descried, from his farm not far from the spot where Martin had first come ashore at St. David's, two frigates, a corvette and a lugger sailing up-Channel, past the Bishop and Clerks. To his experienced eye they bore the appearance of Frenchmen, but when he reinforced that eye with a telescope he saw that the colours they flew were British.

* * * * *

Martin set off from Fishguard in the worst of tempers. Even had he not planned to spend his free time to-day very differently, his present errand was unpleasant, and probably quite useless as well. Had it not been for his companion he would have shirked the whole journey and made a false report about this confounded Dumaresq. Whether or no the selection of himself as the leading spirit of the expedition owed anything to malice on the part of the mate, it certainly had an ironical tinge unknown to that seafarer, who was, of course, unaware that he was setting a deserter to catch a deserter.

Tom Pelley (whose name was properly Le Pelley) was almost equally disgusted at this method of spending a holiday, but he was a rather silent man and said little. As his acquaintance with the neighbourhood turned out to be limited to a visit during childhood to an aunt who had lived at Manorowen, his guidance was more misleading than complete ignorance would have been. The couple had naturally made enquiries before leaving Fishguard, but they found the lanes into which their quest led them bewilderingly similar, and their banks too high to see over as they walked. From time to time one of them would climb up and scan the countryside, but the outlook seemed always the same-fields and more fields, and in the distance the low swelling range of hills which the county called mountains-Mynedd Precelly. There were no signposts, and it was hot. On they went and on, except when, steering partly by the sun and partly by these glimpses of the hills, they corrected their course and tramped back to some branch lane about taking which they had generally argued already.

"When I catches that Dumaresq," observed Le Pelley at last, mopping his brow, " 'tis a clout on the head as I shall catch him!"

These were Martin's sentiments also, and he said so. They had no doubt been the sentiments, too, of the three hands from the *Vrijheid* who had searched for him in this same county last July.

At last, at long last, they came through a tree-shadowed hollow, grateful after the shadeless lanes, to the hamlet of St. Dogwells. The first person of whom they enquired for Pen-y-coed Farm could not understand English; the second, after thought, replied (as far as the seekers could make out) that there was no farm of that name in the neighbourhood; the third, a woman at a farm door who had evidently seen something of the world outside Pembrokeshire, suggested that the farm of which they were in search might be Mr. Lewis's of that name at St. Dogmells, not St. Dogwells.

"And how much further is St. Dogmells?" enquired Martin crossly, conscious of a desire that was almost a determination to rest in her kitchen.

The woman stared at him. "How much further? *Dyn anwyl* , I declare to goodness you must be joking! St. Dogmells, look you, is close to Aberteivi-which the English call Cardigan-and you have been coming away from it ass hard ass you can!" She broke into a hoot of shrill laughter. "Sarah Ann, Sarah Ann, d'ye hear there-how much further iss it to St. Dogmells?"

* * * * *

Martin and his comrade in misfortune did rest in the woman's kitchen, and besides bread and cheese absorbed some generous draughts of *cwrw dda* . The not unnatural result of the strength of the home-brewed ale was that after about half a mile of their homeward journey they both climbed over the omnipresent bank into the field beyond and went to sleep. Martin had remembered by this time that he had come across a mention of St. Dogmells in the *Itinerary* of Giraldus. But, since it was quite impossible to get there now, unless heaven suddenly endued them with wings, there was no purpose in hurrying back. Whatever happened, however, he *would* go to Trehowell to-morrow.

Even this excessively fine day must have an end, and, since the month was February, that ending was upon it by the time the defeated search party began to approach Fishguard. Martin had become extremely silent, while Le Pelley had blossomed out into a loquacity occupied at the moment in enlarging upon the succulence of the ormer, the edible shell fish of his native isle, when he suddenly stopped. There was a puzzling sound not only of people coming, but of dogs and poultry coming, too; and round a bend in the lane suddenly appeared a man pushing a large wheelbarrow at a rate at which that vehicle is not usually propelled, especially if loaded with bedding, saucepans, crockery, and all kinds of domestic objects, including a timepiece in action. The whole was topped by a couple of hens tied by the legs, one pecking placidly at a blanket, the other testifying loudly to its dislike of travel in this equipage. Beside the man, who was crimson in the face, shuffled quickly a perspiring woman with a child tucked Welsh fashion into her shawl, and a sack over her shoulder bulging with wearing apparel. A dog was harrying with loud barks a couple of frightened goats; and last of all came a boy about ten, dragging as best he could a lesser sack.

This group, suggestive in miniature of the patriarch Abraham in transit, came on in such a hurry that Martin and his companion almost automatically stood aside to let it pass; but Martin called out to ask what was amiss.

The answer came back at the highest pitch of the high national voice.

"The French have landed-the French are in Fishguard-it will all be burnt down by morning whatever . . ." And as the two seamen stared open-mouthed another throng of fugitives, all women this time, rushed round the corner.

(4)

The tidings thus delivered by the man with the wheelbarrow afforded a fair specimen of the hundred-and-one rumours and exaggerations of those first hours of panic, and to nobody did they administer a greater shock than to Martin Tyrrell. Yet the truth, though bad enough, was not quite so spectacular. Fishguard was not burning, nor were the French in it-as yet.

At first it was difficult, in the dusk and turmoil, to discover what exactly was the calamity which had fallen upon the neighbourhood while Martin and his shipmate had been plodding to and from St. Dogwells. Fishguard was in the most complete confusion; some were fleeing out of it, and some into it-these mostly fugitives from the Pencaer countryside. For it seemed that it was in Pencaer that the French had landed; near Strumble Head, said some-thousands and thousands of them there were! No, nearer than Strumble Head, said others; at Careg Gwastad point; landing was still going on up those cliffs. Yes, as near as that, look you, because it was not until the fort at Fishguard Harbour mouth had fired a salute to the British colours which the enemy were so deceitfully flying, that those colours came down, and up went the bloody French flag with the blue, white and red that they called "the trickler"... and then all Fishguard *knew*!

"*Careg Gwastad!*" gasped Martin, hardly believing what he heard; and he clutched the excited shopkeeper (or whatever he was), his present informant. "Up the cliffs there, you say... but Careg Gwastad is near Trehowell Farm-near Mr. Mortimer's!"

"Yes, indeed; and they do say that the French general is making Trehowell his headquarters, and ——"

"Good God! Then are Mortimer and Miss Mere ——"

"No, Mr. Mortimer and his daughter are safe here in Fishguard," put in another voice, a woman's. "At the 'Royal Oak' they are indeed; they came driving in this afternoon before them villains landed."

"And Miss Meredith with them, I trust?" But this new informant had been swallowed up in the frightened crowd which surged about the street, and his original one had vanished. With Le Pelley Martin had long ago parted company. In desperation he next seized hold of an old Druid-like man with a long beard declaiming something of an apocalyptic character in Welsh. "Show me where the 'Royal Oak' is!" he commanded, shaking him. But the ancestral voice went on undeterred, prophesying, no doubt, war, rapine and the end of the world.

And then, through a break in the crowd, Martin saw that he was quite close to the hostelry in question, a small unpretentious-looking place, and he succeeded in getting across to it. But it was difficult to force his way in, and he forgot that to all outward seeming he was merely a common seaman in a jersey, so that his pushing and his clamorous enquiries for Miss Meredith passed unregarded in the general gabble of alarmed conversation. Then he tried using the name of Mortimer instead; and on that a burly-looking man with the appearance of a farmer did give him some information, though it was far from comforting.

"Mortimer of Trehowell-poor fellow, God knows what is come to him by this time, for he did go back to Trehowell, though we tried to stop him-terrible 'tis for his daughter, for likely enough the French will cut his head off... there's a man here says he saw one of those machines of theirs landed up Careg Gwastad ——"

"But Miss Meredith? Did Mr. Mortimer say nothing about her?... Then, please God, she is here with Miss Mortimer. Where *is* Miss Mortimer? I must see her!"

It took him another quarter of an hour and a substantial money gift before he was allowed to enter a tidy little room heavily furnished with a reserve store of pewter pots and a smell of ale, where the lady he had seen the day before in Mrs. Powell's shop sat upon a horse-hair sofa with her handkerchief to her eyes.

* * * * *

Full of worry, general patriotism and a burning desire to fight the insolent Mounseers (and wishing, though he liked him well enough, that the master of the *Raymonde* were not one too, albeit of a species friendly to England), Mr. Jonas Challacombe stood upon the quay in the gloom listening with one ear to the noise in Fishguard town, perched high on the further side of the harbour, and with the other for the sound of that master's returning footfalls.

For the "Chevaleer" had not yet come back from Cardigan, and was probably quite unaware of the earth-shaking event which had taken place since his departure. The *Raymonde* could not slip out to sea, for she would have to run the gauntlet of the French frigates and smaller fry lying off Careg Gwastad, and, in any case, she was unarmed. Before she was captured in harbour, however, a fate which seemed quite likely to overtake her in the end, Challacombe was disposed to set her afire with his own hands. But, since she did not belong to him, he could only pray for the speedy return of her actual owner in order that measures of some kind might be taken for her safety.

Someone was running along the quay. At last! But into the circle of quavering light cast by a lantern on a post came not the missing captain, but the missing cook, Gregson, panting with haste.

"I'm glad to see 'ee back, my lad," said Challacombe gruffly. "Yu've heerd, o' course?" He jerked a thumb in the direction of Goodwick.

"My lad" nodded, his breath coming fast. "Is the captain back?" he managed to get out.

"No, he bain't . . . I only wish he was!"

"Not back? Damnation!" cried Mr. Gregson, recovering some of his wind. "However, it can't wait for him. I want as many of the crew as you can spare, Challacombe-most of them, in fact-to come with me at once to Trehowell Farm where ——"

"What's that yu say?"

"Where Miss Meredith is alone in the hands of those scoundrels. Mr. Mortimer has gone back to try to reach her, but ——"

A large hand here took him by the front of the jersey, almost indeed by the throat. "Be yu making game o' me?" demanded its owner in the voice of an outraged lion, "or have 'ee took leave of thy senses? The crew of this schooner desert her for to go and get themselves took and murdered by them bloody French dogs-for to go to Trehowell, the very place they'm making their headquarters? Yu'm mad drunk, Gregson, drunker than that Dumaresq when he came back this arternoon!"

"I am neither mad nor drunk," protested Martin, trying to twist himself away. "If M. de la Vireville were here he would give me the men at once . . . there's the Precentor of St. David's daughter, a mere girl, alone in the farm, alone with those men! . . . Oh, for God's sake, Challacombe, let me have someone! I can't get a soul in Fishguard to come with me, they are all too distracted . . ."

"Well, *I* bain't distracted!" bellowed Challacombe, "and I du knaw what's my duty to my ship if yu don't. Let 'ee take the hands for to go arter a maid, when we'm got all we can du to save the schooner. Get on board at once!" He loosed him with a push.

The altercation had drawn several figures to the *Raymonde's* side. Martin recognised among them the sodden face of Dumaresq; he had almost forgotten about him. He suddenly raised his voice in appeal. "Men, if you have any of you daughters or sweethearts, will you leave a young lady in deadly peril in the hands of the French? Isn't there one of you will come with me to her rescue? If you call yourselves Englishm ——"

The mate sprang at him with an imprecation and a doubled fist, which would have felled him had he encountered it. Martin ducked, turned, and vanished into the darkness.

* * * * *

His little Nausicaa, his little Nest, alone, except for servants, in the very spot where the invaders were landing-the idea was too horrible! Poor Miss Mortimer, waiting for news at the "Royal Oak," had been almost in hysterics, partly on Miss Meredith's, partly on her father's account. The worthy man had started back to Trehowell directly it became certain that the vessels were not English but French, yet if ever he succeeded in getting there, would he be in time? There was a dreadful rumour flying about that the invaders were convicts just released from the galleys ... And what could he, Martin Tyrrell, do, one man against hundreds? Nevertheless, winged with rage and despair, he had no thought-there seemed no other necessity in the world-but to get to Trehowell as quickly as possible. Again he arrived, with sobbing breath, in the steep panic-struck streets of Fishguard; again he uttered vain appeals for a few men to accompany him. But all assured him that they had their own families to protect. . . .

It would take him at least an hour to get to Trehowell on foot-more, with pickets to avoid. If only —— But there, there, in front of that house, stood a horse and cart, unattended! The cart was laden with household goods, of which the owner was no doubt within, collecting more. Provided that he did not come out for a moment or two no one else would interfere with the borrower. Martin began feverishly to tug at the harness, got it unfastened, gathered up the long reins, took the horse clear of the shafts and turned it, then, scrambling on to its back, urged the stout, surprised animal as fast as he could down the street. As its hoofs clattered and slipped on the cobbles he was picturing French troops clambering up that very headland where he had sat yesterday in the sun. *French troops!* It seemed incredible, fantastic . . . and yet it was only what had long been feared.

(5)

Was this herself, Nest Meredith, who lived in the Close at St. David's, and had a dog named Bran, and went to church every Sunday in the Cathedral, and had this winter helped her aunt to make twenty-three flannel petticoats for the poor-this girl sitting in the big kitchen at Trehowell, at the head of a table ringed with noisy French officers? It could not be; it was someone else? Or she would wake from this too-vivid dream . . . yes, please God, she would wake!

But the dream went on . . . the horrible, horrible nightmare, rather. The candles flared and guttered; snatches of song smote her ears out of the din; one officer, unsteadily holding up a glass, evidently not his first, of the wrecked port, was toasting her; another was trying to capture one of the hands which, tightly clutched together, she kept resolutely below the table. "*Mademoiselle*," he was saying thickly, "*chère petite galloise . . . que tu es jolie!*" Then, not finding Nest's hand, he hit one of his own against the table in his clumsiness, and carried it grumbling to his mouth, calling her a foul name (which she did not understand), and saying that she had struck him. For he was very drunk.

Here she was, then, and had small remembrance of how she had come here, only a confused recollection of being pulled, though not roughly, out of her corner by the press in her room, of a voice saying, first in broken English, and then in French, slowly, for her better comprehension, that there was nothing for Mademoiselle to be frightened of, for they were gentlemen; but that they must beg her to come downstairs, since there was no lady of the house to welcome them, and every servant had fled. She had not shrieked any more, and she did not think that she had fainted, though certainly she had remembered little (save cries and thumpings on the table) when her escort had brought her into the kitchen, and an elder officer sitting at the head of the table had at once jumped up and surrendered his place to her with a bow.

As little did Nest understand how these Frenchmen were here, save that she gathered they were from the supposed "British" ships, and that they had come up over the cliffs. They told her that; they told her too that they would soon be in Fishguard, and afterwards march on Liverpool, burning and destroying; and that she should go with them always, to bring them luck, the first pretty girl whom they had found on English soil-or rather Welsh-whom indeed they had found actually in their headquarters, whence every soul had fled before their arrival, leaving them this excellent supper. For General Tate, whom she had not yet seen, proposed to make this farm his *quartier général*. But she was Welsh, was she not; and Wales, as one knew, was ripe to throw off the tyrant yoke of England. She should be sacred to them, their oriflamme, their Jeanne d'Arc.

It was a young officer, standing on his chair, one foot on the table, who had proclaimed these lofty and flattering sentiments, which had led to great applause. But that was earlier; there were signs now that she might not be held so sacred. There was, for instance, that leering man on her right who had tried to seize her hand. Nest shut her eyes and prayed harder; and, since there seemed no possibility of deliverance, prayed that she might die. . . . A window in the room had been broken, and she could hear much more noise now outside, uproar indeed, and singing, the crackling as of a bonfire, and the agonised squeals which she knew meant that a pig was being killed . . .

"Mademoiselle," said a voice in her ear, "you shut your eyes! But you must not go to sleep before the General comes. You have eaten nothing; pledge me then in this wine!" And he bent over her, a glass in his hand, young, rather handsome, and not nearly so drunk as her right-hand neighbour, but with that in his gaze which frightened Nest even more. Mutely she shook her head.

"*Belle enfant*, do not be so alarmed! We are Frenchmen-save our General, who is an American-and we do not war with women. At least put your pretty lips to the glass, and let me drink after you!" The officer bent nearer, holding the wine, but his face was still closer than the glass. In a moment she would feel his abhorrent lips on her cheek-she knew it! To die could not be worse than this!

Suddenly the face was removed; the wine slopped forward upon her dress. Another officer had roughly swung away the first. Nest covered her eyes. "Here, name of a name, Didier, you are terrifying the *fillette*! Come, my dear, take down those hands, and give me a smile-no, indeed, you shall, my pretty one!" Laying hold of her wrists this second Frenchman pulled away her hands.

And then what little remained of Nest's nerve went entirely. She jumped up and shrieked for help; vain as it was, the scream, the appeal were instinctive. She called, too, instinctively upon the potentate who had always ruled her life, far away in Somerset though he was. "Papa, papa! . . . O, let me go, let me go!"

But, far from being released, she felt hands upon her shoulders also, from behind, and the voice of the dispossessed admirer saying, "I'm damned if you shall have the first kiss, Gavel- it's mine!"

Yet Providence had heard her. At that very moment a door at the far end of the kitchen opened and an indignant voice cried-in French, like all the other voices: "Gentlemen, what is this? A woman here —a girl? Captain Didier, let her go at once!"

The hands dropped off Nest's shoulders, removed themselves from her wrists, and she saw coming towards her out of a kind of haze a middle-aged man in a cocked hat with a tricolour plume, at sight of whom all the officers there, including her own assailants, stood to attention. He was followed by a younger officer.

"How does this girl come to be here?" he demanded severely. "This, gentlemen, is not the way to be conducting yourselves, when the landing, too, is not fully completed!" And then with equal severity he addressed the shaking Nest herself, but in English. "How did ye find your way in here, girl?"

"Find her way!" Her mouth was so dry that she could hardly speak. Speak she must, however, for this General used her own tongue, and her sharpened senses told her a thing she would never normally have perceived-that he was not naturally a severe man. (Indeed he did not look it.) But his displeasure with his officers was her own best protection.

"I . . . I was staying here, sir, with the people of the farm," she got out. "I was asleep in my room upstairs." And then, seeing from his expression that it was dawning upon him that she was not a mere country girl, she added, with a gleam of hope, "I am Miss Meredith, the daughter of the Precentor of St. David's Cathedral, and I implore you, sir, to release me at once! Pray, pray, sir, let me go!" And with an effort she succeeded in choking back a sob.

"Is this true-that this young lady is the daughter of some dignitary of the Cathedral of St. David's?" asked General Tate, looking round upon his officers. Some shrugged their shoulders; one said, "It may be true, *mon général*, but we knew nothing of it."

"Ye say ye were in your bedchamber, madam," remarked Tate, turning again to Nest, whose heart revived a little further at the formal address. "Why then did ye leave ut?"

Nest hesitated to give the reason; but evidently her face must have been a sufficient guide to the truth.

"Is it possible," asked the General of his officers, in French again, "that you brought this young lady downstairs against her will?"

"Afraid it is, *mon général*," replied the stout Gavel, with a slightly tipsy smile. "At least, someone did-not I, 'pon my honour!"

His superior looked angrily upon him, and turned away with a gesture of disgust. "Madam," he said to Nest, "I deeply regret this occurrence. I am sorry that I cannot release ye at present — 'twould be out of the question to carry through the matter to-night, but I assure ye that ye shall henceforth be treated with all respect." Seeing how she was trembling (and indeed the relief from the intolerable strain had brought her nearer fainting than she had yet been) he said very politely, even gallantly, "Permit me, madam!" and handed her back with courtesy into the chair from which she had just risen, adding, " 'Twould be well, I'm thinking, if ye could take a sup of wine. Faucon, *un verre propre*!"

Nest subsided again limply into the big chair. God had not entirely deserted her, then, in spite of her past wickedness (that wickedness which was really the cause of her being here at all), for He had heard her prayer and sent this American general-but he sounded like an Irishman-to save her in the nick of time. She lifted a white, not much reassured face and tried to thank him as he himself brought her a glass of wine; and, chiefly from gratitude, she put her lips to it. While she tried to swallow the wine she heard him speaking again, still with that uneasy severity, and caught some of his remarks-that it was no way to commend themselves to the Welsh, to ill-treat and frighten a Welsh lady, and she, it seemed, the daughter of an important ecclesiastic; it might have the worst possible effect upon local opinion, which they were so anxious to conciliate. And he concluded by saying, "I shall write her a safe-conduct now, to be in readiness for to-morrow, when she shall be escorted away from here."

Pen and ink were in fact brought, and the general, in his plumed hat, sat down to write among the half-eaten viands-actually just in front of a large apple pasty which Nest remembered Miss Mortimer making . . . in another existence. When he had dashed off something or other, the young officer addressed as "Faucon," evidently his aide-de-camp, not finding a sand-box, snatched up the big hour-glass on the chimney shelf, broke one end, and grinning, sifted the sand from that over the paper. Meanwhile a place was being cleared for the general's repast; but before he could sit down to it another officer entered and came up to him.

"There is a man here, *mon général*, a sailor or a fisherman of these parts, who asks if you have need of a guide."

"A Welshman?"

"I suppose so, sir."

"Ah!" said Tate, with an air of satisfaction, "I am glad to hear that. Not that we particularly require a guide, having with us, as you know, that transported horse thief who was formerly a servant at this farm, but I take the offer as evidence of the goodwill of the natives. I will see him for a moment; have him brought in here." Leaving the table he thereupon went towards the door at the further end of the room.

In another moment there had entered two very villainous-looking soldiers clad in brown uniforms, which bore the unmistakable imprint of the dye tub, and wearing upon their heads, very oddly, the crested helmets of the cavalry. Between them was a young man in a sailor's jersey, a slim, dark young man with a nascent beard and brass ear-rings. At him Nest found herself looking with a sad curiosity, feeling thankful that she was not likely to know personally this traitor to his country.

But . . . O Heavens . . . she did! The room swirled. Was she mad, dreaming, dying? Despite the little beard she knew him; it was Martin Tyrrell, whom she thought miles and miles away! He was here-and would save her! But when she tried to say his name, to rise from the chair, she could not; she was held there as immovably as though her limbs, her tongue, her very brain had been turned to lead. For it was true, then; he *was* hand in glove with the Irish and the French; he *had* been rightly pursued by the law; he had lied to her, he had been deceiving her all these months . . . A spinning darkness enveloped Nest, and for a moment she slipped back in Mr. Mortimer's big chair only half conscious.

But a deep instinct fought the blackness off; she knew she must not swoon with no other woman near. And perhaps there was some mistake; or, even if he had come to give information, yet, when he found that she was here, alone in the hands of the French, he would help her. He had wanted to come back into danger for her at Haverford, and her situation now was a hundred times worse than then! She could not see him clearly at the other end of the room, for there were officers between, and the General was talking to him in English about the help which he could be to the expedition: but she could hear his well-remembered, pleasant voice, answering in a feigned Welsh accent; he was, it seemed pretending not to understand English very well . . . Why, why? Oh, it must be because he was so accustomed to feigning, to pretending to be something he was not . . . he was so clever-much too clever for a simple country girl like her! She bit her lips, until they almost bled, to keep back the slow, bitter tears, for not only she herself, but her hero was in the dust.

(6)

This method of obtaining access to Trehowell had come to Martin, so he thought, as a real heaven-sent inspiration; and it had come not long after he had parted from his stolen cart-horse, which he had done soon after reaching the top of the hill above Goodwick. He realised that it would then be easier, because quieter, to slip along in the darkness on foot, now that he was nearing the enemies' lines-if they had any. Definitely placed outposts they apparently had not, and every fugitive he met had some hurried screaming tale to tell of slain pigs and poultry and gutted barrels, which seemed to argue that the rank and file were more pleasantly employed than in guarding their position. And though this increased his fears for Nest, it seemed to lessen the difficulty of getting into the French headquarters, especially now that he had thought of this stratagem.

To such pickets therefore as he had come across, and to the sentries outside the gate of Trehowell itself he had announced in French that he was-what Nest had just heard. The ex-convicts (for such they really were) not being disposed, luckily, to criticise the surprising possession of their tongue by a Welsh fisherman, Martin was hailed at the farmhouse as "camarade," and no obstacles were raised to his seeing the general. Once within he would lay his plans, the first step in which would be to discover Nest's whereabouts in the farmhouse.

But he had never expected this: to find Nest down here, in this heated room full of the fumes of food and wine and half drunken French officers, a solitary and terrified little figure; nor to have his supposed errand announced in front of her; nor to be prevented, by reasons of strategy, not merely from rushing to her side, but even from giving her some sign of encouragement. It seemed to Martin the hardest thing he had ever done in his life to remain there by the door taking no notice of her, when he was almost consumed with wrath and with a wild desire to rush up to the big chair where she was so piteously installed, snatch her up in his arms and leap with her through the broken window or something equally dramatic and useless.

This, then, was the General. The other officers, crowding round to view the informer, now blocked out the chair at the end of the table from his sight. Martin's object was to keep these infernal Frenchman in play, and to make himself seem likely to be of real use, and consequently retained on the premises, without actually telling them the way to anywhere. He would pretend, in his character of a Welshman, not to understand French-luckily the two soldiers who had brought him in here were not the sentries whom he had originally addressed in that language.

But-curse it all! —this general of theirs was English-or Irish, from the inflection of his speech-and did not address him in French.

"So ye're wishful to help us, me man?"

Martin nodded.

"Ye belong to these parts?"

"Yess, I am a sailor whateffer," replied Martin, affecting as best he could a Welsh intonation, and reflecting that if he were asked his name, he must manufacture yet a fourth alias, since he must give a Welsh one.

"That's not what I was afther asking ye. But maybe ye do not understand English very well?"

"Not fery well, sir." And Martin shook his head until the ear-rings swung. (Had Nest recognised him? He had no idea.)

"But-listen now, for ut's important; ye came to help us because ye are Welsh, because the Welsh are desirous of helping us against the English. Is that not so?" General Tate spoke slowly and carefully, raising his voice in the belief, common in the British Isles, that so will those of an alien speech be granted better comprehension.

Martin smiled and nodded. "I will take you anywhere that you shall wish to go," he announced amiably if irrelevantly.

"He certainly seems a willing fellow," observed Tate to his staff, in French. "We will keep him, and see of what use he proves himself to-morrow."

"Ask him, sir," suggested someone, "if the young lady there is what she says she is; he may know her."

"Move aside then." And Nest, staring with great eyes down the table at the group, eyes that looked as if they hardly knew what they stared at, was fully revealed to her intending rescuer. "D'ye know, me good man, who that young lady is?"

Martin gave but the most cursory glance; he was afraid of Nest's appealing to him and spoiling his ultimate chances. "Yes, indeed, sir; she iss the daughter of Dr. Meredith, the Precentor of St. David's Cathedral. You must take great care of her, General; otherwise my people shall be fery angry with you and shall not help you."

"You hear that, gentlemen!" said Tate warningly. And he went at once back to the head of the table. "Madam, I suggest that ye retire now to your room, where I guarantee that ye will not be molested again. Here is the safe-conduct; if ye will have the kindness to take charge of ut I will see in the morning that ye are taken to your friends. Faucon, give Miss Meredith your arm as far as the stairs."

Nest rose like an automaton. *His* voice again, coolly stating who she was, not even pretending, from shame, that he did not know her! But no wonder that he dare not look her in the face. . . .

Another officer opened the door. The aide-de-camp bowed as she withdrew her hand and went slowly up the stairs alone. She was safe now . . . and did not seem to care.

* * * * *

Downstairs General Tate, urged by his officers to partake of the good cheer, or what they had left of it, installed himself in Nest's vacated place at the head of the table. Martin's escort, who had not yet been dismissed, still stood awkwardly in the corner, doubtless with watering mouths, while he, having never been inside Trehowell before, was mentally noting its geography. That door, then, led to the stairs, and up those stairs was Nest's bedroom; that other door — —

Even as he looked at it this door was thrust open and another officer appeared. He seemed in haste.

"*Mon général* , I am sorry, but your presence, if only for a moment, is indispensable at the landing-place. A little misunderstanding has arisen. Two of the Irish officers — —"

The hungry commander-in-chief, who had hardly swallowed a mouthful, said crossly, "Major Le Brun must go!"

"He is there already, sir, and can do nothing."

"The devil take ut!" exclaimed General Tate in English, threw down his knife and fork and went out. What an extraordinary army, thought Martin, where the officers feast and the general does all the work-except, apparently, the Irish officers whom they seem to have brought with them, and they do not feast, but quarrel. And yet these people had managed to effect a landing, on a very dark night, up a slippery headland of a most difficult coast. To think that a hundred, a score even of determined men at the top of the cliffs could have stopped them, had they been there. But there had been no one to organise that timely resistance.

His critical reflections, however, upon invaders and invaded were abruptly cut short by a development which began almost immediately Tate had left the room. Two officers-they were the very two, young Didier and the stout intoxicated Gavel, who had previously been disputing for a kiss, but this Martin did not know—were bickering by the fireplace. Now the door leading to the stairs was not far from the hearth, and it was their proximity to this door rather than the subject of their difference (which he did not at first grasp) that led Martin to keep his eye upon them. And then all at once, to his horror, he gathered that they were disputing which of them, now that the general was out of the way, should follow *la petite galloise* upstairs and snatch that kiss of which Tate's advent had defrauded him.

"But she will surely have locked her door," thought Martin in a panic. "She will surely have done that!" He started to edge almost imperceptibly along the wall.

"I tell you the first claim's mine!" affirmed the stout captain. "I tell you — —"

"Oh, shut up, Gavel!" protested someone from the table. "If you were not so drunk you would realise that the girl is not your sort; she is a lady, and under the general's protection now. For heaven's sake drop the subject, you and Didier there!"

"And you might also realise," another voice pointed out, "that pretty Miss will have locked her door. Sit down again, there's a good fellow; there's an excellent ham over there!"

"Pretty Miss won't have locked her door," retorted Gavel with a fatuous smile. " 'Cause why? There's no key in the lock! Ha, ha, ha! Didier here took it out, the dog, when he fetched her down-got it now, he has! So she can't lock her door-see, she can't lock it!"

"No," said Captain Didier smoothly, "she can't, you drunken brute. But I can . . . from the inside too!" He gave his rival a sudden push, slipped round him, plucked open the door leading to the staircase and was gone from the room. But before Gavel could recover a figure in a blue jersey had shot through it also, and the two pairs of feet could be heard running up the uncarpeted stairs.

Captain Brémond, one of the recent protestors, jumped up from the table. "Stop him, stop him!" he cried. "It's the Welshman-and he has a knife!"

It was true that Martin had a knife, but he had not yet drawn it, as he pelted up the narrow, enclosed staircase after the disappearing figure of Captain Didier. The former, reaching the bedroom door first, had not time to do more than open it when he was seized from behind and hurled aside; and next moment, having supposed his assailant to be a brother officer, was considerably surprised to find himself at grips with a ferocious young seaman who was exclaiming in English, "Get out or I'll kill you! Get out and give me the key, you blackguard!"

To and fro they wrestled on the threshold, but not for long. The staircase became full of the thunder of ascending reinforcements, and Martin himself was seized round the waist. By this time, however, he had managed to draw his knife, and with this struck backwards at his new foe-it was the half-intoxicated Gavel-who instantly, with a spluttered curse, relaxed his grip. And Captain Didier also removing his in order to draw his sword, Martin even had a second in which to get actually over the threshold and to catch hold of the open door, with the intention of at least slamming it in the faces of the invaders, even though he could not lock it. But, trying to do this, he could neither guard himself nor move quickly enough to avoid a tremendous boxer's blow, straight from the shoulder, the contribution of a very stalwart newcomer who had taken Gavel's place. It caught Martin on the point of the chin and laid him out as if he had been in the ring, the knife shooting from his hand almost to Nest's feet, where she stood clinging to the bedpost with a face like death.

The noise and trampling of this mêlée were at once succeeded by a remarkable silence. For, now that the episode was over, and a brother officer delivered from the peril of a knife in the back, which some of them thought not entirely undeserved, the invaders could see the cost at which this deliverance had been accomplished. The terrified girl, whose privacy their general had guaranteed, had now sunk to her knees, her head bowed against the bedpost, round which her arms were still entwined; her defender lay motionless on the threshold of her violated room, lay almost as a dead man might lie . . .

Captain Brémond stooped uneasily over him. "I believe you have killed him, Guillerot," he muttered.

"Nonsense," said the stalwart one, but not very confidently. "Moreover, if I have, I could not help it; he was dangerous. Gavel here has a stab in the arm as it is."

Brémond knelt and put his hand on the jersey, while the rest stood round in silence. It was a blow that could kill; they knew that, and in the presence of the young lady they were ashamed, for after all they were not ruffians, even though the troops they had been given were convicts. Rising after a moment, Captain Brémond went a little nearer to the bed and uttered apologies which, from her attitude, he doubted if the young lady even heard. But he continued nevertheless to assure her that her fellow-countryman was only stunned, and that they would take him downstairs and care for him, hinting also that his comrades' high spirits were due to the wine-cup, and that no disrespect to her was intended. She remained, however, huddled and motionless, and he dared not even lay a reassuring hand upon her shoulder.

Meanwhile the others were just about to lift the inert Martin when Guillerot, who had gone downstairs with the wounded Gavel, came running up again. "Come down at once, my friends-here's Tate returning! He must not find us all up here!"

"And he must not find that we have injured the Welshman-perhaps killed him! He will be furious!"

"Then he must not see his body. Stow it away somewhere-but in the devil's name be quick about it; the General's just coming in!"

"Leave the man here, then, for the time," suggested another voice. "He's only stunned. And lock the door, lest he should come down and lodge a complaint. The key, Didier!"

The plight of the young lady was forgotten again in the culprits' almost schoolboy desire to avoid getting into trouble with their commander. The babel ceased; the key turned in the lock, feet ran fast down the stairs again, and Nest was left alone with Martin Tyrrell . . . or with his dead body.

(7)

If she had been some stage heroine of Dryden's or Otway's, had she even been Calista in that very *Fair Penitent* of Rowe's—of whom Dr. Johnson observed that she showed more shame than sorrow, and more rage than shame-Nest would now have flung herself upon the body of her love, and after loud outcries "offered" to kill herself with his dagger. But, much more because she was at first too terrified to move, than because she had never seen Mrs. Siddons, superb in trailing black as Calista, declaiming over the dead Lothario on his bier, she attempted neither of these high gestures. Crouched at the end of the bed, hiding her eyes against the coverlet, she dared not for some minutes even lift her head, and it was a moment or two more before she rose, very shakily, to her feet, and stared again at the result of that wild scrimmage which had taken place in the open doorway, a scrimmage which she had only witnessed because she had been too petrified to avert her eyes. It was only after Martin Tyrrell's overthrow that she had had recourse to hiding them.

Her champion was lying on his back with his arms spread wide, very much as he had fallen, save that, in order to get his feet out of the way when they shut the door, the departing Frenchmen had dragged him a little further into the room. But he had not moved; the girl instinctively felt that. Besides, how could he move if he was, as they had hinted . . . dead?

The word, not the fact, of which she had had so little experience, seemed for a moment actually to dangle before her in the air, as if written gigantically upon some inn-sign—DEAD. Nest swayed and put out her hand again to the bedpost. But no! how could Mr. Tyrrell—"Mr. Towers"—be dead? Such a thing could not happen in a moment, like that! And she had heard someone deny it. He had been knocked down; she had seen it done, and it was horrible enough; but men (she thought) did not die of being knocked down, unless perhaps old men. She had seen no weapon used; the only steel unsheathed had been her defender's own knife; that indeed she had seen glittering for a second or two in the candlelight ere it had flown from his hand-to slide, she believed, under the bed. No, he could not be dead! Yet he lay there quite motionless.

As far as she could tell, however, the worst horror of all was wanting; there was no blood visible. And surely if there were no signs of blood, then she might allow herself to believe that he was merely stunned. Holding her breath she tiptoed over to look-quite sure that she should faint if there were. No, there was none! He was alive, alive! In spite of the fact that he looked so lifeless . . . and so strange, with that beard! in spite of the fact that he had been one against so many, he was alive! And, assured of it, she knelt down by her knight, and forthwith burst into tears.

And while she wept Martin uttered a groan, then another; moved slightly, opened and shut a hand. For though Nest's premises were quite false she had, by the special intuition of her sex, arrived at a correct deduction: he had not been killed. But he had been badly knocked out, and he was feeling extremely shaken and not a little sick, in a state just between the unconscious and the wholly conscious.

Nest checked her sobs. A new fear assailed her; that, though not dead, he was dying. The groans alarmed her very much; also the fact that Mr. Tyrrell's eyes were still shut. Carried out of her natural timidity and the reserve proper to a young lady, she seized hold of his nearer hand with both her own, clutched it to her and said in extreme agitation, "Martin, Martin-dear Martin, you shall not die . . . I will not let you!"

A long way down a revolving tunnel or well-shaft Martin heard his name. With a great effort he opened his eyes. Evidently he had risen to the top of the shaft, since he saw above him in a faint light a rapidly spinning wheel, dark against a lighter background-the beams across the ceiling going round at a great pace. The sight made him feel still more sick, so he sensibly shut his eyes again; on which he seemed to sink anew down the well-shaft. Not particularly wishing to do this, he tried to stretch out his arms to stop himself, and was worried to find that one of his hands appeared to be caught in something or other-not, it was true, immovably, for when he attempted to free it he succeeded. And with the effort he ceased to sink; became in fact aware that in reality he could neither sink nor rise, since he was undoubtedly lying on something solid and hard—a floor perhaps. But what floor?

He opened his eyes once more to candle-lit beams; but these were now only slightly gyratory, and, as he frowned up at them, steadied down almost to immobility. Accomplishing what seemed to him an immensely praiseworthy intellectual feat, he concluded that he was in a room somewhere. Then a slight sound attracted him, and turning his eyes he saw, kneeling at a little distance, the agency which had held captive his right hand. It was gazing at him with an expression of mingled terror, misgiving . . . and something else. Then he remembered.

"Nest," he said thickly, "Nest . . . are you . . ." If only he did not feel so sick! There was much more he wanted to ask-and say. Perhaps if he had a drink of water . . .

Had he uttered this wish aloud? At any rate, here was some water spilling out of a glass over his mouth and chin, the agency's hand shaking so, and it being impossible to drink with one's head flat on the floor. "If . . . you . . . could lift my . . . head up a little . . ." After a moment he felt that it was being supported and lifted, gingerly; so he took a good gulp of the water, then another, and felt much better; and after lying quiet a moment longer, even contrived to raise his head a trifle from the arm which pillowed it.

"Are they gone?"

"Yes." The answer came in a whisper. "But I think they are still in the house."

With some difficulty Martin got on to an elbow. "And you-you are not hurt? They did not touch you?"

She shook her head. "No, no! But you, Mr. Tyrrell . . . that terrible blow! You are injured, perhaps badly, for my sake!"

Martin ran his other hand thoughtfully round his jaw, felt his neck and finally explored the back of his head.

"I do not think it is anything to speak of," he announced slowly. "And I am glad to think that I must have . . . But where *is* my knife?" he finished, thus betraying the subject of his self-congratulation.

"I will look for it."

She got up from his side and Martin relapsed for a moment on to the floor again. From what had he saved her-if he *had* saved her-for she was still in the French camp? Perhaps from nothing worse than a stolen kiss, for it had been clear that the more sober of the invaders below by no means approved the raid of the unspeakable Didier. Yet Didier might make another attempt. . . . And there were always the men outside, the lowest of the low, from what he had seen of them; he could well believe that they were released convicts. If they got out of hand they might sack the farm, and what would happen then? So, though Martin's fervent desire of the two last days was granted, and he was having an interview with Nest Meredith, he most sincerely wished that it were taking place anywhere but here. He must indeed be ready still to protect her with what forces were left to him.

Starting therefore to crawl to his feet-there was no other word for the process-he accomplished this manœuvre not too ill, subsiding rapidly on to a chair, and sitting there, elbows at first on knees and head on hands, for he felt dizzier than he had anticipated. And when that physical dizziness slowly cleared, another, of quite a different kind, came upon him, when he saw his little Nest kneeling compassionately by him, tendering a handkerchief which she had evidently soaked in her ewer, and murmuring something about putting it to his head.

But *that* dizziness he had felt ever since he had seen her sitting at the end of the table downstairs, the captive guest of those brutes. He disregarded the hand and its offering. "Oh, Nest!" he sighed brokenly, and drawing her to him as she knelt there, let his head sink upon her shoulder. How blind he had been not to have known long ago!

Nest did not resist, but he felt a tremor go through her. She allowed him to do this, he thought, because she knew he was giddy and temporarily disabled; and perhaps she permitted it from gratitude also. But what would she say when in a moment more he got to his feet and clasped her in his arms, first asking her for the kiss which he would have taken without asking, but for what she had been through this evening; and then telling her — —

But how could he possibly propose marriage to her, he, the proscribed outlaw, he, still hunted, still bearing a fake name? It was crazy and dishonourable even to think of such a thing!

Martin lifted his head from its brief resting place, loosed his hold, and uttering a sound like a groan, got to his feet. Nest rose too. Without looking at her-he could not-he took the sodden handkerchief with a word of thanks, and pressed it for a moment to his forehead. Then, with no more than a slight sensation of walking on a swaying floor, he went over to the window and cautiously peered through the curtain at the firelit avenue.

"They are still here," he said in a low voice; and indeed the noise penetrating the shut window could have told him that. He went, quite steadily this time, to the door of the room, and gently tried it.

As he had feared, it was locked. He listened, and could distinguish voices downstairs, but voices neither noisy nor numerous; listening more intently he came to the conclusion that there were not more than two or three men down there now. But he and Nest were prisoners, and, as far as he could see, must spend the remainder of the night here . . . in her bedroom. He hoped that fact was not troubling her; probably she had been through too much for ideas of propriety to occur to her now, and he certainly did not intend for the sake of those ideas to go away, even if it were feasible to do so, and leave her unprotected.

As he softly came back from the door he saw Nest standing in the middle of the room looking at him in a way he found hard to bear. Gently he asked her-for it was important to know it-why the scoundrels had withdrawn after knocking him down, and why they had left him there? She told him, to the best of her ability; and when he again enquired about his knife she fetched it from the bed where she had laid it. "Here it is, Mr. Tyrrell."

Someone, when he was down in that well-shaft, had called him "Martin," even as he just now had called her by her own short sweet name. But he must not do that again, save in his heart. He took the knife.

"You must forgive me if I stay here with you," he said. "Perhaps you will repose yourself a little in that chair, which does not look too uncomfortable; and I will station myself over by the door, lest anyone should . . . frighten you again. I do not think they will," he added hastily. "But even if I could climb out of the window unseen by the soldiers down there, I could not bring myself to leave you-for in that case of what avail to have come here after you at all?" (Though even as he said it he knew and thanked God that it had been of avail.) "See, this big chair — —"

But Nest broke in agitatedly, "You did, you did come here on my account then-you knew, somehow, that I was here? That was all a pretence downstairs, that you had come to guide the French — —"

Martin swung round from pulling forward the chair. "Surely that device did not deceive you too," he exclaimed in astonishment and some horror. "Did you really believe — —" But she had turned away and begun to cry-the most heartbreaking little tired sobbing it was, like a child's, which could not, could not, be left uncomforted.

"Nest, Nest!" he whispered; caught her in his arms and drew the small disordered head to his breast. "Nest, you must not cry like that!"

"I . . . I thought . . ." She gulped back a sob, struggling to control her tears (since tears were not for that place where she found herself now), and in another moment, for all his resolve, Martin's kiss would have fallen upon her hair at all events, when he suddenly stiffened.

"Listen, listen!" he said under his breath; and then adding, "Do not be alarmed, 'tis probably nothing!" put her gently from him into the chair and went on tiptoe to the door, pulling his recovered knife from its sheath. For in that second or two of silence he had heard footsteps stealing very softly and cautiously up the creaking stairs.

(8)

In Pencaer that night, from Llanwnda to Pen Brush, from Strumble Head to St. Nicholas, there was more universal (and unprepared for) feasting, much of it in the open, than had taken place there in the memory of man. Thirty-six raided farms yielded supplies of poultry and quantities of the recently wrecked port, of which almost every dwelling had a barrel or even a pipe (which widespread and copious distribution of wine was afterwards, owing to its incapacitating effects on the marauders, ascribed by the pious to an overruling Providence). The amazing fact was that the convict-invaders did little other damage and inflicted practically no personal injuries, and when the inhabitants who had not already left their homes fled before the pillagers, the latter were better occupied than in pursuing. Possibly they felt that after their really remarkable feat, not only in scrambling up a steep and slippery grass-clothed headland from boats of which only one had been lost in the surf, but also in propelling or dragging up it nearly fifty barrels of ammunition, a sheet full of ball cartridges and twelve boxes of hand grenades, they deserved a good feed. And such they undoubtedly had, though their culinary methods were wasteful as well as rough, for some of the ducks and geese they boiled in butter.

Trehowell, it was true, had a substantial and varied meal prepared, but then this meal had nearly all been eaten by General Tate's staff. The troops round Mr. Mortimer's homestead feasted in the avenue and the outbuildings, and some were still satisfying their appetites, though a trifle languidly, at two in the morning. The officers within, all save one, had however dispersed by this time, some to supervise the last of the landing operations, some to assist in the consolidation of the position chosen at Carnwnda, above the hamlet of Llanwnda; and, their control being temporarily removed, only the somewhat precarious authority of a sergeant and a couple of corporals, both regulars, restrained the more active spirits from searching the farmhouse from roof to cellar for more viands and drink and anything else they could lay their hands upon. Some of the sailors who had come up with them from the flotilla had already contrived to slip in unobserved, had secured two or three feather beds, cut them open and carried off the ticking in order to make themselves fresh trousers, so that from a great mound of feathers against an outhouse wall there arose occasional flurries like snowflakes, which drifted across the light from the camp fires. Mr. Mortimer's grandfather clock, too, had some time ago slid down Careg Gwastad at the end of a rope on its way to the lugger *Vautour*.

By the embers of one of these fires a party of the invaders were picking and sucking the denuded bones of the last goose, and discussing the feasibility of entering the farmhouse and helping themselves also to some of its contents, when out of the darkness a voice said, in French, "*Eh bien, les copains*, one hopes that you have eaten well!" And to this salutation one of the revellers replied muzzily, "Afraid there's nothing left for you, comrade-who are you, by the way?"

"Why, a Frenchman like yourself," replied the newcomer; and indeed there could from his command of the tongue be no doubt about his nationality. He came forward into the firelight, a tall man in a blue coat. "I wish to see the General."

"He's not here; there's no one in the house at the moment except Captain Gavel, and he's — —" The speaker laughed and broke off; but another completed the information by draining an imaginary glass.

"Hallo, who's this?" asked a sergeant, suddenly coming up. "Who is this customer, and how did he get here?"

"I have come from Fishguard," replied the tall man. "I have business with General Tate; but if he is not here I can wait."

The sergeant eyed him suspiciously. "Who are you?"

"That I am afraid I must not tell you," replied his compatriot. "But you can probably guess that the Directory has been preparing the ground in these parts for you others, and I have a report to make on the subject. With your permission I will go inside and wait for the General's return."

For a moment it was touch-and-go whether this permission would be given, but there could not be the slightest doubt that the visitor was a Frenchman, and it never occurred to the sergeant that he might be a Frenchman of a different taste in politics. "Very good; go in," he said, waving his hand towards the dimly seen porch. "I suppose the General will be back some time. But you will find Captain Gavel within; he is composing himself after some accident or other." And armed with this authorisation the self-styled agent of the Directory made his way past the sleepy sentry into the farmhouse.

Perhaps in all that night of surprises there was no individual more violently taken aback than was Jonas Challacombe, mate of the *Raymonde*, when her captain, returning from Cardigan soon after Gregson's dash from the quay, and learning the motive of this desertion, immediately announced his intention of following him. The horrified Devonian had then suggested that he should at least take some of the crew with him, but La Vireville had refused. "I can pass easily, being French," he had explained, "but they would only get captured."

"But that there crazy Gregson can't pass for French!" Challacombe had objected.

"No; that is just why I am going after him-he is a lad of spirit. Moreover, I have met the young lady, and if she is really there . . ." He finished with a gesture, and forthwith departed, leaving the honest mate with a tiny thistledown of doubt floating about his mind, of which he was ashamed. Yes, the Chevalier was French, worse luck; was it possible that he was secretly in league after all with the villains who flew the "trickler"? And there was that young Gregson, too, gone off to their headquarters, Gregson, between whom and the Chevalier there undoubtedly existed an understanding of some kind!

Challacombe's suspicions might indeed have been strengthened if he had been in a position to witness the ease with which La Vireville carried out his intention of "slipping through" such groups of marauders as he encountered. He had but to speak his native tongue and to represent himself to these half bewildered gaol-birds as whatever he pleased; it was enough for them that he was indubitably a compatriot. His chief difficulty-the night being a particularly dark one-had been to find his way to Trehowell, which, unlike Martin, he had not previously located. In fact, he twice lost his way, and a good deal of time as well.

Inside the farmhouse kitchen he now stood, like Martin before him, noting its geography. Yet its aspect was different from when Martin had entered, for the table had now a disorderly and even wrecked appearance, covered as it was with used plates, fragments of food and a forest of empty bottles. The sole occupant of this banquet hall deserted looked rather wrecked too — a stout officer seated sideways at the table, with his legs on another chair, his lolling head supported by one hand. His other arm was in a sling. Looking up, he stared in a very owlish manner at the intruder.

"Hallo!" he said sleepily. "Come up from the squadron, have you?" The marine-looking blue coat had evidently deceived his bemused senses.

La Vireville, quick to take advantage, nodded. "I thought the General was here."

"Don't know where Tate is," replied the solitary officer, pouring himself out another glass. "Don't know and don't care. May be at landing place with outlandish name, may be up at position with outlandish name. Was unable to acc-accompany him . . . owing to severe wound." He pointed to his bandaged arm.

"Ah?" said the Royalist with interest. "And how did you receive that?"

"Devil of a Welshman stuck a knife into me. Must tell you there's a girl here-pretty piece she is too. Didier and somebody else had her down-enliven supper. Then the General — —" Herewith he launched into the tale, and, despite the half-intoxicated condition of the narrator, M. de la Vireville shortly had a fairly correct idea of what had occurred; save that, even if the "Welshman" really were Tyrrell, it was not clear whether he should find him alive or dead. At any rate it seemed obvious that, whatever his condition, he was locked in with the girl he had come to rescue, in the room at the top of the stairs.

"I shall go up-pay her a little visit," announced Gavel at the conclusion. "When I feel better, that is. Pretty girl, like to reassure her . . . But *you're* not to go!" he added thickly. "No business of yours!"

"But naturally!" agreed the Chouan readily. "I was not thinking of it. I haven't got the key, for one thing." This warrior was in such a confidential stage of drunkenness that he would quite probably respond to the mention of the key by revealing its whereabouts.

He did. "Have glass of wine!" he said, pushing a nearly empty bottle unsteadily towards the newcomer. "As matter of fact, key's just where you wouldn't expect it, as far as I know-still in the lock. But you're not to go up; you're to go back squadron. Which frigate do you belong to?"

"To neither," said Fortuné prudently. "To the corvette."

"Ah-thought I hadn't seen you before. Lost your arm, I see; poor fellow, very sad, very sad! . . . Tell you in conf-confidence, as you're naval officer lost arm-not very likely that Castagnier will get his sailing orders yet awhile!" And he shook his head with an immense and stupid solemnity.

La Vireville pricked up his ears, though he knew not what this announcement might signify. "You think not?"

"Well, man, is it likely?" retorted Gavel with a still more portentous gravity, directing a wavering stream from the bottle in his hand at his glass, with so ill an aim that scarcely a drop entered it. "You musht have seen for yourself-men as drunk as pigs out there-dishgushting sight! You know ships are to leave if things going well on shore. General can hardly say that, can he? Great mistake of Hoche's, picking convicts for this expet —" he struggled, "expedition when what's wanted 'bove all is dish'pline, strict, strict dish'pline!"

"No, I suppose we cannot expect our discharge yet awhile," agreed the bogus naval officer, looking musingly at the author of this disclosure. So that was the plan; very interesting! "I wonder," he went on, tilting up the bottle, "*how* well things must go before General Tate gives Castagnier" (evidently that was the commodore's name), "his sailing orders? Not, of course, that we sailors want to desert you."

Captain Gavel stared into his empty glass as if to find the answer there. "Difficult to say." He held the glass up to the light, and there was puzzlement in his bleared gaze, for he knew that he had recently tried to refill it. "Tate's Irishman, you know-calls himself American, though," he said, putting down the glass with a sigh. "Never know what Irishman will do-so damned impulsive, the Irish. What ye looking for?"

For the visitor had risen. "Another bottle. There's deuced little left in my glass, or in yours." One more glass and the man would be under the table, a consummation which there was not a moment to lose in bringing about, since Tate or some members of his staff might reappear at any moment (it seemed a miracle that they had not already done so) or, if they did not, the convict troops outside might carry out the intention which he had overheard some of them express of ransacking the farmhouse. As La Vireville drew the cork of the bottle which he had found, the fuddled Gavel abruptly sat up and looked about.

"What was that—a shot? Fighting begun already?"

"No, no. Something less alarming. Where's your glass; let's make sure that the wine goes into it this time! . . . Well, here's to the success of the expedition!"

"Shuccess!" Gavel held up the glass, drained it, murmured something about having been up all night and requiring sleep, put his head down on the table, and in less than sixty seconds was snoring, by which time Fortuné de la Vireville had his hand on the half-open door leading to the stairs. But as he never neglected an opportunity, he cast a last look round the disorderly kitchen, and observing a paper propped up on the mantelpiece near a broken hour-glass, he went quickly and took it down. It seemed to be a proclamation drawn up ready for printing, an "Appel au Peuple Gallois," four sides of a double quarto sheet of flamboyant rhetoric in French and English. The last few lines and the signatures-Tate's and a couple of his officers-were on a separate sheet. The Royalist folded both sheets of this composition and put them in his pocket.

Then, with a last look to see that he was unobserved, he went stealthily up the stairs, trusting that the key *was* in the lock.

It was; yet it was fortunate that after turning it he only opened the door a little way, saying softly in English, "Mademoiselle, may I enter? It is a friend!" The precaution was all to avoid alarming the fair inmate, but it possibly saved La Vireville himself a knife thrust. For just inside the door, looking haggard and murderous, stood Martin Tyrrell, a seaman's knife clutched ready in his right hand. Beyond him, huddled in a chair, was a female form.

"Good God!" exclaimed the defender under his breath, his arm relaxing, "*You* , Chevalier!"

La Vireville slid quietly in and closed the door. "I am glad to see, *mon cher* , that you are not a corpse. *De grâce* , do not make me one!"

Martin sheathed his knife. "You know what has been happening, then? How on earth did you get in?"

"If you mean into this room, I turned the key, which was in the lock outside. The drunken sot, your victim, who is the only occupant of the kitchen, took me for one of their own naval officers . . . Would it be possible to remove Mademoiselle before any others of Tate's staff return, which may happen *à tout moment* ?"

They both looked across at Nest, who had now raised a ghostlike countenance. Obviously she was pretty well at the end of her powers. The Frenchman went over to her and kissed her hand.

"Mademoiselle," he said, with great gentleness, "I had the honour of meeting you once, outside the Cathedral. I hope you will allow me the further privilege of helping Mr. Tyrrell to restore you to your friends, when we can think of a way to do it."

Nest made a great effort. Her hand went to the bosom of her gown. "The . . . the General gave me this paper and said that to-morrow he would send me home; but after that those . . . those men came up here, and if it had not been . . ." Her eyes turned to Martin.

In her hand by now was Tate's safe-conduct. La Vireville, taking it out of her fingers, was so much surprised and pleased that he automatically expressed his feelings to Martin in rapid French.

"Un laisser-passer du général lui-même! La chose est faite-pourvu qu'aucun officier ne revienne le disputer, et que les autres gueux respectent la signature de leur chef! Mais-pas un moment à perdre! Que Mademoiselle mette son manteau pendant que je fais une petite reconnaissance!" And as noiselessly as he had entered he left the room again.

Everything was to Nest now more phantasmagoric than real, and she was so tired that she could hardly remember where her bonnet and cloak were hanging; divining which Martin went and rather timidly opened the door of the press where he guessed them to be, returned apologetically with them, and murmuring: "You will permit me, will you not, for we must be as quick as possible?" slipped the bonnet over her bright, tangled hair, and while she, almost crying from fatigue, mechanically tied the strings, put her cloak round her shoulders. These intimacies certainly gave him a delightful thrill; but then alleged traitors ought not to have thrills of that kind. Nor certainly, as he whispered, "A little more courage-it is nearly over now!" ought he to have added fervently, "My dearest one!" and to have clasped her for a second to him. (But that was, perhaps, because she seemed a little unsteady on her feet.)

La Vireville was back in the doorway beckoning to him. "All's well! I have found a side door leading to a little lane. There is a sentry, but I have shown him the safe-conduct, and explained that we are Mademoiselle's qualified escort. And the sot still sleeps. *Allons!* "

"Miss Meredith is worn out," whispered Martin. "I think we may have to carry her."

"It will be an honour. —But, if you can, Mademoiselle, walk out now as composedly as possible between us! There is nothing to be afraid of while we have this paper." But over Nest's head he made a significant grimace at Martin expressive both of some doubt upon this point, and of the necessity of carrying out the flight with the minimum of delay.

It was at least a good omen for the start that the sleepy sentry at the side door made a show of presenting arms to La Vireville in his naval-seeming uniform. "*Bien jolie fille, quoi!* " he muttered to himself, looking after the trio as they vanished from his ken in the darkness. "*Je *vais boire une coupe à sa santé.* " And letting his musket slide to the ground he went in search of more *cwrw dda* .

(9)

Llanwnda churchyard, whence on Tuesday evening Martin Tyrrell had admired the view, held a strange congregation at dawn that Thursday morning, some groups of the oddly-clad foreign soldiery-though it was on the rocky outcrop of Carnwnda above it that Tate had concentrated most of his forces. The sky was lightening a trifle already as the General himself, standing in the porch of the little church (whence the communion plate had already been looted), folded up the map at which he and one of the Irish officers, Lieutenant St. Leger, had been looking.

As the General had just been remarking to his compatriot, the position here was good, a better one perhaps after all than they would have found so quickly had that mule of a Castagnier consented to land them on the North Devon or Somerset coast when, last Monday, they had got so far up the Bristol Channel as to be abreast of Porlock. Their orders had been to land, if possible, within reach of Bristol. But Castagnier was so careful of his precious ships, so vehement about the persistence of the contrary wind and the little assistance given by the tide, that one had had to agree to withdraw and to make for the alternative goal, Cardigan Bay, with a view to the destruction of Liverpool instead. And indeed it might prove more advantageous to have landed in Wales, where the inhabitants, like the Irish, would, with a little encouragement, be ready to rise. He must, when he got back to Trehowell, take steps about the proclamation to the natives which he now discovered had been left in the farmhouse.

At this point there appeared in the porch his aide-de-camp, Captain Faucon.

"There is a man here, *mon général*, of a well-to-do kind, who was captured by a patrol last evening, he and the gig he was driving, and shut up in some farm or other here. The patrol has now brought him out, for it seems that he declares he is Mr. Mortimer, the owner of Trehowell, and he demands insistently to see you."

"Mr. Mortimer, you say? I'll see him," quoth Tate, shivering slightly. "Bring him in here."

And so Mr. Mortimer, who, if his captors had not chanced to decree otherwise, would have been taken a prisoner to his own house, had the interview with the chief of the invaders which he had for hours been demanding with passion, half-way up this windy excrescence only a mile from Trehowell, whose roofs (not yet, thank God, in flames) he could see down among the trees not very far away. His home, his possessions, the young lady entrusted to his care, all in the hands of the invaders; what wonder that the rage and anxiety bottled up since his capture burst out in spate at first sight of the General in his great tricolour-bedecked hat, standing in the porch of the little church round which slept so many of Mr. Mortimer's own forbears.

"They tell me you can speak English," he began, standing up very straight as he faced this alien figure. "I will say nothing about your ragamuffins having robbed me of my watch and my shoe-buckles, and put my horse and gig I don't know where! But I demand to be allowed to go at once to my house yonder, which I understand you are unlawfully occupying!"

"I grant ye we have made a little free with the victuals, Mr. Mortimer," responded the General pacifically, "but I assure ye that the house is safe entirely, and shall be restored to ye without a stone of ut damaged, all in good time."

"It's not the house-for the moment-it's the safety of the young lady under my care, Miss Meredith, the Precentor's daughter. Why are you not at Trehowell yourself, sir? They told me you were. If you have let your scoundrels loose may the curse — —"

The General interrupted him. "I'll trouble you, Mr. Mortimer," he said, with dignity, "to kape a civil tongue in your head! I have seen the young lady and reassured her; she is safe within her room, with me own safe-conduct in her pockut, and whin day comes 'twill be put into execution. How could I be sending her off home in the middle of the night?"

"Is that the truth, as in God's sight?"

"As in God's sight, ut is!"

The worthy farmer drew a long, long breath of relief, and taking out his handkerchief wiped his forehead.

"Sure I'll give ye a pass too," went on Tate, "if ye'll go back to Fishguard-ye shall have your horse and gig-and tell thim what ye've seen here, the thousands of throops I have, disperate men all of 'um, and the strong position we have here, that the redcoats'll niver dhrive us out of. Will ye be telling thim that?"

But Mr. Mortimer was staring at him in a displeased perplexity. "God bless my soul!" he exclaimed, "I believe you are an Irishman!"

Tate drew himself up. "It's an American citizen I am. But it's thrue I was born in Wexford." Here he smiled a little. "Sure, then, that's all to the good, Ireland helping Wales!"

"Helping!" ejaculated Mr. Mortimer, with a snort. "Ravaging our farms, killing our stock, terrifying our women and children, robbing, murdering for all I know, you call that ——"

"Have patience now, sir, and ye shall have your buckles and watch again, if ye can point out the men that tuck them! They're meaning no harm, and there's not a hand been laid on any Welshman-or woman either! Sure we have no wish to injure the Welsh; 'tis the English are our inimies, and whin we get to Liverpool ——"

Mr. Mortimer permitted no more. "And you think the Welsh are going to allow you to get there!" he demanded volcanically. "You're very much mistaken, my fine Paddy from America, you and your dirty gaol sweepings, that dare to land here —*here*—and think we men of Dyfed are such white-livered curs as to put up with it! You'll all be swept back into the sea"—he threw out his arm towards it—"the whole lousy crew of you, when the troops come up! To help Wales! Pah!" And Mr. Mortimer's Celtic blood getting the better of his good yeoman breeding, he spat upon the ground.

Considering that "General" Tate, if he really came from Wexford, was presumably a Celt likewise, he kept his temper well. With some magnificence he said, also indicating the ocean: "Ye're forgetting, sir, that we have a fleet!" Then, without condescending to more exchanges, he beckoned to his aide-de-camp, ordered him to see that Mr. Mortimer had his horse and gig restored to him and that he went in the direction of Fishguard; and himself crossed the church-yard towards the rocky knell above, swarming with his brown uniformed followers, demanding loudly as he went the attendance of the *chef de bataillon* or major, Le Brun.

So Mr. Mortimer, still at boiling-point, was left with no alternative but to follow Captain Faucon, though to be actually within sight of Trehowell was to encourage a hope of getting to it after all. But Faucon carried out his orders to the letter. Mr. Mortimer was so sedulously assisted into his recovered gig, and the horse's head so firmly turned towards Goodwick-with a line of soldiers drawn up across the road behind him-that he gave in. Irish or American, this Tate was at least in possession of the English tongue, and that fact, as well as his assurance about the safe-conduct, did quiet the worst of Mr. Mortimer's anxiety about Miss Meredith's situation. Since he had been set at liberty, it was perhaps best to hurry back to Fishguard, find out what preparations were being made for attack on the French position, relieve his daughter's fears and report to Colonel Knox of Llanstinan, in command of the Fishguard Fencibles, what he had seen of the invaders-nothing, indeed, to make him think much of them . . . except their numbers. They seemed like ants-or monkeys-all over Pencaer.

Behind Dinas Head and Carn Engli the sky was all flushed now. Mr. Mortimer's wheels trundled steadily along the lane; here there were none of those ants, for he was nearing the sidelong descent into Goodwick, and apparently they had not yet spread so far. And here came in the lane which skirted Carnwnda on the other side, that away from the church and the hamlet, and at the junction the farmer pulled up for a moment. This route also led, though more circuitously, back to Trehowell; should he make an attempt to follow it?

Then he saw that there were three people a short way along the lane, two men and a woman, belated fugitives perhaps. They were resting against the bank, the woman drooping on the shoulder of one of the men; and when he himself was observed, the other man sprang up and waved to him. No doubt they wanted a lift, poor souls; he could take the woman, at least, but his gig only held two persons. He turned it at once in their direction; but it was not until he was abreast of the group, and the young sailor who was supporting her had lifted his companion gently to her feet, that Mr. Mortimer recognised the face within the bonnet as Miss Meredith's.

VIII
UP ANCHOR!

"They swear they'll invade us, these terrible foes!
They frighten our women, our children, and beaux;
But should their flat bottoms in darkness get o'er
Still Britons they'll find to receive them on shore."

Hearts of Oak.

"Quick, rouse you, gallants! catch the gale;
Sit to the oar, unfurl the sail!
A god, commissioned from on high.

   Commands us cut our cords and fly."

Æneid IV (Conington's translation).

VIII
UP ANCHOR!

(1)

Martin stood staring after Mr. Mortimer's disappearing gig with an expression at once rapt and stupefied.

"She's safe!" he ejaculated after a moment.

His companion touched his arm. "Yes, *mon preux chevalier*, your task is accomplished."

"It could not have been carried through without you," said Martin, blinking. "Had you not come after me, which was extraordinarily — —"

La Vireville stopped him. "This is not the place to discuss the apportionment of the laurel, nor are you in a state to do it." He slipped his hand under Martin's arm. "A glass of eau-de-vie would not come amiss to you, I fancy, my paladin, and perhaps an hour or two's sleep. We shall find both, I hope, in this Goodwick *là-bas*. *Allons-y!*"

"Goodwick? I thought we were going back to the *Raymonde*?"

"All in good time," said the Chouan, as they began to trudge along in the wake of the now vanished gig. "But there is something that I wish to do in Goodwick while you repose yourself. An idea has come to me."

Martin was at present but little interested in ideas. Now that the mental tension was over, and Nest really out of the invaders' hands, he was beginning increasingly to feel the physical strain of the business, and that in the most literal sense of the word, since, owing to the jar of the heavy blow which he had received, his neck, as he now realised, was so stiff that he could only turn his head with difficulty. An hour or two's rest and sleep-yes, it was a blessing which he would willingly have enjoyed here and now by the roadside save for the risk of falling anew into the hands of the French. He hurried along uncomplaining and bemused, vignettes of their clandestine journey from the farmhouse unrolling one after another in his tired brain: their challenge by a patrol into which they stumbled, from which strait the production of the safe-conduct had with some difficulty extracted them; the detour they had then made and the banks they had climbed to avoid another such encounter, and the moment when Nest collapsed entirely, and he had to carry her-reluctantly, at last, light though she was, relinquishing her to his companion.

Soon the two adventurers were at the top of the hill, and saw across the wet sands below Fishguard reared upon the other slope. The sun came up as they were descending among the houses of Goodwick with their sloping, sheltered gardens, which provided vegetables for the Fishguard market —a prosperous little colony clinging to the hillside. But no smoke drifted this morning from any chimney; Goodwick was wrapped in utter silence, for every inhabitant had fled.

This, however, seemed very little to discompose the Chevalier de la Vireville. With the half-dazed Martin on his arm he very cheerfully selected a little house whose panic-struck owners had omitted to lock their front door, led him within, installed him like a guest in a large chair, disappeared to forage, and finally reappeared with some hot soup, which Martin drank without questioning how he had procured or heated it at such short notice. Equally without protest did he submit to be led upstairs and to clamber on to a bed. He did, it is true, observe: "What if the French should occupy Goodwick and find us here?"

To this the Chevalier, who had insisted upon rubbing the sufferer's neck with butter (in default of oil), replied: "I have Mademoiselle's safe-conduct in my pocket. We are her escort, returned from delivering her to her friends; *donc*, we are quite in order. It is *we* who have occupied Goodwick, and when you have slept a little I will tell you the reason for it."

Martin thereupon slept-uncomfortably.

When he awoke his head felt a little clearer, but his neck still had affinities with a poker. However, he got off the bed, noticing for the first time an empty cradle and a child's toy upon the floor, and, descending into the living-room, found M. de la Vireville busy at a table with pen and ink.

"Sit down," said the latter, "and have the goodness to wait a moment. You can amuse yourself by reading this nonsense." And he pushed across to him a sheet of manuscript headed "Appel au Peuple Gallois."

"What, are the enemy in Goodwick now?" asked Martin, puzzled.

"No, and not much sign of it. On the other hand, I can see troops coming into Fishguard. I acquired that treasure at Trehowell."

He went on writing. And Martin's eyes, on the paper given to him, encountered high-flown phrases which seemed to indicate a belief that the Welsh, proud of their ancestors, the golden-sickled Druids (*fiers de leurs ancêtres, ces druides aux faucilles d'or*) were pining for an opportunity to shake off the yoke (*le joug insupportable*) of tyrant Albion, and more than ready to join those who in the name of liberty and fraternity were come to assist them in this righteous endeavour. Whether this rhodomontade (presented in English as well as in French) had come originally from the pen of Wolfe Tone or had its birth in a Gallic imagination Martin could not know; but it struck him as much more absurd than dangerous.

"What nonsense!" he said hotly. "Nevertheless, I dare say it is as well to suppress it. But perhaps it is already printed."

La Vireville finished reading over what he had just written on another double sheet nearly identical in size to that of the "Appel."

"Printed or not," he said, "it is a godsend. Give me your attention, *mon ami*. It is evident, is it not, that, as they have made no move forward, the enemy intend to await attack on the strong ground which they have taken up. I know not what may be the military resources which can be assembled in the district, but I imagine that they are not great. In any case, there will be lives lost-perhaps many lives. For my part, I am not anxious that these should be the lives of Englishmen, whose country shelters me, an *émigré*; nor, as a Frenchman, am I anxious that they should be the lives of these poor devils of convicts, herded out of their galleys and thrown upon this coast like so many sheep. For, after all, they are my fellow-countrymen."

"I appreciate your feelings, Monsieur de la Vireville," replied Martin, "but I do not see how bloodshed can be avoided. This Irish-American filibuster could hardly be persuaded to withdraw and go off again; he would not dare to encounter the wrath of the Directory."

"*Entendu*; but he might be induced to surrender, either by the menace of a superior force, or by having his retreat cut off-or by both these misfortunes *à la fois*!"

"But before a superior force can be brought against him he will have sacked Fishguard and be marching inland. Nor can his retreat be cut off without a naval action. Till that takes place, he has his frigates and what not waiting for him off the headland-though I grant that re-embarkation in daylight might be rendered dangerous for him."

La Vireville gave a cryptic little smile. "The frigates and 'what not' could be sent away," he countered.

"I should like to know who is going to send them! Not Tate, that's certain!"

"*Si*, Tate *lui-même*! Or rather, I!" announced the Chevalier, with great composure. "No, my dear Gregson, I am not mad. *Ecoutez!* If things go well with this ridiculous Tate —*cette vraie tête de mouton* —the ships will receive an order to leave, since their presence off the coast will no longer be required; I learnt that last night from my drunken but communicative friend. In fact, they await that order; it may be with some impatience, lest a much stronger English squadron appear and trap them. *Eh bien*, they are going to receive it. Here it is!"

With the suspicion of a flourish he handed his companion the other sheet, and Martin read an order, couched in French, authorising Captain Castagnier, commanding the flotilla of the Republic now lying off the coast of Pembrokeshire, to weigh anchor upon its receipt, since his services, for which he was thanked, would no longer be required. The document concluded with expressions of fraternity and the signatures of Tate and two other officers. Martin stared at the whole uncomprehending.

"You found this, too, at Trehowell?" he enquired.

"*Nenni*. I wrote it myself just now."

"But the signatures-the signatures look genuine!"

"They *are* genuine. They are the signatures to that preposterous 'Appel.' By great good luck," explained La Vireville, demonstrating with his forgery, "the last few lines of that effusion ran over on to a second double sheet of paper, for which reason the signatures were on that extra sheet. I had merely to cut off the nonsense at the top, refold the entire sheet so that the first page became the third, write my order on what was now the first —*et voilà* !"

Martin spent a few moments examining this ingenious transposition. Except that the signatures did not directly follow upon the order-though they were on the same sheet of paper-there seemed no fault to find with it. The French was, naturally, impeccable; even the handwriting had the foreign characteristics which no Englishman could have hoped to imitate with success. The forgery certainly looked most convincing.

"But who will take this order to Captain Castagnier?"

"You and I," replied the Chevalier de la Vireville gaily. "Or, at least, I."

But Martin, though he could not withhold appreciation, was not brought to assent to this audacious plan without a good deal of argument. In the first place he doubted the discharge, for all its speciousness, being received as genuine: against this La Vireville urged that the signatures *were* genuine, and that Castagnier was expecting just such a discharge-the very strongest point in favour of the scheme. But, objected Martin, how could one account for the order's being entrusted, not to Tate's aide-de-camp or a member of his staff, but to an absolute stranger? La Vireville retorted that in an enterprise of so essentially amateur a nature, with convicts for troops, anything was possible, and Castagnier would probably not be in the least surprised; moreover, he could represent himself (as last night, with success, to the sergeant at Trehowell) in the guise of an agent of the Directory. And in any case, one must take *some* small risk! Yes; and how, queried Martin, if suspicions were aroused, were they going to escape being captured themselves? The Royalist replied that only he should go aboard with the order; and even that he hoped to avoid doing.

"You seem to have an answer to everything," conceded Martin, with half unwilling admiration. "But, listen now, Chevalier: Tate would surely have arranged to *signal* this order from the shore; why should he trouble to send a messenger by boat?"

"You must put yourself in the shoes of Castagnier as well as in the boots of Tate, *mon ami* . Castagnier is not going to risk sailing away without a written discharge from the General; he might get into trouble with his superiors. I have been in the Navy myself," added La Vireville. "*On prend ses précautions.* "

Martin sat looking at him meditatively. "I suppose, if you really contemplate doing this, that you intend to take a small boat from the harbour here? Have you tried to find a Goodwick man to accompany you?"

"*Dieu m'en garde!* " replied the *émigré* , with what seemed unnecessary fervour. "This is a strictly private expedition, designed for us two alone-that is, if you feel moved to come. (You may set your mind at rest about your unfortunate *torticolis* —your neck which is so stiff-for you shall not labour at the oar. The boat which I design to employ has a little sail.) There is a certain amount of risk in the business; I cannot disguise it, but it is not much, and the game is worth the candle-at least I hope you will think so." He looked down, smiling, at the paper for a moment; then raised his head and added "But there is naturally no obligation upon you to accompany me."

"You intend to go in any case-even if I do not?"

"But certainly! It would be a crime to waste those signatures!"

Martin got up. "I am with you, then. Only, I warn you, Chevalier, that I feel as stupid as a donkey—besides not being able to turn my head with any comfort. It is you who will have to answer any questions."

"That is understood. You are only my boatman—a fisherman of the place, whom I have hired to convey me to the squadron. You will remain in the boat, where I very much hope to remain also. *Allons donc!* "

In high spirits the Royalist put his fictitious despatch into his pocket, and Martin, infected by his enthusiasm, but not wholly convinced, followed him out of the abandoned house and down to the equally deserted little quay.

(2)

To Mr. Jerome Salt, as to most of the citizens of St. David's, the staggering news of the invasion of Pencaer had penetrated in the dusk of the same February evening, when the landing was still in progress, though, of course, the fact that an "English" squadron was sailing in that direction had been common property since about eleven in the morning. The owner of Bowen's Folly was not backward in warlike preparations, though he neither mounted a ladder to strip lead from the Cathedral roof in order to cast bullets, nor countenanced those who did. Indeed when he heard of this over-zealous feat, which neither the Treasurer nor the Chancellor was able to prevent, he was conscious of great sympathy for the absent Precentor when he should learn of it.

But Mr. Salt was still ignorant of the vastly sharper and more personal agitation which would soon engulf that dignitary amid the amenities of Bath, for he did not know that it was to Pencaer-to Trehowell itself-that Nest Meredith had been exiled. He learnt it, to his horror, early next morning, on the march up to Fishguard, in the stream of volunteer warriors, composed of townsfolk, local gentry and their servants, farmers and farm labourers, the latter armed for the most part with the sharper agricultural instruments.

On arrival at Fishguard, therefore, Mr. Salt's concern (and a very burning one it was) was less to learn the present position of affairs, which indeed no one in that distracted town appeared to know, but the whereabouts of the owners of Trehowell, and whether they and their guest had fled in time. Finally, to his immense relief, he discovered that they were all safe, Mr. Mortimer and his daughter and the young lady visiting them, whom Mr. Mortimer had gone back to Trehowell to fetch, and whom he had brought in his gig to Fishguard this morning at sunrise, having rescued her from the clutches of the insolent invaders.

Mr. Salt upon this offered fervent thanks to Providence, even though it sounded somewhat as if Nest had been all night at Trehowell. His next task was to interview Mr. Mortimer, to hear further details and to thank the worthy man, who must surely have run considerable risks. The "Royal Oak," where he heard that he should find him, was all a babel and a confusion of militia and fencible officers, and was expecting Lord Cawdor, who was known to be hastening to the scene of action from Stackpole Court, some thirty miles away, and who, it was rumoured, had been requested by Lord Milford, the Lord Lieutenant, to take command of the troops, since the latter was himself too infirm to do so, though he was making his way to Fishguard with the rest.

Mr. Mortimer, when at last Mr. Salt came at him, explained the situation, and that the actual rescue of Miss Meredith, at present under his daughter's care at the house of some old relatives of theirs, was due not to him, but to two men, sailors-at least, one of them, though looking like a common seaman, spoke like a gentleman, while the other seemed to be a foreigner, and Mr. Mortimer had since thought that he might be the master of the Jersey schooner in the harbour, and the young man, perhaps, one of his crew. At any rate, it was they who had penetrated into Trehowell and got Miss Meredith away unharmed. He had not seen them since.

"The Jersey schooner!" exclaimed Mr. Salt, almost gaping. "A foreigner, you say, and a younger sailor? What was the young man like?"

Mr. Mortimer attempted a description, adding that his daughter had said something about a young seaman who seemed to know Miss Meredith personally, having distractedly demanded news of her the evening before, after he, Mortimer, had set off on his frustrated return to Trehowell. He now mentioned further that the "foreigner" had but one arm.

"By gad!" exclaimed his hearer. "By Jupiter, Neptune . . . and Cupid! I would call at your relatives' house now, but that I hope Miss Meredith is asleep. But ask your daughter, Mr. Mortimer, to be so good as to inform her when the occasion offers that I am in Fishguard, if she have need of me-for the Precentor, as you probably know, is away in England. I hope, by the by, that the damage and loss of property you have sustained at Trehowell will prove not to be too great!"

"If my house isn't burnt to the ground, sir, it's all I can expect," replied Mr. Mortimer, shaking his head. "They say that the ruffians have slit open all the feather beds for the sake of the covers!"

"Well," observed the antiquary grimly, "they may find something else slit open before we have finished with them. I hear that the Castlemartin yeomanry cavalry will soon be here; and meanwhile scythes upon poles, such as accompanied me from St. David's, have their uses." He wrung Mr. Mortimer's hand and hurried off down to the harbour.

On the deck of the *Raymonde* a large, red-bearded man was putting the crew through some kind of cutlass drill, though but few of them had cutlasses. "Schooner ahoy!" called Mr. Salt. "Is that the *Raymonde* of St. Helier's, and is the master aboard?"

Challacombe turned, saw the questioner and swung on to the quay, cutlass in hand. "No, sir, he'm not, I'm main sorry to say. He went off last night after one of the hands that was crazy to get to that farm that the French has occupied-some maid or other in danger-and neither of 'em's been seen since. Took by the Mounseers, the both of 'em, and their throats cut by now, I warrant!"

"No," replied Mr. Salt, "their throats have not been cut-at least they were intact at sunrise this morning, for they succeeded in rescuing the young lady in question, and delivered her over to the owner of Trehowell, a little above Goodwick, at that hour. I expected to find them here; why, in heaven's name, are they not returned?"

(3)

It was perhaps as well that Mr. Salt could not learn the answer to this question.

Martin had followed the Chevalier into the small boat lying at Goodwick's little pier tucked under the cliff, rather like a somnambulist, though he was perfectly willing to share in his audacious plan, whose almost impertinent boldness might well call down success. If it did and the French were thereby brought to surrender-well, his darling would be out of any further danger. Personally, he would have preferred to help drive these impudent hordes back over the cliffs into the sea, there to drown; but, like his companion, he very much doubted whether the troops which could be brought up, joined to half-armed farmers, would be able to accomplish this, especially as one had little idea of the actual numbers of the enemy.

The breeze was light, and their progress out of Fishguard Bay rather slow. Martin, as supposed owner of the boat, steered under direction from La Vireville. When they rounded the sharp nose of Pen Anglas, they were able to see the French ships lying at anchor within the ten fathom line, two frigates, a corvette and a lugger, looking, the frigates at least, large and formidable in the extreme. Their own little craft, as it made its way towards them must, Martin thought, appear very small from the cliffs, and from the frigates, too, where no doubt its advance was being closely scrutinised-the only sail, and so tiny a sail, on that wide blue expanse! And when they were near enough to see the black grin of the men-of-war's gunports the impulse surged through all Martin's blood to send the ships away at any cost! Why, in half an hour, if they chose, they might be in the bay firing round-shot into Fishguard town and frightening his little Nest again!

He steered, as directed, round the stern of the larger frigate. They were observed from her upper deck, that was evident, but not challenged. Martin could see her name now under the lazily moving tricolour, *La Vengeance*. Her accommodation ladder was down, with a boat made fast at the bottom; and as their own sail fell the sentry at the top did shout down a demand to know their business.

La Vireville held up his despatch and waved it as Martin brought the boat alongside and held on. The man beckoned to him to come up, but the Chevalier (making a secret grimace down at his companion) continued to wave, and shouted up in French that he had a despatch for Captain Castagnier, on which the man came half-way down.

"But mount, then, kind of a sluggard!" he cried. "Do you expect the Captain to come down to you?"

"No help for it, I'm afraid," said La Vireville under his breath, and stepped on to the ladder. But before he had ascended more than a few steps a youngish officer appeared at the top and ran down to the sentry.

"What is all this? Who is this man, and why are you admitting him on board?"

"Because he says he has a despatch for the Captain, my officer."

The officer passed him and came further down the side. "You have a despatch for the Captain, eh? From whom?"

"From General Tate," responded La Vireville, holding it out. "If you will take it, sir ——"

"From General Tate!" interrupted the officer in tones of astonishment and incredulity. "That's a likely story, considering that the General is himself on board at this moment!"

Martin's heart leapt into his mouth. Good God, that dare-devil had over-reached himself! Even the dare-devil himself, who had been in many unpleasant places in his time, took a step backwards down the ladder. But only one.

"How very extraordinary!" he observed, with just the appropriate amount of surprise. "He must have changed his mind, then, after I saw him. The despatch is, naturally, cancelled, and I need not trouble you further." Replacing his forgery in his pocket, he prepared to descend to the boat.

"Not so fast!" cried the officer, coming down after him. "If you really have a despatch for the commodore then, *corbleu*, you must deliver it! Who are you, by the way —I do not remember to have seen you before? Did you come over in the *Résistance*?"

"No," replied La Vireville. "I——" (here he dropped his voice and directed a quick suspicious glance at his boatman below) "I have been preparing the ground here on behalf of the Directory. That is why General Tate entrusted me with this communication. However, if he is here himself——" He shrugged his shoulders in the true Gallic manner, and therewith came unobtrusively down a few more steps of the ladder.

All they could hope for now was to get away unchallenged-and even that did not seem very likely. Martin was glad that *he* had not to decide what was best to do-whether to tear up the forged order and drop it into the sea (a desperate and suspicious move) or to make another effort to get the officer to take it, spring into the boat and push off. Yet, of course, that would be madness, for the sentry could shoot them down at a word, or the frigate blow them out of the water if they succeeded in leaving her side. Yet to be confronted with Tate. . . .

But that, evidently, was what was going to happen. La Vireville, still quite cool and leisurely, had his foot on the gunwale when the officer plucked out a pistol and pointed it at him. "No, you don't go off like that, my one-armed friend!" he observed. "There may be nothing wrong with you, but you may equally well be a spy, for all your command of French. Up with you and your despatch; and the General will soon tell us if it is genuine. Both of you-your man there, too!" He beckoned imperatively to Martin. "Look sharp now!"

There was no help for it. Martin made fast the painter without a word, and followed the Chevalier up the frigate's side, wondering what he was feeling like, for *he* was undoubtedly in a position of acute peril. Royalist *émigrés*, as Martin knew, were liable to instant execution without trial if they set foot upon their native soil; and presumably the quarterdeck of a French frigate was French territory. As yet, of course, his compatriots were not aware of his real status . . . As for himself, he must hope for the best; but it did seem, now, extraordinarily crazy to have landed oneself so gratuitously in this very unpleasant position. He wished he did not feel so stupid, the result of the blow he had received; for they would require all the wits they could muster to extricate themselves from this den of lions. He must remember that he did not understand French (so La Vireville had decreed) and not much English. Centuries ago-yet only yesterday evening-he had exhibited exactly the same deficiencies at Trehowell . . . and to Tate! What would Tate say when he confronted him again? Heavens above, who could have dreamt of such a piece of ill-luck as that the General himself should be here to repudiate the forged order? They had taken for granted that he had his hands full-more than full-on land!

* * * * *

But was he here after all? The officer preceded them into a large cabin, but even before Martin, bringing up the rear, could see who was speaking, he caught something, in an argumentative and excited French voice, which was certainly not Tate's as he remembered it, about "drunk as pigs, I tell you, and completely out of hand, so that even the General——"

"*Chut!*" cut in another, deeper voice warningly; and Martin found himself side by side with his too ingenious accomplice in the big stern-cabin of the *Vengeance*, through whose windows the sea-sparkle threw moving lights on the painted ceiling. At a table were sitting a bronzed sailor-like man in uniform, presumably Captain Castagnier, and a young, thin-faced soldier-most certainly not Tate. There was no one else there.

"I . . . I beg your pardon, sir," stammered their captor, evidently taken aback. "The General—I understood that he was with you, and this man——"

"You have been misinformed," said his commander curtly. "One of his officers, not the General himself. What do you want-and who are these men?"

Recovering himself the naval lieutenant explained.

"A despatch from the General, you say, and brought by a civilian who claims to be an agent of the Directory-how very odd!" Captain Castagnier looked searchingly at its bearer. "Give it to me, if you please."

La Vireville put his hand into his pocket. Yes, thought Martin, he was wise to have kept it. For, since Tate was not on board after all, it did at least serve as something of a credential; and so its author silently produced it and handed it to its destined recipient.

The sailor opened it, cast a glance down it and uttered an exclamation.

"*Parbleu!* Captain Guériel, things are not after all going so ill as you have led me to believe, for here is my discharge!"

"What!" cried the soldier, almost leaping from his seat. "But that is impossible!"

"Not at all. The General orders us away, as arranged. You can go," he said to his subordinate. The officer hesitated. "These men, sir, are you sure ——"

"You can go, I said," repeated Castagnier. "Do you think I was born yesterday? But it is for me, not for you, to investigate the *bona fides* of the messengers."

"Surely it is rather the *bona fides* of the order which needs investigating, sir," said Captain Guériel protestingly, as the naval officer left the cabin. "It cannot possibly be genuine! The General ——"

Castagnier pushed the paper over to him. "Look for yourself! Is not that General Tate's signature, and Major Le Brun's and Captain Brémond's too?"

Guériel looked carefully. "Yes, I think so; but the order itself is not in General Tate's handwriting."

"That is hardly essential, is it? Why should it not be genuine? The question is rather why it was sent in this irregular manner, and not by an aide-de-camp or one of the staff." He turned a dark, penetrating gaze upon La Vireville, standing quietly there, and kept it on him for several seconds before he spoke. "You say that you are a secret agent of the Directory. What proof can you give me of that?"

"Why," answered the Chouan, with a little smile, "that very despatch in your hand, citizen Captain. Would General Tate have entrusted it to me otherwise?"

"That is begging the question entirely," put in Captain Guériel hotly. "It is just the point which you have to prove-that he did give it to you! It is so extraordinary and improbable a proceeding," he went on, appealing to Castagnier, "when, if General Tate had wished to send such a preposterous order, he could have done so, for example, by my hand!"

"Perhaps he knew that you would consider it preposterous, and preferred another messenger," retorted Castagnier coolly, and once more turned his deep-set eyes upon its actual bearer. "Now first, monsieur the secret agent, I should like to know how you, a palpable Frenchman, have contrived to pass among the people here-if that is what you have been doing."

"But I am not a Frenchman, Captain Castagnier," replied Fortuné de la Vireville. "I am a native of Jersey, a British subject, speaking English as well as French, and free to go where I choose." (But Martin thought he had another reason as well for claiming English nationality.) "And on my going early this morning to make my confidential report on the state of the district to the General, up at the position on the hill called Carnwnda, he asked me if I would convey this despatch to you."

"Up at Carnwnda?" said Captain Guériel. "How was it that I never saw you there?"

La Vireville shrugged his shoulders.

"What report did you make to the General?" asked Castagnier abruptly.

"You must excuse me, Captain, but it was confidential," replied La Vireville respectfully.

Castagnier frowned. Guériel, frowning too, demanded whether it was his report which had induced the General to send "this very premature order," to which La Vireville answered that he was unable to say.

"If it is so," went on the soldier, a scowl upon his dark, narrow face, "then let me tell you that you have done a great disservice to the cause which you have embraced-which you claim to have embraced. —And, by the way, may one ask why you turned traitor?"

"You use hard words, my officer," protested the *émigré*. "Surely a Jerseyman is nearer to a Frenchman than to an Englishman!"

"The Republic does not find it so!" grumbled Captain Guériel. "Jersey is a perfect nest of Chouans and *émigrés* and their sympathisers. Is that not so, Captain Castagnier? . . . This whole business is most suspicious; I parted from the General not an hour ago at Trehowell, and there was no word, no breath of any intention to dismiss the squadron. Indeed, how could there be, with the troops almost mutinous?"

Castagnier shrugged his epauletted shoulders. "Nevertheless, here is the order, and since it is genuine it is not for me to discuss it, but to obey."

"It is not genuine!" rapped out the soldier. "I deny that, I deny it outright! The whole thing is too fantastic; and it makes the General appear both stupid and treacherous, to take such a step behind his officers' backs and to say no word of his intention!"

"Major Le Brun has signed it, too," Castagnier reminded him shortly, tapping his finger upon the disputed document.

Captain Guériel rose from his chair. "I shall take the paper and go ashore to investigate its genuineness," he announced.

Castagnier folded up the order. "Go ashore by all means, and investigate as much as you please, Captain Guériel! But you will not take this discharge with you. It is addressed to me!"

For a moment they almost glared at one another, and it dawned more fully upon Martin that for some reason Castagnier was not really displeased at having the order; that, in fact, he would like to obey it if only he could. . . .

"I shall go at once," reiterated the soldier, hitching up his sword. "And I will signal the result to you from the cliffs."

"Do so by all means," said Castagnier stiffly. "Not that I should have waited for a confirmatory signal had the despatch come by a less unusual channel." He looked once more at La Vireville, directing a speculative glance at his left sleeve, but he said nothing. "But how will you signal? There is no semaphore upon the headland, not even a flagstaff."

"On my way to the farmhouse of Trehowell I will order a temporary flagstaff to be erected. To see the General and return to the cliff will take me — —" Guériel pulled out his watch and made calculations. "Be on the look-out, if you please, in three quarters of an hour's time from now . . . though it may take me longer. The tricolour shall be run up and dipped thrice; if the order is not genuine-and you are in consequence to remain-it will return to the masthead and continue flying; but if the order is authentic, and you are to obey it and sail off, the flag will then be hauled down and fly no longer. Is that clear?"

"Perfectly," said Castagnier coldly. "If it remains flying I stay, the order having been repudiated; if it falls I weigh anchor, the order being genuine. But since I am convinced that the order is genuine, I shall now signal to the *Résistance*, *Constance* and *Vautour* to stand by in readiness for departure."

"You may spare yourself and them the trouble, Captain Castagnier," was Guériel's retort as he left the cabin.

And now ensued for the two adventurers a period which thoroughly initiated Martin into the meaning of the French phrase about a bad quarter of an hour. For nearly that length of time Castagnier attempted to draw from their own lips admissions which would damn them. In this battle of wits La Vireville naturally bore the chief part, and the commodore got very little out of him, save, as the young man admiringly recognised, a great wealth of corroborative detail of the rôle which he had assumed as a confidential agent of the French Directory, detail which must all have been invented on the spur of the moment. Yet the sailor never succeeded in actually catching him out in an inconsistency or a contradiction. As for Martin himself, affirmed by La Vireville to be merely a hired boatman, all he had to do was to answer in halting English the questions put to him either through the medium of the supposed Jerseyman, or occasionally in an execrable version of that tongue by Castagnier himself.

But Castagnier, too, was equally impenetrable, for at the end, without giving any sign whether he believed what he had been told or guessed it to be fiction, he announced that as everything with regard to the couple must depend upon what was signalled to him from the shore (of which the couple in question were only too painfully aware) they would be kept under guard, and that separately, until the signal was made; and so dismissed them in that condition.

As they were marched out of the big stern-cabin La Vireville gave his companion a very pregnant look, which, almost as clearly as if he had spoken, asked his forgiveness for having brought him into this unpleasant situation. Martin responded by a smile and a barely perceptible movement of the head. He knew that the Frenchman had refrained from speech because it might proclaim them accomplices, and endanger what chance his supposed boatman had of going free. La Vireville's own chances began to seem very slender.

It was a blow, their being separated like this at the crucial moment; yet, once thrust into a dark little cabin with a sentry at the door, Martin, engulfed by fatigue and a curious feeling of indifference, sat down, leant his stiff neck against the bulkhead, and closed his eyes. It was true that their plight was uncommonly nasty, for what slightest hope was there of Tate's confirming an order which he must know to be a forgery? But somehow Martin could not bring himself to believe that his present circumstances were real, and that he was once more in the hands of the French, having come there, of his own free will, for the second time in less than twenty-four hours. But this time there was no safe-conduct to help him and La Vireville away. Yet there really seemed no good reason why Castagnier should proceed to extreme measures with a harmless fisherman, and La Vireville was so resourceful that he might still contrive to extricate himself on some plea or other. Thinking of Nest, and of what means he could employ to see her again, Martin went off into a kind of waking dream.

And when, some twenty minutes later, he was bidden to come forth, he obeyed with the same nonchalance, and was marched up to the quarterdeck, where most of the ship's officers appeared to be assembled, before the dream fell from him. But there, suddenly and acutely, the lost sense of reality returned as unpleasantly as circulation to a numbed limb . . . recalled by the sight of two suggestively dangling ropes, brand-new and swaying delicately in the breeze, each with a neat stiffish noose at the end-two of them. Martin stared at them fascinated.

"A running bowline, I suppose," he found himself thinking, back suddenly in those days of curse-accompanied instruction in knot-making on board the *Fair Penitent*.

La Vireville also had been brought up on deck, and the guard marched them both to within a few paces of the commodore, whose mood, it was evident, had not softened-and indeed why should they expect it?

"Prisoners, you see those ropes!" he said harshly. "If you are what you claim to be, there is no danger of your making closer acquaintance with them. You know best with what feelings, therefore, to regard them; and I shall learn what those feelings are in about five minutes' time. The flagstaff erected on the headland yonder is fully visible; I recommend you to keep your eyes on it!"

"Commodore," broke in La Vireville sharply, "I recommend *you* to reflect on your feelings when you are brought to book by the Republic for murdering one of her agents on no more valid ground than the flutter of a flag. If the signal should be made that the ships are to remain, it does not falsify the despatch, signed, as you admit, by the General himself, which I brought you; it merely means that, worked upon perhaps by Captain Guériel, General Tate has changed his mind since early this morning. Should he now wish to withdraw his order, that does not mean that he never sent it!"

"Good!" thought Martin. "That must surely carry weight, for it is sound logic." And indeed, from their looks, the argument did not seem to be without effect upon the assembled officers.

Yet all that Castagnier said was: "Very specious! But if the signal is made to remain, you will hang!"

"You have not the right to hang me," retorted the Chouan. "I am a British subject!"

"In that case you are a spy-an agent of Pitt's; and spies are hanged whatever nationality they claim. But as for this young fisherman," he turned towards Martin, "since you declare that you merely hired him to bring you here-though for all I know he may be an accomplice —I will give him one chance of not swinging there beside you. If he is really a Welshman from the bay he must know what are the defences of the town of Fishguard, and what reinforcements it is expecting."

But at those words Martin, entirely forgetting that he was not supposed to know any French, and not even waiting for the signal to confirm Castagnier's suspicions, burst out angrily in English: "Enough to blow you and your ships out of the water three times over!"

Castagnier's grizzled eyebrows went up. "My congratulations, young man; you have learnt to understand French very quickly!" he said, with a sour smile. "The Welsh fishermen must be unusually intelligent! —But I do not want bombast like that. I know perfectly well that the fort at Fishguard is small and not formidable, but I require details."

"I know none. I have never been inside it," answered Martin, a little less pugnaciously. "But in a few hours," he added, giving rein to his imagination-and his hopes, "you will have a British squadron surrounding you, and it will be too late then to sail away!"

"It is never too late to get away from a British squadron which remains at a safe distance," retorted the Frenchman coolly, and his officers guffawed. "What of Bantry Bay, where our ships stayed for five days and reached home unmolested by your vaunted sailors? You will not save your neck by bluster about your invincible navy . . . which takes such care to keep out of the way!"

"Who says that I want to save it?" riposted Martin, stung by this taunt, and thrilling with the intemperate and desperate joy of wholly useless defiance; and, for all that La Vireville was frowning at him, would probably have gone on to add something still more crazy had not the crack of a musket shot come sharply at that moment over the water. It was evidently designed to attract attention, for next instant an officer stepped forward to Castagnier and offered him a telescope. The signal was going up on the cliff.

It could be seen without the aid of any telescope. Yes, on that headland where Martin had sat the day before yesterday and so fondly imagined that Nest would shortly sit with him, that piece of bunting was rising which would condemn him and his comrade in this crazy undertaking to extinction. His mood fell from him and he clenched his hands. Oh, why could not the English ships, which must surely be on their way, arrive a little quicker!

Above the group of men on the headland, among whom Guériel was almost distinguishable, the tricolour fluttered jerkily up, dipped once, twice, thrice . . . and returned to the masthead, where it blew out cheerfully in the easterly breeze —a death-warrant. The order *was* repudiated, and not until that moment did Martin Tyrrell know how much he had been counting, weakly enough, upon a miracle which could not happen.

He heard himself draw a long breath, and hoped that no one else heard it. It was a pity that the sea was so blue, the day so fine . . . and that he had not kissed Nest after all. So Careg Gwastad-from the sea-would be the last of earth that his eyes would rest upon. Of what was the man by his side thinking? It was only last year that he had been married. He stole a glance at him, but from his face he could tell nothing. The ancient scar on his cheek seemed a little more noticeable, that was all.

"Lieutenant Cazeaux!" Castagnier's voice came at last, cold and abrupt as ever, but with a ring of satisfaction in it. "That signal yonder means that the General has no longer need of us, as indeed his despatch had already informed me, only, as you are aware, I had doubts of the bearer. Those doubts are now happily at rest. Signal to the *Résistance*, *Constance* and *Vautour* to prepare for instant departure. I hope also to see how smartly the *Vengeance* herself can get under way."

It was like last night's smashing blow over again. Martin almost felt himself reeling. But what nonsense! Had Castagnier taken leave of his senses? The signal flying there meant exactly the reverse of what he had just said! It had been arranged with Guériel that . . . He had, he afterwards believed, half opened his idiotic mouth to say so, when he received an emphatic dig in the side from the end of La Vireville's hook, and looking round saw the Royalist's expressive gaze fixed upon him. "Be quiet, you triple fool!" it seemed to say.

And then everything was swallowed up in a deadly anxiety lest Castagnier should recognise his mistake, or some officer venture to set him right. But quite soon Martin realised, with an extraordinary shock of hope, that in all probability not a soul on board save Castagnier and they, the prisoners, knew the true significance of the signal; there had been no one else in the cabin when the arrangement was made with Captain Guériel.

After that-was he gone mad too? —he seemed to be hearing what sounded like a rather stiff apology being made to La Vireville for doubting his honesty and the *bona fides* of the order he carried, since the flag there had proved the despatch to be genuine. The commodore was saying that he hoped the Directory's secret agent would understand and not bear malice; the circumstances had seemed a little unusual . . .

"But as for your boatman," and here Castagnier looked with very little favour upon Martin, "you seem to have made a strange choice in him. His sentiments and attainments do not at all bear out the character you gave of him, and it appears to me that for your own safety I had better retain him on board; for on your return you may find his knowledge of your movements this morning inconvenient. I imagine he may well denounce you to the authorities at Fishguard!"

Once more Martin's blood ran cold. Fool, fool-if only he had held his tongue!

"Ah, Captain," he heard La Vireville say, half laughing, "you must not take the poor fellow's outburst too seriously! You frightened him, you know. I doubt if he knew what he was saying. And if you keep him here, how am I to get back to Goodwick? I cannot sail a boat alone-with this." And he touched his maimed left arm.

"Yes, that is true," admitted the Republican unwillingly. "I must let him go, then; but I advise you to find some means of stopping his mouth."

"Trust me for that, *mon capitaine*!" And the Chevalier played out the farce to the end with superb aplomb and gravity, even going to the length of saying that he would not inform the General of the kind of reception which he had received. And so, amid the shrilling of the bo'sun's whistle, the shouting of orders, the bustle of running feet, they went down the frigate's side and cast off, La Vireville, a grim but silent amusement on his face, at the helm this time. But when once their little sail was up and drawing, and they were breasting the slight swell away from the *Vengeance* and her consorts, Martin hastily clambered forward across a pile of wicker lobster pots, and there, hanging over the bow, was most unheroically sick.

(4)

Never had the world seemed so lovely. Not only was a gull dipping by a miracle of beauty, but there was charm (now that Martin's attack of nausea had passed) even in the slight smell of old fish rising from the bottom of the boat, a fascination in the rusty little anchor with one fluke broken off. Even his recent deplorable exhibition proved to the young man that he was at least alive . . . And there, now that they were once more rounding Pen Anglas, there was Goodwick under its hill, and the sands with the sun on them, and Fishguard Harbour at the other extremity-he fancied that he could see the masts of the *Raymonde* —and Fishguard town looking down upon its green waters, Fishguard, where Nest lay asleep. Half an hour ago he had never thought to see any of these again; still less, probably, had M. de la Vireville expected to do so.

He looked back towards the French ships. On board the other frigate, *La Résistance* , a sail could be observed creeping up already.

"Smart work, *ma foi* ," observed the Chevalier, who had been looking that way too. Then he turned his gaze upon Martin. "That is my best justification for having taken you into greater danger than I anticipated, for though you do not perhaps realise it, *mon cher camarade* , we *have* succeeded in what we set out to do?"

And indeed the young man's somewhat battered senses had hardly grasped the fact. He stared stupidly towards the big ships, so black and white against the cliffs, and thought that he could still see the signal fluttering unregarded from Careg Gwastad. Getting up he came and sat down opposite the steersman.

"It's a mystery to me still," he said seriously. "I thought that Castagnier had gone mad-no, I thought that he had made a mistake which he would find out and rectify at any moment . . . and then it would still have been all over with us."

"There was no fear of his rectifying his 'mistake,' " replied La Vireville with a grin. If he was aware of the tribute which Martin had recently paid to physical and mental stress, he acted as though he were not. "No, there was no fear of his rectifying it, and there was no one else who could do so . . . though you, *mon ami* , showed at one moment a leaning towards it! It was a magnificent chance for him, and he took it; he ought to go far, *cet homme-là* !"

"A chance?" stammered Martin stupidly.

"Why, *mort de ma vie* , he *wanted* to sail off!" explained the Frenchman. "Did you not guess that, when you saw how curiously eager he was, before Captain Guériel went ashore, to obey the order, or at least to believe it genuine? He had no fancy for having to re-embark a horde of drunken convicts, probably under fire-you must remember that Guériel had just been telling him how drunk they were-and he snatched at the chance of getting his ships and crew away untouched. I wager that in his heart he loathed the whole expedition. And now his position, when he gets back to Brest, or wherever he came from, is unassailable, for he has his discharge with Tate's signature to it, and not a soul in the flotilla can gainsay him over the meaning of the signal. Even if an enquiry were ever held, it is only Guériel's word against his as to what they arranged together; and Castagnier has, *en plus* , the General's order. *Ma foi* , we have done him good service, and it was not kind of him to dangle those ropes in our faces. —My congratulations to you, by the way, on your bold bearing in the crisis!"

Martin got very red. "Chevalier, you are mocking me!" he protested. "I am deeply ashamed of the way I behaved, and have been wanting to apologise for being such a fool. It is true that I lost my head. I thought that matters could not well be worse, and so — —"

"I understand. I do not blame you in the least for wanting-what is it you English call it? —a run for your money. At your age I should probably have done the same."

"But I nearly wrecked the whole situation," groaned Martin. "I made it most difficult for Castagnier to let us go, since his officers had overheard my foolish bombast. —But you" —he added ingenuously —"you are never at a loss, Monsieur de la Vireville!" And as the Chouan laughed and shook his head, Martin continued: "Yet, granted that, once he had pretended to believe the order genuine, and carried out by the signal, Castagnier could not justifiably hang us, I still do not fully understand why he went to the length of letting us go!"

"Why," said the Royalist, as he put the tiller over and they went about, "what else could he do? Once he asserted that the order was genuine, what possible grounds could he advance for taking steps against its bearers? He could not carry us off as prisoners, much as he may have longed to do so, without falsifying his whole position."

"Then, since he had resolved to misread the signal, why that extremely unpleasant comedy with the ropes? —By the way, did *you* know that it was merely a comedy?"

"No, for though I suspected him of the desire to read the signal in the way which suited himself, I did not believe that he would really venture to do so. Until the moment when he actually took that step, therefore, I certainly thought that one, at least of those nooses would have an occupant. Why did he play the comedy? Because he too wished to have 'a run for his money.' He knew of course that we were fooling him (although it happened to suit him very well) and he determined for his part to fool us as long as he could, in which he certainly succeeded." He looked back over his shoulder for a moment and added appreciatively, "Yet the individual who will look most foolish is the unfortunate *Tête de mouton*, who is probably even now dancing with rage and apprehension as he sees what is happening under his very nose and is powerless to stop it; for if he sends off any amount of aides-de-camp, Castagnier will not admit them on board now! And it is you and I, Monsieur Martin Tyrrell, who have dealt him this blow. The sooner we let the authorities at Fishguard know about it the better. —For we *have* sent the squadron away!"

But Martin could still hardly believe it. Again he looked back, but they were too far round to see the French ships now. "If it is so, we must make it known at Fishguard, as you say. But you understand, do you not, Chevalier, that I do not wish to put in an appearance before any authorities. My disposition just now is extremely retiring."

"But certainly your modesty shall be respected-for the present." There was a twinkle in La Vireville's eye. "And *parbleu*, we had best get to land as quickly as possible! Look there!"

Martin looked and gave an exclamation. Across the sands of the bay were moving, in the direction of Goodwick, what looked like several blocks of toy soldiers, scarlet and white; the sun struck sparks from the invisible bayonets on their muskets, and now and then the beat of drums came irregularly to the ear. And more were coming down from Fishguard-cavalry too.

"I expect that most of the tackle in this boat is rotten," said La Vireville hastily, "but we had better try to get some more sail on to her. Your countrymen are evidently marching to the attack, and we must put a stop to that if possible."

(5)

Half an hour later Martin sailed alone into Fishguard harbour, having landed La Vireville at Goodwick and left him to make his way as quickly as he could to the advancing troops, with the object of gaining the ear of their commander, whoever he might be, and convincing him, if possible, of the probable advantages of delay. And that the Frenchman had succeeded was obvious, for no longer were the toy soldiers moving forward. After some prancing about of mounted officers they had halted, and as far as Martin could make out, had faced round once more towards Fishguard. It was extraordinary to think that he was partly responsible for this! Yet how nearly had he and the Chevalier not only missed their *coup*, but paid the extreme price for attempting it! He *had* looked upon the gallows after all . . .

As Martin made the harbour a voice shouted down an enquiry from the fort at its entrance, and he realised that its garrison must have witnessed something of the voyage of this little craft, and that this voyage might bear a suspicious interpretation. But he was at once too tired and too exultant to care. He ran up on to the quay; and there at the top of the steps was standing no less a person than Mr. Salt, wearing a sword, and with two pistols stuck into his belt. Delighted, he grasped both that gentleman's hands.

His late employer seemed equally pleased to see him, for his first words were: "I almost regret that I am not a Frenchman, for in that case I should feel it permissible to embrace you. May I ask where you have been since rescuing your Nausicaa? —Yes, I know about that, for I have talked to Mr. Mortimer."

"How *is* Miss Meredith?" demanded Martin eagerly.

"I have not seen her; but I trust that she is in bed and asleep. Answer my question, Odysseus of the many voyages!"

"M. de la Vireville and I have just been out to the French ships, sir, to induce them to go away."

"What is this joke?" enquired Mr. Salt, pleased and expectant.

" 'Tis not a joke, sir. We have succeeded, what is more! When we left they were preparing to raise anchor. The Chevalier is somewhere on the sands informing the authorities, since he hopes that, in consequence, Tate may surrender; and, as you see, the advance has been stopped."

"But what in the name of——"

"I will tell you," said Martin; and had only begun to do so when he broke off and said in an exasperated voice, "Damn it, there's the mate coming!"

Indeed Mr. Challacombe, looking enormous, was bearing down upon him in the manner of an outraged Viking. "Yu'm back at last, then, ye varmint!" he roared. "And wheer's the Chevaleer?"

"I landed him at Goodwick," replied Martin rather casually. "He will be here before long. — After that, Mr. Salt——"

"Then yu goo aboard at once, Jem Gregson!" commanded Challacombe, "or——"

"Mr. Mate," put in Mr. Salt, "I must ask your forgiveness, but this young man originally shipped with me as secretary, and I think my claim to his services is paramount."

"Seckertary, eh?" queried Challacombe, turning a wrathful eye upon this neat, professional-looking yet well-armed gentleman. "Seckertary! I knawed as he were something useless-least-ways not a ship's cook!"

"You have suffered under him, I can see," observed Mr. Salt, sympathetically. "But you must allow me his society a little longer, for I wish to hear more about his recent doings."

"So do I!" said a fresh voice, and a hand, emerging from a uniformed cuff, tapped Martin on the shoulder. He turned, and there stood, in a rather new uniform, an officer of the Fishguard Fencibles, who garrisoned the fort. "I should like to know what you were about in that boat out there, young man. What business had you with the French ships?"

Martin began to laugh just a trifle hysterically. "Will you too threaten to hang me? My business with the French ships-you'll learn it soon enough, I hope!"

The officer eyed this disreputable-looking, laughing young man very suspiciously, aware no doubt of the rumours of local complicity with the invaders which were already going about. "I think," he said, "that you had best render an account of yourself to the governor." He indicated the fort behind him and put his hand firmly on Martin's shoulder. "Come along!"

"Nonsense!" said Mr. Salt quickly. "Your suspicions, sir, are quite unfounded. I know this young man personally, and from what he has just told me, his errand to the French flotilla has resulted in an amazing——"

But now another voice broke in. None of the four had observed the swift, almost stealthy approach of its owner.

"I thank you, Mr. Salt, for your identification," observed this voice with unction. "This time you have helped me in the performance of my duty! Martin Tyrrell, I arrest you in the name of His Majesty King George-and I am glad to see, sir," he observed to the startled Fencible officer, "that you were already taking the man into custody. If you will keep him for me for a few hours I shall be obliged to you-but look out he don't give you the slip! I will show you the warrant."

But Martin was making no attempt to give anyone the slip, and this not because he was encircled by three persons all wanting him at once, though for different reasons, and that he observed a couple of Fencibles also advancing at the double. His fate had chosen so delicately ironical a moment to come upon him; the man Manisty-he supposed it was he-had timed his appearance with such exquisite justice and precision, and poor Mr. Salt, for once, was looking so crestfallen, as well as angry, that the young man stood quite still and went off into peal after peal of laughter, so that the Fencible officer actually began, to shake him, ejaculating, "Stop that, stop that-the fellow's crazy!"

Between his paroxysms Martin attempted to say that it was other people who were crazy. But then he suddenly caught sight of Challacombe's face, a study, in its less hirsute areas, of such varied emotions that it sent him off again. And then things went as quickly as, at the end, they had done on board the *Vengeance*. He was between two Fencibles; he saw Mr. Manisty displaying the warrant to the gaze of his timely ally, their officer, heard him stating that he would follow in a moment and see the governor about the prisoner; Mr. Salt, at his ear, too much shaken to remember prudence in nomenclature, was saying, "Martin, Martin, it will be all right—I shall go at once to Lord Milford . . . though if only I knew a little better what you have been doing out there——"

Martin controlled his mirth sufficiently to say, "Find La Vireville-he'll tell you!" and adding, in a half-choked voice, "The French commodore nearly strung us up at the yard-arm—now this!" walked off, limp with merriment, between the Fencibles, the officer following.

It was Mr. Manisty's hour of triumph; and considering the trick which had been played upon him by Mr. Salt, the many weary miles he had gone upon a false trail-even hunting a perfectly innocent and unconscious traveller from Cardigan as far as Shrewsbury; the resolution with which he had returned upon it to Fishguard, intending indeed to go back as far as St. David's in the hope of picking up the right scent; the instinct which had stayed his steps at Fishguard on hearing the news of the French invasion (which instantly seemed to him to have some sinister connection with the stay of the man Tyrrell in Pembrokeshire, and led him almost to believe that he *had* come to the Fishguard neighbourhood after all); the acumen he displayed when, upon seeing Mr. Salt emerge from the "Royal Oak," he had not accosted him, but had carefully tracked him instead, first to the *Raymonde* and then to his vigil on the quay; the patient circumspection with which he had observed this vigil (which was long) from a distance: considering these trials and his perseverance, one may admit that he deserved his successful *coup*
. In the ultimate outcome, circumstances had undeniably favoured him, for when he saw from his post behind a pile of timber Mr. Salt greeting with cordiality a young man from a boat whom he himself had never set eyes on, and who was further transformed by a slight beard from the description which he possessed of him-whom, therefore, but for this greeting, he might never have identified-he uttered a joyful cry and set forward. And meanwhile that most

useful Fencible officer had started to net his prisoner for him, drawing thereby from Mr. Salt's lips a most damaging admission . . .

Yes, it was his hour of triumph, and not the least pleasant of its elements was the fact that the owner of Bowen's Folly, who (as he had since become convinced) had so disgracefully gulled him, was now himself the chief contributor to it. Folding up his warrant, Mr. Manisty surveyed that frowning gentleman with a lofty smile upon his large and solid features.

"You would have done better, sir," he observed, "to be frank with me when I came to your house. As it is, you have not only betrayed Tyrrell, but by your lies about him have involved yourself in suspicion of complicity with him!"

But on that Mr. Salt, rousing himself, told him in a gentle voice, but with a blistering wealth of detail, what he thought of his origin, career and ultimate destination, concluding with a vehement adjuration to betake himself swiftly to the latter. The outraged Mr. Manisty, conscious of the grinningly appreciative face of the great red-bearded seaman who seemed to be mixed up in the matter, was so astounded at this command of invective in the mild bookworm who had once blinked at him through his glasses with so ineffectual an air, that he attempted no answer; and Mr. Salt, announcing sharply, "I am going straight to the Lord Lieutenant," walked swiftly away.

Mr. Manisty, nettled, then thrust the warrant into a side-pocket and directed his steps towards the *Raymonde*, followed instantly by Challacombe, who demanded to know where he was going.

"I understand from what you said," replied Manisty shortly, "that the man Tyrrell is, or pretends to be, a member of the crew of this vessel."

"The man Gregson is. But that has nowt to du wi' ee!"

Mr. Manisty disregarded this statement. "That being so, I wish to come on board and investigate his belongings. He is a dangerous traitor and may have papers."

"He may and he mayn't," retorted Jonas Challacombe, placing his large person between Mr. Manisty and the gang plank. "And I'm not upholding him, nor I'm not saying aught against him, for I knaws nothing about him, save that he'm a main bad cook! But goo aboard this schooner in the absence of the owner and master, and start hunting about in her so sharp as a ferret is a thing yu won't du as long as I'm here to stop 'ee."

And even to Manisty, who was not a small man, the mate looked a sufficiently valid obstacle to his intention.

"But, my good man — —"

"I'm the mate of this here schooner, not a hand," corrected the Viking, seeming to become even larger with the words.

"Well, Mr. Mate, then," said Manisty impatiently, "I require you by virtue of this warrant," he pulled it up for a moment from his coat pocket and then thrust it down again, "to give me all the assistance in your power. In fact, if you stop me from coming on board you will have to answer for it to the Law."

It was never wise to threaten Mr. Challacombe. "Yu won't search this schooner, and Law don't say 'ee can! Come poking that long nose o' thine . . . Don't 'ee try to du it, or — —"

For Mr. Manisty having taken a step nearer, Challacombe doubled that mighty fist which Martin last night had also seen displayed, but had evaded. Mr. Manisty's evasion of it was not so happy, even though the giant was not in this case offering to strike him. But he certainly gesticulated . . . Mr. Manisty involuntarily retreated a pace or two, caught his foot against the *Raymonde's* hawser, staggered, tried vainly to recover himself, and in another second had gone backwards over the edge of the quay.

A faint echo of the mighty splash came to the ears of Mr. Salt, hurrying wrathfully up the slope to the town. The wish crossed his mind, "Would that were the infernal tipstaff fallen in!" but it never occurred to him that his desire was gratified; he did not even look back at the harbour.

The streets of Fishguard were more or less deserted, everybody having hurried towards the points whence they could have a good view of the sands below, whereon the gallant forces had set forward to attack the French position. Yet it appeared that these valiant warriors were advancing no longer, but were actually returning! Why, in the name of goodness whatever? Mr. Salt, however, never arrived at the edge of the town in time to witness these retrograde manœuvres, for he suddenly observed, coming towards him, a man in a blue coat who had lost his left arm. He stopped him.

* * * * *

The Chevalier de la Vireville's conversation with Mr. Salt, though pregnant, was not lengthy, and the ex-Chouan, wrath in his heart also, arrived back at his schooner to be greeted by Challacombe, not only with the tidings of Gregson's arrest, which he knew already, but by those of the involuntary immersion of his captor, who, it appeared from the mate's account, had swallowed a mort of water before he was got out.

"What did you do with him?" enquired his superior, not too sympathetically. "Send him to the fort yonder to be cared for?"

But it appeared that the unfortunate bather had seemed in too bad a way for that, and that he had been stripped, rolled on a barrel, then enveloped in blankets and put in Challacombe's own berth, where the hot grog which had been administered had already begun to take effect, for the patient was very drowsy, if not asleep.

"I told Tom Pelley to hang his clothes up to dry, sir," continued the cause, though not the author, of this accident, "but I kep' his coat wi' his money and pocket-book and such like under my own eye, and I'll give et over to 'ee, sir." In a moment he returned with a sodden brown garment heavy with sea-water. "It han't been touched save to wring et out a bit."

He held it up while the master of the *Raymonde* searched its dragging pockets, removing therefrom a wet pocket-book, the purse which Mr. Manisty had jangled at Mrs. Morris, and a tinderbox. Last of all he fished out a sodden pocket handkerchief and a folded document so stuck together that it took careful handling to pull it open without tearing. La Vireville looked at it curiously; it bore the Royal arms, and though such portions as were in ink had run, quite enough remained to tell him what it was.

"That will do, Challacombe," he said. "You can give the coat to Le Pelley now. I will take charge of these effects. And, by the way, the French frigates are making off, and, if I am not mistaken, the French will not show fight. I have just been interviewing Lord Cawdor and Major Knox on the point, and the British advance is stopped for the present."

"I'm main sorry to hear et!" observed the Viking, and went off.

Fortuné de la Vireville once more thoughtfully surveyed the very damp paper which he held. "It seems a pity that this did not remain in the harbour," he said to himself. Going to the main hatch he spread it carefully upon it, weighting it down with the tinderbox; stood there a moment, looked aloft, as if judging the force and direction of the wind, and then in an absent-minded manner picked up the box again, put it with the rest of Mr. Manisty's possessions in his pocket, and went away.

At the same hour someone else beside Jonas Challacombe was expressing a certain amount of doubt, if not of disappointment, on the subject of the postponed attack, even though he had consented to the delay.

"No, my dear Jerome," Lord Milford was saying, in his private room at the "Black Bull," the other Fishguard hostelry, "I gave way, it is true, to Lord Cawdor and Colonel Knox, as they seemed impressed by this French Royalist's rather wild tale — —"

"But, dash it all, Milford," broke in his old friend impetuously, "the ships *have* sailed off! What more do you want-for the moment?"

Lord Milford, Lord Lieutenant of Pembrokeshire (who one-and-twenty years ago had been Sir Richard Philipps, of Picton Castle), shook his head. Although only in the fifties his bad health made him look much older than his years, certainly much older than Mr. Salt, who was, in fact, slightly his senior, and it well justified him in handing over active command on this occasion to the recently ennobled John Campbell, of Stackpole and Cawdor. "Yes, I know that they have sailed-or appear to have done so. But I fear a ruse. I feel sure that the commodore will discover somehow the . . . well, I must call it the extremely curious cock-and-bull device by which he appears to have been taken in."

"But, my dear Richard, surely that dare-devil Frenchman who, with my young friend's assistance, carried it out, explained to you and Cawdor that the man was not in the least taken in; that it suited his book to go-exactly fell in with his own desires! If he can deliberately raise anchor with the signal to remain flying all the time from the cliff, is he likely ever to come back?"

"Even if that be so," said Lord Milford, blinking a little at this vehemence, "I doubt if the situation is much improved thereby. I admit that with the small forces just now at our disposal-not more, as you know, than seven hundred and fifty men-the issue of an attack on the unknown strength of the French in their commanding position up there would be doubtful. But how long are we to wait to see the result upon the mind of this so-called General of theirs of the departure of his flotilla?"

"And of the drunkenness and indiscipline of his troops of which we have heard," put in Mr. Salt. "Not long, I think. And meanwhile the delay gives time for the arrival of the reinforcements which we know are upon their way."

"Well, well," admitted Lord Milford, sighing, "Cawdor and Knox are satisfied, and I am getting old and not of much use. . . . To think of such a blow falling upon us here-to think of Pencaer in a state of rapine and plunder ——"

He went on for some time in this vein, concluding by saying regretfully, as he looked at Mr. Salt's personal armoury: "Even you, Jerome, can bear weapons with some prospect of using them!"

"Even I!" said the antiquarian, with a smile. "But, Richard, you carry guns of much heavier calibre than I do; you, my dear fellow, have influence. (By the way, let me say how deuced public-spirited I think it of you to have come all the way from Picton Castle here!) Yes, you have influence, and I want you to use it to right an injustice, and to reward this courageous deed, which may well result in the discomfiture of the French. You realise that the *émigré* who risked his life by going on board the flotilla to carry out his ingenious *coup* was not alone?"

"Yes, for he said as much; in fact, he seemed to me, as well as I could gather, to be attributing the inception of the scheme to some young Englishman who accompanied him. I don't quite know why this young man did not put in an appearance on the sands there."

"Would you like to know where he is now?" asked Mr. Salt, offering no direct explanation of this absence. "Absurdly enough, having risked his neck also to send the ships away, my young friend is now a prisoner in Fishguard fort, snapped up by a fool of a Fencible officer (I was there) on suspicion, if you please, of complicity with the French or something equally ridiculous!"

"Arrested for what he had done! But that is, as you say, Salt, ridiculous-for even if I cannot take quite so rosy a view of the *results* of these men's scheme as you do, I can see that their *intention* was excellent-and their bravery undoubted. I will send at once to the governor and have this young man released; moreover, I should like to see him, and to thank him. You seem to know him well?"

"Until a short time ago he was my secretary-had been so since last summer."

"You don't say so! What is his name?"

"Tyrrell-Martin Tyrrell-the son of a parson in Northamptonshire."

"I wonder," observed Lord Milford thoughtfully, "whether he is a relative of a gentleman with whom I was once quite intimate-Sir Sumner Tyrrell of Hartley Castle."

"I don't know. But Fishguard, the whole of Pembrokeshire, owes much to him-or will owe much, I hope, very shortly. And, in any case, he risked his life. —There is even more than this, Milford; do you know that to him, and to the Chevalier de la Vireville, the *émigré*, is due the rescue from Trehowell of the Precentor's daughter. But perhaps you have not yet heard of that?"

231

"I have heard something. That was the same young man, you say? But he is a hero, Salt! I must certainly get him released from the fort at once, and apologies must be tendered to him for the over-zealous action of the Fencible officer. Where is my aide-de-camp got to? —I will send an order forthwith! There's paper and ink at your elbow, Jerome, if you will pass it to me."

But "Jerome" did not comply. "There is," he said slowly, "another difficulty about my brave Martin Tyrrell. He suffered, so to speak, a double arrest just now in the harbour, for I must tell you that he is under a cloud, and that cloud —I might call it a thunder-cloud —burst upon him at the same moment. There happened to be a warrant out against him-oh yes, I knew of it-and though your command is sufficient to release him from the charge of a Fencible officer, it will require a little more . . . pressure in high quarters to get a warrant withdrawn."

"For what was the warrant issued? Debt, I suppose, or something of the sort-some young man's peccadillo."

Mr. Salt rubbed his chin. "Perhaps peccadillo is not quite the right term-even though Martin Tyrrell is as innocent as you or I of what he is charged with. But the warrant is for treason."

"What!" Lord Milford sat up. "Treason! My dear Salt, that is a very different matter. *Treason!* Are you sure?"

"I have seen the warrant-twice."

"You did not know this when you employed him, naturally!"

"Indeed I did! It was just why I made him my secretary."

"My dear Jerome!" The Lord Lieutenant sounded a little annoyed. "You carry your love of quizzing too far! If you are not careful you too will find yourself under arrest!"

"I should deserve it quite as much-or as little-as Martin Tyrrell!"

"That would be for a court of law to decide. Naturally I cannot take steps for his release if the young man, whatever heroic action he have since performed, is under arrest for treason. Do you know on what grounds he is accused of so grave a crime?"

"None better, my dear Milford. I will tell you."

He began, and had almost finished the story of his late secretary's misfortunes when a knock at the door heralded the entry of Lord Cawdor's aide-de-camp.

"My lord," he said, saluting with an air of great satisfaction, "I have the honour to announce that two French officers have just come in under a flag of truce. Lord Cawdor presents his compliments, and asks if your lordship would be good enough to give yourself the trouble of stepping over to the "Royal Oak" for a council of war, there being, he believes, no room here large enough for the purpose."

Lord Milford seemed a moment incredulous. "Two French officers! —Yes, I will come at once, tell Lord Cawdor. Be good enough, Captain Edwardes, to inform my aide-de-camp."

"What did I say!" exclaimed Mr. Salt in high glee. "Now, remember, Richard, whom you have to thank for this!"

"I will, I will," promised the Lord Lieutenant; "that is, if anything comes of it."

"But something *has* come of it! And for it two men have risked their lives."

Lord Milford got slowly out of his chair, stood looking a little doubtfully at his old friend, and finally said: "I think, Salt, that you had better accompany me to the "Royal Oak." I fancy there would be no objection to your presence at a council of war provided that ——"

"Provided that I hold my tongue, eh? I engage to be dumb, then-unless I am spoken to!"

(6)

"To be sent back to Brest at the expense of the British Government!" exclaimed Lord Cawdor. "I never heard such a piece of impertinence!"

In the general whole-hearted murmur of assent even the group of candles in their pewter sticks at the end of the table seemed to join, for their flames bent towards him as if in concurrence. But that was perhaps only because Mr. Salt, with his passion for fresh air even in winter, had surreptitiously opened a window. Indeed, the room at the "Royal Oak" was exceedingly hot, for the council of war had crammed it quite full. There was Lord Milford, looking rather tired, Lord Cawdor, alert and capable, with his reddish-fair Campbell colouring, Colonel Knox of Llanstinan in his Fencible uniform, and Major Ackland of Llannion in that of the Ninety-first Foot, Colonel Colby and Colonel James, the two Colonel Vaughans, and that veteran of Bunker's Hill, Captain William Davies, in whose experience of actual warfare Lord Cawdor was known to repose much confidence. If all these and other warriors, not to speak of the two French officers, could endure the stifling atmosphere, a civilian like Mr. Salt might have put up with it; yet no doubt his action pleased the groundlings outside, that whispering and thick-pressed crowd in the dark street, waiting wedged together for gleanings of eye or ear.

The two French officers whose advent under a flag of truce was the cause of this gathering sat side by side at the table, their blue and white regimentals (for they were regulars) contrasting with the British scarlet. Captain Brémond was one of them. They maintained a correct attitude and sufficiently concealed their chagrin; correctness was also observed by the other side, and a tolerable attempt made to conceal gratification.

"Those were our instructions," said Captain Brémond rather shortly.

"They are not in General Tate's letter," responded Lord Cawdor, glancing down at the missive on the table in front of him. "And indeed I am not surprised that he hesitated to put such a monstrous suggestion into writing!"

"Would you have the goodness, my lord," asked Colonel Colby, "to read us the letter again?"

Lord Cawdor took it up and complied. The letter was in English.

> *Sir,*
>
> *The circumstances under which the body of troops under my command were landed at this place render it unnecessary to attempt any military operations, as they would lead only to bloodshed and pillage. The officers of the whole corps have, therefore, intimated their desire of entering into a negotiation upon principles of humanity for a surrender. If you are influenced by similar considerations you may signify the same to the bearer, and in the meantime hostilities shall cease.*
>
> *Health and respect,*
>
> *Tate, Chef de Brigade.*

Lord Milford leant forward from his place at the head of the table and addressed Captain Brémond in French.

"What exactly, sir, does your General mean by 'the circumstances of the landing'?"

"He means, I think," interpreted Lord Cawdor contemptuously, "that he cannot control his gaol-birds now that he has landed them!"

Again a murmur went round as various colonels were heard to express *sotto voce* their opinion of an enemy who could deliberately pick out and release felons in order to loose them on an unprotected countryside. And Captain Brémond, not looking too comfortable, made haste to reply:

"As you may be aware, Monsieur, we have, owing to the misinterpretation of a signal, been deprived of the support of our squadron-an unforeseen piece of ill-fortune."

"Or of good fortune," interpolated Colonel Knox of Llanstinan loudly. "Good fortune, if it leads General Tate to surrender before he is surrounded by twenty thousand men!"

Mr. Salt was here heard by his next neighbour to ejaculate softly to himself something about Falstaff and Gad's Hill, which the soldier, not understanding, took for a mere expletive.

"You deal in very large numbers, Monsieur," observed Captain Brémond, looking rather startled-as indeed did also Lord Milford, placed at the nominal head of an army of such proportions and of such mushroom speed of growth.

"I do not say that these troops are all in Fishguard at the moment," supplemented Colonel Knox. "But half of them are here, the rest upon the way." He appealed to Lord Cawdor for corroboration. "Is that not so, my lord?"

"Oh-er-undoubtedly," replied his lordship, passing his handkerchief across his lips. "What with local levies . . . and the militia . . . I think you do not understand," he said, addressing himself to the French officers, and making an effort to justify these figures, "the bitter resentment and hostility of the brave folk among whom you have so rashly ventured. They are rallying from their first surprise, and together with the immense Government forces upon their way . . . however, as this communication informs us, General Tate is desirous of coming to terms, and indeed he is very wise. —Will you allow me, gentlemen, a word apart with the Lord Lieutenant?"

It was impossible for so crowded a room to afford any seclusion, but Lord Cawdor went and whispered for a few seconds to Lord Milford, and the latter was seen to nod several times. Returning to his place the younger nobleman looked round the gathering.

"If you agree, gentlemen, I shall inform these officers that an answer, embodying the terms of surrender, shall be returned in due course to General Tate at his headquarters, but that they may meanwhile inform him, by word of mouth, that his troops will be expected to parade for surrender to-morrow afternoon. Does that meet with your acceptance?"

There was no dissentient voice to that; indeed it was hard to keep a decent veil over elation until the French officers, with due courtesy, were once more blindfolded as when they had been admitted, conducted through the crowd outside (not so well acquainted with military etiquette as to abstain from hissing and clenching of fists), and set upon their way outside the town. But when the emissaries were fairly gone, noise, laughter and congratulations broke out even in the council of war within; Lord Milford himself agreed that the circumstances called for wine. The occasion had already been pledged when Lord Cawdor rose to his feet.

"I think, gentlemen, that before we go any further you will like to thank and drink the health of the gallant and resourceful man who has contributed so largely to this promising state of affairs by contriving to send away the French ships, whose abandoning of General Tate is, I am convinced, the main cause of his so quickly asking for terms. I requested this gentleman to be in attendance. Captain Edwardes, kindly go into the next room and ask the Chevalier de la Vireville to be good enough to come in here."

"But the name, surely, is French, my lord!" exclaimed someone in surprise as the aide-de-camp left the room.

"Yes; M. de la Vireville is a Royalist, a Chouan leader who fought at Quiberon," explained Lord Cawdor. "And that is fortunate, for who but a Frenchman could have penned the order which, incredible though it seems, induced the flotilla to sail off?"

"And who, gentlemen, but an Englishman would have assisted and accompanied him?" asked a voice with a foreign intonation at the door. "Lord Cawdor will remember that I told him this morning on the sands that I was not alone, that a young compatriot of his had voluntarily accompanied me into peril, though his modesty kept him from appearing with me, and he was not anxious even to have his name mentioned." And in came a tall, lean, one-armed man with a scar and a smile. When the acclamations which greeted him had subsided, and he had been presented to Lord Milford, Lord Cawdor assented.

"You did indeed say that you had a companion, sir-insisted upon the fact, egad! It had only slipped my mind for a moment. But we must have his name; he must come to receive the thanks of this council of war equally with you. Modesty should not be encouraged too far, eh, gentlemen? Where is the young man to be found?"

In order to keep his vow of silence Mr. Salt was here obliged to put his hand hard over his mouth. But from what he had seen of him he judged M. de la Vireville to be equal to the occasion.

"My lord," replied that adventurer, "he is now, I regret to say, a prisoner in Fishguard fort, an officer of the garrison having in his zeal mistaken the purpose of his errand to the French squadron."

"A prisoner? A prisoner, did you say?" ejaculated his lordship, while loud expressions of disgust and concern arose. "Good Gad, we'll have him out at once! Captain Edwardes-did you say something, Milford?"

"I? No, no, nothing," said the Lord Lieutenant, drawing his breath a little as if a hand had been laid over *his* mouth.

Lord Cawdor began to scribble. "The young man's name, if you please, Monsieur?" he asked, without raising his head, and one person in the audience, with his eyes fixed upon the Frenchman, wondered which of his late secretary's aliases was going to be offered to Lord Cawdor. But without hesitation the Chevalier answered, as though there had never been any Gregson, let alone Towers: "Tyrrell, my lord, Mr. Martin Tyrrell." And Mr. Salt considered that the choice was a judicious one.

"Tyrrell," murmured Lord Cawdor. "Go then, Captain Edwardes, as speedily as you can, with this note to the governor of the fort, and ask Mr. Martin Tyrrell with my compliments to give us the pleasure of his society here, if he be not abed. And now, Monsieur le Chevalier, pray be seated, and give us some account of your courageous and successful ruse."

Knowing that the distance down to the fort was not inconsiderable, and aware of the value of a good entry for Mr. Martin Tyrrell, the Chevalier began by the story of the setting off entirely alone of the young man to Trehowell in order to attempt the rescue of Miss Meredith, which indeed was not irrelevant, since it accounted for his own presence in Trehowell and the securing of Tate's signature. And it might almost have been supposed, from the Frenchman's account, that it was Martin who first caught sight of the "Appel" upon the chimneypiece and divined that some use might be made of it; although La Vireville admitted that it had been necessary for him to forge the actual order to Castagnier. To many there the peril of the Precentor's daughter was unknown; all listened breathless and admiring. And then on top of this chivalrous rescue of a helpless girl from Tate's doubtless licentious hordes came the even more hazardous exploit which, Lord Cawdor had assured them, was the prime cause of the French general's recent appeal for terms. In the corner Mr. Salt, smiling to himself, rubbed his hands together; the Frenchman was really extraordinarily generous as well as skilful; but Lord Milford played with a pen and looked unhappy. Every other gaze was directed absorbedly upon the narrator, and when La Vireville's narrative reached the episode upon the quarterdeck of the *Vengeance*, when, with some slight artistic embellishment, he narrated the young Englishman's indignant refusal to save his life by revealing the state of the defences of Fishguard-and this in face of a rope already dangling for him at the yard-arm —an uncontrollable roar of applause almost drowned his voice.

So that Martin could not have had a better entry, even though he was escorted prisoner-fashion by a couple of Fencibles, though he looked dazed, weary, dirty and pale, and had not at all the proud port of a conscious hero.

"*Messieurs, le voilà!*" cried La Vireville histrionically; and many in the room sprang to their feet crying "Huzza!"

* * * * *

Nor had Martin the feelings of a hero either, when he found himself confronting this small, hot room full of uniformed men in a state of excitement. Indeed for a moment he was conscious of almost petulant irritation because he had not been allowed the opportunity of at least a wash and a shave before being brought up in this fashion before all these gentlemen, to do-what? To make his defence? But oddly enough there seemed no call for that. Lord Cawdor (if it were he) was shaking him by the hand, was presenting him to Lord Milford; some officer in that by now much disliked Fencible uniform was saying loudly: "Well done, young man, well done!" Only the less enthusiastic Lord Milford was looking at him, he thought, dubiously. In a corner stood the Chevalier, smiling, and by him Mr. Salt, smiling too. What had the indefatigable La Vireville been up to now?

But soon it broke upon him, for Lord Cawdor was saying something about: "Thanks of the country ... gallant co-operation with our French Royalist friend here ... should like to drink your health, Mr. Tyrrell ..."

But, thought Martin, I must explain; it is of no use their continuing in that vein! He tried several times, and at last got in a word.

"My lords, you must please understand that I am not a fit person to sit down and drink with you, as you honour me by suggesting that I should do. I have not only been arrested by a very natural mistake on the part of an officer of the fort, but also on a warrant-which I must beg you to believe was issued in error—a warrant for treason."

"Treason!" exclaimed Lord Cawdor incredulously. "*Treason!* You, sir, who have just at great personal risk rendered this service to your country! Indeed the warrant must have been issued in error! There must have been a disgraceful, a ludicrous mistake! Pray tell us, Mr. Tyrrell, on what grounds, and when, such a mistake was made, that steps may immediately be taken to rectify it!"

But the tired and battered Martin, as he himself well knew, was in no fit state to embark upon such a version of his misfortunes as it would be necessary to lay before these persons in authority—a version which should somehow leave out Gerald Roche. His brain was not sufficiently alert. He looked appealingly and rather despairingly at Mr. Salt in his corner. But Mr. Salt in his turn had directed upon Lord Milford an almost mesmeric stare, and after enduring it for a few seconds the Lord Lieutenant, to Martin's astonishment, rose in his place at the head of the table.

"I happen, Lord Cawdor," he said rather ponderously, "to be cognisant of the grounds upon which the warrant was issued, and I can assure you and these gentlemen that a great mistake does seem to have been made, a mistake to which I hope presently to call attention in the proper quarter. Meanwhile as Mr. Tyrrell-besides having given an account of himself to-day which should silence all detractors-is vouched for by my good friend Mr. Jerome Salt, of St. David's, under whose roof he has lived continuously for the last seven months, I think we need not require any account of the circumstances which led to the unfortunate mistake being made." Rather stiffly he resumed his seat; but Martin, for his part, could have embraced him-or rather Mr. Salt, who had undoubtedly worked the oracle.

"Then that is happily settled," said Lord Cawdor, with satisfaction. "And indeed any other outcome is not to be thought of. Let us drink a joint health to both these heroes. Fill your glasses, gentlemen all!"

But amid the acclamation with which he was obeyed Lord Milford left his place and came and stooped over him.

"My dear Campbell," he said in a low voice, "let us nevertheless remember that as loyal citizens we cannot disregard the King's warrant if it is presented to us. Whatever our own convictions or wishes, neither you nor I—certainly not I, as Lord Lieutenant of the county-can disobey it!"

Martin overheard. "That is exactly what I recognise, my lord," he said wearily, so wearily that Lord Milford himself quickly filled a glass of wine and held it out to him.

"Mr. Tyrrell, sit down! I think it will be more to the point if, instead of our drinking your health, you yourself take some refreshment. When did you last have a meal?"

Martin sank gratefully into a chair, while the Lord Lieutenant continued to make kind enquiries, among which floated the name of Sir Sumner Tyrrell. It seemed very strange nevertheless that he, the outlaw, should receive such solicitous treatment from those in high places. And yet it could only end in one way, in his being dragged off again by Manisty. It was perfectly true; not even the Lord Lieutenant could flout a warrant.

However, he drank; drank a second glass which someone filled for him; was conscious, amid the buzz of conversation and the slight vertigo produced by wine upon an empty stomach, of some fresh disturbance-some commotion at the door. Looking up, he groaned inwardly as he beheld what he half expected-Manisty, a Manisty much agitated, wearing a suit of clothes very evidently not his own, and gasping out:

"My lords-gentlemen-that man there is my prisoner . . . I have only just heard . . . release from fort . . . but my lord . . . beg you . . . restore him to my custody . . . have just arrested him . . . for treason!"

"Mr. Tyrrell has already informed us of that unfortunate occurrence," said Lord Cawdor calmly. "The warrant, of course, was issued in error; Lord Milford, who knows the circumstances, assures us that the imputation of treason against this gentleman is quite unfounded, and, once this present crisis is over, we shall take steps to procure the withdrawal of the warrant."

Mr. Manisty had sunk uninvited into a chair and was mopping his brow. "I wonder what the prisoner has been telling you, my lord. He's a good liar if ever there was one! . . . he and the antiquary gentleman at St. David's who abetted him. But I may remind your lordships, with all respect, that the warrant has not been withdrawn yet-if ever it is!—and that I am here to carry it out."

This aroused protestations, and even murmurs of "Shame!"

"We cannot obstruct the law, sir," observed Lord Cawdor coldly, "nor do we wish to do so, but I put it to you that there must obviously be a grievous mistake. Why, Mr. Tyrrell has just performed a most heroic and patriotic act-has succeeded, in company with an equally courageous French gentleman, in sending away the invaders' ships!"

Mr. Manisty restored his handkerchief to his pocket. "So that's the tale the prisoner has been pitching, is it?" he remarked unpleasantly. It was a strange fact that his immersion (or some other cause) seemed to have washed away the veneer of superior speech and bearing which had been his at St. David's. "It would be better if your lordships were to consider whether it was not Tyrrell who arranged the whole affair-after the failure of the Bantry Bay invasion in which he had a hand. —Here he's been in Pembrokeshire all these months, holding communication with the French very like, and slung his hook from St. David's just as I ———"

Lord Cawdor stopped him. "Your remarks, sir, are offensive! Let me also remind you that you are not a judge making his charge to a jury, nor even an advocate for the prosecution. You are merely an officer of the Crown charged with the execution of a warrant. I would, however, beg of you, on my own behalf, and upon that of the rest of the gentlemen here, at least to postpone the carrying out of it to-night. Mr. Tyrrell has been through a great deal in the course of the two several gallant actions he has performed."

"I'm sorry, my lord," replied Martin's pursuer, "but I can't risk his giving me the slip again. I must take him now whatever he's been through. And," he added significantly, "he's not the only man who has been through something!"

"If you insist," said Lord Cawdor, evidently deeply annoyed at this uncompromising attitude, "the formal course of justice shall not be impeded. Produce your warrant, and you may then remove your prisoner. Mr. Tyrrell will understand our regrets."

"I have already produced the warrant," said Manisty surlily. "There's no call, my lord, to do it again. The prisoner Tyrrell has seen it, and the party there"—he indicated Mr. Salt—"who broke the law by sheltering him!"

"The point is," said Lord Cawdor, with considerable sharpness, "that Lord Milford and I would like to see it!"

Beads of sweat might have been observed above Mr. Manisty's mouth. "It is not necessary," he reiterated. "The prisoner has seen it-he can't deny it, liar though he is-and that's enough."

"You are mistaken, sir," said Lord Milford, intervening at last. "The circumstances are highly exceptional, and Lord Cawdor is right in saying that I wish to see the warrant. Without it, indeed, you have no claim to the person of Mr. Tyrrell."

Mr. Manisty got very red. "Is your lordship hinting that I am an impostor?"

"Certainly not," replied Lord Milford mildly. "Why, therefore, are you so reluctant to produce the warrant with which you are armed?"

"The prisoner can tell you that I am armed with it!" repeated Manisty, angrily returning to his former defence, "and so can Mr. Talkative Salt of St. David's, and that great redheaded ruffian belonging to the schooner, and ——" His eyes were suddenly fixed and his speech arrested, even before Lord Cawdor said sharply:

"Sir, you are strangely forgetting yourself to bluster thus! You are required not to tell us who has seen the warrant, but to let us see it! For you shall not take Mr. Tyrrell into custody without it!"

And at that Manisty sprang up, tears of rage in his eyes. "Ask *him* to show it to you!" he cried, pointing an accusing finger at the just discovered La Vireville. "In my coat pocket it was when that brutal bully of his tumbled me into the harbour, and in my coat pocket it still was, I'll take my oath, when I was hauled out more dead than alive. But my coat was taken away, and when I was sufficiently recovered to ask for the warrant——"

"In short, sir," broke in Lord Cawdor, "you cannot now produce it?"

"Because it's been made away with," spat out Manisty. "Because that damned Frenchman there-Frenchman, mind you! —has destroyed it! But the man Tyrrell's my prisoner for all that, because the warrant's been executed on him already, and I'm within my rights——"

"Monsieur de la Vireville, is this true, that the warrant was made away with?"

"My lord," answered Fortuné de la Vireville, in a quiet, shocked tone, "I hope I should make a better return to the country which shelters me than to flout her justice! When this zealous gentleman was recovered by the crew of my schooner from the harbour-into which, I give you my word, he fell and was not thrown —I myself took charge of the objects in his pockets. Among them was some document or other —I could not tell what its nature was, since it was nearly ruined by sea-water; nevertheless, I spread it carefully in a safe place to dry, intending to return it to its owner, then asleep, with his purse and pocket-book. Most unfortunately some stupid or careless member of the crew must have removed the article with which I had weighted it; the breeze is fresh in the harbour . . . and the paper must have blown back into the water, for when I searched for it it was gone."

"*Gone!* Oh, my God!" whispered Martin. The hot room began (though for a very different reason) to tilt and spin like that sailors' den at Liverpool, and Manisty's furious face, La Vireville's, with its diverting expression of concern, apology and innocence, Lord Cawdor's, keeping gratification still under lock and key, all swirled round against a tapestry of uniforms, candle flames and other faces. . . . Then a hand gripped his arm.

"Better sit awhile by the window," said a well-known voice in his ear. "Damnably hot in here. . . . There! You have finished with your travels, I think, Martin de Turribus!"

The sash went up with a bang, and the crowd outside had a full view of a neat, grey-haired gentleman in a blue coat with gilt buttons looking down in a satisfied manner at a very pale, untidy young man in a jersey, with a dirty smear on one cheek, who smiled up at him rather uncertainly-to-morrow's hero, though neither he nor they knew it.

IX
THE CLEAR HORIZON

"I will never be a truant, love,
Till I have learn'd thy language; for thy tongue
Makes Welsh as sweet as ditties highly penn'd,
Sung by a fair queen in a summer's bower,
With ravishing division, to her lute."

First part of *King Henry IV*. Act iii, sc. 1.

"Wha ever heard, in ony times,
Siccan an outlaw in his degree
Sic favour get before a King,

   As did Outlaw Murray of the forest free?"

The Outlaw Murray.

IX
THE CLEAR HORIZON

(1)

"What was that noise?" asked a sleepy voice, which was nevertheless not quite free from alarm. "And . . . where the devil am I?"

Mr. Salt, who had just gently drawn aside the window curtains and let in the February daylight, replied: "You are occupying half my bed at the 'Black Bull' in Fishguard. If you want also to know *who* you are, your name is Martin Tyrrell, and you can claim it without fear of consequences. I am sorry if I startled you."

The tousled head sank back again on to the pillow, and the sleeper surveyed with puzzled surprise that trim figure-for Mr. Salt had been up an hour or more. " 'Pon my soul, I was uncertain for a moment whether I was on board the privateer, or the *Raymonde*, or in irons in the lazaret of the French frigate!"

"A little uncertainty is excusable," returned Mr. Salt, putting down a small jug of hot water. "You might also have added 'or in a dark corner of Fishguard fort, or even in a cell in Newgate.' I always said, Martin, that you were Protean in character; I might have said in your choice of residence also."

"*Choice!* " ejaculated Martin, sitting up in bed. In so doing he caught sight of his face in the mirror of the dressing-table, and remained a moment staring at it in horror. "Good God! is that what I look like?"

Mr. Salt laughed. "I should have covered that looking-glass. However, I have brought you some shaving water-for everything in this hostelry is at sixes and sevens-and here is my razor. Not but what your present swashbuckling appearance is more striking. I have always admired that touch of the ear-rings; I hope you will not give them up!"

"They were some foolery of La Vireville's," growled Martin, by now sitting on the edge of the bed. "Thank you, sir, a thousand times for bringing me that hot water. Where is La Vireville, by the way? What should I have done without him-or without you, sir! Had ever a man better friends? And where is that fellow Manisty?"

"Gone to the devil, I should suppose. At least you need not trouble about him. He had hard luck, nevertheless."

"And the French? Have they taken that road, too?"

"Not yet. Major Ackland set out for Pencaer at dawn under a flag of truce, carrying Lord Cawdor's ultimatum informing Tate that he should expect him to signify by ten o'clock his willingness to surrender. It is now nine. I suppose we may assume that he will; if not, then the twenty thousand men in buckram whom Colonel Knox called into being last night ——"

"And of whom I shall hope to be one," interposed Martin, lathering.

"—will march against them. But as I say, it is only nine o'clock, and you have ample time to break your fast and for . . . any other enquiries which you may wish to prosecute. Shall I order you some breakfast? There is nobody to cook it save Lord Milford's body-servant. I was forgetting, you are fully competent to cook your own."

"I would much prefer," said Martin, scraping away painfully, "—damn it, why was I ever persuaded to let my beard grow!—I would much prefer, sir, that someone else should cook for me. Immediately after I have eaten I must go and enquire for Miss Meredith, if she is still in Fishguard. You have seen her, perhaps."

"No; Miss Mortimer put her at once to bed, but not at the "Royal Oak." She took her to some friends of theirs in the town of the name of Davies. But I have not seen the child, though Miss Mortimer tells me that she is none the worse for her experiences. Martin"—there was more feeling in Mr. Salt's voice than Martin could imagine him showing—"if ever a debt was discharged with interest yours has been, for which all who love Nest Meredith may thank God!"

"I am glad that I was able to get to Trehowell in time," said Martin quietly. One half of his face had now assumed a more civilised aspect. "There is just one more thing, sir; would it be possible for me to procure writing materials? In case I cannot see Miss Meredith in person I should wish to leave a letter for her. I suppose that she will be returning to St. David's as soon as she is fit for it-that indeed Dr. Meredith is probably on his way to fetch her?"

Mr. Salt produced out of a pocket-book a sheet of paper, a pencil and a wafer. "I doubt if I can find pen and ink in this confusion, unless Lord Milford can supply them."

"This is all I need. By the way, am I not under a sort of parole to Lord Milford? But he will not object to my leaving the "Black Bull"?"

"Not at all. All you undertook was not to leave Fishguard. But as for that, my boy, you need not trouble yourself. There will be no fresh warrant issued against you-particularly if the French do surrender. Well, I'll go see about your breakfast. I was forgetting to tell you, the Chevalier sent up your more reputable attire from the schooner early this morning. He appears to think of everything, that ingenious gentleman."

It was not until he had finished shaving, washing and dressing that Martin allowed the tide surging at the back of his mind to rush resistlessly to shore and to sweep away all thoughts even of his own now assured safety. Not even to Mr. Salt could he give more than a hint of how overwhelming was that tide, even though he knew that the avowal would not have met with quizzing, but with approbation. La Vireville's quiet disposal of the warrant-for, of course, he *had* disposed of it-had done more for his companion in adventure than merely to free him from material shackles; it had set him free to attempt the carrying out of that which the night of dismay at Trehowell had shown him to be his dearest wish. He sat down at the dressing-table, the only place available, and with no jewelled pen, but only a small and rather blunt pencil, began his first love-letter.

(2)

The friends, indeed relatives, to whose little house in Fishguard the Mortimers had yesterday taken their charge, were two small twittering maiden ladies, sisters, of the name of Davies. They were not unlike canaries. Yet for all their twittering and their undoubted timidity they had stayed (like canaries) in their cage when the great danger approached, too timid, perhaps, to leave its shelter. The large presence of Mr. Mortimer (dispossessed though he was) had encouraged them to remain, and when the rescued Miss Meredith was brought under their roof they accepted her as a direct charge from heaven.

In the little bedroom assigned to her by the fluttered cage-birds, Nest had remained the whole of yesterday, sleeping a great part of the time. The shock of her experiences at Trehowell was not, so Miss Mortimer hoped, going to have the profound and disastrous effect which might have been anticipated. By the evening, indeed, Miss Meredith had appeared to be not only rested in body, but a great deal calmer in mind than Myfanwy Mortimer would have thought possible. She had pictured a young lady of the delicate upbringing of the Precentor's daughter suffering, and justifiably after so terrible an adventure, from fit after fit of hysterics and the most unremitting vapours.

But the truth was that the Precentor's daughter had a talisman to cherish, a picture to look at, a sensation to revive; and she spent a good deal of that Thursday doing all these things in secret. Of all people in the world it was Martin Tyrrell who had rescued her, displaying the most incredible resource and braving the most horrid danger for her sake; and he had not done it out of mere chivalry or gratitude, for he had put his head upon her shoulder and called her "Nest," and twice after that he had taken her in his arms. Out of all the welter of the night's impressions those memories were paramount, and she continually brought them out and looked at them.

Yet though, as she was told, both Mr. Salt and the brave and resourceful Frenchman-and even Mr. Perrot-had been to enquire for her, Martin had not come, which was curious, for if M. de la Vireville knew her present whereabouts, he must know it too. What if, after all, she had been mistaken? The circumstances were highly unusual; he had been moved by her danger. If he did not feel for her what she did for him-and indeed how could he? —was he to be blamed? Was not his conduct all the more chivalrous and noble? At least she had had her few moments of bliss in the midst of the acutest terror she would probably ever know.

Mr. Mortimer had at once despatched a messenger to Mrs. Pennefather at the Precentory with the news of Miss Meredith's safety; and it had been arranged that he should take or send her back to St. David's later to-day, Thursday. The French surrender was expected, but since it had not yet taken place it would be wiser for her to go. Nest, however, displayed a most surprising reluctance to leave Fishguard, alleging as one reason that by this time dear Papa was probably hastening as fast as posthorses could bring him direct from Haverfordwest, and that if she started for St. David's she would miss him, and cause him to journey to Fishguard in vain. The canaries and the Mortimers did not like to cross her, and could not do more than exercise pressure; and so far had Nest defeated them that Miss Mortimer had agreed not to start with her until the afternoon.

But *he* was not coming; that was certain. Nest sat in the window with a volume of Welsh sermons-all the literature which she could find. Miss Mortimer was helping the two ladies; Mr. Mortimer was out-like all the males in Fishguard and many of the females. The street was alternately full of people and empty again, as they drained off to some new point of interest or heard some fresh rumour. The French had surrendered: they were not going to surrender: Lord Milford had had a stroke: Colonel Knox and Lord Cawdor had quarrelled (this, indeed, though incorrect, was prophetic). So when Nest heard a louder uproar than usual, and a more swollen tramp of feet, she did not pay much attention, though she was certainly not deeply immersed in the Welsh divine. She was rather sadly fingering her memories.

Miss Mortimer suddenly opened the door. "Miss Meredith *bach*, if you come upstairs," said she, sounding somewhat excited, "you will be able to see the crowd that is coming down the street whatever with the young man who went out to the French ships and persuaded them to go away-so a boy has just told us. They say that if the French surrender 'twill be due to him. 'Tis worth looking at; they are carrying him on their shoulders!"

Glad to escape from the sermons, Nest followed Miss Mortimer upstairs to her own bedroom, and, looking out, saw a noisy knot of people carrying shoulder-high a laughing and apparently protesting young man. Nest had heard something of this sending away of the French ships, and, realising that she must be looking at a hero, wished that she could see his face. Suddenly he turned his head. . . .

"Why," exclaimed Miss Mortimer, "though he is dressed very differently, it looks like the young seaman who came ——"

"It is!" cried Nest. "It is he-Mr. Tyrrell!" Her eyes shone; she gazed enchanted; then, as the crowd, hurrahing and shouting, went past, that figure high in their midst, she came away from the window, and, throwing herself down in a chair, began very quietly to cry.

For Miss Mortimer this was, of course, but one of the natural symptoms of her charge's overwrought condition. Fussing over her, she finally conducted her to her bed, and urging her to lie upon it, departed to seek some specific. Nest obeyed; but she continued to cry, though not at all violently. The hero of the hour-her hero-no wonder he had no thought to spare for her, did not even know that she had seen his triumph, that it was past her window that he was being carried! It was foolish to cry; she ought rather to rejoice, for surely now he would never be arrested! All the time since the episode of the haycock began to unroll in a series of flashes. . . .

Most abruptly Miss Mortimer burst in again, without the cordial, but with something else in her hand.

"Miss Meredith, he's come here-the young man-Mr. Tyrrell! He has come to ask for you! It seems he was on his way to enquire after you when the crowd overtook him. He said-he asked-in case you were not able to see him, I was to give you this." She held up a letter. "Will you read it now, my dear?"

Nest was sitting up, a vivid colour in her cheeks. "Yes. Give it to me, please! Has Mr. Tyrrell gone again, then?"

"No, indeed. He is waiting downstairs until I should tell him if you would see him." Tactfully she went to the window as she heard the letter torn open.

A moment passed.

"Where is he, dear Miss Mortimer? I will . . . see him at once!" Nest had slipped off the bed. By her appearance she had drunk deep of her specific (indeed for all that was now to be seen of it she might really have swallowed the letter).

"He's in the back parlour, *cariad*; I took him there, because every one in the street is trying to look into the other room. Now, no harm to keep him waiting for a moment or two while you put some cold water to your eyes. He'll not go away, whatever; don't you be fearing it!"

* * * * *

Down to the back parlour, a little room she had never seen, cold and prim. And he was standing in the middle, waiting. He took a step forward, holding out his hands.

"Have you read my letter. . . . *anwyl* ?"

Suddenly overcome by shyness, Nest remained by the door. ". . . You have learnt a Welsh word, Mr. Tyrrell!" she said, with some idea of fending off the sweet, ineffable moment.

Her evasion had not at all that result. One more stride and Martin had her hands fast prisoners.

"I think I have always known it, Nausicaa! But it was only at Trehowell that I learnt its meaning. And only you can tell me if I learnt it rightly. . . . Nest, do you mean by it what I do?"

She drooped her head. "I . . . I think so."

"What is it, then? . . . Oh, my little Nest. . . ."

Indistinctly, Nest translated. *"Dearest!"*

243

(3)

The postchaise with its smoking horses had to draw up at the side of the road to let them pass.

"What is it-what is this delay?" exclaimed the agitated ecclesiastic within, and he put his head out. A sprinkling of cavalry, of a corps he knew-Castlemartin Yeomanry-then rank upon rank of trudging figures in rusty brown uniforms, soldiers without weapons, strange, unmilitary-looking and dejected men . . .

"Good God!" exclaimed the Precentor. "But are they captured then, these wretches?" Poking his head further out of the window he shouted to the postillion, who had dismounted and was holding one of the horses which was manifesting an aversion from the "wretches," to find out what had happened; and then himself caught sight of a slowly advancing mounted officer in the midst of the marching ranks. Unable to get out of the chaise, since there was no room to open the door, he beckoned to the horseman and was seen, for the officer, coming abreast, edged his horse through the stream and pulled up.

"Perrot, where's my daughter?"

"Safe in Fishguard, sir."

"Safe? Thank God, thank God! She was out of Trehowell then before . . . or is it untrue that these scoundrels landed in Pencaer?"

"No, it is true. Trehowell was their headquarters. Miss Meredith, fortunately, was rescued by a French Royalist emigrant —a sea-captain, I believe-and, so far as I can make out (though it seems improbable), by that secretary of Mr. Salt's. If I had had the least idea that she was at Trehowell— —"

"What!" interrupted the Precentor. "That secretary of Salt's! But that's impossible, quite impossible! Perrot, tell me— —"

"I fear I must get on at once," said Mr. Perrot. "Have to march these fellows to Haverfordwest-we shall not be there before the small hours as it is." He touched his horse.

"One moment-one moment! Has there been a battle?"

"No. The French surrendered. They were deserted by their ships." He moved off.

Tramp, tramp-the procession continued to go past. The Precentor was unaware that many of these captured troops still bore the marks of the galley-irons on their wrists, but he did think that they looked an extraordinary horde, some chattering, some silent and gloomy, some distinctly rude. Dr. Meredith could not remember ever having had a tongue put out at him before, and even in the midst of his almost unbearable relief about Nest, he was conscious of resentment. But nothing-not even that-mattered so that Nesta was safe. Only, by what means? That secretary of Salt's —arrant nonsense, of course! He was, one might hope, in Newgate by now.

After a while he was able to proceed, but about a mile short of Fishguard had another encounter. This time it was he who was stopped by a mounted officer, one of a stationary group, who, after shouting an enquiry to the postillion, swung off his horse and appeared at the chaise window. It was Lord Cawdor, all triumph and exhilaration.

"I thought it might be you, Mr. Precentor, hastening to have news of your daughter, and I wished to be the first to tell you that she is perfectly safe and unharmed, thanks to the courage and address of a young man whom I think you must have met in St. David's, Mr. Martin Tyrrell, and a French friend of his."

"I have heard that she is safe, and I thank Heaven most fervently for it. But I cannot believe . . ." Dr. Meredith stammered.

"No, I dare wager you cannot," replied Lord Cawdor, misapprehending the point on which he felt incredulity. "Yet, though she was actually in Trehowell when the French landed-however, you will hear about it soon enough, for Milford will present the rescuers to you . . . that is if they can be rescued themselves from the townsfolk, for Mr. Tyrrell is become the hero of the hour, for another reason! (It appears, by the way, that he is a kinsman of an old friend of Lord

Milford's.) Well, I will not keep you from your daughter; she is here with the Miss Davies. You will find the town greatly elated at the happy issue of this outrageous attempt."

* * * * *

The two best friends-save one-of the hero of the hour, between whom there had sprung up a mutual liking, were still down upon Goodwick Sands, where, after the great spectacle of the formal capitulation, a sprinkling of onlookers still lingered, gazing at the piled weapons of the Frenchmen. Spare arms and ammunition had been left up in the camp, when, with drums beating, but without their colours, the "Légion seconde des Francs" had marched (not very unwillingly perhaps) down the steep hill to their surrender on the shore.

The brilliant weather had departed, the wind had shifted to the south-east, and the tide, far out, was crawling in grey and complaining.

"That was a remarkable sight," observed Mr. Salt reminiscently. "And perhaps the most remarkable part of it was the fierceness of the women folk. Tate looked quite frightened at those farmers' wives screaming for his blood."

"It must indeed have been a disagreeable surprise for him if he had really expected to be welcomed by the Welsh," agreed Fortuné de la Vireville. His tone was rather absent, he looked grave, and, meeting Mr. Salt's somewhat enquiring glance, said slowly, "The last surrender I saw I was taking part in, I and my friends. It was on a seashore too. But it did not end as this will do. England does not shoot prisoners made upon terms."

Mr. Salt knew that he was referring to the tragedy of Quiberon. "I hope we are more civilized," he murmured.

"Even the uniforms these gaol-birds were wearing have to do with that chapter of blood," went on La Vireville sadly and fiercely.

"But they were English," exclaimed Mr. Salt —"dyed, it is true, yet with British buttons still on, for I examined one. I could not understand where they came from, for they seemed new."

"I can tell you that," said the *émigré*. "They were once landed from Sir John Warren's squadron for the use of us Royalists in that fatal peninsula. . . . Ah, well, it is a small, a very small compensation to have checkmated this expedition of the Directory's, and without bloodshed."

"You ran a very great risk," said Mr. Salt, "and nearly paid the penalty of your audacity. —Tell me, why did you take my young Tyrrell with you? From what I have seen of you, Monsieur le Chevalier, I could better imagine you setting out on that perilous errand alone!"

The Frenchman gave a little smile. "You see too far, Mr. Salt! I suggested that he should accompany me because, though I did not tell him so, I thought it might be very useful to a young man accused of having helped to bring a French fleet to Ireland to take part, at some risk-greater risk indeed than I anticipated-in sending one away from Wales!"

"So that was it! Egad, your ingenuity seems to have been successful! And then you completed your benefaction. In confidence, now, how *did* you dispose of that warrant?"

"Dispose?" repeated La Vireville, raising his eyebrows. "*Mon cher Monsieur* Salt, I did not dispose of it. It was exactly as I told the *conseil de guerre* : some careless person removed the weight from it, and *le bon Dieu* did the rest with His wind-exactly as with the fleet in Bantry Bay!"

"But you must admit that it is as well to know when to assist *le bon Dieu* ! —What's this?"

Behind them came a shouting. A man was hurrying over the firm sand towards them. "Is that the French gentleman? Sir, you are looked for everywhere; your presence is required at the "Black Bull." There is a feeling that some public acknowledgment should be made to you and Mr. Tyrrell for what you did; but Mr. Tyrrell swears he will not accept it unless you are there too."

"Come on, Chevalier," said Mr. Salt, laying hold of his arm. "You must not be modest-the plan was yours and you know it!"

"My worst enemy could not call me modest," retorted his companion. "But somehow I do not feel in the mood for receiving public acknowledgments. Let the young British hero receive them alone; a British crowd will prefer that. I only wish *l'archiprélat* could be there to see it!"

"If you mean the Precentor, so do I," said Mr. Salt warmly. "I would give my best Aldine for that consummation. But he can hardly be arrived in Fishguard yet.—Come on, Chevalier; if you will not share the honours, at least let us witness their bestowal."

* * * * *

Although the extreme and long-drawn anxiety of Dr. Meredith was indeed allayed, he desired to get into Fishguard as soon as possible; but this proved difficult, for the place was beside itself with joy and relief, and, since the general return from witnessing the surrender upon Goodwick Sands, a good deal of *cwrw dda* had not unnaturally been drunk. Because the chaise could advance even less easily through the packed and narrow street than through the ranks of the captured foe on the road, the Precentor was at last constrained to alight and to attempt to penetrate on foot. At first some of the populace either recognised him or made way for him because they were awed by his dignified appearance, but he soon got swept into an unregarding human torrent which bore him, very unwillingly, towards the "Black Bull."

"Let me out, good people!" he exclaimed, struggling. "I wish to find my daughter—I am Dr. Meredith of St. David's Cathedral!"

His words were wasted. The enthusiastic ranks carried him on, wedged in their midst, and one half tipsy sailor from Solva, who was singing snatches of *Rule Britannia*, even threw his arms about the Precentorial shoulders and invited their owner to sing too.

"This is unseemly . . . highly improper . . . and what is the meaning of it?" demanded Dr. Meredith several times with indignation, for though he realised that the collapse of the invasion was certainly an occasion for popular rejoicing, he did not understand this purposeful if confused setting of the tide in which he found himself towards one particular point. And at last a more sober individual, tight pressed against him, enlightened him on the subject.

"They are going to show themselves at a window in the "Black Bull," sir."

"They? Who? And why?" panted the Precentor.

"Why, sir, the two gentlemen that sent the French ships away whatever; 'tis they that caused the surrender of the frog-eating villains . . . and one of them a French gentleman too!"

"A French gentleman?" said the Precentor faintly, apprehensive at that of who the other might be. "You mean, surely, that these gentlemen are said to have rescued my daughter, Miss Meredith, from Trehowell?"

"I do not know . . . about any daughter, sir . . ."—the crowd was getting more tightly packed as it surged nearer to its goal—"but this young man from St. David's . . . he had the Frenchman to do the parley-vooing . . . here, Thomas Lloyd, take your elbow out of my back!"

The breath was not more squeezed out of the Precentor's frame than was sense, he felt, from his brain. *Could* the man mean Martin Tyrrell! This business was a mental as well as a physical nightmare. The loud shouts and acclamations which now burst out did not disperse it. The crowd was by this time within sight of the "Black Bull," a mean little hostelry in Dr. Meredith's eyes; and something was taking place there, but not even he, with his height, could see what it was. However, the tumult suddenly stilled, and there uprose (from some invisible source on the "Black Bull's" doorstep) a loud voice announcing in Welsh that an opportunity was now at hand to return thanks to the two valiant courageous brave loyal men who had contributed to this happy end to a wicked attempt against the liberties of Dyfed and of Britain; but that as at the moment only one of these heroes could be found, the speaker would present that one for their acclamations, and was only sorry that he could not claim him as a Welshman; but at any rate he had for some time been resident in their Cathedral city of St. David's. And here he was; or rather if they would look up at that window they would see him, for he was too modest to come down-Mr. Martin Tyrrell, of Northamptonshire.

All eyes-even the Precentor's—went to that window. Yes, it *was* that impudent secretary of Salt's, smiling rather shame-facedly and apparently trying to say something. But he could not make himself heard in the roar which instantly went up. Every hat came off and was flourished. And though the poor Precentor did not wave his, someone sacrilegiously snatched it off from that august wig and waved it for him.

And as he indignantly looked round for the perpetrator of this outrage he felt his arm firmly clutched, and in his ear sounded the mocking voice of Mr. Jerome Salt, shouting through the din:

"Meredith, Meredith, you should have listened to St. Paul and me! What did I tell you about charity? And *I* had faith and hope into the bargain. . . . John Jones, give Mr. Precentor back his hat!"

THE END

NOTE

To most people, save to those familiar with north-west Pembrokeshire, it may come as a surprise to learn that a French invading force actually landed near Fishguard in February 1797, in an enterprise which might easily have run less upon the lines of comic opera than it fortunately did. But even by those who, on this side of the Channel, have written accounts of it, no explanation has ever been found for the sudden and mysterious departure of its transports on the day after the descent, and these are always held to have left Tate in the lurch. It is evident, however, from Castagnier's report of the expedition, which survives in the *Archives de la Marine*, that the withdrawal was due, after all, to Tate himself, though what could have impelled him, in view of his own far from satisfactory situation, to dismiss the ships is still an enigma. The foregoing pages provide an explanation which the novel-reader, if not the historian, may perhaps accept.

For the rest, the details of the landing and of the surrender, the fact of the occupation of Trehowell (where Mr. Mortimer actually did prepare a feast for the supposed Englishmen), the names of Tate's officers and of Castagnier's ships, as well as of the British leaders and officers, are all historical.

There was really at that date a privateer of Liverpool named the *Fair Penitent*.

www.ingramcontent.com/pod-product-compliance
Ingram Content Group UK Ltd.
Pitfield, Milton Keynes, MK11 3LW, UK
UKHW022228230426
12048UKWH00016BA/1132